# ENEMY INVASION

## A. G. TAYLOR

USBORNE

For Sandra

First published in the UK in 2011 by Usborne Publishing Ltd., Usborne House, 83-85
Saffron Hill, London EC1N 8RT, England. www.usborne.com

Copyright © A.G. Taylor, 2011

A CIP catalogue record for this book is available from the British Library.

JFM MJJASOND/11 00658/1 ISBN 9781409526711
Printed in Reading, Berkshire, UK.

# HIDRA INFO SHEET
## CONFIDENTIAL:
## LEVEL 5+ OPERATIVE EYES ONLY

*THINK!*

*Do you have security clearance to view this document?*

*If in doubt, contact your supervisor immediately.*

*Viewing confidential HIDRA material without*

*permission will lead to automatic suspension,*

*court martial and a possible jail sentence.*

## OVERVIEW

As a new military and/or scientific operative at the HIDRA UK and/or Asia-Pacific base, this document is designed to bring you quickly up to speed with the events of the past twelve months. *If you are a returning HIDRA operative or have already been briefed, please skip to the next section of this induction booklet.* All material is strictly confidential and only to be discussed with operatives with an equal or higher security clearance.

## BACKGROUND: THE FALL VIRUS

The virus is known to be of alien origin, carried to earth by space-born debris. Twelve months ago, a meteorite strike in central Australia led to a significant fall virus outbreak, with several thousand people affected. Adults exposed to the virus fall into a deep coma for which there is no known cure at this time. However, among a small percentage of children, remarkable side effects have been noted.

## SIDE EFFECTS: PSYCHIC/TELEKINETIC POWERS

Current data suggests that 0.01% of those under the age of sixteen exposed to the virus develop a number of incredible side effects: mind-control abilities, teleportation, invisibility, pyrokinesis (fire-starting) and telekinesis (the ability to move objects with one's mind). All these subjects develop the ability to communicate telepathically. With time, these subjects (hereafter referred to as *superhumans*) can learn to control and even develop their powers, although at first their manifestation can be disturbing and potentially dangerous for themselves and others.

## RECENT EVENTS: THE MAKAROV INCIDENT

Six months ago, a storm of fall virus-bearing meteors was detected on collision course with earth. It soon became clear these objects were being controlled by Nikolai Makarov, the Russian billionaire/genius, who wished to cause global infection for his own gain. With the help of a small team of superhuman children, Makarov's base of operations (the skyscraper in eastern Russia known as *the Spire*) was destroyed and the alien storm deflected. Theories of an alien intelligence controlling Makarov and the meteors remain unconfirmed at this time.

## SPECIAL OPERATIVES: SUPERHUMANS AT HIDRA

Following their assistance in the Makarov incident, the members of the superhuman team led by Sarah Williams have been designated *special operatives* within HIDRA, reporting directly to Colonel Rachel Andersen. Please talk to your supervisor for operational guidelines for working with superhumans. For quick reference, here is the current list of special operatives and their associated powers:

Sarah Williams – Mind-control
Robert Williams – Teleportation
Alex Fisher – Invisibility
Louise Bates – Telekinesis
Sikong Wei – Pyrokinesis
Nestor del Fuentes – Aerokinesis
Octavio del Fuentes – Telekinesis

## ONGOING THREATS: MAJOR BRIGHT

The former second-in-command of HIDRA Asia–Pacific was stripped of his position and is currently wanted for trial for his actions during and after the Australian fall virus outbreak. His obsession with harnessing the powers of the superhumans has led him to various illegal activities, including kidnapping and attacking HIDRA personnel. He was originally believed killed in the Spire collapse, but images have recently come to light of the major alive and well and attempting to purchase weapons from a black-market dealer in Indonesia.

Current whereabouts: unknown.

## Prologue
*Wilkes Land, Antarctica*

The helicopters came just after dawn, two of them flying low along the coast from the direction of the Shackleton Ice Shelf. Dr. Jan Petersen spotted them as he was prepping the snowcat for his weekly trip to the Casey Research Station, twenty kilometres west. Squinting against the brilliant blue of the Antarctic sky, he watched the helicopters make a circle of the three single-storey buildings that made up the Wolfe Station and then touch down on the snow.

Helen Brooks walked out of the communications

shack to get a look at the unexpected visitors. Winter had set in and the Wolfe Station was preparing to close until spring, so they were the only two researchers left on site. Normally the station, an offshoot of Casey, would have closed weeks before.

But the discovery out on the ice had changed all that...

"Who are they?" Helen asked.

Jan shook his head. "Beats me. There's no flag on the helicopters."

Men wearing heavy-duty thermal coats, gloves and boots piled out of the machines. Jan started towards them as the chopper rotors slowed. Three of the men ran to meet him, bent low so their heads wouldn't be taken off by the still-spinning blades. As they straightened up, Jan noted they were all tall, but the man in the middle was a giant, well over two metres. Despite the sub-zero cold, this man pulled back the hood of his coat. Jan was immediately struck by his piercing blue eyes and the scar running down the right side of his face. The crew cut and lack of a beard indicated that he hadn't spent much time in Antarctica, where facial hair was a must if you wanted to stay warm.

"Hi," Jan said, glancing over the two men flanking the blue-eyed one. They looked back at him expressionlessly, eyes hidden by mirrored goggles. He noted the automatic rifles slung over their shoulders.

Blue-eyes gave him a smart salute and said, "Dr. Petersen?"

"Yes."

"My name's Major Bright," he said with the unplaceable accent of a man who had lived all over the world. "We're here to take over this operation."

"Take over?" Helen spluttered from behind Jan, always quick to anger. "Why?"

Bright gave her a look like the question was stupid. "Why do you think?"

She began to say something else, but Jan held up a hand for her to be calm. "On whose authority are you doing this, Major?" he asked.

"HIDRA's. I'm sure you've heard of the Hyper Infectious Disease—"

"I've heard of your organization," Jan interrupted. "You have no authority here. This is a research station run by the Australian government—"

"Not any more. We have reason to believe there's a contamination risk from the object you discovered."

"You're talking about the fall virus? There's absolutely no reason to believe—"

"It's a done deal, doctor," Bright cut him dead. "You're

under my authority now. Both of you."

"We'll see what the guys at Casey Station have to say about that," Helen said, bristling. "I'm getting them on the radio."

She started stomping back towards the communications shack before anyone could argue. Bright nodded to his men, both of whom followed. Jan looked after them, taken aback at how quickly things were moving. Major Bright took his arm and began to lead him towards the helicopter.

"Don't worry about your partner, doctor. My men will make sure everything is taken care of. Right now I need you to guide us to the discovery site." Jan tried to protest, but Major Bright's hand was firm on his arm. "I won't take no for an answer."

Before the doctor knew what was happening, he'd been bundled into the back of the nearest chopper. Two burly men sat on either side of him, as if worried he might try to jump out. Major Bright took a seat opposite and produced a tablet PC as the helicopter took off.

"Mark the location of the crater," Bright shouted above the noise of the rotors.

He handed Jan the tablet, which showed a map of Wilkes Land – the 2.5 million kilometre square area of Antarctica claimed by Australia. Seeing he had little choice, Jan tapped the screen at the point thirty kilometres south of Wolfe Station where the object had been discovered two weeks before. A flashing marker appeared.

"Very good," Bright said, passing the tablet through to the pilot. "Now, who else knows about the object?"

Jan shrugged. "Well, apart from Helen and me, just a few people at the Casey Station. We kept it as confidential as possible."

"What about other research stations in the area?"

"There's the Russians at Vostok and the French at Concordia Station. But they have no reason to be looking for anything in that sector."

Bright smiled thinly. "We'll see."

"Where did you guys come in from?" Jan asked. "Is your ship close by? Are there HIDRA scientists on board?"

Major Bright gave no response. They sat in silence for the rest of the ten-minute trip, Jan feeling more and more uncomfortable sandwiched between the men with the mirrored goggles. None of the members of Major Bright's group looked or acted like scientists. They were soldiers. HIDRA or not, it was clear to Jan that the military was moving in to claim the amazing find they'd made on the ice. And all he could do was grin and bear it.

Finally, the crater in the ice appeared through the windows on the right. "That's it," Jan said, although it was pretty obvious they'd reached their destination – the crater was almost two hundred metres across. The helicopter descended and made landing near the edge. The soldiers pushed Jan out after Major Bright and they walked the snowy incline to the rim of the giant bowl.

"Amazing," Major Bright said as they looked across the indentation.

Jan nodded in agreement. A meteorite strike on a continent the size of Antarctica was common enough, although the size of the crater was unusual. (As was the fact that none of the global monitoring stations had picked it up, but given the amount of meteorite activity in the last six months, that was forgivable.) No, the truly interesting thing about this crater was under the ice itself. It was as if the meteorite had hit the permafrost and burrowed deep inside. In the centre of the crater the ice had turned the deepest black and it was possible to see a spherical object under the surface. From this object spread dark, slender veins, as if the matter at the centre was bleeding material out through the frozen Antarctic ground. It looked like a giant spider preserved in ice.

The second helicopter landed on the other side of the crater and Jan saw that there was some kind of camp over there. Bright scanned the opposite rim with a pair of binoculars then handed them to Jan for a look.

"The Russians!" Jan said. "I might have known the Vostok boys would come sniffing around." He shook his head. "Those sneaky—"

The unmistakable sound of gunfire echoed across the crater. Jan brought the binoculars back to his face. A Russian scientist he recognized was running along the edge of the crater. One of the soldiers aimed a rifle at his back and fired a burst of rounds. The man's body jerked and went down. Bright's men were shooting the members of the Russian scientific party. Gunning them down in cold blood.

"What is this?'" Jan demanded, hardly believing what he was seeing.

Bright smiled coldly. "Just protecting our find, Dr. Petersen."

Jan lowered the binoculars and backed along the edge of the crater. "You're not from HIDRA."

"Duh. You think?"

Jan's legs felt too weak to run. "Helen is calling the Casey Station, you can't get away with this."

"No one from Casey is going to answer that call, doctor," Bright said, producing an automatic pistol from the folds of his coat.

Jan stammered, "W-why?"

"Because we've already been there."

Major Bright shot Jan three times in the chest. The scientist staggered back over the edge of the crater and slid down the curved edge, leaving a smear of crimson blood on the ice, all the way to the bottom.

One of the soldiers appeared at Major Bright's side. "The Russian team has been neutralized, sir," he reported. "As has the woman at Wolfe."

"Very good."

"Orders, sir?"

Major Bright looked across the crater and surveyed the dark, spider-like infection running through the ice. His gaze focused on the hard, black mass in the centre.

"Dig it up," he said.

### HIDRA Mobile Base, Pacific Ocean

The empty cargo bay at the rear of the aircraft carrier was the place Sarah Williams went when the voices in her head buzzed so loud they took on the intensity of a migraine. The power to read and even control people's minds had been steadily growing in strength during the last six months (ever since her encounter with an infinitely more powerful being known as the Entity), but this increased ability came at a price. Sometimes the constant stream of thoughts, visions and images from the people around her was impossible to control – like a television playing at full volume that could never be turned off. Only in the bay's dark stillness could she shut out the world for a while and focus in on the important voices.✷

The ones with something to say.

Understanding what Sarah was going through, Colonel Rachel Andersen had ordered the crew of the HS *Ulysses*, HIDRA's mobile base in the Pacific, to keep Bay 6 empty at all times. Therefore, no one batted an eyelid when they saw the dark-haired fifteen-year-old walk through the lower levels of the ship, turn the heavy wheel on the entrance hatch and slip inside.

The cargo bay door closed with a clunk behind her...

There were no windows in the bay, so the darkness here was absolute. Sarah didn't hit the light switches by the door, however, choosing instead to find her way to the centre using a flashlight. When she reached what she assumed to be the middle of the bay – which was half the size of a football pitch – she sat cross-legged on the floor.

And turned off the torch.

Darkness flooded in.

The images and disembodied voices that had plagued her all day came on stronger with the sensory deprivation. She caught glimpses of her friends – Robert, Louise, Wei – studying, practising their skills or just hanging out on the *Ulysses*.

But she also saw further afield…

…to kids she'd never met, in foreign countries, often using languages she could not speak but could somehow understand in the visions. They were all like her: given special abilities of some kind or another by their exposure to the alien fall virus. Some were trying to be found. Others were running away. All were attempting to come to grips with the changes their new powers brought.

Sarah zeroed in on the image that had been disturbing her – shutting out the irrelevant clutter and voices one by one until…

…she saw a vast city sprawl of skyscrapers, neon lights and traffic. Amidst the mass of millions of people crammed together she focused upon one boy… A tall, black-haired Chinese kid, who looked about fourteen…

He was on the run, desperate… Pursued by men with guns…

And also by other, darker forces that would not yet reveal themselves…

She saw a high tower… Bullets exploding through a window… And the boy falling, falling, falling…

"Are you okay, sis?"

Sarah's eyes flicked open, but she didn't look round. She'd been so intent on trying to capture the vision, that she hadn't even heard her younger brother, Robert, enter the bay.

"Someone's in trouble," she said. "A boy – just a little older than you. His life's in danger."

Robert crouched and held up his own torch so he could see her eyes amidst the darkness. "Do we know him? What kind of danger?"

Sarah frowned. "Unclear. We don't know him yet, but he's one of us."

Robert took his sister's hand in his. Whenever she was like this – alone in the dark, so distant, almost alien – it worried him desperately. He squeezed her fingers, trying to bring her back to him somehow.

"It's okay," he said. "What do you want me to do?"

"You have to find him," Sarah replied. In the light of the torch, her eyes snapped into focus, like a sleeper awaking from a dream. "I'll try to guide you."

"Why me?"

"Because you're the only one who can save him from dying."

PART ONE

## 1

In the last week of the school holidays, when Hong Kong's summer was at its most oppressively hot and humid, Hack developed the unshakeable feeling he was being followed.

First there was the guy wearing the ankle-length coat (even though it was over thirty degrees outside) waiting for the MTR train at Tung Chung station and again when he changed to the Tsuen Wan line. Later, after trawling the electronics stalls in the city all afternoon, Hack spotted him again – sitting on the train back to Lantau

Island, head buried in a book. Probably just a coincidence.

Or so he thought at that point.

On Tuesday he spent the day fishing with his friend Danny and wandering the narrow alleyways of Tai-O, the fishing village where he lived with his grandfather. It was high season and by midday the place was bustling with tourists, but there was one thin woman who seemed to follow wherever they went. Every time he looked round, she had her camera pointed in their direction. *Why would she be taking a picture of us?* Danny laughed when Hack voiced his suspicions.

He let it go at that.

On Thursday the guy with the coat was back. Hack caught a glimpse of him in the crowd as he ascended the steps into the IFC mall on another city trip. Their eyes met and the man melted into the throng of lunchtime shoppers like a ghost.

By Friday, Hack was looking over his shoulder constantly, attempting to work out who was a tail and who was not. He tried staying in the house, but found himself checking the blinds every five minutes to see who was passing by outside. School wasn't back for two weeks and for the first time in his life, Hack actually found himself wishing he was there, just to take his mind off things. Sick of watching him pace the floor, Grandfather sent Hack on an errand to the market stalls by the bay, where he became convinced that everyone was eyeballing him: housewives, pensioners, even little kids.

*Had his secret finally been discovered?*

Hack thought he'd been careful enough: he never used his power in public and had only told a few trusted friends. But had one of them ratted him out? And to who?

These questions whirled through his mind like a tornado until he finally fled back to the city and the place where he felt most at home: the Golden Chip. He needed to talk to someone, and Jonesey, one of the few people who knew about his secret, was the obvious choice.


The Golden Chip, or GC as it was known to the regulars, was a computer and software market that sprawled across six floors of a high-rise in the Kowloon area of Hong Kong.

Two basement levels bustled with stalls selling every imaginable piece of junk. If you were looking for a component for a thirty-year-old games console or wanted to buy a box of motherboards for five dollars (some of which might actually work), the basement was the place for you. On Levels 1, 2 and 3, pushy sellers touted laptops,

PCs, fake iPhones, real iPads and just about any gadget you could name (and a few that you couldn't) at half the price of the malls. Levels 4 and 5 were the place for Nintendo cartridges loaded with fifty games, PS3 and X-Box titles selling for cents and copies of any operating system you wanted – complete with fake seals of authenticity. Nothing had a price tag, everything was up for negotiation, and the air buzzed from dawn to dusk with the sound of haggling.

Hack rode the escalators past all the noise, casting his eyes over LCD screens showing a cornucopia of images and messages written in Cantonese, English, Mandarin, and often a mix of all three. He breathed a sigh of relief. For most people, the incessant chatter, computer noise and harsh lighting would have been headache-inducing, but not to him.

This was home.

Level 6 was his ultimate destination – the repairs and upgrades area of the GC. A customer could start at the bottom of the building and ride the escalators to the top, picking up components on the way, and have them assembled into any machine he or she desired. Level 6 was markedly less noisy than the other levels and divided up into little cubicles like an office building. Some of these cubicles contained little more than a workbench and a few tools. Others were crammed with spare components, discs, and shelves groaning with manuals. Each cubicle had a technician, and to get a space here you had to be a kind of magician at building, repairing or upgrading computers – a master of your craft.

Hack's friend, Jonesey, had a cubicle at the far corner of the floor and it was one of the untidy ones. This was Jonesey's work and sometimes living space (mainly when he'd had an argument with his mum and she threw him out of her flat). He was a pudgy kid (and getting pudgier by the day, due to a diet that consisted mainly of McDonald's and chocolate bars) whose long, greasy black hair wasn't made any better by the fact he cut it himself with a pair of paper-scissors. Jonesey wasn't a big one for personal appearance.

"*Ni hao*," Hack said as he pushed a stack of magazines off a swivel chair, flopped down and wiped the sweat from his forehead. The air con on the sixth floor just never seemed to work well enough in the summer.

"Speak English," Jonesey replied. He spoke with a thick American accent although, as with Hack, Cantonese was his first language and he'd never set foot outside Hong Kong. Jonesey was only a year older than Hack, but he'd dropped out of school at the age of fourteen – he was making too much money building and selling his own computer systems to waste time away from the GC. That Friday afternoon, he had a laptop balanced on his knees and was working at its exposed innards with a tiny screwdriver.

Hack noticed a brand new LCD TV hanging from the back wall of the cubicle. It was playing a Blu-ray: some blockbuster that wouldn't be released in the cinema for another month.

"What's wrong with the picture?" Hack asked, squinting at the distorted colours.

Jonesey grabbed a pair of plastic glasses from the bench and tossed them over. "3D version."

Hack looked at the TV through the specs as a spaceship seemed to fly off the screen at him with perfect clarity. "Cool."

With a groan, Jonesey threw the laptop on the desk. "I can't get this piece of junk to work."

Hack got up and walked over to the machine. "What's wrong with it?"

"Someone spilled a glass of Coke over the keyboard."

"That will cause issues."

Jonesey smiled persuasively. "Think you could…you know…use the magic on it?"

Hack frowned and looked back at the cubicle entrance. "I don't know. This place is too public. I've been seeing people following me. I think someone has found out about...the thing..."

Jonesey punched him on the arm. "Getting paranoid, man! Have you been playing too much *Left 4 Dead* again? Survival horror always freaks you out."

"I know what I saw, Jonesey."

"Come on! No one is watching! Look at this place. No one cares!" He put his hands together like he was praying. "It's for that girl who works at the Asus stall on 3. She is going to be soooo grateful if I fix it."

Hack pointed to a sauce stain on his friend's T-shirt. "Maybe you'd have more luck if you washed your clothes for once."

"Who has the time? Pleeeeease!"

Hack groaned. "You owe me."

Taking a final look back at the walkway, Hack crouched and placed his right hand on the exposed innards of the laptop. Jonesey leaned in, fascinated.

"This is my favourite bit."

"*Shut up!*"

"Sorry."

Focusing all his attention, Hack pressed his hand against the motherboard. Blue electricity leaped around his fingertips and licked the components. Hack closed his eyes...

*...and became one with the machine. He sensed the data stored in the hard drive, the dormant operating system, damaged chips. Mentally flying through the computer, Hack visualized its processors healing, repairing and becoming healthy again – like a body mending itself.*

He opened his eyes, removed his hand and pressed the *on* button. The screen flickered into life and Windows started to boot. Jonesey threw an arm around him.

"You're a genius! A complete freak, but a genius!"

Hack shushed him. "Keep it down!"

"Sorry, *Tony Stark!*" Jonesey said as he closed the laptop. "Forgot it has to be a big secret!"

"Have you looked at the net recently? Beijing is talking about registering kids with virus-related powers. So is Washington. I think that's who's been watching me. Some government organization."

"Chinese? American?"

Hack shrugged. "Who knows?"

Jonesey snapped his fingers and turned to his desktop PC. "Check this out," he said, and brought up a series of saved images and web grabs. "Been doing some research for you."

Hack leaned in as his friend flicked through the pages in rapid succession: images of military personnel walking alongside a group of teenagers, a grainy photograph of an aircraft carrier, satellite photos of a base in a desert, and endless blog entries on the subject of the fall virus, kids with superhuman powers and an organization calling itself HIDRA.

"HIDRA," he read aloud. "What's that?"

Jonesey sniggered. "Stands for Hyper-Infectious Disease Response Agency. Can you believe it? The UN created it ten years ago to investigate virus outbreaks. It was intended as a scientific operation, but it got taken over by the military pretty fast. This guy's name keeps coming up." Jonesey flicked to an image of a hard-faced man with a crew cut so short he was practically bald. The man looked directly at the camera – blue eyes flashing with a kind of fury. "Major Bright. He used to work for HIDRA but went rogue – sounds like a real lunatic. HIDRA arrested him for crimes against humanity or something, but he disappeared six months ago, presumed dead. Word is he's alive but in hiding. There's, like, a gazillion conspiracy blogs about this guy and HIDRA."

Now Hack laughed. "Yeah. All rumour, hearsay and pure fiction."

"No smoke without fire," Jonesey said. "In fact—"

He stopped as a commotion broke out near the escalators. One of the stallholders was screaming at a stranger dressed like an American tourist. The stallholder had snatched a pair of sunglasses from the man's head and brandished them in the air. There was some kind of micro-device attached to one arm – a camera? The stallholder thought so.

"You like to take pictures, huh? You spying on me? Who you from?"

The tourist held up his hands and backed towards the escalators. The stallholder and his friends had other ideas, however, moving in to block his escape route.

"I said, who you from?" the little man said, jabbing a finger in the tall American's chest.

Hack and Jonesey watched this from the cubicle opening. "Another corporate spy," Jonesey said with a shake of his head. "We speed up their systems, fix glitches in their software, then they come down here and try to steal our tricks. Goddamned big business. And they call us pirates!"

"I don't think that's what this guy is after."

"Why do you say that?"

"Because I've seen him before." Hack hadn't been sure at first because the clothes and haircut were different, but now he was: the "tourist" was the coat guy he'd seen four times on the MTR underground system. "I'm out of here."

He moved to the back of the stall, planning to jump

the cubicle wall and exit via the emergency stairwell just a few metres away. If he was lucky, the fake tourist wouldn't even notice him leave.

"Wait!" Jonesey said, grabbing his arm. "What about tomorrow night? The IFC infiltration, remember?"

*IFC infiltration* – typical Jonesey, making everything sound like a stealth mission. Hack had almost forgotten his promise to help with the Goodware Inc. issue.

"I don't know," he said. "I should be laying low. I'm going to keep my head down in Tai-O for the rest of the holidays. Give it a month, okay?"

"Aw, come on!" Jonesey pleaded. "Goodware stole my game and now they're shutting up shop and shipping out to Europe! If we don't hit them this weekend, there won't be any evidence left by next week!"

Hack looked back at his tail – the stallholders were still keeping him occupied. Jonesey got down on his knees and did the praying thing again.

"Okay, okay," Hack relented. "But if I see anyone following me, we abort. Right?"

"Right!" Jonesey said as he went over the wall. "8.30 p.m. tomorrow at the usual place..."

But Hack was already through the fire escape door and two flights down...

2

Hack's "power" was a result of the meteor shower six months before. Or, at least, that was his explanation.

It had been an unusually warm March night, so he and Danny had run down to the beach after a day's fishing and plunged into the sea, screaming and hollering against the water's coldness. They swam for a while and then floated on their backs in the stillness, bodies quickly adjusting to the temperature. A shooting star (in fact a meteor burning up as it hit the earth's upper atmosphere, Hack knew from his science classes) streaked across the sky from east to west. This sight, although spectacular, was quite common.

What happened next was not.

A multitude of shooting stars lit up the night in the full spectrum of colours: whites, reds, oranges, even blues. Sometimes the paths of the exploding meteor fragments would intersect at a point, creating a larger dot of light that quickly extinguished.

"It's like the stars are falling," Danny said, floating by Hack's side.

"Yeah," he agreed, although he well knew that the light show was merely debris from a larger meteor storm that had destroyed itself several days before. There'd been panic that the storm was headed straight for earth, a possible extinction level event. Then the storm simply collided with itself – the result of a lucky burst of solar radiation, both NASA and the Chinese National Space Administration claimed. There were plenty of other explanations buzzing around online, however: from nuclear missiles being fired into the storm, to stories of kids with superhuman powers being used to deflect its course.

It was hard to know what to believe.

Hack didn't mention any of this to Danny, however. He could talk to Jonesey and the guys at GC about all of that, but Danny was different. He was a village kid who knew the alleyways through the seafood markets and the best fishing holes like Jonesey knew his way around the innards of a PC. Danny would go to work on the fishing boats, settle down with one of the girls from the market and probably stay in Tai-O for the rest of his life. Hack, in contrast, was already on the move. Increasingly he spent his free time at the GC or the other tech-dens in the city. In a couple of years there would be exams, university and opportunities that would take him far from the sleepy village. They lay on their backs in the sea that night, watching the light show above them, each processing the event differently.

Eventually, the cold got the better of them and they moved their numb arms and legs back to shore where a crowd of people had gathered to stare at the sky.

"You boys ought to be careful," one old man called after them as they pushed their way through and went to their piles of clothes. "It's too cold for swimming."

Picking up his jeans, Hack turned to say something smart, but he didn't get a word out. Pins and needles shot up his arm, as if he'd stuck his finger in a light socket. Looking down, he saw blue veins of electricity shooting from the iPhone in the pocket of his jeans, along his fingers and up to his shoulder. For a brief moment Hack's mind flooded with an unstoppable gibberish flow of data.

Then he hit the sand...

He was vaguely aware of being carried from the beach back to his grandfather's house... Of being laid on his bed and a doctor standing over him... Of noticing the hairs along his forearm standing on end...

He awoke just before dawn, feeling thirstier than he ever had in his life. After staggering to the kitchen and downing three glasses of water in quick succession, he returned to the bedroom and found his iPhone (in fact a pretty good copy he'd bought six months before) lying by the reading light. The white back casing was blackened, as if it had been plugged into a power supply with too much voltage. Wiping the carbon residue away with his thumb, he sat on the side of the bed and tried holding the buttons in the reset sequence, to no effect. Then he recalled the final seconds before he collapsed at the beach: the data that burst through his mind, almost as if he had been linked to the machine.

Feeling just a little silly, Hack held the iPhone in both hands and closed his eyes. He concentrated on making some kind of connection; on plugging into the machine somehow.

For a moment nothing happened…

Then images began to form behind his eyelids, just flashes at first, growing in complexity. He sensed the internal flash drive, practically burned out by the earlier power surge. He imagined it coming to life again, and sure enough the process began. Within a few seconds the machine felt warm in his hands and he opened his eyes. The screen was illuminated and the usual apps were present.

He'd repaired it.

Over the next few days Hack excitedly experimented with other pieces of electronic equipment around the house. In terms of computing power, it didn't come much smaller than a phone, but Hack was mindful that his first experience of connection with the machine had knocked him off his feet. Therefore, he took it slowly, trying to connect with simpler items such as the television and the Blu-ray player before he moved onto more complex things.

Soon enough he felt ready to connect with his laptop. The greater complexity of data, components and structure left him feeling drained upon his first attempt and almost led to another burnout, but he soon learned how to control the flow between himself and the machine. When connected, he found that he could control and manipulate the computer's inner workings with his mind alone. He could also download data from the laptop and hold it in his brain – as if he had some kind of internal storage in his head, something akin to photographic memory.

Growing comfortable with his own new power, Hack began to research the meteorite storm and found out about the fall virus in Australia – how it put most people into a coma for which there was no cure and how it also gifted a small number of immune children with incredible abilities. Following the meteorite showers, it seemed such children were turning up all over the world.

A girl in Paris seen flying over the Eiffel Tower...

A student in Beijing who could punch holes in solid metal just by thinking about it...

A kid who disappeared on a passenger jet over the Atlantic and turned up thousands of kilometres away in Poland...

Hack realized he was one of them. One of the new breed of humans touched by the fall virus. And he understood that this was something he had to keep a secret. In Hong Kong, there had been stories of kids with suspected powers being picked up and transported to the Chinese mainland – never to be seen again. There were similar stories coming out of America. The CIA. The PSB. Why wouldn't they want a piece of kids with such powers?

So, apart from the times when he helped Jonesey and a couple of other trusted friends at the GC with particularly tricky hardware problems, Hack kept his power under wraps. Being able to change channels on the TV without the remote or carry files around in your head was fun at first, but no great shakes. The power almost became an afterthought. A skill Hack had, but never used. It was just safer that way – he had no urge to end up in Guantanamo Bay or anywhere like it.

But then Jonesey got him involved in the Goodware situation...

Goodware Inc. was just ten years old, but in that time it had risen to the top of the gaming business, swallowing up a whole load of smaller companies in the process. Its founder, Marlon Good, was some kind of geek genius. He came from an American family that was already super-rich (from dried goods or something boring), but made his first million by the time he was sixteen – by writing a very addictive bead puzzle game and selling the rights to Nintendo. He created Goodware the next year and never looked back. The key to Goodware's success was one of Marlon Good's later creations: *Portal War*, the most popular online shooter of the decade.

Six months before, Marlon Good had set the gaming community alive by sending out an invitation to coders all over the world to send in their game ideas to their head office in Hong Kong, stating he "wanted to encourage the next generation of game designers". What Good hadn't revealed was that he intended to take the best of those ideas and claim them for himself. Jonesey had been one of the people who submitted, sending in the code to a daft little flash game he'd written for the net: *Ridge Run Rabbit* (an endless platform jumper with a theme tune that stuck in your head).

Three months after Jonesey sent in his plans, an almost identical copy, renamed *Widge Wun Wabbit,* went on sale as an iPhone app under the Goodware banner. It was an immediate hit, selling almost 100,000 copies in two months. The first Jonesey heard of it was when someone at the GC congratulated him on becoming an app millionaire. He tried to contact Goodware but received no reply.

Then he contacted a lawyer.

The next day, his mother's apartment was burgled and his computer equipment stolen – along with all the evidence he had originally created the game. His lawyer dropped the case after a similar break-in at his office. After his family began to receive threatening phone calls, Jonesey dropped the case too.

Until Hack told him about his power.

Jonesey was convinced there had to be evidence of his original work kept somewhere in the Goodware Inc. offices. The only problem was that Goodware utilized some of the most advanced security technology in the world. Their office on Hong Kong Island was practically a fortress, but that didn't deter Jonesey.

He intended to get the evidence that Marlon Good stole his game.

And he'd persuaded Hack to help him.

3

There were three ways to cross the bay that separated Hong Kong's two major islands: by road through the tunnels, by the MTR train system, and by ferry. The last option was by far the slowest, noisiest and most crowded. It was also Hack's favourite, because of the spectacular views it gave of the 'scraper-lined waterfront of Hong Kong Island.

Hack stood by the ferry's observation rail and looked across Kowloon Bay. It was just past 8 p.m. and the nightly light show was in full swing. On either side of the bay, multi-coloured lasers stretched from the tops of the skyscrapers into the night. Cruisers crammed with tourists circled as people snapped away with cameras. The muffled sounds of cheesy music and the recorded *History of Hong Kong* commentary floated across the water from speakers.

He wasn't riding one of the tourist boats, however, and all too soon the Star Ferry Pier loomed ahead. The boat engine screamed as it was put into reverse. Passengers crowded for the exits, but Hack remained at the rail, looking up at his destination for that evening: the towering skyscraper called Two IFC. The tower exuded brilliant, white light – steel and glass gleaming brighter than its neighbours'. Two IFC was eighty-eight storeys tall, double the height of its twin tower, One IFC, just across the street. Whenever Hack looked at the buildings, he thought of the scene in *The Dark Knight* where Batman jumps off the top of Two IFC, glides over the city and smashes his way into an office in One IFC. A very cool scene – but probably suicide for anyone other than Bruce Wayne, Hack reflected.

The buffers around the side of the ferry squealed as they touched the pier. Seconds later the gangway descended and people shuffled towards the mall in search of shopping, cinema and food. Hack joined the back of the herd and followed them through the ferry terminal and into the shiny environment of the mall. Here everything was pristine – even the rubber plants in their pots looked as if they'd just been polished. Hack passed shops filled with designer goods and overpriced electronics towards one of the central hubs – a circular area with escalators going up and down. Through the glass atrium ceiling, he caught a glimpse of Two IFC tower extending above like a needle. The reality of the situation began to hit home. After months of planning and discussion with Jonesey, they were actually going to do it.

They were going to break into the Goodware offices on Level 77.

Hack checked his watch – almost 8.30 – right on time for his meeting. On Saturday night the mall hummed with thousands of people. Every restaurant had a queue stretching out the door. Groups of students hung around the entrance to the cinema. He saw a couple of school friends and waved to them, but didn't have time to stop, carrying on to the meeting place.

Honeymoon Dessert was a chain of ice-cream restaurants that had places all over the city. Due to Jonesey's sweet tooth, whenever they arranged a meeting outside the GC, it was usually at one of them. The place was packed and Hack had to look around for a moment before he spotted his friend, seated at a stall at the very back. The rest of the clientele were either dating couples or groups of teenage girls. Hack pushed his way through, feeling a little self-conscious, and took a seat opposite.

"What is that?" Hack asked, looking at the white and black liquid in the yellow bowl.

"Lychee and black bean soup," Jonesey replied, spooning another helping into his mouth.

Hack shook his head as he noticed an untouched bowl of the same dessert on the table. "I thought I said not to get me anything."

Jonesey looked sheepish. "Uh, it's not for you. Someone else is joining us."

Hack took a second to process the information, before leaning in towards his friend. "Someone else is coming tonight?"

"Take it easy!" Jonesey said, waving a hand for him to lower his voice. "How do you think I got my hands on all those security schematics? I needed someone with connections. We can trust this guy. He's got more reason to want to keep this secret than we have."

"What is he? Some kind of criminal?"

"No!" Jonesey insisted. "Just a guy with an interest in Goodware."

"He works for a rival software developer? Are we talking about industrial espionage—"

Jonesey coughed. "Here he is."

Hack looked round as a well-built guy in his twenties approached the table. He wore an immaculate grey suit, a white shirt open at the neck and looked like Chow Yun-Fat in *The Killer*. At first glance he might have been mistaken for a businessman on his night off, but then Hack spotted the edge of a tattoo at his neck, unmistakably the curving tail of a dragon. It was a fair bet that if the man removed his shirt, you'd see an upper body covered in such artwork. Hack had never met a member of the Triad, the network of criminal gangs that had controlled Hong Kong's underworld for centuries, but this guy fitted his mental image to a T. He took a seat beside Jonesey.

"Hack, meet Hui," Jonesey said by way of introduction, switching to Cantonese for once.

The man turned his dark eyes on him. Hack tried to hold his intense gaze, but had to look away. "Nice to meet you," Hui said, also using Chinese, his voice deep and measured. "Jonesey has told me so much about you."

"Yeah," Hack replied, "perhaps a little too much."

Hui laughed softly. "There's no need for concern. You'll find I'm very discreet. In fact, discretion is my business." He glanced at his watch – a Rolex that was probably genuine. "So, the shift change to the night-time security team in the corporate levels of the tower is at 9.00. We should make a move."

Hack gritted his teeth in annoyance. Clearly Jonesey had told the man everything about their plan. "Do you mind if we have a quick word in private?"

Hui's mouth widened into a smile, but his eyes didn't join in. "Why should I mind?"

"Just let me finish this," Jonesey said as he continued to spoon the soup into his mouth. Hack kicked his shin. "Or maybe I'll finish it later."

As the two boys rose, Hui leaned back and his suit jacket fell open, allowing the briefest glimpse of an automatic hanging in a holster under his left arm. Hack's blood ran cold as he and Jonesey crossed to the restaurant entrance.

"What were you thinking?" Hack whispered. "That guy's Triad!"

"Oh, come on! Just because he's got a tailored suit, doesn't make him a gangster."

"He's carrying a gun! When we left the table he opened his jacket so I could see it." Hack grabbed Jonesey's arm and shook him. "Do you understand? He *wanted* me to see it."

Jonesey looked away at the crowds of families, couples and groups of friends traipsing through the mall. The air was full of laughter and shouting and friendly arguments. When he turned back, his face was even paler than normal and his eyes were watery.

"I'm sorry, Hack," he said. "I went to him to buy the IFC security plans, but he wouldn't leave it at that. Pressed me for information. When he heard about Goodware, he wanted in. Wouldn't take no for an answer."

"What does he want?"

"The beta version of *Portal War 2* from the Goodware server. Creating a pirate copy months before release would be worth millions to them."

Hack looked at him incredulously. "No! You think? How could you have been so stupid?" He took a deep breath, trying to calm down. "Now at least I know who's been following me all week."

Jonesey shook his head. "If the Triad were following, you wouldn't have seen them. Look, let's just get this over with. All we care about is getting proof of my original game design, right? Let the Triad have their pirate copy – in a few weeks, the real thing will be in the shops for the punters dumb enough to pay full price. Goodware won't lose anything. It's a victimless crime!"

"And you think it's going to stop here? Hui knows about my power now. What about when he wants to bypass another security system or break into another building? Who do you think he'll come looking for?"

"All he knows is your name, I swear."

That assurance didn't make Hack feel much better – he was certain that if the Triad wanted to find someone, they had ways of doing it. He glanced back at their table. Hui sat impassively, hands clasped together before him like a terracotta soldier waiting to be brought to life.

"Okay," he said finally. "We walk away right now. Lose him in the crowd. What's he going to do, start shooting at us in the middle of the mall? He can't make us go through with the break-in."

His friend looked at his feet. "It's not that simple. I made promises to them. Borrowed some money, just for the 3D LCD and some other components—"

"Jonesey!"

"I know! I was stupid! He wanted me to take an advance. Up capitalize my business or something."

"He wanted you in his debt."

"They're not going to let me walk away."

The two friends looked at one another for a moment. Jonesey gave a lopsided grin. "It's okay. You can leave. I should have told you what was going on."

"Yes, you should."

"I'll muddle through somehow."

"And how are you going to get past the Goodware security systems without me?"

Jonesey looked at his feet again. Hui approached them from the restaurant.

"We should get on with the job," he said.

Jonesey opened his mouth to say something, but Hack cut him dead. "Yeah, let's get this over with. In and out fast, that's the plan, right?"

His friend looked like he could have hugged him. Hui gave a mocking laugh.

"*In and out fast,*" he repeated. "You two sound like real professionals. You're not...*bad men,* are you?"

Hack ignored him and started in the direction of the express lift to Level 77, closely followed by the other two.

"Your friend should lighten up," Hui told Jonesey as they wove through the crowd. "He's too serious for his own good."

4

Two IFC tower was accessible by public lifts and several keycard-controlled express lifts to the upper financial trading floors. A dedicated lift for Levels 75, 76 and 77 wasn't marked on any of the official maps of the building. Its entrance was located in an anonymous, dimly-lit corner of the basement level. Goodware occupied the floors serviced by this lift – the three most secure in the entire building.

At 9 p.m. every evening, the general security detail for the tower changed over to the night shift, making it the perfect time for any type of incursion. During the changeover, the eyes of the security guards studying the CCTV cameras positioned around the tower were most likely to be distracted.

"Stop here," Hack said, as they stepped off the escalator from the mall levels and walked into the corridor containing the access lift. He pointed to a CCTV camera in the ceiling opposite the doors. Jonesey and Hui waited as he moved forward, keeping close to the wall and out of the line of vision of the camera. He stopped level with the lift doors and placed his hand flat against the wall. If the architectural plans Jonesey had provided were correct, his palm was over a cavity containing electrical wires for the light fittings, sockets and the camera itself.

Closing his eyes and channelling his power, Hack was able to visualize the wires as he made contact with them. Quickly isolating the coaxial cable that delivered the camera feed back to the security control room on Level 5 of the tower, Hack sent a surge of energy along the wire. He looked up. The green operation light on the side of the camera had gone out. The malfunction would bring one of the guards to investigate eventually, but not before they'd conducted their business. Hack ran over to the lift and beckoned for the others to join him.

The lift doors were plain grey metal with a numeric keypad in place of a call button. Access for the lift was controlled by a ten-digit keycode that changed every seven days (and sometimes at shorter intervals). Hack had no idea what the code was that week, but he didn't need to know. He placed his hand over the pad. Blue electricity flashed around his fingers as he accessed the encrypted code within the device. The doors opened.

"Nice work," Jonesey said, slapping Hack on the shoulder.

"We're not there yet," he replied as they stepped into the lift. Hui leaned against the back of the car as the doors closed. There were only three buttons to choose from. Hack pressed for Level 77 – the software development lab of Goodware Inc. – and the lift zipped up the shaft towards one of the most protected locations in the city.

"So, there are no security guards on this floor?" Hui said.

"The tower guards only cover the entrance to the lift," Jonesey replied. "Everything on these floors is run by Goodware's personal security team. They don't trust the IFC employees."

"And they don't have any private guards on patrol?"

Jonesey shook his head. "Uh-uh. The Goodware board

doesn't trust human beings in general. Everything is automated: motion sensors, sound traps, laser trip wires. If an alarm gets triggered, there's a fast-response security team located on Level 50 – they only get access to these levels in the event of an alert. Then there's a second response team located in One IFC whose job it is to monitor the actions of the first team – just in case one of the guards created a false alarm in order to gain access to the software on this level."

Hui nodded approvingly. "There are many dishonest people out there."

"That's not all," Jonesey continued, talking a mile a minute, just like he always did when nervous. "The ceiling has halon/$CO_2$ gas canisters fitted in the air vents. Halon is used to put out electrical fires because it doesn't damage computer equipment, but it's toxic to humans if inhaled. In the event of any alarm, the level floods with halon – whether there's a fire detected or not."

Hui grinned. "So, their fire system is also an effective way of disabling any intruders."

"Nice people, huh?" Jonesey said. "I can't believe I was ever stupid enough to trust them with *Ridge Run Rabbit*."

"Don't worry, kid, we'll get your little game back," Hui replied, with little sincerity.

Hack met his friend's eye and gave the slightest shake of his head. His heart had been racing since they first entered the lift and he could see sweat beads standing out on Jonesey's forehead. Hui, in contrast, was as cool as a cucumber – as if breaking into a high security building was all in a night's work. Which it probably was.

The lift reached its destination and the doors slid open onto a bland-looking reception area.

"Okay," Hack said, eyeing the sliding glass doors that marked the entrance to the office area. "I'm only going to shut down the security systems that I absolutely have to. That way, there's less chance of triggering any of the anti-tamper devices built into the network. Walk exactly where I walk and do what I do. We're spending no more than five minutes in here. Any longer and there's a serious risk of something going wrong."

Hui nodded approvingly. "Very good. You know, when Jonesey told me about you, I was sceptical. But from your attitude and performance so far I can see you have a very bright future ahead of you."

Hack wiped his palms, which were damp with perspiration, against his jeans. "There's no *future* for me in doing things like this," he said. "I'm here for Jonesey and that's all. After we get what we want, you can forget you ever met me."

Hui smiled. "Sure."

"It's okay, Hack," Jonesey reassured. "Let's just get this over with as fast as possible."

Hack went to the glass doors and placed his hand against the card reader on the wall. Seconds later, the reader beeped and the doors opened. Hack looked back at his companions and placed a finger against his lips. The main floor had sound as well as motion sensors. They both nodded to show their comprehension and followed Hack into the open-plan office area.

Over fifty employees worked on this level – a mixture of the company's best programmers, designers and testers, all of them dedicated to refining the current build of Goodware's cash cow, *Portal War*, and working on the follow-up. Each employee had a desk and terminal, but to cut down on privacy there were no cubicle walls or any piece of furniture above waist height. From his study of Goodware's working methods, Hack knew that each of the terminals was a slave device linked to a central server under the control of the head administrator. Email and internet access outside the local area network was strictly controlled. Random spot searches of employees were conducted daily to make sure flash drives or other storage devices weren't being smuggled into the office. The administrator could tap into any of the terminals at any time to spy on what employees were doing.

Goodware Inc. was a paranoid business – with good reason.

The *Portal War* online community numbered over twenty million worldwide and through subscriptions and product placement (advertising posters and objects within the gaming environment which Marlon Good said "added realism") had generated close to a billion dollars' revenue. The sequel was expected to earn double that during its lifetime. This made the pre-release game a very precious commodity. It would be only too tempting for an employee to steal part of the code, new character designs or level maps and sell them on for a fast profit. Goodware spent millions of dollars every year planning so that didn't happen.

*But they weren't planning on me,* Hack thought as he swiped his hand over a laser grid protecting the route through the centre of the office. He sensed the beams fail and moved forward, keeping as low as possible. Directly behind him, Jonesey and Hui did the same.

They progressed across the office towards a room in the very centre: a cube of black glass with no visible entry point. This was the main testing room and the office of the system administrator. It also contained the control server for all the work terminals and it was here that they would find evidence of Jonesey's original game designs – if indeed it still existed.

Disabling more lasers, cameras, a directional mic designed to pick up the sound of breathing, and a pressure sensitive pad under the carpet, Hack reached the edge of the cube. The glass room exuded brilliant blue light, stretching out in ever-changing spikes and arcs. This electronic aura was only visible to Hack, however – an indication of the ultra-powerful technology housed within. He placed his hand on the glass, creating swirling patterns of energy across the dark surface. The rectangular outline of a door appeared a metre to his right and swung outwards, allowing access.

Hack smiled at Jonesey, despite the seriousness of their position. The goal they'd been talking about ever since Goodware's theft of *Ridge Run Rabbit* was within their reach.

"We're almost there," Hack said. He led the way into the cube.

The interior of the room was exactly six by six by six metres. Although the glass on the outside was opaque, inside it appeared clear – allowing 360 degree views of the office. Against one wall stood the server tower – a black monolith with green lights flashing rhythmically along one side. An LCD screen took up most of the opposite wall. Directly before this was a work desk with a terminal linked to the server, an unfamiliar games console and two swivel chairs. This was the administrator's work area and the place where the overall build of the game was tested. Many programmers worked on different components of the game, but only a few were ever allowed to run the full draft version, and then only under the watchful eyes of the administrator.

Jonesey and Hui entered the cube. The door closed behind them with a faint click.

"This is amazing," Jonesey said breathlessly.

Hack didn't intend to waste time. He estimated they'd already spent three minutes inside the office, which meant they had another two to find what they wanted and get out. He sat and placed his hand on the terminal keyboard. Rather than pressing the power button on the monitor (which would set off an alarm) he instead accessed the server through touch alone – stretching out with his mind via the keyboard's wireless connection to the machine. In seconds, he had pushed through layers of encryption and protection that would take an experienced computer criminal months to crack (if ever) and gained access to the hard drive.

For a moment his thoughts tumbled, trying to sort the confusing depths of code, images and information stored on the server. Employee data was here, as were entire obsolete versions of the game and swathes of security reports. He had never accessed a computer with a tenth of the capacity and speed of this machine – it was remarkable. Hack tried to focus. He had to find Jonesey's original designs. Searching the information was like swimming through murky water – so much irrelevant information that it was hard to find what he was looking for.

"Is it there?" Jonesey asked at his shoulder. "The original concept maps? Code fragments? My submission email? Anything!"

"I can't find it," Hack replied, shaking his head. "There's just too much junk."

Jonesey groaned in frustration and paced behind him. Hack decided to try a different approach – accessing the vast abyss of trash files collected in the depths of the server's memory. Here was material that had been long since deleted, but still existed in fragments waiting to be reassembled – like photographs torn into a million pieces and thrown into the wind – a practically impossible task for all but the most sophisticated software. Putting them together again was no problem for Hack, however. He cast his mind across the ocean floor of corrupted data and it sprang back into life before him.

Then he saw it – a file named *Ridge_run_jones* shining like the light of a candle amidst the flow. Reaching out, he grabbed it and held it tight, along with a whole load of tagged files relating to it. The file properties indicated that the last user to access the files was none other than Marlon Good himself. *Gotcha!* Hack thought triumphantly. This was the evidence they needed to prove the company's theft of the original idea. Good had tried to destroy it, but he hadn't done a thorough enough job – no doubt assuming that no one would ever get their hands on the server.

Hack said, "Give me the USB."

With shaking fingers, Jonesey removed a 128 gig flash drive from his pocket and placed the metal contact in Hack's free hand. In an instant, Hack transferred the files from the server, through his body and into the drive. Then, remembering Hui's interests, he snatched up a large folder marked *Portal War 2* and put that on the portable drive as well.

"Done," he said, opening his eyes and tossing the USB drive to Jonesey. He rose from the swivel chair. "Now, let's get out of here."

"Not so fast."

Hui had spoken. He stood at the far end of the desk, looking down at the games console. "Is that thing alarmed?" he asked.

Hack turned his attention to the console for the first time. It was surprisingly thin, had a silver and black casing and no apparent place to insert a games disc. The blue lettering on the top read *PlayStation5*.

"I don't believe it," Jonesey said quietly.

"It must be a prototype used for game development," Hack replied. He'd read online that the console wasn't scheduled for release for another year at least. The artists' drawings he'd seen looked completely different to the machine sitting before them, however. Goodware had obviously been allowed access to an early version in order to facilitate their programming development.

"I said," Hui repeated, his voice taking on a harder edge, "is it alarmed?"

Hack scanned it quickly and detected no attached security devices. He shook his head.

Hui picked up the console, ripped the HDMI cable from the back and tucked it under his arm. "Let's go."

Hack and Jonesey exchanged glances. Suddenly everything was becoming clear: Hui and his employers weren't interested in *Portal War 2* – that was small fry compared to what he now had in his hand. A prototype of a next generation console would be worth billions. The technology could be reverse-engineered, cloned and put on the market. Within weeks, cheap copies would be available in every city around the world and they all knew it. The Triad would make a fortune and all of it would go back into their criminal activities.

"I'm not going to let you take that," Hack said, trying to keep the fear from his voice. "It's stealing."

Hui laughed. "That's very noble, coming from someone who just ripped off Goodware's central server."

"That's different. We're just taking what belongs to us! We're not criminals."

Hui patted the PS5. "Possession is nine-tenths of the law, as the Americans say."

He turned and pushed the section of wall where the door had been. The glass didn't budge. Hui looked back at Hack.

"Do that thing you did before. Open the door."

"No."

Jonesey took a step closer to his friend and whispered, "Just let him take it! Remember the gun?"

"Listen to your friend," Hui said. "You'll live longer."

Hack shook his head. "If you want to get out of this room, you'll put the console down. Try anything funny and I'll trigger every alarm in this building. Like I said, we're not thieves."

"Really? Well, I think you'll have a hard job convincing the cops of that." With a lightning-fast motion, Hui raised his left hand towards Hack's throat. "When you wake up."

Cold metal fangs pressed against the exposed skin of Hack's neck and a burst of electricity jolted his entire body. For a moment he remained standing, every muscle dancing as the current ran through him. Then Hui released the button on the taser concealed in his sleeve and Hack fell against the server.

"Hack!" Jonesey cried, but Hui rounded on him with the weapon.

"Keep your voice down or you're next."

Jonesey looked on helplessly as Hui placed the taser in his pocket and removed his automatic. He pointed the weapon at the area through which they'd entered and pulled the trigger. With a deafening blast, the entire wall shattered. Ceiling lights flicked on blindingly full and an alarm began to screech. Hui thrust the PS5 into Jonesey's arms, grabbed him by the shoulder and manhandled him through the shattered wall of the cube.

"What about Hack?" he protested weakly.

"Let him work it out," Hui snapped. "He's the one with superpowers…"

On the floor by the server, Hack lay helpless, his body continuing to jolt in the aftermath of the electric shock. Above the sound of the alarm, he heard a hissing sound and remembered Jonesey's story about the halon gas.

The canisters were releasing their poison.

Summoning all of his strength, and fighting against the muscular spasms running through his arms and legs, Hack rolled onto his stomach and began to crawl for his life.

5

The hovercopter was almost fifty kilometres from the outskirts of Hong Kong when Sarah Williams's voice sounded in her brother's head.

*Are you almost there?* she asked. *The target is in danger.*

Robert looked at the pilot sitting beside him in the cockpit. "How much longer?"

"Ten minutes," the pilot said.

Robert relayed this information to his sister.

*He doesn't have ten minutes!* Sarah replied. She was

back in the cargo bay of the *Ulysses*, keeping track of the boy as best she could.

Robert looked through the curved windscreen of the hovercopter. On the ocean's horizon, the lights of the city glittered in the darkness. It was still quite a distance away – further than he'd ever teleported before. But he heard the desperation in his sister's thoughts.

*Can you get a definite lock on the kid?* Robert asked. *I'll try a teleport.*

*Okay,* Sarah replied. *I'll guide you.*

Robert unclipped his seat belt and spoke to the pilot again. "I'm teleporting out. I'll call in our location as soon as I make contact."

The pilot nodded. "Just remember the prearranged extraction point—"

But Robert Williams had already disappeared.


Less than a minute after the alarms triggered, the doors of the express elevator opened. Five security guards emerged, fanning out across the reception area, machine guns in their hands. Dressed in lightweight Kevlar body armour, they also sported full-face breathing masks to protect themselves against the halon gas already pouring out of open doors to the office area. The leader of the security detail gave a hand signal to the two men on his right, indicating they should stay at the lift in case any of the intruders attempted to slip past. He then waved for the other two to follow him into the office.

He advanced into the thick, white cloud of halon gas, which had cut visibility down to a metre. The other two guards took positions to his left and right and they went forward in a line.

"Stay close," the leader whispered into his comm. "Keep to your firing vectors." He wasn't so much worried about the intruders – the halon would have knocked any fight out of them by now – as getting shot in the smog by one of his own men.

His earpiece crackled and his second-in-command, who was leading a second team up the emergency stairwell (the only other way off the level), barked an urgent message. The leader shook his head and spoke to his men. "Beta team has been fired upon in the stairwell. One man down." Then he added, "Shoot anything that moves in here."

His men nodded and they carried on, reaching the centre of the floor where the glass cube stood, only half intact. Halon hung densely here, but the leader spied something at the far end of the office space – a shadow moving through the mist.

"Target, two o'clock!" he barked, firing at the shape. His men spotted it and also went "weapons free". Computer terminals and office chairs exploded as their bullets cut a swathe through everything in their path. Ten seconds later, the leader held up his fist for them to cease firing.

Inside the halon cloud, nothing moved.

The leader gave the *forward* signal and they continued their advance.

Hack removed his T-shirt and held it over his mouth and nose as he staggered towards the far end of the office, where the halon was less thick. Seconds before, he'd considered approaching the guards as his only way out of the gas – then they'd opened fire indiscriminately. Now, heart racing, Hack staggered in the other direction, still trying to process what was happening: between the poisonous gas and the trigger-happy idiots on the other side of the room, his chances for survival were looking pretty slim.

He reached the back wall of the office and followed it towards a door, praying it wasn't locked. It wasn't. He collapsed into the adjoining room on his hands and knees and kicked the door shut. His lungs were on fire from the gas he'd inhaled, but Hack fought the urge to crawl into a ball and lie there on the floor. He was in a conference room with a long table and floor-to-ceiling windows along one wall. The halon was pouring under the door and through several holes in the wall made by stray bullets, so he moved to the other side of the table and leaned against the window.

Outside, the skyline of Hong Kong Island glittered, its shimmering skyscrapers distant and unreachable. One IFC was lit up directly ahead and Hack thought of Batman again – not much chance of making it off the building without a glider or parachute, and even then it would probably be suicide. There was, however, a thin ledge that ran around the edge of the level. It was less than a metre across, but Hack guessed it would be possible to walk round the ledge to the other side of the building and maybe even climb down to one of the lower levels. He touched the window – thickened safety glass that would take a sledgehammer to break.

Another volley of bullets burst through the wall of the conference room. Hack hit the carpet as a round tore over his head and through the window. The glass went opaque as the bullet punched a one-centimetre hole in the middle of the pane.

Wasting no time, Hack threw the T-shirt over his head,

grabbed one of the leather chairs from the table and heaved it at the weakened pane. The chair sailed through the glass and over the side of the building. Gulping down some of the halon-free air blasting through the gap, Hack struggled forwards and stepped out onto the ledge.

Standing on the side of a building, seventy-seven floors above the earth, a half-metre ledge doesn't seem very wide at all. The window panes provided no purchase, so Hack pressed his back against the glass and slid along towards the corner of the building. His plan was to walk round to the other side, hopefully out of the immediate view of the guards, and then try to climb down. This was easier said than done, what with the force of the wind at this height, which threatened to catch him and sweep him off the side at any moment. Centimetre by centimetre, he edged his way along to the comparative safety of the other side of the building...

Inside the conference room, one of the guards kicked the door open. Taking a quick glance over his shoulder, Hack started moving faster as the man entered the room and swept his gun around. He was almost two thirds of the way to the corner when the guard spotted him.

Sacrificing caution, Hack ran the remaining few metres as gunfire split the air. The windows behind him exploded. Hack made the metal support at the edge and threw himself round as glass splinters flew. Somehow he managed to keep his balance, but then a powerful crosswind hit and he staggered back, feet on the edge of the ledge. He caught a glimpse of IFC plaza, over three hundred metres below. Turning from the vertigo-inducing sight, he grabbed the support and pulled himself against the building. He looked at the ledge along the other side of the building and tried to get his feet moving, but they just wouldn't obey.

Another volley of bullets ricocheted off the metal.

"I'm not a thief!" Hack screamed. "You've got the wrong guy!"

He was answered by more gunfire.

Holding on for dear life, Hack looked at his feet and wondered just how far the drop was to the level below.

"It's too far to jump," a voice said at his side, as if in answer to his thoughts.

Hack turned and saw a blond-haired kid just a little younger than himself leaning casually against the glass right beside him. In shock, Hack's grip on the support loosened. He took a step back—

And fell off the side of the building...

Hack tried to scream, but found it impossible as he fought to get air into his lungs. Two seconds after going over the ledge, he passed the fiftieth floor of Two IFC, picking up speed as he went. His arms and legs flailed uselessly as he spun round. The side of the building raced past like a track and the illuminated plaza rushed up to meet him at terrifying speed. His mind was filled with the awful certainty of death approaching.

Four seconds down, passing the thirtieth floor, Hack finally managed a scream that came out as a strangulated gurgle.

A second figure blinked into existence directly beside him...

Hack recognized the face of the boy from the ledge as he reached out to grab his arm...

The world disappeared. For a split second, they were nowhere at all. *So, this is what it's like to be dead,* Hack thought.

Then reality rushed back as he and the other boy rematerialized less than a metre above the ground. Hack slammed against the concrete of IFC plaza, every bone in his body jarred by the impact, and lay still for a second. With a groan, he looked over at the body of the blond kid, lying beside him on the ground. They should have been dead – pulverized by the fall – but somehow that hadn't happened. Around them, people were murmuring and pointing. Someone ran over and crouched beside him.

"I'm okay," Hack said, pushing himself into a sitting position. He looked up at the skyscraper and shook his head at the hundreds of metres he'd just fallen. "Somehow I'm okay."

"They're calling an ambulance," the woman reassured. The other kid snatched Hack's wrist and they disappeared again…

Teleporting back into existence on the far side of the plaza, hidden in the shadows of a tree. Hack yanked his arm free and rounded on the kid.

"Will you stop doing that?" he snapped, still aching from the impact.

"Sorry," the boy said, sitting heavily on a low wall in the semi-darkness. It was clear from the look on his face that he was in pain also. Across the plaza, the crowd that had seen their original fall was now in complete turmoil at their disappearance. "We were generating a little too much interest."

Hack sat down and rubbed his aching shoulder, which had hit the concrete hardest. "Who are you?"

"My name's Robert Williams," he answered. "And I'm here to make sure you don't get yourself killed tonight."

6

"So, let me get this straight," Hack said. "You came here looking for me because your sister had a premonition I was in trouble. She just knew I'd be there on the 77th floor needing someone to save me from the men with guns?"

Robert nodded. "Something like that. Sarah has advanced telepathic abilities and she uses them to track down kids like you. Kids who've been given powers by the fall virus."

"Track down?" Hack said. "Or do you mean *hunt* down?"

"We're with a scientific organization called HIDRA. It stands for the Hyper-Infectious—"

"I know what it stands for. I've read the blogs."

"Then you'll know we're working to find a cure for the fall virus," Robert continued. "We're also a safe haven for kids who've been persecuted because of their abilities. We give shelter if necessary, advice on controlling and developing your powers—"

"And all I have to do in return is help out your private army from time to time, right?" Hack interrupted. "I've heard all about Colonel Moss. And what was the other guy called? Major Bright?"

"That's in the past. Colonel Moss is in jail. The military doesn't call the shots at HIDRA any more."

"I'll take your word for that," Hack said. In the middle of the plaza, a couple of uniformed cops had arrived and were listening to the woman's story. He got to his feet, keeping in the shadows. "Well, thanks for saving me from getting squished. Maybe I'll look you up sometime—"

"Hey, you can't just walk away!" Robert protested, standing also.

"That's exactly what I'm doing," Hack said and he started across the plaza, keeping to the edge.

His thoughts had turned to Jonesey, who was still in the hands of Hui. They could be anywhere in the city, but if he knew his friend he'd go to the Golden Chip. The only question was, would Hui let him? Thankfully, the crowd was too busy bending the ears of the cops to notice him as he approached the entrance to the MTR station. The teleporting kid, Robert, seemed to have taken the hint and wasn't following him either.

Hack ran down the escalator into the station, waved his Octopus card at the turnstile reader and made the platform for the Tsuen Wan line just as the train was arriving. The protective doors, designed to stop the rush hour crush of passengers pushing themselves onto the tracks, opened and he slipped inside, grabbing a post in the middle of the carriage. A few seconds later the train pulled away smoothly on its high-speed trip under the bay towards Kowloon.

Glancing down the carriage, Hack saw someone he recognized: the fake tourist guy from the GC. He cursed inwardly and looked in the other direction. Sure enough, there was camera woman from that day in Tai-O. Both of them were staring directly at him, making no effort at pretence now. How had they found him again?

"Friends of yours?"

Hack turned. Robert stood beside him, holding onto the pole as if he'd just appeared out of nowhere – which he probably had.

"You don't give up, do you?"

Robert shook his head. "I told you I wasn't going to let you get yourself killed, and I meant it. My sister sensed people are after you because of your powers – people who don't have your best interests at heart."

"And did she *sense* that before or after your HIDRA spies started following me?" Hack pointed at the man down the carriage and then the woman. "I spotted my tails a week ago, so you can stop with the telepathy story."

*I've never seen those two before in my life,* Robert replied, using his mind to communicate directly for the first time. *But judging by the way that guy is talking into his wrist, I'd say they're not alone.*

Hack turned his attention back to the man. Robert was right – he was whispering into a mic concealed in the sleeve of his coat. There was a receiver in his left ear.

*They're not with you?* Hack thought. He'd never had the chance to use the telepathic communication all fall virus-altered kids shared, but in the presence of the other boy it seemed completely natural.

*Believe me, it's not our style,* Robert replied. *You're picking a fight with the wrong person. Whoever those two are, they know how to find you. How much do you want to bet that guy's calling in backup? When you get off this train, you'll find more of them waiting and there's nothing—*

"Okay, okay," Hack said. "I get the idea." His head was spinning. The man and woman weren't Triad and they weren't HIDRA either, so who were they? The train began to slow as it approached Tsim Sha Tsui station, the closest stop to the GC.

"All right," Hack said, "let's say I want your help. What's the big plan?"

"I teleport us to street level this minute. Two HIDRA hovercopters are en route to the city. I'll call in our position and they'll pick us up for transport to our mobile base."

"There's something I need to do first," Hack said. "A friend of mine is in trouble and I'm not leaving the city until I know he's safe."

He fully expected the other kid to make some argument about how they didn't have time or how it was too risky to go after Jonesey when people were following them. But Robert merely nodded.

"Fine. We'll help your friend."

Hack said, "Okay, let's get out of here then."

Robert took his wrist… The brightly-lit, enclosed space of the carriage faded away and was replaced by humid night air and a darkened alleyway. Hack felt momentarily disorientated by the teleport and just a little nauseous. He bent over and took a couple of deep breaths.

"You okay?" Robert asked.

Hack nodded. "Yeah, still getting used to that."

"Do you know where we are?"

Hack looked left and right, spotting the buses crowding Nathan Road at the far end of the alley. He estimated they were only a few streets away from the GC.

"This way."

Hack led Robert through the backstreets at a run, checking behind to make sure they were no longer being followed. Teleporting directly out of the subway system seemed to have done the trick.

"That's a pretty useful ability," he told Robert as they ran. "Have you done that before? Jumping off a building to save someone, I mean?"

"Never," Robert said.

"Then how did you know it was going to work?"

"I didn't."

As they reached the ground level entrance to the GC, Hack stopped and gave his companion a look. "You didn't know it was going to work? Then you could have been smashed to a pulp along with me."

Robert shrugged. "My sister told me to look after you. Didn't want to let her down. She's real mean when she's angry."

Hack was suddenly a whole lot more grateful for what the other kid had done for him that night. There weren't many people for whom he'd jump off a building, especially not if he'd just met them.

"If he's here, Jonesey will be on Level 6," Hack said, indicating the open entrance to the GC. It was almost 10 p.m. and the market was shutting down. Evening shoppers and stallholders poured out of the building.

"Okay, let's get going."

"We're not teleporting up?"

Robert shook his head. "Best to take the stairs. I'm getting tired and we might need to get out of there fast. I've probably got a couple of 'ports left in me this evening, but let's save them."

Hack understood what Robert meant: using his own power for any extended length of time left him feeling drained. He could only imagine the amount of mental energy expended in jumping from one physical location to another.

They entered the GC and rode the elevators past the floors of gadgets and software. Lights and screens were shutting down everywhere. Hack always found the market a little eerie at this time of night – without the hustle and bustle, the GC became a place of shadows. Level 6 was in near darkness. The upgrades area never stayed open as late as the computer stalls below. Hack scanned the empty cubicles, eyes adjusting to the light, and then turned to Robert.

"Wait here. I need to deal with this myself."

He and Jonesey had gotten themselves into their present situation. And if Hui was there, as Hack somehow sensed he was, it was up to them to sort it out. Robert seemed to understand this, because he nodded and leaned against the wall by the escalator.

"Just shout if you need me," he said. "I'll be there quick."

"I bet."

Hack headed across the floor towards Jonesey's cubicle. Sure enough, he found his friend sitting in the middle of his workspace – wrists and ankles secured to the swivel chair with duct tape. Jonesey's eyes widened as Hack approached and ripped away the piece of tape covering his mouth.

"You escaped!"

"Yeah. I had a guardian angel."

"You shouldn't have come here. It's a trap!"

Hack nodded and looked around the cubicle. The PS5

sat on the workbench, linked up to the LCD. Jonesey read his mind.

"It works."

"Let's get you free." Hack kneeled and tore away the tape around the other kid's ankles.

"Just go!" Jonesey protested. "All this is my fault."

Hack started on the wrist bindings. "We got the evidence that Goodware stole your idea. It was worth it. Right?"

Jonesey shook his head as Hack removed the final piece of tape. "He's here."

Hack straightened up and turned slowly. Hui stood in the cubicle doorway. In his right hand he held a squat weapon that Hack recognized from a lifetime of first-person shooters as an Uzi 9mm.

"Well, you are a talented young man," Hui said, aiming the machine gun in their general direction. "Even I would have found it difficult to escape that tower in the position I left you. I'm beginning to think that shooting you would be a terrible waste." He studied Hack with his dark, calculating eyes. "Come with me. I'll make you a billionaire before you're twenty."

Hack played for time. "What about Jonesey?"

Hui chuckled. "He's a fat slob with a moderate talent for fixing laptops. Toss a rock in this city and you'll hit ten kids just like him. You, however, are truly unique."

Hack picked up the PS5 from the workbench. "And what about this?"

"Just something my bosses want," Hui said with a shrug. "Sony will pay to get the prototype back rather than have it cloned, just like Microsoft did when we stole theirs. Everyone will be happy."

Hack looked at Jonesey from the corner of his eye and then turned his attention back to Hui. "So, I guess if it got full of bullets, your bosses would be pretty annoyed, huh?" He stepped in front of Jonesey, holding the PS5 before them like a shield.

Hui gave an exasperated sigh. "You're really starting to—"

Hack threw the PS5 at Hui, making him choose between catching the console and shooting them. He chose the former. As he grabbed the machine, both Hack and Jonesey went for the back of the cubicle.

They vaulted the wall and landed on the other side. Hack grabbed his friend's arm and pulled him in the direction of the fire escape. The back of the cubicle exploded as Hui fired a burst of rounds. The two boys staggered back. Bullets impacted the plasterwork ahead. They ducked round the side of another cubicle and crouched there, all too aware that the cardboard walls were no protection at all.

"You disappoint me, kid!" Hui shouted. "I'm offering you the chance to make some real money!"

"You've got the console!" Hack shouted back. "Just take it and go!"

Hui laughed. "That's not how things work in my business. We tie up our loose ends!"

Hack pulled Jonesey into another cubicle. Hui fired again – cutting through the wall where they'd crouched seconds before.

"Go for the fire exit," Hack whispered. "I'll keep him distracted."

Jonesey opened his mouth to protest, but Hack pushed him out of the cubicle and went in the other direction, moving towards the escalators where he knew Robert was waiting.

"You're gonna have to do better than that!" he shouted.

Hui responded with gunfire, more prolonged this time. Hack threw himself onto the floor of another cubicle as computer manuals exploded above his head.

"I can keep this up all night!" Hui screamed when he finally stopped firing. There was a *click* as he ejected an empty clip and slotted another into the Uzi.

Hack looked up. Bullet holes riddled the cubicle walls and paper fragments filled the air. He rose into a crouch, ready to run, but a hand touched his shoulder…

"Let's get out of here," Robert said.

Hack pulled away. "Not until I know my friend's safe!"

Robert began to argue, but was cut short as Jonesey's voice called across the floor.

"Hack! He's got me!"

Robert and Hack looked at one another. Hack sighed and moved to the cubicle entrance.

"You're not actually going out there?" Robert hissed. "He'll kill you."

Hack thought it over. Then he said, "You've still got a couple of teleports in you, right?"

7

Hack walked between the cubicles with his arms outstretched. Dead ahead, Hui stood with the snub-nosed Uzi pressed into his friend's ear and the PS5 tucked under his other arm. Jonesey's face was drenched with sweat.

"I'm sorry," he said. "He was too fast."

"Don't worry," Hack replied. "It's going to be okay."

Hui pushed Jonesey down onto his knees and placed the gun against the back of his head.

"I'll give you one last chance to walk away," Hack

said. He held Hui's eyes this time.

Hui actually smiled. "You've got a lot of spirit, kid. But not much of a brain. What a waste."

He raised the Uzi at Hack…

…who closed his eyes and scanned the surrounding electronics that hadn't been destroyed by Hui's bullets – hard drives, LCD screens, adapter sockets stuffed with far too many plugs, even the PS5 console. Summoning all his strength, he prepared to send a blast of mental energy to every device.

"Jonesey!" he yelled. "Hit the deck!"

The other boy flopped face down as Hack threw his arms forward. An invisible wave of energy swept out in all directions from his body. Every piece of machinery within a five-metre radius overloaded, as if their electrical supply had increased tenfold. Tower casings burst open in showers of sparks… Screens exploded… Electrical sockets spewed fire… Broken components filled the air, tearing through the cardboard-thin walls of the cubicles…

In the path of the shockwave, Hui threw his gun hand up to protect his eyes from the flying plastic and metal. Something was burning his other arm. He looked down at the casing of the PS5, which was glowing red-hot. With a cry of pain, he tried to throw it from his grasp, but the plastic had already melted around the skin of his hand. Dropping the Uzi, he desperately tried to pull his burning fingers free, but they had fused into the machine. It had literally become a part of him.

Someone materialized out of nowhere by his side. Hui looked round and saw a European-looking kid. The kid grabbed his elbow.

"Bet you wish you'd left while you had the chance, huh?" Robert said.

The world shifted and Hui blinked in surprise as the shattered cubicles shimmered and faded away. He had the strangest feeling he'd travelled some distance. The unfamiliar kid let go of his arm and slapped his hands together, as if wiping them clean.

He grinned.

And then he disappeared again.

Hui looked left and right. He saw the half-shattered glass cube, the wrecked computer terminals and the remnants of the halon cloud. Somehow he was back in the Goodware office.

"You!" someone shouted at him. "Knees! Now!"

Hui turned his head fractionally. The butt of a gun hit the back of his neck. He went down. A booted foot kicked him over.

"Move again and you're dead," spat a guard in body

armour, aiming a machine gun at his face. The guard touched a mic at his throat. "Got one of them, sir."

Hui's eyes tracked down the left side of his body – the cooling plastic of the PS5 console was now fully melded to his fingers.

"Yessir," the guard said. "Caught him red-handed."

Hack helped Jonesey to his feet and brushed the blast wreckage from his shoulders. "Are you okay?"

Jonesey nodded. "Yeah. What about you?"

"Not a scratch."

Jonesey started as Robert rematerialized beside them.

"It's okay," Hack said. "He's a friend."

"That guy won't be bothering you any more," Robert said. "I left him in the middle of a dozen armed guards. All the same, we shouldn't hang around here."

Hack nodded and turned his attention to Jonesey. "You need to get out of the city. Go and lay low with my grandfather in Tai-O. He'll understand – you can take my room for as long as you need it. Just do me a favour: forget about Goodware Inc. and *Ridge Run Rabbit* for a while."

"I've had it with them," Jonesey replied ruefully. Then he frowned. "Where will you be?"

Hack glanced at Robert quickly and then looked back at his friend. "There are other kids like me out there. I have to meet them. See what they have to offer."

Jonesey threw his arms around him. "Just make sure you come back," he whispered in his ear.

"Look after my grandfather. Now get out of here."

Jonesey turned and ran for the fire escape, leaving Hack and Robert alone amid the ruined cubicles. In the distance a police siren whooped and howled, getting closer.

"We should move," Hack said. "Want to make that call?"

Robert removed a mobile phone from the back pocket of his jeans. Flipping it open, his face fell as the screen remained dark. He pressed a couple of buttons, to no effect.

"I think it got fried by my energy blast," Hack said sheepishly. He sensed the innards of the machine fused beyond even his repair abilities. "Sorry."

Robert put the phone away. "Not a problem. There's a pre-arranged extraction point about a kilometre from here. Tin Hau temple. Do you know it?"

Hack nodded. It was a small Buddhist temple just off Nathan Road – probably about ten minutes away on foot. "I take it a teleport is out of the question?"

"I'm pretty much out of energy for tonight."

"Then let's get going."

They took the fire escape down to ground level and exited via the back entrance of the GC. It was the long way round, but Hack decided that it was best to keep to the side streets as much as possible. For all they knew, Hui had accomplices watching the GC for their exit. Despite the heat of the night, they made a good pace, running side by side through the back alleys, which were all but deserted now that the markets and shops had closed.

"You really saved Jonesey and me tonight," Hack said as they ran across an intersection. "Sorry for trying to ditch you earlier."

"Don't worry," Robert said. He looked drained after the last two teleports. "I know it's hard to trust people. That trick back there was pretty cool, by the way. What did you call it?"

"The energy wave?" Hack said. "It was just something I thought would work. I'm still learning what I can do with my power."

"We all are," Robert replied with a grin.

Hack took a left towards Nathan Road. Kowloon's main drag was as busy as ever – cars, buses and scooters fought for space across four lanes of traffic. The street was ablaze with the neon light of a thousand adverts. Every direction was an assault on the eyes, but Hack knew exactly where he was going. The Tin Hau temple was directly opposite. The pedestrian crossing went green and they ran across the street and down the narrow alley that led to the main entrance of the temple.

When it was built in the nineteenth century, the temple had overlooked the bay. Now two kilometres of reclaimed land separated it from the water. It stood amid the noise and chaos of one of Hong Kong's busiest districts. High-rise buildings overlooked it on all sides. Nevertheless, it retained a strange kind of quietness. The Buddhist temple stood at the far end of a square surrounded by trees and a wall that ran the perimeter. The place was typically deserted this late in the evening, which is why it had been chosen as the extraction point, Hack guessed.

As they entered through the south gate, it appeared they were alone – then Hack noticed something completely out of place and almost hidden in the shadows of one of the trees...

In the centre of the square sat a small, black helicopter – albeit one with no visible rotor blades. A hovercopter. It looked like a fat-bodied beetle sitting in the darkness.

A pilot in a jumpsuit stepped from behind the machine as they approached. He had a gun in his hand.

"It's okay," Robert told Hack. "He's with us." He held up a hand and waved at the pilot. "Our communicator got fried!"

The man ran to meet them, shouting something... Hack looked up and saw the lights of another vehicle floating above the trees... A second hovercopter...

A whooshing sound filled the air as a rocket tore through the trees and hit the vehicle on the ground. The machine exploded in a brilliant ball of flame that threw out lumps of red-hot shrapnel. The blast knocked the pilot forward onto his face. Hack and Robert were hurled backwards as the force of the explosion hit them.

Momentarily stunned, Hack lay on his back looking up at the branches above. A rocket streaked through the air and there was a second explosion – one which lit up the night sky. The second hovercopter was hit.

Robert grabbed Hack's arm. "It's coming down!"

Sure enough, the vehicle that had been hovering almost silently above them had become a fiery lump of metal hurtling to earth. The two boys scrambled for their lives, running blindly in the direction of the temple at the far end of the park. As they reached the steps leading up to the building, Hack looked over his shoulder – and saw the second hovercopter fall through the tree, setting its branches ablaze. It hit the ground with a mighty crash, showering more shrapnel about. Hack thought of the pilot with the gun and wondered if he'd managed to avoid the impact – it was impossible to tell in the inferno.

"In here!" Robert exclaimed, kicking open the temple door.

They both ran in and crouched in the shadows on either side of the entrance. The interior of the temple was almost pitch-black. The smell of incense hung thick in the air. Hack pressed his face against the gap where the door met the wall and scanned the fiery mess outside.

"What just happened?" he said, breathing heavily. "I thought HIDRA was supposed to be like a private army or something. Why are people shooting at you?"

"We've got powerful enemies," Robert replied.

"Great. You could have told me that before—"

Gunfire cut him short. Both boys hit the floor as bullets ripped into the brickwork and through the wooden door. A second later, the firing stopped. Hack and Robert exchanged a glance and then looked back through the door. The fire was still blazing, but Hack counted at least four figures crouched by the temple steps.

"Robert Williams!" a man's voice yelled. The accent was British. "All Major Bright wants is the kid. Send him out and we'll leave you alone. Make us come in there and you'll get hurt."

*Major Bright.* Hack recognized the name instantly: the scary-looking guy from Jonesey's internet research. Even in the darkness he was able to see the shock on Robert's face.

"Bright," Robert whispered to himself.

"Well, guess we know who's been following me all week," Hack said. "So, what's the plan?"

Robert looked at him with a pained expression. "I don't have enough energy to teleport both of us out of here…"

Hack understood. "Just yourself, right?"

Robert nodded. "But I'm not leaving you."

"Oh, yes you are—"

More gunfire flayed the front of the temple.

"You've got thirty seconds!" the man yelled.

"You saved me twice tonight, Robert," he said. "Looks like we're outgunned this time." He considered their situation. "What do you think this Bright guy wants with me?"

"I don't know," Robert said, "but he's bad news. If Bright's taking an interest, it can't be for anything good."

"Thanks," Hack said wryly, "don't try to sugar-coat it or anything."

"*Twenty seconds!*"

"Are you going to get out of here or not?"

Robert hesitated just a moment longer, before reaching inside his jeans pocket and removing a metal object that looked like a miniature gun.

"Give me your arm," he ordered. Hack rolled up the sleeve of his shirt. Robert held the object against his skin and pressed a trigger. Hack winced as a needle darted in and out of his skin.

"I've just injected you with a GPS tracker," Robert explained. "We're going to find you and rescue you. I promise."

"*Ten seconds!*"

Hack rubbed his arm and pulled his sleeve over the mark. "Okay! Okay! Get out of here!"

Robert nodded – and disappeared.

Suddenly, crouched in the darkness of the temple, Hack felt more alone than he ever had in his life.

"*Time's up!*"

Hack pulled open the temple door and stepped outside. He felt the heat from the burning hovercopters on his skin and held up a hand to shield his eyes from the light. Four towering men approached – each holding a rifle in his hands and dressed in combat gear.

The one whose voice Hack recognized as the leader said, "That's a good boy." He was thin-faced to the point of looking like a skeleton – not a nice look. Two days' worth of greasy stubble adorned his face and a name tag on his chest read *Kotler*. He turned to one of the others. "Prep him for transport."

Two of the men grabbed his arms while another threw a hood over his head, drawing a cord tight around his neck so it stayed in place. They pinned his arms behind his back and secured his wrists with a plastic tie, leaving his ankles free so he could walk unassisted. The hood was heavy and incredibly claustrophobic. Hack's breath came in ragged gasps as he began to panic.

"Take it easy," one of the men said, grabbing his arm and shaking him. "Just breathe slowly."

He did just that and his heart rate regulated. The panic began to subside. He was led away blindly by the soldier as gunfire erupted behind them. Hack assumed they were shooting up the temple and was very glad that Robert had teleported away.

The door of a vehicle slid open noisily and he was thrown onto a metal floor. Seconds later, the engine started and the vehicle screeched away at high speed.

Hack fought to rise into a sitting position, but a heavy boot pushed him back again.

"Keep down," Kotler's voice said. "Or I'll put you down."

Hack did as he was told and lay still. Having survived falling off a building and being shot at by an insane Triad member all in one evening, he now found himself a prisoner.

He just hoped Robert had one more rescue in him.

## 8

Hack tried to keep track of time as he lay on the floor of the van. He estimated that an hour passed before it skidded to a halt – long enough to reach the outskirts of the city. It was impossible to tell for sure with the hood over his head, but he guessed they had driven towards the New Territories in the north, or even the border with mainland China. Doors opened. One of the soldiers pulled him roughly to his feet and guided him along. After a few metres they ascended a slope and, from the sound of engines and the vibration of the room, Hack sensed that he had been loaded aboard a plane.

He was made to sit (not easy with his wrists bound behind his back). The engine noise increased in volume and the plane began to move. As it picked up speed, Hack felt the vehicle angle up and he realized they were taking off. Where was he being taken? It could be anywhere. He began to breathe too fast again as the panic rose. *Keep it together,* he told himself. *You've survived this far.*

The plane levelled off and seconds later boot-steps approached. Someone loosened the cord around his neck and pulled away the hood. Hack's vision swam as his eyes adjusted to the light.

Sure enough, he was inside a plane. This was no passenger jet, however. The interior was a bare cylinder with benches along either side of the fuselage. At one end metal crates stood next to a ramp. Because the cabin was not pressurized, the engines were deafening. Hack realized that he was on some kind of military transport – in the rear cargo bay, by the looks of it. Directly in front of him, a bearded soldier stood with the hood in one hand.

"I'm gonna cut your wrist bindings," he said. "Try anything stupid and I'll put the hood back on your head. Understand?"

Hack nodded to show he understood very much. The plastic bindings had long since started to dig into his skin, stopping circulation in his arms. The soldier removed a wicked-looking knife from his boot and signalled for Hack to get up. He cut the restraint cleanly and replaced the knife.

Hack rubbed some blood back into his wrists and thanked the man.

"Sit down and behave," the soldier said, giving him a shove towards the bench.

Hack sat and continued to massage his numb arms. The soldier took the bench opposite and stared ahead blankly. The man's uniform was coloured camouflage green, but Hack saw no flag or emblems indicating any country. His accent was British, like the man in charge at the temple, but Hack didn't think he was with the British army – or any army, in fact. He was a mercenary – a soldier for hire to the highest bidder and, as such, could be working for anyone.

"Where are we going?" Hack asked.

The soldier's eyes focused on him. "Shut up or I'll gag you."

Hack looked at his feet. As the feeling came back into his arms he sensed an ache above his left elbow and remembered the tracking device Robert had injected.

The thought that someone knew and cared where he was being taken was the only glimmer of hope he had.

At least half an hour passed before the door at the other end of the cargo bay opened and two more soldiers entered. They took positions on either side of the entrance as a third person stepped into the room: a thin man in his thirties dressed in jeans and a T-shirt, looking completely out of place beside the bulked-up mercenaries. He pushed his thick glasses back on his nose as he scanned the interior of the cargo hold. His eyes fell on Hack and he smiled as if recognizing an old friend. Hack, for his part, knew the man's face well enough, although they'd never met in person…

Marlon Good – the head of Goodware Inc.

"So, you're the kid who bypassed all my security systems," he said. His American-accented voice was reedy and almost drowned out by the roar of the engines, so he moved closer to Hack. He offered his hand for the boy to shake. Hack didn't take it.

Marlon Good said, "No hard feelings, huh?"

"*You…* You stole Jonesey's game."

Good's face fell, as if he were hurt by the accusation. "Oh, come on! Your friend sent me a shoddy little idea ripped off from *Robot Unicorn Attack*. I took it and made it into one of the best-selling apps on the planet! You're not seriously suggesting that he deserves any credit, are you?"

"You stole his idea."

Good shrugged. "Well, we'll just have to agree to disagree on that one."

"Is this why you kidnapped me?" Hack said. "All we wanted was the evidence of Jonesey's original game. We didn't take anything else."

For a moment Marlon Good looked genuinely confused. Then he broke into a high-pitched laugh. "Please! You don't really think that all this is about a *game*, do you?"

He turned and snapped his fingers at one of the soldiers by the door. The man stepped into the other chamber and reappeared with a laptop, which he passed to Good.

"I've been looking for someone like you for a long time," he explained, taking a seat beside Hack. "Ever since the fall virus started ramping up human evolution, I knew there would eventually be someone with a power I could use. A power like being able to interface with computer systems with your mind."

Hack shifted nervously. "I don't know what you're talking about."

"Sure you don't," Marlon Good said with a wink. "But let's say that there *was* a person who could do that... Well, he could influence the future of computer development. And as computers control the world, the possibilities for that person would be endless. Given the right support. You get my point?"

"Not really."

Good carried on regardless. "Imagine my shock when my security operatives informed me about two high-school kids planning to infiltrate Two IFC. *That's right* – we knew what you were planning for weeks. Ever since the office schematics were stolen. After that, it was easy enough to track you down and find out that you were more than just your usual criminals."

Hack thought of the man and woman who had been tailing him – not HIDRA or the Triad, but Goodware operatives.

"We could have stopped you at any time," Good continued, "but I really wanted to see what you could do." He opened the laptop. A film clip showed Hack moving through the Goodware office disabling the lasers. "I had some extra surveillance put in especially – stuff not included on the official plans. After all my searching, in the end you came to me. Such a stroke of luck – it almost seems like fate. Imagine my distress when it looked like those idiot security guards were going to shoot you off the side of the building."

"I was pretty distressed too," Hack said.

Good chuckled. "Well, at least we can laugh about it now."

"What do you want from me?"

Good minimized the video window and brought up a login screen bearing the HIDRA logo. "This is the portal for the HIDRA global network. Only a few people in the world have access and it's protected by some of the best encryption software ever created. I've had a team of genius-level computer criminals working on it for three months and they haven't got further than this screen."

Hack met his eyes. "So, what do you expect me to do?"

"I expect you to cut through the HIDRA firewalls and access the database they've created of children with superpowers like yours. I want names, addresses, details of everything they can do."

Hack folded his arms across his chest. "No way."

"Sure?"

"Yes."

Marlon Good closed the lid of the laptop and rose to his feet. "I wouldn't have expected you to say anything else."

He nodded to the bearded soldier sitting opposite. The mercenary advanced on Hack with a pair of handcuffs. He fixed one bracelet round Hack's left wrist, then pulled the cuffs through a bar on the wall above his head and locked them around his right wrist. The merc walked to the stack of crates, opened one and removed a metal pack with two long cables extending from it. He fitted the unit over his shoulders like a backpack and took a cable in each hand.

"I guess you're wondering what I'm doing here," Good said to Hack conversationally as the merc adjusted the equipment on his back. "I am, after all, an incredibly successful and rich man. One of the richest in the world, in fact."

"The thought had crossed my mind," Hack said nervously as the merc approached. In each of his gloved hands he held a cable end, which Hack could now see had metal contact points like oversized plugs.

"Well, aside from wanting to control the future of the world," Good answered, "I get bored. Terribly, terribly bored. Then I met Major Bright – I'm sure you've heard of him. Now I get to play real soldiers. *It's much more fun than computer games, believe me*."

Hack swallowed heavily. "You're crazy."

"That's what my psychiatrist keeps telling me," Good

said. He turned to the merc and jerked his thumb at Hack. "Would you mind torturing him until he gives us what we want?"

The bearded merc nodded. "Not a problem, sir."

"Great!"

Marlon Good stepped back, eyes sparkling. The merc touched the contact points of the cables together. There was a crackle and a jagged, dancing beam of electricity expanded between the cables as he pulled them apart. Hack shrank back against the wall of the plane. The merc advanced, holding the energy beam before him.

"No, wait!" Hack cried. "You don't have to—"

He screamed as the electricity hit his body. It was like being stunned by the taser again – only a hundred times worse. For a moment he was lost as the energy surged through every fibre of his body. His muscles convulsed, legs thrashing, arms straining against the handcuffs. Then the merc stepped back and the agony ceased. Hack collapsed against the seat, breathing heavily. He tried to say something, but all that came out was an incoherent mumble.

"Give him what he wants, kid," the merc said. "Don't make me hit you up again."

Hack sucked air into his lungs, trying to get control.

"Well, what's it gonna be?" the merc demanded.

Hack looked at him. "Don't do that again. I'm warning you."

Marlon Good clapped his hands together like he was really starting to enjoy himself. A look of annoyance passed over the merc's face.

"All right, son, you asked for it."

The merc stepped forward and brought the energy beam across Hack's chest. This time Hack was ready, however. The moment the beam made contact with his body, he pushed back with his own energy surge – sending a mighty wave of electricity up the cables and into the backpack. The merc howled as he was engulfed in the blast-back. He flew across the plane and hit the opposite wall.

The two soldiers by the door rushed over as their comrade hit the floor face down and lay unmoving. Smoke rose from the backpack. One of the soldiers kneeled down and gingerly felt for a pulse in his neck.

"Is he dead?" Marlon Good asked.

The soldier shook his head. "He ain't well."

Hack looked at Good. "I told him not to do that. The next one who tries the same will really get fried. Or maybe I'll just send an energy surge to the engines and crash this plane."

The excitement drained from Good's face. "If that's

how you want to play it. Bring out the other prisoner."

The soldiers disappeared through the door. Seconds later they pushed a hooded man into the cargo bay. The man's suit was in tatters, but Hack recognized it instantly, along with the Rolex watch on his wrist. One of the soldiers ripped the hood off the man's head, revealing that it was Hui. His face was battered and his left hand clumsily wrapped in a bloody bandage. He struggled against the soldiers holding his arms.

"Well, this is an unexpected reunion," Marlon Good said as he flicked a lever on the wall. The loading ramp at the back of the plane lowered, allowing air to howl into the cargo bay. The soldiers pushed Hui towards the ramp.

"It was the kid!" Hui screamed. "It was his idea! Please!"

The soldiers held Hui in front of Good, who looked him up and down with contempt. "And I thought the Triad were meant to be tough."

"What do you want?" Hui begged.

Marlon Good grinned. "I just want to know one thing: can you fly?"

He gave the nod to the soldiers, who pushed him to the edge of the ramp and then threw him off the side of the plane. Hui's final scream was lost in the roar of the wind and the engines. Hack looked away.

Marlon Good walked over and prodded the semi-conscious merc with the tip of his shoe. "This one doesn't look so good either. Toss him as well."

The two soldiers by the ramp exchanged a look.

"Well?" Good demanded. "Am I paying you to stand around?"

The soldiers grabbed the bearded merc by the ankles and dragged him to the ramp. As they threw him off, Good came to sit beside Hack once more. One of the soldiers flicked the lever and the cargo bay became relatively quiet again as the ramp closed.

"I just had one of my own men thrown into the Pacific," Good said, leaning close to Hack with his voice almost a whisper. "What do you think I'm going to have done to you if you annoy me? Or your friend Jonesey? Or your grandfather in Tai-O?"

Hack looked round at him with wide eyes. "Leave them alone!"

Good reached for the laptop and flipped up the screen showing the HIDRA portal. Hack nodded in defeat.

"I need my hands free."

## 9

"Sarah, are you listening?"

She kept her eyes on the view of the endless Pacific Ocean out the narrow window of the consultation room.

"Sarah?"

Dr. Lesley Smith's voice became more insistent. With a sigh, Sarah looked round at the blonde, thirty-something psychologist sitting across the table from her.

Lesley pointed a manicured fingernail at the half-hour timer ticking away on her desk. "I thought we agreed that during our sessions we would be completely honest and not be mentally reticent."

Sarah had to smile. *Mentally reticent.* She probed just a little with her mind.

"You haven't called your boyfriend this week, Lesley," she said. "Is that because of the Skype argument you had last Thursday?"

The psychologist's eyes narrowed just a little and she sat back in her leather chair. She fiddled with a pen between the index and middle finger of her left hand.

"I know you're dying for a cigarette right now," Sarah went on, unable to help herself. "But you did make a promise to Paul, remember?"

"Stop that!" Lesley slapped the pen down on the desk with a little more force than she probably intended. Taking a breath, she tilted her head to one side and assumed a mask-like expression of calm once more. "Sarah."

"Lesley." Sarah mimicked the woman's delivery.

"You know the rule we agreed for our sessions. No using your psychic ability as a weapon against me or others. You know all I want to do is support you. Help you come to terms with your gift."

Sarah looked out the window again. The weekly sessions with Lesley were part of the price of being with

HIDRA. They were supposed to make sure she and the other kids weren't becoming a danger to themselves. Or going insane. Or something. She knew from experience that annoying Lesley just led to an increase in the number of meetings per week, so she decided to rein it in a little.

"I'm sorry, Lesley," she said. "It was wrong to read your mind. Do you forgive me?"

"It would mean more if you'd look at me when you said that."

Sarah turned to face the psychologist. If she wanted to, she could use her power to make Lesley forget everything that had happened in the previous five minutes. Or even that they had a meeting full stop. Unfortunately, the woman had a hidden camera installed somewhere in the office and she always reviewed the tapes of their sessions. Sarah had found this out after she'd made Lesley dance around the office like a chicken one afternoon and then wiped her memory of the event.

"Sorry, Lesley," she said. "I'm just a little worried about my brother. He's on his way back from a mission. Things went bad."

"Would you like to talk about it?"

"I'd love to. But the mission details are on a strict need-to-know basis. I'm not sure you have the security clearance."

"Why don't you like me, Sarah?" Lesley asked with a note of hurt in her voice. "You know I just have your best interests at heart."

*Because you don't have our best interests at heart,* Sarah thought. *You're just a spy trying to get to the bottom of me and the others.* She had understood this about Lesley from the first moment they met. Although the psychologist reported directly to Colonel Rachel Andersen, Sarah sensed her real allegiances were to other groups within HIDRA. Shadowy figures such as David Wisher, the suited observer who had flown in from the Paris HQ just a few days before. He was a man who made everyone on the *Ulysses* nervous. Sarah remembered her promises to Rachel…

*Play nice with Wisher. Play nice with Lesley.*

"I like you just fine, Lesley," Sarah said. "I guess all the trauma that I've suffered has made me a little prickly at times. There's nothing I'd like more than to bond with a big-sister figure like you. I think it could be really… good for me."

Lesley regarded Sarah with a look that said she knew very well when she was being strung along. An alarm echoed down the corridor outside.

"Incoming flight," Sarah said and rose from her chair. "The rescue choppers they sent to pick up Robert."

"We still have ten minutes in this session."

Sarah paused at the door. "Well, I won't tell anyone if you don't. Should give you time to sneak that cigarette on the loading bay before your next appointment."

Before the psychologist could respond, she slammed the door and went running down the corridor.


The HS *Ulysses* was cutting through the waters of the Pacific Ocean north of the Philippines as the three-hovercopter rescue party approached. Ignoring the protests of the deck commander, Sarah Williams emerged from the command tower and walked out onto the landing deck. The flight crew of the *Ulysses* ran forward as the three copters touched down. The door of the nearest machine swung up and Robert emerged. Sarah breathed a sigh of relief as her brother ran over.

"You're safe," she said, putting her arms around him. "I shouldn't have sent you alone."

"It was Major Bright's men," Robert said, pulling away. "They got the kid you sent me after. His name's Hack. We have to find him!"

"We will," Sarah said. "Bright's been in hiding for six months. Why has he resurfaced now?" It didn't make sense to her: when a HIDRA sweep of the Spire wreckage had failed to find any trace of Bright, they'd suspected he'd escaped the destruction somehow – then secret photos of the major meeting a weapons dealer in Indonesia had confirmed those suspicions. Somehow he'd got out when Makarov's tower came down. "And what does he want with a kid we've never met before?"

"I don't know."

"I think we just got an answer to that question," Commander Craig's voice announced behind them. They turned to see the fair-haired young officer standing in the open doorway to the control tower. He was in charge of the military personnel on the ship, and second-in-command to Rachel Andersen, to whom he was unflinchingly loyal. "Come on. We're in the war room."

A meeting in the war room – both Sarah and Robert knew that meant something big was up. They followed the commander back into the ship and down two levels. Colonel Rachel Andersen, the head of HIDRA Asia–Pacific, stood on one side of the giant computer table, studying a series of images as they entered. She looked up, the worry lines on her face illuminated starkly in the LCD glow. Sarah thought that in the year the doctor had been in charge of HIDRA, she seemed to have aged ten. There was even grey starting to show in her long, dark hair. Rachel smiled briefly, but then her face became grave again.

"Are you okay?" she asked Robert and looked relieved when he nodded. "It was only a matter of time before Major Bright reared his ugly head."

"I placed a tracker on Hack," Robert said urgently. "We have to use it to find him."

A figure stepped out of the shadows in the corner of the room, looking out of place in an immaculate grey suit and blue tie – everyone else was either in HIDRA uniform or dressed in combat trousers and T-shirts. David Wisher. He cast an unimpressed look over Sarah and Robert, little piggy eyes glinting behind round glasses.

"Excuse me, Colonel," Wisher said, rounding on Rachel. "Is it necessary to have these children in the war room during a crisis situation?"

Rachel Andersen's voice was extremely measured as she replied, and Sarah sensed that she was working hard to keep herself under control. "Robert and Sarah have been involved in a mission to retrieve a boy we think is intimately involved in the crisis. It's entirely appropriate that they're here, in my opinion. Do you have an issue with that, Mr. Wisher?"

The man held up his hands. "I'm just an observer, Colonel. Don't let me stop you from running things as you see fit. I'll be sure to note it all down in my final report."

Sarah sensed Rachel controlling her anger, but also her anxiety about the man. Wisher might look like a pipsqueak alongside the HIDRA personnel, but he clearly had the power to make everyone's lives difficult. She sensed he even had the power to have Rachel removed from command if she did the wrong thing.

"Thank you," Rachel replied, casting a quick glance at Commander Craig. Her second-in-command exuded hatred towards Wisher.

"What about Hack?" Robert said again. "We have to find him fast!"

Rachel nodded. "We're on that. Right now, there's a more serious issue at hand."

"But his life is in danger! Who knows what Bright has planned!"

Sarah placed a restraining hand on her brother's shoulder. *It's okay,* she reassured, aware of Wisher's scrutiny. *Let's hear what they have to say.*

Robert looked like he was going to protest further, but Sarah gave him a warning look and spoke to him telepathically. *Do you want to get us thrown out?*

He folded his arms in a semi-sulk, but kept his mouth shut. All eyes turned towards the colonel.

"Judging from what Robert has reported about Hack's skill with computers," Rachel said, "he's connected to our other crisis." She nodded to her assistant, Lt. Kaminski, who stepped up to the table.

"Someone infiltrated the HIDRA global network four hours ago," Kaminski explained. "A significant amount of data was stolen. They knew what they were looking for."

"How was this possible?" Commander Craig said. "We're supposed to have better encryption than the CIA."

Kaminski shrugged. "I'm sorry, sir. It seems there's someone better out there."

He tapped the tabletop computer screen. A new image opened up – a red line bouncing around a world map.

"They walked right through every firewall and server we have. We traced the origin to this point." The screen zoomed into a location in the Pacific, east of China. "There's nothing there but ocean."

"It has to be Hack," Robert said.

Kaminski nodded. "The signal corresponds to the path of the tracking device you placed on the kid."

"So," Rachel said, "what did they get?"

"The target was the superhumans database,"

Kaminski replied. "They managed to download a significant amount of information before we locked down the network."

Sarah placed her hands on the edge of the table and leaned forward. "You're joking, right? I thought that data was supposed to be safe!"

Rachel held up a hand. "Let's try to stay calm here."

"I've spent half a year contacting those kids! We've collected their names, their locations—"

"And for all we know that information *is* still safe," Rachel interrupted.

"Well, it doesn't sound like it," Sarah fumed, no longer worrying about how they appeared in front of the HIDRA personnel. "We promised them anonymity! Protection! We should have just published their names in the paper and have done with it."

"And if we hadn't collected those details," Rachel countered, "the American or the Chinese governments would have done it instead." She walked round the table and faced Sarah. "We'll get the data back, I promise. It sounds as if this kid from Hong Kong—"

"His name's Hack," Robert interjected.

"It sounds as if he's involved in the data theft. This explains Major Bright's interest. The tracking device Robert planted is going to lead us right to him."

She nodded to Commander Craig, who brought up a map showing the path of the tracking device from Hong Kong to a point in the middle of the Philippine Sea.

"The tracker stopped less than an hour ago," he said. "An island called Oshino. It's about ten kilometres across, owned by the Japanese government and supposedly uninhabited. However, one of our spy satellites picked up these images."

He tapped the screen. A black-and-white shot of the island appeared, showing a highlighted set of buildings and a landing strip.

"A base."

Rachel said, "It looks like Bright's assembling his own little army." She pointed to some cross-shaped objects on the screen. "Correct me if I'm wrong, commander, but aren't those helicopters?"

"Black Hawks, I'd say," he agreed and indicated other points of interest. "Looks like he's also got a couple of tanks, some troop carriers and two C-17 military cargo planes. That's about a billion dollars' worth of hardware right there."

"Someone's funding him," Rachel said.

"Someone rich," Sarah added. "This doesn't make any sense. If he's been hiding out in this region, I should have been able to detect his presence using my psychic ability. I've been searching for him ever since those photos confirmed he was alive, but found nothing…"

David Wisher rolled his eyes. "Here we go with the *psychic* mumbo-jumbo…"

"Who knows with Bright?" Rachel said, ignoring the comment. "The main thing is we have his location. And this time he isn't getting away. What's our current status, commander?"

"The *Ulysses* has altered course for the island, sir," Craig said. "Our ETA is thirty hours, but we'll be in drone attack range within eighteen. The crew is on alert for the primary strike. They've been waiting for another crack at Bright ever since we found out he didn't die in the Spire collapse."

"Good work," Rachel said. "We already have permission from the Japanese to attack the island."

"What about Hack?" Robert asked. "Aren't we sending a rescue team for him?"

Rachel and Commander Craig met one another's eyes, but said nothing.

"Well?" Robert persisted.

Unexpectedly, it was Wisher who spoke next. "At present we have the advantage of surprise. We can't risk alerting Bright to our presence by sending in a commando team. I speak for General Wellman and the HIDRA high command when I say that Bright is to be taken out and the base destroyed at any cost. A rescue mission is just too dangerous. We can't jeopardize the lives of HIDRA personnel."

Robert said quietly, "But I promised Hack we'd protect him."

"The evidence suggests this kid was behind the data theft," Wisher said. "For all we know, he's in league with Bright."

"Bright forced him to break into the database!"

"We don't know that," Wisher said. "Didn't you rescue him in the middle of robbing an office building? What kind of kid gives himself a name like *Hack*, anyway? It's practically an admission of juvenile delinquency."

Robert opened his mouth to argue more, but was clearly baffled by the man's logic. He turned instead to Rachel. "I thought you were supposed to be in charge here. Make them rescue Hack!"

"Robert, it's not that simple," she said. "I can't just bypass orders from—"

The boy ignored her and looked to Sarah. "Make them do it. I know you can. Make them do what you want—"

*Robert!* Sarah snapped. *Stop it. Stop it right now. You're making us both look stupid...*

*Well, I wouldn't want to do that.*

With that, Robert pushed past her and ran out of the room.

"Ridiculous behaviour," Wisher said with no little satisfaction. He turned to Rachel. "Colonel, could we please have the war room cleared of non-essential personnel so we can have a proper strategy meeting?"

Rachel looked at Sarah, who was already heading for the door after her brother.

"Don't worry, I'm leaving," she said. "There's a bad smell in this room."

She found Robert in the rec room on the lower deck, punishing the buttons of the ancient *Space Invaders* machine in the corner. Louise and Wei stood by the machine and looked round as Sarah entered. Robert didn't. She smiled at the younger girl and boy.

*He's mad at you,* Wei informed her. He was a round-faced Chinese kid with dark hair and a seemingly inexhaustible supply of sci-fi T-shirts. Today: *Battlestar Galactica*. Beside him, Louise brushed a lock of blonde hair out of her eyes and backed him up with a nod of her head. The two of them were inseparable and, with Wei's ability to control fire and Louise's ever-strengthening telekinetic powers, quite a team.

*I never would have guessed,* Sarah replied with a slight smile.

Robert lost his last life in a tinny explosion from the speakers of the machine and gave the controls a final bash, before turning to face Sarah.

"We had a vote," he said. "We're going after Hack whether HIDRA likes it or not."

"You had a vote." Sarah looked at Wei, who couldn't meet her gaze, and then Louise, who shrugged as if it didn't really matter to her one way or the other. Sarah turned back to Robert. "And how do you intend to do that?"

"Using the stealth jet you stole from Makarov," Robert said. "It's still sitting in Bay 3, right? They keep it flight ready?"

"Yes," Sarah said, "but we don't have permission—"

Robert interrupted, "Since when did we need *permission* to do anything? We made a deal with HIDRA that we can leave any time we want. And that jet is ours."

"He's right, Sarah," Louise said. "That was the deal they gave us after we beat Makarov for them."

Sarah kept her eyes on Robert. "It's not that simple."

"Are you one of them now?"

Sarah was taken aback by his question. "What do you mean?"

"We're supposed to be a team," Robert replied. "Not you and HIDRA. You and us."

Both Louise and Wei nodded. Sarah suddenly felt as ganged up on as she had in the war room. "You don't understand what's going on here. Rachel is in a really difficult position. She can't just send us running off on some suicide mission."

"If Alex and Nestor were here, they'd help."

Louise nodded in agreement. "Even Octavio would."

"Well, they're not here," she said sharply. "They were the ones who wanted to leave, remember?" She took a deep breath, thinking how she was sick of hearing about Alex and the other two.

Up till recently the boys had been part of their team... Alex had helped them escape from the clutches of Major Bright in Melbourne and she'd fought alongside him in the wastes of eastern Russia. The twins, Nestor and Octavio, had been with them since the very beginning, when they had first discovered their new powers in the Australian outback and had taken on a rogue HIDRA colonel. Despite the fact they'd been on the verge of killing one another half of the time (particularly Nestor and Octavio, who had a strained sibling relationship, to say the least), they'd always managed to come through for each other in the end. And after their return to HIDRA,

Sarah had begun to realize that, along with the younger kids, the boys were the closest thing to a family she'd had for a long time. The world had become a dangerous place for kids like them, but at least they had each other to rely on...

And Sarah had become particularly close to Alex – perhaps because of their experience together in Russia, when they'd had to flee into the Arctic waste together, facing death above and below the ice. Which had made his desire to leave so hard to accept. To her, the return to HIDRA was the chance to put an end to the fighting – to concentrate on helping Rachel Andersen and the scientists find a cure for the fall virus and bring their families back. But following their battle against Makarov, Alex had wanted more freedom, more excitement – more opportunities to get them into trouble. When the information came through that Major Bright had been spotted in Europe, he'd wanted to take the others and go running off after him. With Bright still alive, it was only a matter of time before he came after them again, Alex reasoned. Sarah had disagreed – hadn't they all had enough fighting? They were safe. HIDRA could take care of the major...

But Alex was determined to carry on the fight against Bright and, to Sarah's surprise, so were the twins Nestor and Octavio (who could usually be relied upon not to agree on anything at all). After several heated arguments all around the ship, Rachel Andersen had stepped in and moderated a solution: Alex, Nestor and Octavio would transfer to the HIDRA base in England, where they would have the chance to see some duty in the field – maybe even against Major Bright, when he was found. Sarah would stay with the younger members of the team on the *Ulysses* and continue her work tracking down virus-altered kids in the region. That had been almost six months ago and although she'd had occasional video calls with both Nestor and Octavio, Sarah hadn't spoken to Alex since.

Sarah rounded on her brother. "Perhaps you should have run away with them to England. It would have been easier for me. Do you think I want to be in charge all the time?"

Immediately Sarah regretted her words, seeing the hurt look in her brother's eyes. She took a step towards him, but he backed away.

"So you're not going to help us then?"

"Robert, I can't—"

He disappeared…teleporting away to some other part of the ship. With a frustrated sigh, Sarah turned to Louise and Wei, who looked at one another. Some silent understanding passed between them and they walked towards the exit.

"Where are you two going?" Sarah said.

Louise looked over her shoulder. "We're going to find Robert. We're with him."

They left without another word.

Alone in the rec room, Sarah stood completely still for a moment, took a deep breath and tried to process everything that had happened in the last half-hour. When the intelligence had come through that Major Bright was alive, she knew it was only a matter of time before HIDRA would have to go into battle against him again. And she knew that once again her brother and her friends would be dragged into the fight. Now that their mother was gone, along with their father, Daniel (who they had only been starting to get to know when he was taken from them by the fall virus), Sarah was the one responsible for making sure Robert was safe. Sending him to rescue a kid from Hong Kong was one thing, but the thought of him having to face Major Bright once more was something that worried her desperately. She just didn't know if she could face seeing him, or Louise and Wei, in harm's way once again.

"Everything okay?"

She started at the sound of Commander Craig's voice

from the doorway of the rec room. He'd appeared there and she'd been so deep in thought, she hadn't even heard him.

"Just thinking about what's coming," she said. "Another fight with Major Bright. I promised my mum before she died that I'd look after Robert. I'm supposed to be keeping him out of danger."

Craig shook his head. "You worry too much."

Sarah laughed. "He's hell-bent on facing off against an insane military commander with superhuman powers to rescue a kid he hardly knows. Yeah, I guess I am being overcautious."

The commander raised an eyebrow. "Robert seems to understand the risks. He isn't running away from the fight."

"Neither am I," Sarah said indignantly. "I can take on Bright myself. But not Robert..." Her voice cracked and she stopped talking. It was only in moments of danger that she realized just how much she cared for her brother. If something happened to him, she didn't know what she would do...

"Like I said, you worry too much," Craig said. "You need to clear your head. Sparring room. Fifteen minutes."

With that, he turned and left before she could argue.

Alone again, Sarah wondered if she was the only one (contrary to what Lesley the psychologist might think) who hadn't gone crazy on this ship.

10

After the plane landed, Hack was led down the ramp by two of the mercs to a waiting jeep. One took the wheel, while the other bundled him wordlessly into the back. Thankfully Marlon Good had already disembarked and left in his own vehicle. Hack did as he was told without protest. He was intent on taking in every detail of his new surroundings – trying to find some clue as to his location.

Judging by the position of the sun, he estimated it was just before midday. This meant that the plane had been in transit for about nine hours. The air was incredibly humid and the temperature was in the high thirties. Seabirds swooped overhead and Hack thought he heard the sound of waves crashing as the jeep pulled away from the plane, suggesting they were on an island or near the coast. The heat and the vegetation around the runway – palm trees and dense jungle – suggested a semi-tropical location in the Pacific.

The jeep sped along the runway towards a control tower and a pair of hangars in the distance. As they drew closer, Hack counted more mercenaries, all dressed in the same camouflage uniform and heavily-armed. They reached a security check at a chain-link fence and passed into a compound that included two hangars and a group of smaller buildings. Military equipment was parked all around: tanks, trucks, helicopters.

*This Major Bright guy isn't messing around,* he thought. *It's like something out of* Modern Warfare.

The jeep pulled up outside a group of weather-beaten concrete buildings that looked as if they pre-dated the rest of the camp. The merc beside Hack grabbed him by the arm and dragged him out. Opening a steel door, the soldier led him down a corridor to another door. This led into a cell no more than a few metres across. There was no chair. No bed. Just hard, bare walls and floor.

An iron-barred window was set high in the back wall.

"Home sweet home," the merc said and pushed him inside.

Hack spun as the door slammed shut and several bolts slid into place. His heart sank. He would have given anything for an electronic keypad or magnetic locks to subvert, but the cell was as low-tech as you could get. There wasn't even a light fitting in the ceiling.

As the merc's bootsteps echoed away, Hack stepped forward and ran his fingers over the door hinges. They were solid, but the brickwork was crumbling around them. After a second's thought, Hack removed the belt from his jeans and scraped the metal buckle against the brick experimentally. It gave. He pressed harder with the buckle and more of the wall became brick dust.

"Don't do that."

Hack turned. He'd assumed he was alone in the cell, but now he made out a figure sitting against the far wall in the shadows. He strained his eyes and saw that it was a girl, about his age and Asian in appearance, although her accent was Australian. She looked painfully thin and wore a tattered T-shirt and jeans. Black hair hung around her shoulders in straggles. She met his eyes and he could see her face was dirt-smeared, as if she hadn't washed in weeks.

"If you mess with the door, they won't feed us for a day," she said.

Hack took a few steps towards her and kneeled down in the middle of the cell. "Who are you?" he asked.

The girl turned to the wall, avoiding his gaze.

"How long have you been here?"

The girl looked round at him and he could tell from her tear-filled eyes that she'd been in the cell for a very long time.

Most of the Oshino compound consisted either of decrepit brick cells like the one in which Hack had been placed, or prefabs that doubled as weapon storage facilities and barracks for the mercs. There was one exception: a circular, single-storey building in the centre of the camp. Communications masts and dishes adorned the roof and the curved walls were mirrored glass, reflecting back the camp and surrounding jungle. There was only one entrance and this was constantly guarded by two mercs bearing machine guns.

Those few members of the camp allowed access to the command centre found themselves inside an air-conditioned environment kept to a comfortable twenty-two degrees at all times. In a tech room that took up half the building, security operatives monitored air and sea traffic for hundreds of kilometres around the island. The rest of the circular structure was given to Major Bright's personal living quarters.

In a perfectly round chamber in the middle of the building, Major Bright sat in a leather examination chair, not unlike the kind in a dentist's surgery. He was stripped to the waist, revealing an incredibly muscular upper body that bore a strange, black mark spreading across his skin. A grey-haired doctor in a lab coat hovered nervously over the major, an ultrasound scanner in one hand. He pressed the scanner head to Major Bright's chest and moved it up and down. On a monitor beside the chair, a grainy image of Bright's internal organs appeared.

"Is it a boy or a girl, doctor?" the major asked, looking at the screen.

"It's a ten-centimetre-long rock fragment," Dr. Cameron said and indicated a dark object next to Bright's heart. "Lodged inside your ribcage. Frankly, I'm amazed it didn't kill you. Care to tell me how it got there?"

Bright drummed his fingers impatiently on the chair arm. "I tripped on a meteorite. Can you remove it?"

Dr. Cameron replaced the scanner in its cradle. "Well, that would be a little risky."

"*Risky* how?"

"The shard is partially embedded in your heart. Removal could have serious side effects. For the moment, at least, I recommend leaving it where it is."

Major Bright rose from the chair and towered over the other man. "Excuse me?"

Dr. Cameron laughed nervously. "You seem to be doing just fine with it in there."

Bright jabbed his fingers at the black, scaly skin spreading across the right side of his chest and up his neck to his cheek. "*Doing just fine?* Take a look at my face!"

"You could always get a second opinion."

Bright narrowed his eyes. "You *are* the second opinion, doctor. My last physician got…fired."

The merc at the door chuckled. The doctor's face drained of blood.

"I can try to stop the spread of the infection," Dr. Cameron said. "Maybe even reverse the process with a retro-virus. The process is experimental, but—"

Bright slapped the doctor on the shoulder so hard he almost knocked him to his knees. "That's fine, doc. I'm used to experimental." He nodded to the merc. "Take Dr. Cameron to his new lab. Make sure he's well looked after."

As the soldier approached, Cameron's face fell. "You don't expect me to stay here?"

"I absolutely expect you to stay here. Ask for any equipment you need and my men will have it for you within twenty-four hours. Money is not an issue."

"But my practice in Sydney—"

"You work for me now, Dr. Cameron. And I expect you to earn your ten million dollar advance." Major Bright's tone was such that it was clear there would be no argument. The merc took Dr. Cameron by the arm and led him from the room.

Alone in the chamber, Bright walked to a sink against the wall and examined his reflection in the mirror. The black, alien mark had moved further up his face overnight. Ever since the meteorite shard had become embedded in his body, following the destruction of Makarov's tower in Russia, the infection had begun to spread. There was no doubt it would kill him eventually – few beings had the psychic strength to live for long in such close proximity to the alien material, that much he sensed. The shard was keeping him alive, but its massive power was also slowly killing him…

For the time being, however, there were benefits: superpowers stronger than he had ever experienced before, courtesy of the Entity, the alien intelligence that channelled itself through the shard. Where previously he had relied on serum developed from the blood of the superhuman children for his strength, now he had a seemingly limitless pool of power. The shard in his body also provided a psychic link with the ancient, evil being across an immeasurable vastness of space. Again, something that was a blessing and a curse.

*Another doctor?* the Entity's voice rang in his head. *Anyone would think you wanted to get rid of me.*

"The mark is spreading," Bright replied. "It's like a cancer." He wet a sponge under the tap and dabbed at his skin with cooling water – the only thing that seemed to give him any relief from the aching pain of the alien flesh.

*Merely a side effect of close proximity to my power,* the Entity said. *Would you prefer to lose your strength? Go back to relying on the blood of children for your superpowers?*

Bright threw the sponge into the sink and stormed to the medical cabinet by the chair.

"I want to live!" he snapped as he popped a couple of pain pills and washed them down with a glass of water. "What are you turning me into?"

The Entity laughed. *So paranoid. We're a team, remember?*

"I didn't sign up to become a lizard."

*I need a different vessel for my earthly form. The girl, Sarah Williams, is the only human I have encountered with the mental strength to contain me. It is our destiny to be joined.*

"Right," the major said. "And when you've joined with the girl, I get tossed away like Makarov, do I?"

*No, no. You will have your reward: you will retain the superhuman abilities I have gifted you... Gain control over the human enclaves of the world... Your own armies to command... All the power you could ever imagine...*

"Well, I can imagine a lot of power."

A soldier rapped on the half-open door.

"What is it?" Bright demanded, annoyed at the interruption.

"The plane from Hong Kong has arrived, sir. Marlon Good is waiting to see you."

Bright set the empty glass down. "Send the fool in."

*Be nice,* the Entity warned. *We still need his money and technology.*

"For now."

A moment later, Marlon Good appeared in the doorway and gave a funny little salute – like a boy playing soldiers. Major Bright ground his teeth, but made no comment.

"You have the boy?" he said.

"Of course," Good replied. He walked to the middle of the room and flopped into the chair as if he were exhausted. "Hard night's work, though."

"You threw one of my men out of the plane."

"I had to make a point. Shake the kid up a bit."

Bright moved closer. "If you ever touch one of my men again..."

Good's eyes widened and he flinched back, as if certain the major was about to strike him. The blow didn't come. Instead, the anger drained from Bright's expression and he took a long breath before taking a couple of steps back – almost as if something internal had pushed a pause button on his anger.

Good produced a USB drive from his pocket. "I got the HIDRA database," he said hurriedly, eager to please.

Bright's expression hardened again and he snatched the drive from Good's fingers.

"Well?" Good asked. "Did I do okay?"

"Yes," Bright said grudgingly. "You did good, *Good*."

He walked to a computer by the wall, inserted the drive and opened up the stolen datasheets. He scrolled through scores of files giving details of virus-altered children. Everything was here, from details of their special abilities to contact addresses and next of kin.

*Perfect,* the Entity's voice said inside Bright's head. *Perfect.*

"HIDRA's been busy," Bright said aloud.

*They have been using Sarah Williams to track down children with the viral side effects. It appears there has been a significant jump in their numbers since the destruction of the meteor storm.*

"It took us months just to find the kid in Hong Kong," Bright replied. "They've saved us a lot of time."

Marlon Good rose from the chair and approached the computer. "Are you talking to me?"

Bright ignored him and continued to scan through the files.

"Did you get what you wanted?" Good asked.

"Certainly," Bright said.

"Who are these kids? What's so important about them?"

Bright looked round at Marlon Good and smiled a smile so cold, it actually made the American shiver a little.

"When we take over the world, these are the ones who need to die first."

## 11

"Go ahead, Sarah. Use your power. I'll understand. You don't have to prove anything here."

She gritted her teeth against her gumshield and flexed her fingers in the sparring gloves. Commander Craig stood a few metres away on the other side of the training mats, also dressed in a gi and a full set of sparring pads for their weekly karate session. Despite her protests (she was in no mood for a lesson after her altercation with Robert), he was insistent the session go ahead. *Karate stops for no man – not even Major Bright.*

Now Craig taunted her with a grin, exposing his bright red gumshield.

"I mean, why bother learning to defend yourself physically—"

Sarah moved in fast, feinting with a strike at Craig's head, then spinning round and delivering a leg sweep to the back of his knees as he raised his hands. The kick turned out ineffectual. Craig punished her with a back-handed strike to the side of the head that sent her staggering away across the mat.

"Nice idea, poor execution," he said as he began to circle to the right. "You'll have to hit harder than that if you want to take me down."

"You're really starting to annoy me," Sarah hissed through her shield. She circled also, guard up, keeping a constant two metres between them.

Craig grinned. "Really? Then why not use your psychic abilities on me? Eh?"

"Because I want to kick your butt the old-fashioned way."

She moved faster this time, aiming a kick at Craig's stomach, which he blocked easily. Her follow-up move was unexpected, however: a direct punch at his face. The commander had to hustle to block it, by which time she was aiming a chop at his kidneys with her left hand.

She made contact and Craig expelled a little air.

Sarah knew the right thing to do next — back off, reassess, strike again if there was an opening. But her blood was up. *What had happened in the war room, Wisher, the argument with Robert...* She wanted to take it out on someone and had decided that the commander would do just fine... Spinning, she angled her body round to deliver a roundhouse kick to his upper body...

Craig caught her leg and yanked her off balance. *Stupid,* Sarah thought as she was pulled round. The commander threw her with more force than normal for one of their sparring sessions. With a cry of surprise and a little pain, Sarah tumbled across the mat and hit her spine against one of the wooden benches that lined the edge of the unarmed combat classroom.

Groaning, Sarah spat her gumshield into her hand and rubbed her lower back. She got to her feet and turned to where Craig was standing...

He wasn't where he'd been a second ago. Momentarily confused, Sarah looked left, towards the exit...

And that's all Craig needed. He moved in low from the right, locked his left arm around her throat and squeezed. Helpless, Sarah placed her hands against his forearm and tried to pull it away. No use. He increased the pressure in response. Craig was stronger than her, plain and simple. *But you don't have to be the strongest to win a fight,* she reminded herself of his words from a hundred combat sessions. *Just stay focused.*

"You're hurting me," Sarah said as he dragged her back towards the centre of the mats, all the while keeping his arm locked around her throat. "I can't breathe."

"Then do something about it," Craig said. There was a hardness to his voice that she hadn't heard before. "I thought you wanted to kick my butt."

"Let me go and I will."

Craig laughed harshly. "That's not the way it's going to be today."

Her eyes widened as he brought his right hand up, revealing a ten-centimetre-long combat knife clutched in his fist. Where he'd got it from, she didn't know. Training sessions never involved real weapons. Her heart raced. Craig shifted his left arm around her throat slightly, exposing her windpipe as he brought the blade closer.

"Just how fast are you, Sarah? Think you can control my mind before I cut your throat? Can you do it when you're panicking?"

"Stop," she said, trying to control her breathing. "I want to stop this right now."

"If you want it to stop, take me out."

He touched the cool blade against her skin and then held it away, but still at the ready. Sarah wanted to cry out or protest that he'd gone too far – but she could tell the commander would not listen. Whatever point he was trying to make, she wouldn't get out of it like that. Clearly this was some kind of graduation lesson.

Or maybe he really had gone crazy.

She tried to make contact with his mind, but the commander seemed to sense this, because he tightened his grip around her throat yet again.

"That's not going to work, Sarah. You've got one second before I finish you. Let's see—"

Sarah rammed her heel down on Craig's right foot – hard enough to cause him some pain. His grip slackened just fractionally, giving her some wriggle room. She jerked her head back violently, away from the blade, and made contact with his face. There was a crunch of cartilage as the back of her skull crushed his nose. Sarah made her body go loose. She slipped down, out of his arms, and rolled forward and round into a defensive crouch. The commander almost stumbled, but kept his balance. She'd hurt him. *Good,* thought Sarah.

"Are we finished?" she said as Craig wiped at his bloodied nose with his left hand.

"Not by a long shot."

The commander moved with alarming speed, swinging the blade at her. Sarah had anticipated the attack, however, flipping backwards and rising to her feet. As Craig swung and missed, she kicked him in the back of the leg – with enough force to drive him down to one knee. This time she backed off, expecting him to swing at her with the knife, which is exactly what he did. She retreated, keeping her guard up. With a yell, Craig ran at her, trying to break her composure by swiping the knife before him as he came. Sarah sidestepped his wild attack and danced back across the mats. The commander lurched round and the blade whistled through the air just centimetres from her face.

*Enough of this,* she thought. Craig lunged again…

"Stop!"

Sarah held up her hand. The commander carried on moving in her direction for just a second before his entire body locked up. He stopped, still as a statue, knife held out before him. His body was frozen – his mind completely under her control. A single drop of blood fell from his injured nose and hit the mat between his feet. Sarah took a few deep breaths, slowing her heart rate, trying to ease the adrenaline coursing through her veins.

"Are we finished?" she said again.

Craig spoke with some effort. "It's not over...until I say...it's over."

Infuriated, Sarah considered walking out of the training room and leaving him like that – frozen like a statue. It was as much as he deserved for the stunt with the knife. But she wanted to beat him. She concentrated again.

Against his will, Commander Craig began to move his knife arm, bringing the weapon round towards his own throat. Veins on his forehead bulged and Sarah could tell he was resisting her with all his might – but it was no use. She stopped his hand when the blade was just a centimetre from his throat.

"Are we finished?"

The corners of Craig's mouth twitched as he tried to grin. "You'd...better...kill me."

Sarah raised an eyebrow. "Sure you really mean that?"

She made him move the knife so the blade was actually making contact with his neck, just to prove her point.

"You...won't...do it..."

The blade pressed into his throat. Sarah felt him fighting back, but wouldn't let him off. However, she sensed if she pressed any harder, she would really injure him.

A thin line of blood appeared at the edge of the blade and trickled along the metal…

"Relent!" Craig said.

Sarah released him immediately. The commander dropped the weapon from his neck and staggered forward, although he managed to keep his balance. He touched a hand to his throat.

"Did I hurt you?" Sarah asked with real concern.

Breathing deeply, Craig shook his head. "Barely a paper cut."

Sarah was relieved to see his tone of voice and expression had returned to normal: the cool, always-in-control teacher she recognized from their training sessions. But that didn't make her any less angry – whatever point there was in bringing a real knife to a lesson, she didn't see it. Sarah ripped off her sparring gloves and threw them at her feet. "I don't want any more sessions if that's the way you intend to run them. What was that with the knife?"

"The most important lesson you can learn," Craig replied. "Outside this room, there are no rules. No backing down. You want to fight men like Major Bright, you'd better be prepared to go all the way."

"You don't have to tell me that," Sarah said petulantly. Craig's words reminded her of the argument she'd had with Robert – and she didn't like it. "I've fought and beaten Bright before. And Makarov. I saved your life in the process, I might add."

She strode past him on the way to the door.

"Going to sit in the dark again, Sarah?" Craig called after her. "Hide out in Bay 6?"

She stopped and turned back to him.

"It's time to make up your mind what you're doing here, Sarah. Are you in the fight or sitting it out? There's no middle ground."

"What do you mean?"

"Nobody's asking anything of you, Sarah. You want a normal life? You want to be a normal kid? Fine. Say the word, and we'll have you shipped out to a place where you'll never have to worry about Bright or the Entity or HIDRA ever again." He turned the knife over in his hand and then threw it at the floor. It embedded itself, point first, in the mat between his feet. "But if you're going to be here, you'd better be prepared to finish the fight. Simple enough for you?"

Sarah reddened – partly from embarrassment, partly from anger at Craig's words.

"Why do you need us anyway?" she asked. "My brother is eleven years old. Can't HIDRA fight its own battles?"

Craig wiped the blood from his nose. "I saw what Bright could do in Russia. And I saw what you kids can do as well. We can't fight him with guns and hovercopters alone. We need you. And if you don't get involved in the fight, the whole world is going to suffer." He walked forward and placed a hand on her shoulder. "I know you want to protect Robert and the others, but if our enemies aren't stopped, none of you will be safe. You have to lead your team, Sarah—"

"What about Alex," she interrupted. "He was the one who wanted to join the action—"

"*You're* the leader, Sarah," Craig said emphatically. "It's time you started acting like one – for all of us."

As the commander's words sank in, Sarah once again felt the terrible responsibility that had been put on her and her friends. They hadn't asked for their powers, but now they had them it was time to decide once and for all how they were going to use them. And as much as she hated to admit it, Craig was right: she was the leader. Alex had never really wanted to go to England – all he'd wanted was to fight alongside her, but she'd driven him away, thinking that he was putting them in danger. Well, it seemed like danger had found them once again.

"I'll think about it," she said and turned swiftly. She made the end of the corridor, threw open the hatch and ran into the next, almost knocking down a red-suited technician as she went. Then she ran, down corridor after corridor, until she stopped, breathless, against a locked hatch. Craig's words echoed in her mind.

*You're the leader. It's time you started acting like one. For all of us.*

Sarah took a deep breath. For some time she just stood, getting control again.

*Robert,* she thought, casting her mind towards his cabin, where she sensed him sitting on the bed with a book in his lap.

There was just a second before her brother responded. *What do you want?*

*Get Louise and Wei,* Sarah responded. *We've got work to do.*

12

Her name was May. Hack had learned that from what little information he'd been able to extract from his cellmate. She was an Australian, born of Chinese parents who had emigrated there before she was born. She'd been snatched by Major Bright's men from the street right outside her house, but she wasn't sure how long ago that had been. Weeks? Months? When Hack tried to press her for information she became quickly irritable and then confused, before falling into a kind of stupor that left her incapable of answering any more questions.

As she half-slept against the cell wall, Hack kneeled before the girl and assessed her physical condition with concern. In addition to her unwashed appearance, she seemed to be suffering from dehydration – no surprise given the heat in the cell. Hack wiped the perspiration from his forehead. Already he was beginning to feel weak from the loss of fluids. The guards had provided no water. Clearly this was what lay in store for him if he didn't escape or get rescued.

Something caught his eye on May's right arm and he carefully lifted the sleeve of her T-shirt. The skin above her elbow was bruised black and purple – rough circular patterns, as if something had been pressed into her flesh repeatedly and with force.

"Oww," May said as he accidentally brushed her damaged skin. The pain seemed to bring her round a little, because her eyes focused and flashed with an intelligence that Hack hadn't seen before.

"How did you get these bruises?"

She frowned, as if concentrating on every word. "Injection marks. They keep me drugged." She looked into his eyes as if seeing him for the first time. "What's your name?"

"Hack. Remember? I told you earlier."

"Right."

"Do you know why they're holding us here?" Hack asked. "What do they want from us?"

May shook her head. "I've asked them again and again. But they never give an answer. Ask too much and...well, you'll see."

"What do you mean? Have they hurt you?"

She raised an eyebrow. "No, just locked me in a cell for a month and stuck about a million needles in me."

"Right, sorry," Hack said, feeling stupid for what he'd said.

May's expression softened. "It's okay. Being kidnapped makes me cranky."

Hack laughed and wondered if he'd be cracking jokes after all she'd been through. "Well, we must have something they want," he said.

May placed her hand against the brickwork and pulled herself to her feet. She wobbled a little and looked ready to fall right back down again, so Hack reached out and grabbed her arm in support.

"Jesus!" May exclaimed as his fingers closed around her tender upper arm.

"Sorry!" Hack said, removing his hand.

She gave him a withering look, but then smiled. "Nothing broken." May looked around the cell and blinked up at the high window. The sun was descending in the west.

"It's the afternoon," she said. "They haven't been yet. Late again."

Hack looked at her in confusion. "Late? For what?"

She ignored his question, jerking her head round to look at him. "What's special about you? I mean, what could Bright want with you?"

He shrugged. "I don't know. I can do stuff with computers, electronics. Y'know, control them with my mind."

"Then you're one of us. A superhuman."

Hack had heard the word used before to describe kids with fall virus powers. "I guess so. Uh, what's your power?"

"Let me show you." May placed the palm of her free hand against the wall and splayed her fingers. "If I get us out of this cell, think you can get us off this island, Hack? Or at least do something useful?"

He considered for a second. "If we can get to a computer, I'll be able to let the whole planet know we're here. Good enough?"

"Good enough."

May closed her eyes and Hack knew from his own power that she was channelling her ability, whatever that was. With surprise, he thought he saw a ripple pass through the bricks of the wall. He blinked, wondering if it was just an effect of the heat. Was he hallucinating? No. The wall rippled again – spreading out from the point where May's hand was touching it. It was as if the solid bricks had become no more substantial than the surface of a pond.

"Cool," Hack whispered.

May opened her eyes and gave him a quick glance. "This is what I do."

She concentrated again and the wall became a raging river – undulating under her control. Hack's eyes widened as he saw gaps starting to form through which he could see the jungle beyond—

The cell door slammed open and rebounded off the wall. They'd been so focused upon the liquefied wall that they hadn't heard the approach of the guards. A merc grabbed Hack's shoulders and pushed him down on the floor. He struggled to get up, but the soldier placed a heavy boot on his chest and pinned him.

Concentration broken, May staggered away from the wall, which had once again become solid brick.

"Please, no," she said as the other merc approached her. Kotler, the merc leader, appeared in the doorway to the cell.

"Getting a resistance to the inhibitor drugs, are we?" he said to May, a grimace-like smile on his lips. It made his skeletal features even less appealing. "Guess we'd better up that dose again."

The merc standing before May removed a metal cylinder from his belt and held it in his fist. The girl stood helplessly before him. Her eyes showed she wanted to fight, but her body made no move – as if conditioned that resistance was pointless.

"What are you doing to her?" Hack shouted, straining to get from under the boot holding him down. The merc pressed down harder and Hack gasped for breath.

Kotler nodded to the merc with the cylinder, who stepped forward and jabbed it against May's arm with no effort at finesse. She cried out in pain. There was a faint hiss as a dose of some drug was administered from a hidden needle.

"Give the brat a second shot," Kotler ordered. "I don't want to be watching her all evening."

The merc obeyed without question, jabbing the cylinder at the same spot. May gave a more muffled cry and then slid down the wall into a sitting position. The merc turned to his commander.

"What about the boy, sir? Should I inject him with the inhibitor as well?"

Kotler walked into the room and stood over Hack, who lay helpless on the floor.

"Why waste the drugs?" Kotler said with a sneer. "This one's no risk. Not like the girl."

With that, Kotler strode out, closely followed by the two mercs. As the door slammed shut and the bolts shot, Hack pulled himself up.

"We need water!" he yelled, slamming a fist against the metal door. No response. The mercs either didn't hear or didn't care.

Deciding it was pointless to waste his energy shouting after them, Hack turned his attention to May. Her head lolled forward onto her chest now. He went over and crouched beside her. Carefully, he placed a hand under her chin and lifted her head.

"May? Are you all right?"

Her eyes were open but they were glazed, unseeing. The girl he had spoken to a few minutes before had retreated again, forced deep down by the drugs. Hack glanced at the wall she had turned to liquid and understood that, unchecked, no prison would hold her. Placing a hand on her good arm, he gently eased her down into a foetal position on the floor, pulled off his T-shirt and rolled it up to form a kind of pillow for her head.

"It's okay, May," he whispered, running a finger over the mark on his own arm where Robert had injected the tracking device. "People are coming for us. Just hold on."

13

The stealth jet sat, sleek and black, in the centre of Bay 3, which was directly under the flight deck of the *Ulysses*. The machine looked like a cross between a stealth bomber and a private jet, its shape roughly triangular, with two large afterburners at the back. Lines of little blue lights set into the floor were the only illumination inside the bay, leading Sarah, Robert, Louise and Wei towards the waiting jet as they slipped inside the hangar. Each of them carried a backpack with a dart-gun and basic supplies.

"Is it ready to fly?" Wei asked.

"They keep it ready for me," Sarah replied.

"The difficult bit will be getting it out of here," Louise said, pointing to the darkened ceiling. The roof could open to allow access to the deck, but at present it was locked shut.

"Don't worry," Sarah said, running under the wing. She pressed a button on the fuselage and the entry hatch slid down. "The tower will do exactly as I tell them—"

The hangar lights flicked on full.

Sarah and her friends spun round as doors slammed open and armed soldiers poured into the hangar. They formed a semicircle around the jet, dart rifles trained on the children. With the troops in position, lighter footsteps clicked across the floor: David Wisher, closely followed by Lesley the psychologist.

*Teleport on board and start flight prep,* Sarah said to Robert. He disappeared. Louise and Wei took positions on either side of her.

*Want us to take care of them?* Louise asked, looking around the circle of soldiers.

*Long time since I've started a decent fire,* Wei added, cracking his knuckles.

Sarah shook her head. *No. We don't want to hurt anyone. They're just following orders.*

Wisher stopped a few metres from the jet, as if afraid to get nearer despite the twenty or so dart rifles backing him up. At his side, Lesley smiled triumphantly.

"Just like I anticipated, sir," she said. "They were bound to try something after your altercation this afternoon." She looked at Sarah. "It seems you're not the only one who can read minds around here."

"Very clever," Sarah said, then turned her attention to Wisher. "All we want is the jet. I have a deal with Colonel Andersen that I can take it whenever I want."

He gave a sniggering little laugh and clasped his hands behind his back. "Really? You're not old enough to drive a car. Do you really think you're going to fly that jet out of here?"

"Just watch me."

"I don't think so. I'm confining you and your friends to quarters for the duration of this emergency. Then we'll reassess your status as HIDRA operatives. Colonel Andersen has clearly allowed things to get seriously out of control on this boat."

"It's a ship," Wei corrected.

Wisher gave him a withering *children should be seen and not heard* look.

Lesley shook her head. "You see what we've come to, Sarah? If only you'd opened up to me a little more."

Sarah regarded the psychologist coolly. "I feel the chicken dance coming on again, don't you?"

Lesley placed a warning hand on Wisher's arm and whispered in his ear. "She's a powerful mind controller, sir. I suggest we don't take any risks here."

Wisher glanced back at the soldiers. "Everyone target Ms. Williams." He turned to Sarah. "I don't think even you can control the minds of twenty soldiers at once. We can do this the easy way or the hard way. Your choice."

Louise nudged Sarah's arm. *Please let us do it the hard way.*

Commander Craig appeared, pushing his way through the line of soldiers. "What's going on here?"

Wisher waved a hand at the jet. "As you can see, *team superhuman* has stepped completely over the line. It's one thing to have them listening in on strategy meetings, another entirely to let them play with classified military equipment."

"No, Mr. Wisher," Craig said, "I meant, why have you requisitioned twenty of my men? I don't remember giving the order."

The suit didn't blink an eye. "Don't pull the rank card with me, mister. I'll have you busted down to private and assigned to HIDRA Alaska by the end of the day." He glanced round at Sarah with a sneer of contempt.

"Now, put a leash on these freaks or I'll find someone who will."

Craig looked at Sarah and shrugged, as if to say *what can I do?* Lesley placed her hands against the side of her skull and screamed.

"Help me! She's targeting my brain! I can feel it!"

Sarah rolled her eyes. "For goodness' sake! I'm not doing anything."

Lesley pointed an accusing finger at her and spoke hysterically. "You stole my mind!" It was a convincing play-act. Her little revenge.

"First I'd have to find something to steal," Sarah shot back. "She's making it up."

Wisher rounded on Commander Craig. "Take that girl down now!"

"Fine," Craig replied, reaching for the dart pistol on his belt. He aimed and pulled the trigger.

The dart embedded itself in Lesley's neck.

The psychologist let out a little yelp and hit the floor, unconscious. Commander Craig pointed the pistol at Wisher and shot him also.

"You're finished—" Wisher managed, outraged eyes bulging, before he fell backwards over Lesley's prone body.

Nobody moved in the hangar. Sarah and Commander

Craig looked at one another and then round at the twenty HIDRA soldiers in a line. Finally, Craig broke the silence, addressing a group of four at the end.

"Take these two to sickbay. Everyone else clear out."

Still nobody moved. For a terrible moment, Sarah was convinced the soldiers would turn their weapons on the commander.

"That's an order!" Craig shouted. "NOW!"

The soldiers snapped into action, as if they'd awoken from a daze. Four ran to collect Wisher and Lesley while the rest ran for the exits. Craig gave an audible sigh of relief and holstered his pistol.

"You didn't have to do that," Sarah said as the unconscious Wisher and Lesley were carried away.

"I didn't," Commander Craig said matter-of-factly. "*You* made me do it. Controlled my mind. That's what I'm going to say at the court martial, anyway. I'd be grateful if you'd back me up on that when the time comes."

Sarah grinned and ran for the ramp after Louise and Wei. On the threshold of the jet, she turned back as Craig began to follow.

"I'm coming with you," he said. "That's non-negotiable. You won't get out of this hangar without me on board. Promise."

She considered arguing, but could see it was no use. Craig was one of the few people at HIDRA she didn't want to mess with.

She said, "You can come along for the ride. But this is my plane and I'm flying it. Right?"

Craig held up his hands. "Your plane. Your rules."

"Okay."

They hurried through the cabin area of the jet. The plane had once been the private jet of Nikolai Makarov, a Russian billionaire in league with the Entity, and had all the trimmings: plush carpets, antique tables and chairs and a giant LCD TV. The military technology of the jet was cutting edge as well, using a stealth device decades ahead of anything the US military had. Over the last six months, HIDRA technicians had been busy trying to discover the secrets behind the jet's most incredible features: its amazingly short take-off and landing distances, the on-board computer systems that approached artificial intelligence, and the stealth drive itself. Many times they'd begged Rachel Andersen to be allowed to dismantle the machine, but she had stayed good to her word to Sarah and kept the jet operational.

"Prepped and ready to go," Robert said as Sarah and Craig entered the cockpit.

*Strap yourselves in back there,* Sarah sent to Louise

and Wei as she took the pilot's seat. *This could be a bumpy ride.*

She ran her hands over the main control panel. It had been over half a year since she'd flown the jet, but she'd made a point of refamiliarizing herself with the controls once a month. The knowledge of how to control it came back like riding a bike. Part of this knowledge (the basic skills of piloting a jet aircraft) had been culled from Commander Craig's mind as he lay injured during their escape from Russia. However, the alien technology of the Entity that had been put into the jet required a different type of intelligence – something she had picked up during her meeting with that alien force under the Russian ice.

"Sure you don't want me to take the stick?" Craig asked, not sounding too certain as he looked over the array of unfamiliar control panels.

Sarah placed her hand on the joystick and the panels lit up around her. She felt the instant, easy connection with the on-board systems of the jet. *This machine was designed to be thought-controlled,* she reminded herself. *And I was designed to fly it.*

*Jets, power up,* she thought and immediately the engines at the back of the plane roared into life. She gave Commander Craig a glance.

"I think I'll manage."

She put on the pilot's headset. "*Ulysses* tower, this is stealth jet. Open Bay 3's roof and raise us to the deck."

There was no response. Sarah tried again.

"Tower, this is—"

Hydraulics squealed outside. The hangar roof split open. The jet juddered as the platform upon which it sat began to rise. Sarah was more than a little relieved. She'd anticipated having to take control of at least one of the tower operatives in order to get the jet to the runway, but then there would be the problem of the deck crew getting in the way if they didn't want her taking off. Someone in the tower was helping out and suddenly she had a good idea who.

The jet cleared the ceiling of the hangar and the platform slotted into place with a *clunk*, forming part of the deck. Evening sunlight cast a golden glow over the wide expanse of the aircraft carrier's deck. Men and women in orange jumpsuits scurried around, preparing the area for take-off. One of the men ran to the front of the jet and held up a flashing signal beacon. He waved it over his head to get Sarah's attention and then pointed it towards the end of the ship, indicating where she should place the jet. Sarah manipulated the joystick and the plane taxied towards take-off position.

In less than a minute she had the vehicle in the correct spot – nose pointed directly down the deck. The runway was a dark rectangle stretching ahead, high contrast against the reddish gold sky on either side. Perfect flying conditions. The deck crew scrambled as they completed their final tasks and cleared the way ahead.

Sarah and the others sat in the cockpit, waiting for the final confirmation from the tower. Robert shifted nervously in the seat behind Commander Craig.

"What's taking them so long? Perhaps we should just take off."

"Calm down," Sarah said.

Her headphones crackled as a message came through from the tower.

"Stealth jet, this is the tower. Deck crew is away. You're cleared for take-off when ready." Sarah smiled to hear Rachel Andersen's voice. "But it's not too late to abort this mission. Nobody's asking you to put your lives at risk here."

Sarah looked at Robert sitting in the seat behind and gave him a reassuring nod. "We're keeping a promise we made," Sarah told Rachel as she turned her attention back to the open runway. "Wisher's going to be crazy when he wakes up, you know. I don't think he'll buy that I controlled you as well."

"Let me worry about him," Rachel replied. "Just make sure you're off that island by dawn tomorrow. There isn't going to be much left after we send in the predator drones."

"Understood… And thanks, Rachel."

"Good luck."

The connection closed. Sarah placed her right hand on the stick and thought, *Jets to full power*. The howling of the engines increased threefold. The entire plane began to shudder, vibrating from the massive forward force from the back of the vehicle to the elongated tip, like some beast desperate to break free of bonds holding it back. Sarah took a deep breath.

*Brakes release.*

The engines whined and the jet shot forward. The world in Sarah's peripheral vision became a motion blur as the massive G-force pushed her back in her seat. Sarah focused directly ahead – on the solid blackness of the runway. The jet tore forward. In less than a second it had covered half the ship, but Sarah sensed that it was not at take-off speed.

"Gonna be close!" Craig yelled over the engines.

The end of the runway was less than a second away. Sarah pulled back on the stick and the nose lifted…

Then the runway and the *Ulysses* raced past and there

was only blue water and red sky on either side. Sarah's heart leaped and for a terrible instant she was convinced the jet was simply going to plough right into the ocean. But the world angled down as she forced the stick back. The ocean disappeared, replaced by sky through every window of the cockpit as the jet executed an incredibly steep climb. Golden light bathed the cockpit. Altitude information flashed through Sarah's mind directly from the on-board computer...

*5,000... 10,000... 15,000 feet...*

At 20,000 feet she pushed forward on the stick and the plane levelled out. She ordered the engines down to cruising power, not wanting to burn through all their fuel on the outward journey. Sarah took a calming breath as she sensed the jet's on-board systems settle into a perfectly stable flight.

"So, how did I do?" she asked, glancing at Commander Craig in the seat beside her.

Craig, whose face was just a little pale, wiped the sheen of sweat from his face. "Textbook stuff."

"I thought we were going to die," Robert said, a little more honestly.

"Thanks," Sarah said.

*Can Wei and I watch a Blu-ray?* Louise asked from the back.

*Yes,* Sarah replied, and then added, *But nothing too adult.*

She looked round at Robert. "Keep an eye on those two, will you?"

With just a little eye-roll, Robert unstrapped himself from the seat and went through to the back of the jet. Sarah turned her attention to Craig, who had removed the dart pistol from his belt and was in the process of placing it in a backpack at his feet. He produced an automatic pistol – the bullet-firing variety – checked the clip and then placed it in his holster.

"Darts don't seem so effective against Major Bright," the commander said as he noticed Sarah watching him. He removed a second weapon from the bag: a chunky, black machine gun with a laser sight clipped to the top.

"I was wondering why Rachel let us go so easily," Sarah said. "And why you were so eager to come along. You wanted this, didn't you? All that talk in the sparring room – you needed me to steal the jet because it was the only way you were going to get to the island."

The briefest smile flickered across his lips. "You've got your mission, I've got mine."

"And that is?"

Craig met her enquiring eyes. "Take down Bright by any means necessary."

"Won't the drone bombers take care of that?"

Craig slotted a curved bullet clip into the front of the machine gun. "Call this a belt and braces approach. HIDRA dropped the ball with Bright three times, Sarah. Now Colonel Andersen wants him dealt with for good. When the bombs hit the island, he'll already be dead if I have anything to say about it."

"And what if Bright gets to you first?"

"That's my business. All you have to worry about is retrieving Hack and getting off the island – with or without me."

Sarah shook her head. "We don't leave anyone behind."

Craig laid the gun on the panel in front of him and spun his chair to face her. He leaned forward, holding her eyes with the same intensity he had shown in the sparring room. "This isn't a game, Sarah. I thought we went through that before."

"I've faced Bright."

"Not like this," Craig said. "Mercenaries... Weaponry... Bright on his own territory. Colonel Andersen let you take the jet only because she suspected there wasn't much she could do to stop you either way. And because she wanted me along for the ride."

"As our babysitter, right?"

Craig shook his head slowly. "Be under no illusion: my primary mission is Bright. All other concerns are secondary – and that includes you and your friends."

She studied Craig's face carefully and didn't have to read his mind to know that he was being deadly serious. If it came to a choice between them and Bright, the commander would follow his directives. He was a soldier – an assassin if necessary – and his first loyalty was to the mission. Sarah shivered involuntarily, suddenly cold, despite the temperature-controlled interior of the jet. She wanted to say something, but couldn't think what.

Craig rose from his seat and went to the cockpit door. "Our ETA on the island is six hours. I'm going to get some sleep before then. Maybe you should put on the autopilot and try to do the same."

"Okay," Sarah said as he left. The feeling of coldness hadn't gone away – in fact, it was spreading through her body.

A bad feeling that wasn't going away any time soon.

## 14

The soldiers returned as the last light of the day was fading through the cell window. There was no electric lighting in the room, so Kotler shone a torch into the cell as they opened the door. Hack held up a hand against the beam.

"On your feet."

Hack did as he was told. "We need water."

The merc leader grabbed his arm and pushed him towards the door, then shone the torch on May. She lay sleeping by the wall, her head still on Hack's T-shirt.

Two more soldiers entered, grabbed her by the arms and dragged her out of the cell.

"Be careful with her!" Hack protested.

Kotler scooped up the T-shirt and tossed it over. "Dress yourself and keep your mouth shut."

Hack made to protest at their treatment once more, but Kotler slapped the torch head against his open palm. It was a heavy-duty metal Maglite, equally effective as a club. Hack had no doubt the man would use it on him if he made trouble. Pulling the T-shirt over his head, he followed the other soldiers down the corridor and out into the compound beyond.

The night was alive with the sound of insects and still incredibly hot. Mosquitoes danced in the beams of the lights strung along the wire perimeter fence. Hack slapped a bloodsucker on his cheek as he kept pace behind the soldiers dragging May, semi-conscious, between them. He cast another look around the camp – at the military vehicles stood waiting for action, and the patrolling guards. A merc in a tower flicked a searchlight beam around the buildings, illuminating the shadowy areas in a regular pattern.

"Keep up, scum." Kotler jabbed him in the spine with the Maglite as extra incentive.

Hack bristled, but kept walking. *Scum.* He wondered

if it was necessary for men like Kotler to hate the people they guarded. Presumably it made it easier to abuse and hurt them. He knew one thing: whether Robert and HIDRA came or not, he would escape the island prison and tell the world what had been done to him and May. Somehow he would bring these men to justice for what they were doing.

All he had to do was escape.

They approached their destination: the largest buildings in the camp – two massive aircraft hangars standing side by side. The twenty-metre high doors of the nearest hangar were half-open, revealing a brilliantly lit interior. As they passed inside, Hack blinked against the light and took in the scene.

The hangar was relatively empty. Hack had expected to see the transport plane that carried him to the island, but it was not there – perhaps in the other building. There were only a couple of vehicles – a pair of Humvees standing against the closed doors on the other side. Apart from that, the hangar was one giant open space, all the more impressive because of its emptiness. Metal steps on either side led up to balconies, while a network of catwalks criss-crossed the ceiling. Hack made out soldiers stationed around these walkways, sniper rifles cradled in their arms. He counted four of them.

Kotler gave him another shove and they crossed the hangar floor towards the centre, their footsteps echoing in the emptiness. Directly ahead was an even more brightly lit area: a square about twenty metres by twenty, demarcated by yellow and black tape on the floor. High-powered lamps were mounted on stands at each corner of the square – the type you'd expect to see in a television studio. There were also three cameras mounted on tripods pointed into the middle, enhancing the feeling of being in a studio. Cables trailed across the floor, some of them taped down, some merely a tangled mess on the ground.

Hack's heart leaped as he walked into the area. *Electronics.* The place hummed with connectivity. After the technological cold turkey of the cell, this area made his head throb. The machinery sang to him. *Now, this I can use,* Hack thought, looking around…

"Ah, ah, ah. I know what you're thinking."

Hack turned in the direction of Marlon Good's mocking voice. Now dressed in a white suit and trainers, the man appeared beside one of the tripod-mounted cameras.

"I bet all this tech must look like Christmas come early to you," Good said, flipping the camera's view screen open and angling the unit on Hack. "But I wouldn't mess with anything. Those guys up top have orders to take you out at the first sign of trouble."

Good pointed a finger at the ceiling. Hack looked up and saw that one of the snipers had moved to the edge of a catwalk and was leaning over to watch him through the sights of his rifle.

"I've never seen anyone head-tapped outside of a computer game, have you?" Marlon Good asked with his characteristic giggle.

Hack looked at the man and wondered if he was truly mad or if it was just some kind of act. He had a nasty feeling he'd find out soon enough. The area was clearly set up to film something, but what? "What is all this?" he asked.

"We're going to make history tonight," Good replied. "And I want to make sure it's caught on camera. You know, for posterity. What we film here will become one of the most important documents in history: the moment the world changed for ever."

*Delusions of grandeur,* Hack thought, but before he could ask any more questions, two soldiers approached with May between them and sat her down in a metal chair off to one side. She mumbled something, but sat limply as the soldiers backed off. Hack started towards her, but Kotler smacked him in the chest with the torch.

"Don't move."

Marlon Good walked towards May, waving a hand at the merc as he went. "It's okay, Kotler. I think the boy knows better than to try anything when he's got four rifles aimed at his head. Be a pal and kill the main lights, will you?"

A muscle twitched in Kotler's right cheek, but he turned and marched out of the square without a word. The other two soldiers retreated to the edge of the area. Marlon Good stood over May and touched a hand to her chin. The girl's head flopped over to the other side.

"You can come over," Good said, looking round at Hack.

Hack moved to the side of the chair and kneeled down beside May. He took her right hand in his and tried to make some kind of contact. *May, can you hear me? Are you okay?* All he got in response was a series of fuzzy, jumbled thoughts.

"You've become friends already, I see," Marlon Good said. He wheeled a small cabinet over to the chair. "How sweet."

There was a *shunk* as Kotler cut the lights set into the hangar ceiling. The area beyond the square was thrown into absolute darkness relative to the brightness of the mounted lights. Marlon Good smiled to see

Hack look at the pitch-black surrounding them like a shroud.

"Dramatic, ain't it?" he said.

Hack didn't let go of May's hand. "Why are you doing this to her?" he demanded.

Good opened the cabinet doors, revealing drawers packed with medical equipment. He extracted a slim aluminium case and laid it on the top of the cabinet.

"May's ability is even more remarkable than yours," Good explained as he opened the lid. "The power to alter matter at the subatomic level with her mind. When we first brought her here, we did try to be reasonable, but she just wouldn't be contained. Kept turning our prison walls into water and the like. In the end, drugs were the only solution."

"It's inhuman."

Good nodded. "I completely agree. Which is why I've had my technicians in Silicon Valley working on a more…efficient solution. One that won't cause long-term damage to her talent. Something for you and May to wear that should help us to keep tabs on you both without having to dull your abilities. Check it out."

He removed a circular item from the case and held it up for Hack to see. It was a collar made of some kind of titanium alloy. A box with flashing status lights along the side protruded from the back. Hack sensed electronics, GPS equipment and anti-tamper technology built into the item – along with something else...

*An explosive charge linked to a detonator.*

Marlon Good smiled as Hack's eyes widened. "Ah, I see you've found the surprise."

He opened the collar from the back and placed it around May's neck. He snapped it closed and the device emitted a high-pitched beep. A light on the side flashed from red to green. Beneath this light, a signal indicator bar like that on a mobile phone appeared – it displayed five bars. Some kind of wireless signal.

"There, now it's armed," Good said. He reached for the case and removed a second, identical collar. "Time to put yours on."

Hack took a step back. "I'm not wearing that. It's got explosives inside."

Good sighed in an exaggerated fashion as Hack retreated. "You will wear it. In fact, you're going to put it on yourself. Of your own free will."

"I don't think so."

The collar around May's neck began to emit a series of warning beeps, spaced about a second apart. Marlon Good grinned nastily at Hack.

"That's the sound of the detonation alert," he

explained. "Each collar has a twin. If that twin isn't activated within thirty seconds of the other, a countdown begins."

Hack glanced at May as the beeps started to sound closer together. Good snapped open the collar and held it out.

"The charge in each device is relatively small, as I'm sure you've sensed. But it's enough to turn a person's head into a soccer ball." He waved the collar tauntingly. "What's it gonna be?"

"You won't do it," Hack replied. "You need us for something. You won't let May die."

"Do you really want to put that to the test?"

The beeps increased in speed. Hack held Good's gaze, trying to work out if he was bluffing or not. The beeps started to come so close together, they were almost a continuous tone...

Hack snatched the collar and placed it around his neck. The device locked shut with a magnetic click at the back. The collar gave the activation sound and in response the device around May's throat ceased beeping. Hack breathed a sigh of relief. Marlon Good regarded him with a triumphant little glint in his eyes.

*He likes to play cruel games,* Hack thought. *And he likes to win.*

"Now, that wasn't so bad, was it?" Good said, giving Hack a slap on the shoulder. "You should feel privileged. You're wearing a prisoner containment system that cost about half a billion dollars to develop. State of the art. How's that for expensive neckwear?"

Hack ran a finger around the edge of the collar. The device was lightweight, but he could tell that over time the heat of the island would make it intensely irritating to wear. He felt round the back to the box-like protuberance. His fingertips brushed the magnetic lock.

"Few things you should know about the collar," Good said conversationally as he closed the case and put it back in the cabinet. "Don't even think about tampering with it – either with your mind or your hands. Try to take it off, or trigger one of the thousand anti-removal sensors, and the countdown begins. For both you and May. Two seconds to boom-time."

Hack lowered his hand from the collar.

"You might think you can bypass the security," Good went on, "but bear in mind it's been designed to hold someone with just such a skill as your own. Don't feel self-conscious about wearing it, soon everyone will have one. Anyone who needs one, that is." Good giggled, as if at some private joke.

"So how do we take them off?" Hack asked.

"You don't," Good replied. "Ever. Wherever you go, it goes. The collars work worldwide. I have my own dedicated satellite network in place to monitor them." He reached inside his shirt and pulled out a rectangular silver object on a chain. "This is the only key. It's also a trigger."

Good pressed something on the side of the key and both Hack's and May's collars started to beep. He pressed it again and they stopped.

"Get the picture? You do as you're told or it's goodbye, sweet neck."

Hack regarded Marlon Good with real hatred as the man replaced the key in his shirt. The collar was a massive complication to any escape plan. Hack's mind raced. What were the odds of rushing Good right now? Blow up the electronics, grab the key, get the collars off. He glanced around at the two soldiers, barely visible in the darkness at the edge of the square. Take them out somehow. Then he remembered the snipers above.

Impossible.

Then another thought occurred to Hack. Marlon Good had become even more animated than normal when describing the collars and how they worked. He wanted to show them off. Like a child with a new toy. And Marlon Good clearly enjoyed playing with his toys. He might need May and Hack for whatever plot he and Major Bright had hatched, but eventually he would want to see the collars in action. He'd trigger them before he took them off his prisoners – Hack was certain of it.

The realization made his blood run cold.

"One last thing," Good said. "The collars are linked wirelessly. If they ever get more than a kilometre apart… boom! Should give you enough wriggle room to move about the camp, but don't think about taking any solo jaunts around the island. An extra incentive in case one of you decides to make a break for it alone."

Hack shook his head with disgust. "I'd never leave May with you monsters."

"Very admirable," a new voice said.

Both Hack and Marlon Good turned as the towering figure of Major Bright walked out of the darkness. He wore a pristine black and gold uniform – the same colours as his old HIDRA special forces, but a new design for a new army. One of his own making. An insignia on the side showed a serpent coiled around a Kalashnikov rifle. Hack recognized the hard, angular features and cropped hair revealing a network of old skull scars from the pictures Jonesey had shown him. Now, however, the lower right side of Bright's face was covered with scaly, black skin – like something was spreading over his body. If anything, it made his appearance more threatening and Hack found himself taking an involuntary step back. Even the crazy Marlon Good seemed to shrink a little in stature as the monolithic military man entered the light.

Major Bright smiled, as if pleased by their reaction. He clapped his giant hands together, creating a sound that echoed through the darkened hangar.

"Right. When do we begin?"

15

Two hundred kilometres from the island of Oshino, Sarah engaged full stealth mode. The jet, always invisible to radar, switched on anti-detection systems designed to cloak its heat, motion and electronic signatures. Light distortion cells built into the fuselage became operational, making it all but invisible to the naked eye as well. *Autopilot disengage,* Sarah ordered and took the stick. She needed to be in full control for the final approach.

"Let's take a better look at where we're headed," Commander Craig said as he eased himself into the co-pilot's chair. He touched a series of controls and a blue-tinted holographic image of the island appeared between them. Craig reached up and tapped the image with his index finger – it responded with a slow spin, revealing a jungle terrain peppered with a few mountains and rivers. Robert appeared at Craig's shoulder.

"There's Major Bright's camp," Craig said. He touched the area around the camp and it zoomed in, revealing buildings, fences and a runway to the south.

"How accurate is this?" Sarah asked.

"Modelled around existing maps and real-time satellite data fed directly to the jet," the commander responded. "Pretty accurate, I'd say."

"Well, there's a runway," she said, "but it's too close to the camp to land without drawing some attention to ourselves. Even in the stealth jet."

Craig nodded his agreement. "Let's look for another point of entry."

He pinched and the holographic model zoomed out. He gave it another flick and it spun again.

"There!" Robert exclaimed, pointing to an area on the other side of the island as it came round.

Craig stopped the image and zoomed in. There was a cleared area in the jungle near the beach and a flat strip of land that looked very much like another runway.

"Good spot, Robert!" Craig said as he examined the site. "Must be a backup landing strip. No evidence of current use. The runway's short and it might be in serious disrepair. Could be a dangerous landing."

"I guess we won't find out until we try," Sarah said. "I'd rather put down there than on Bright's doorstep. How far do you think it is from the camp?"

Craig rubbed his chin. "A few kilometres through the jungle."

"Not too far," Robert said.

"Maybe not for someone who can teleport across the island. For the rest of us it could be a hike through some very rough terrain."

"It's our best option," Sarah said, settling the matter. "I'm putting us down there. Robert, go back and make sure Louise and Wei are strapped in. We land in fifteen."

Her brother nodded and disappeared into the cabin. Craig locked the location of the second runway into the jet's instrument landing system and a marker beacon appeared on the HUD. He closed the holomap, dimmed the cockpit lights and strapped himself into his seat.

"Great flying, Sarah," he said. "You handle this jet like you've been at the stick for twenty years."

She glanced over at him. "I had a good teacher."

In the instrument-illuminated darkness, Craig's face was serious. "When we reach that island we're in the combat zone. If I say we abort the mission, we abort – no questions asked. Okay?"

"Okay."

They sat in silence after that. Sarah took the jet down to the deck – flying less than fifty metres above the ocean. Through the window the water raced by, blacker than the night sky. A shadow appeared on the horizon – an irregular lump that could only be Oshino. The appearance of the ILS beacon, flashing on the HUD, confirmed this. Sarah sent the jet round the island in a wide arc, steering clear of the side on which Bright's camp was situated. As the beacon came round, she angled the nose in for a direct approach, perfectly lined up with the angle of the disused runway in the jungle.

*Jets, fifty per cent power down,* she ordered and the plane slowed, beginning to descend...

The island approached at speed. In the darkness it became possible to make out beach and jungle...

*Undercarriage.*

Landing wheels extended. Suddenly they were passing over the tops of trees, dense and impenetrable...

The beacon symbol flashed on the HUD, rhythmically tracing the outline of the unlit runway, which was otherwise invisible. Sarah pushed forward on the stick and...

The jet touched down, bumping and jolting violently against the broken surface of the landing strip...

*Airbrakes engage. Full reverse thrust.*

There was an amazing pull as the jet came to a sudden and definite halt less than fifty metres from where the wheels had first touched – a feat impossible in any normal plane.

*Engines power down,* Sarah ordered. *All flight systems, stand-by mode.*

Craig touched another control and a scan showing a kilometre radius around the jet opened up. It showed no life-signs big enough to be a person in the area. Satisfied, the commander unstrapped himself from his seat, picked up the machine gun and moved to the cockpit door.

"It's clear. Let's not hang around."

Sarah followed him through to the dimmed interior of the main cabin where Robert, Louise and Wei were preparing to exit the plane.

"Okay," Craig said, looking round them all with a *don't mess with me* expression, "when we set foot outside this jet you follow my lead. Walk where I walk. Stop when I stop."

Robert protested, "Why can't I just teleport directly into the camp? I can grab Hack and we'll be out of here."

Craig shook his head. "Too risky. We don't know the kid's exact location or enough about the camp defences. You could teleport right into a group of guards."

Sarah nodded. "He's right, Robert. We need to be careful."

For once her brother didn't argue. They each grabbed their backpacks. Louise and Wei were already at the exit door, eager to get outside after being cooped up in the jet for hours. Craig walked over, operated the hatch and went out first.

It was approaching midnight, but the air was still amazingly warm and humid. Sarah felt the sweat prickling her skin within seconds of stepping off the jet.

"Let's move," Craig ordered, and started off across towards the treeline at a half-run, closely followed by Robert, Louise and Wei. Sarah paused only to give a final command to the jet.

*Defensive systems engage.*

The ramp retracted into the jet and the door closed. Sarah moved away as motion detectors linked to gun turrets concealed by the undercarriage went operational. In the darkness, the jet was practically invisible up to a few metres away, but anyone who did go snooping around would get a nasty shock. Satisfied their way off the island was as safe as she could make it, Sarah ran off after the others.

Running, as it turned out, was not an easy task in the intense humidity of the island night. By the time Sarah reached the trees, she was panting as if she'd run a full kilometre. She looked at the jungle ahead – uneven ground, vines draped at head-height and roots underfoot – and understood that a few kilometres' hike was going to be quite an undertaking. Maybe Robert's instinct about teleporting to the camp hadn't been so bad after all – at least they could get closer. She mentally projected ahead, scanning for the camp to the north of the island and sensed…

*Nothing.*

With a frown, she tried again – attempting to make contact with the minds of the soldiers in the camp or anything that would give them a handle on their target.

*Again nothing.*

It was as if a blanket had been thrown over her psychic senses, and she didn't like it. It was like going suddenly deaf or blind. The closeness of the night and the jungle pressing in around them seemed instantly more threatening…

A low chuckle echoed through the back of her mind, like something she had heard before but couldn't quite remember where…

"Sarah?" Robert said, placing a hand on her arm. "Are you all right?"

She came back into the moment and gave him a smile. "I'm fine. I just felt…"

"What?"

"Nothing," she said. There was no point in worrying him just because she got spooked by the jungle. "Just feeling a little light-headed from the heat, I guess."

"This level of humidity will do that," Craig said. "You've all got water in your packs, so keep hydrating. Walk steadily, no unnecessary movements. We're all about conserving energy. Sarah, I take it you'll be able to sense any enemies hanging around in the bush?"

She felt sheepish as the eyes of the others fell upon her. "Uh, maybe not at the moment. Feeling a little bit off my game. Sorry."

If Craig was worried by this information, he didn't show it. He removed a set of night-vision goggles from his belt and put them over his head. "Okay, I'll take point," he said. "Robert, bring up the rear. Louise stick close to me – be ready for action in case I need you."

She gave him a little salute. Wei put up his hand like

a kid in a classroom. "What about me?"

"Maybe not such a good idea to start a fire in a jungle," Craig said, referring to Wei's pyrokinetic power. Then, when he saw the boy's face fall, added, "You can light up the camp before we leave."

Wei grinned. Craig turned and started forward into the jungle, machine gun at the ready, brushing aside vines and moving almost silently despite the carpet of leaves and debris on the ground. The others followed, a little less expertly. As Sarah brought up the rear with Robert, she had the feeling of a presence out in the jungle once more…

Something watching…

And drawing them in…

# 16

"How much longer is this going to take?" Major Bright demanded as technicians weaved around the cameras and other equipment packed into the lit square. Bright regarded them with contempt – they were Good's people, nerdy, nervous types, not soldiers. And as such, they'd needed paying ten times a soldier's wage just to get them out of their air-conditioned offices in California and to the island.

Marlon Good, who was poring over a computer screen, didn't look round. "It will take as long as it takes.

You want to get this right, don't you?"

"I want to get this done." Bright began to pace the centre of the lit area.

*Have patience,* the Entity warned in his head. *This is why we need Good. Let him do his job.*

*I'd like to break that runt's neck.*

The Entity chuckled. *Eventually you'll get your chance. But not tonight. Think of our plans. Think of the future.*

Bright clenched and unclenched his fists. *I don't like waiting.*

*Don't worry. There will be plenty for you to do soon enough.*

*Meaning?*

The Entity chuckled again. *I'll leave it as a surprise. Something for later...*

Before Bright could press further, one of the technicians gave Good the thumbs up from a computer on the other side of the square.

"Excellent," Good said. He walked over to the medical cabinet and removed an injection tube.

"What are you doing?" Hack said, rising to his feet.

"Giving sleeping beauty something to perk her up. Just a little stimulant."

He jabbed May's arm with the tube. The effect was instantaneous: with a gasp, she half-rose from the chair, eyes wide, hands gripping the armrests. Her entire body was shaking, muscles taut. Hack placed his hands on her shoulders and gently eased her back down.

"It's okay, it's okay," he said.

May looked at him wildly, but then some recognition came into her eyes. "Where…are…we?" she asked, barely able to talk because of her racing heart.

"In one of the hangars," Hack explained. He gave her a bottle of water to drink from. "Just try to breathe. You've been given a shot."

May nodded. She touched the collar around her throat and looked at Hack with alarm.

"Don't try to take it off," Hack warned, pointing to his matching collar. "Explosives. Mine too."

Again May nodded her understanding. She bent forward and stared at the floor between her feet, trying to get herself under control. Hack looked up at Marlon Good accusingly.

"You're going to kill her like this."

"She can take it." Good tossed the injection tube back in the cabinet as he walked to the computer, neglecting to close the cabinet doors. Hack considered for a split second – everyone at ground level was occupied with the cameras and computers, but were the snipers watching him every second? The chance had to be worth taking. He moved round so he was crouching on the other side of May, then reached back with his hand, shielding the motion as much as possible with his body. His fingers brushed the smooth metal of the injection tube. He grabbed it and stuffed it in the pocket of his jeans. For a moment he didn't breathe – expecting the report of a rifle, or the heavy hand of Major Bright to close on his shoulder.

Seconds passed.

It didn't happen.

Hack had to stop himself from laughing with relief. Now he had a weapon.

"What are they doing?" May asked, her voice barely a whisper. If she'd noticed him grab the stimulant, she didn't show it.

"I don't know," Hack said, looking round, "but I think we're about to find out what all this is about."

Marlon Good had moved into the centre of the square as the technicians took positions at the cameras and computers. A kind of hushed anticipation fell over the area. Even Major Bright took a step to the edge of the light and waited in silence, giant arms folded across his chest. Good brushed a speck of dust from the lapel of his jacket and turned to face the largest of the cameras. He pointed to the technician behind it.

"Action." Then…

"Citizens of the world," Marlon Good said to the camera, basking in the imagined attention, "good evening. And welcome to my secret lair somewhere in the Pacific Ocean."

Good laughed to himself. In the corner, Major Bright rolled his eyes, but he said nothing.

Good snapped his fingers and held up his right hand before him, palm open. A blue-tinged holographic image of a rotating globe appeared above his hand. Hack sensed he had a mini holo-projector concealed up his sleeve. *Very clever – he's quite the showman,* he thought. In addition to his money, was this why Bright needed the American? To be the public face of whatever terrible plans they had for the world?

"Consider the earth," Marlon Good said, eyeing the planet rotating above his hand as if it was a precious jewel. "So very fragmented. Different languages. Different governments. Different cultures. Bad for unity. And bad for progress."

He touched the index finger of his right hand to the image and it slowly began to turn red, until the entire globe had changed colour.

"We intend to put an end to this disunity. We have the means to create a new world order. The old factionalism of individual countries and companies will be swept away and in its place we will install a single government." He closed his fist over the image and the world disappeared. "By the time this message is broadcast, we will already have demonstrated the awesome power at our command by taking over a major capital city in less than a day. We call upon the remaining nations of the world that have not already fallen to surrender unconditionally. You will be treated with…mercy."

Good paused for a moment and clasped his hands behind his back.

"Tonight you will be witness to the greatest technological revolution since the invention of the internal combustion engine. Let our children and our children's children know that this is where the new world began." Good's face cracked into a grin and he waved his arms wildly, surprising even Major Bright with his sudden change in tone. "I know, booooring! But don't you want to see the demonstration? Wouldn't you like to see how we're going to take over the world?"

Good signalled to his people waiting in the darkness surrounding the square. "Bring in the hypersphere!" He winked at the camera. "Trust me, this is cool."

Technicians appeared, wheeling a huge, circular trolley before the cameras. On this trolley stood a metal frame and within the frame a black sphere the size of a small car was suspended, perhaps by some kind of magnetic field. The surface of this sphere was perfectly smooth and it was possible to make out etched patterns, almost like letters, but of a totally alien language. As the technicians backed off, Marlon Good stepped forward and tapped the sphere with his finger. It began to rotate slowly on its axis, the perfect, dark surface reflecting the studio lights.

"An object of alien origin – salvaged from the recent meteorite storm that almost ended life on earth," he explained. "I'm sure you all heard about it. Most of the meteors collided in space, broke into pieces and burned up harmlessly in our atmosphere. A few larger fragments did manage to survive, however. This piece was retrieved from an area of Antarctica so remote, even the penguins don't go there. We call it the hypersphere."

At the edge of the area, Major Bright wound his index finger in a *hurry up* motion. Marlon Good took the hint and started speaking even faster.

"This rock is possessed of amazing properties beyond the science of our time. In its natural state, it's perfectly harmless – dormant, as you see here. But with the right catalyst, it can become one of the most powerful forces this world has ever seen. Now we have that catalyst."

Good looked round. "Major Bright, would you care to begin the demonstration?"

Bright unfolded his arms and strode across the square. Three cameras followed his movement, but he acknowledged none of them – almost as if they were beneath his attention. He headed directly for Hack and May and stopped before them, arms held out to them.

"Take my hands, children," he ordered. "It's showtime."

## 17

The two mercs patrolling the eastern perimeter never knew what hit them. As they passed one another on their circuit of the area an invisible force grabbed them both and dragged them twenty metres into the jungle. One smacked head first into a tree and was immediately out for the count. The other skidded to his knees at the feet of a nine-year-old girl standing amid the trailing vines. His rifle was lost, so the merc reached for his pistol. Something heavy hit him on the back of the head and he went down.

"I'm only going to ask you once," Commander Craig hissed as he pressed the machine-gun muzzle into the merc's skull. "Where are you keeping the boy?"

The merc glared back at him. "Shoot me and you'll bring the whole base down on yourself."

Craig nodded at Louise. "That girl can turn you inside out with a thought. Don't make me tell her to demonstrate."

The merc swallowed heavily and looked at Louise with widening eyes. She smiled sweetly at him.

"There's a set of brick buildings to the south of the camp," the merc said. "Cells. That's where we're holding him."

"Thanks," Craig said, and smashed him across the face with the butt of his gun. He looked at Sarah and the others. "He should be out for a while."

They headed to the metal fence. Wei stepped forward and put his fingers through the chain links. His hand glowed red-hot and the metal around it began to melt. He waited until a suitably large hole had been burned in the fence and then removed his hand. He gestured for the others to go through.

Craig grinned as he passed. "Nice work, Wei."

They ran to the cover of a set of crates as a searchlight swept the area, illuminating the shadows.

"This is where we split up," Craig said. "Go to the cells and get the kid. If anyone gets in your way, you know what to do. I'm going after Bright."

Robert shook his head. "We should stay together. You can't face Bright by yourself—"

Commander Craig laid a hand on the boy's shoulder. "That is the way it's going to be, Robert. Go and save your friend."

With that, he disappeared round the side of the crates.

"Do as he told you," Sarah said urgently. "And be careful about it. I'll meet up with you soon."

"Where are you going?" Robert demanded in exasperation.

"To help him take care of Bright," she said over her shoulder as she disappeared after the commander.

"Typical," Robert muttered. Becoming aware that both Louise and Wei were looking at him for direction, he drew himself up a little taller. "Okay, let's go rescue Hack," he said, trying to sound more purposeful than he felt.

"Place your hands on it," Major Bright commanded as he led Hack and May over to where the hypersphere was suspended. He held hands with each of them, his grip like a vice. For a moment, both kids hesitated, until Bright tightened the vice painfully. "Do as you're told!"

Hack glanced past the major's bulk and met May's eyes. *It's going to be okay,* he told her. *Just go along with what he wants.*

May nodded and placed her left hand on the glass-like surface of the sphere. It stopped rotating. Hack did the same with his right hand. Major Bright looked at the camera for the first time.

"Now," he said, "let me show you real power."

For a moment, Hack felt nothing. The sphere felt oddly cool to the touch, but nothing more. It felt at once like a metal and a rock; a substance not of the world. Then Hack sensed it: a vibration passing up through his arm from the rock and through his body. Suddenly, in his mind, there was another presence...

*...A presence that is at once incredibly ancient and powerful without measure. Hack senses the intruder comes from Major Bright somehow, but it is not him. He wants to let go of the major's hand, to break the connection, but finds that he is completely unable to move. Paralysed.*

*"Yes, at last. Don't be afraid. This is what you were born to do."*

*The alien voice in his head is at once beguiling and terrifying. Hack senses both May and the major and the alien intelligence – almost as if they are one consciousness.*

*"Who are you?" he asks.*

*"I am the Entity," comes the reply. "The devourer of worlds. All things become me in time."*

*Hack wants to scream, but he has no control over his body. The world around him has receded to a pinpoint in the distance. The thing calling itself the Entity is everything – everywhere.*

*"Now, do my bidding," the voice commands.*

*Hack senses May's power being channelled into the hypersphere – although she is clearly not in control of what she is doing any more than he is. The molecular structure of the rock begins to change, shift and become amorphous. It's as if the matter is alive and, chameleon-like, able to transform itself into any form it chooses...*

*Now the Entity turns its attention to Hack, assuming his power like it's putting on a glove. Images, schematics and coding flash through his mind at a dizzying rate: like looking at all the computer code in the world in less than a few seconds. Hack makes out instructions for machines – horrific machines of death and destruction...*

*The Entity uses him to imprint these instructions into the very fabric of the rock May has just activated – like DNA in the cells of an embryo...*

*The hypersphere begins to shift and change yet again...*

*The Entity gives a satisfied sigh...*

And the world around Hack flooded back in as Major Bright released both his and May's hands. The link with the alien force was broken. His knees buckled and he almost fell to the floor. He felt mentally and physically drained – as if contact with the thing...the Entity...had sucked the life force from him. He looked left and noticed something about the major. The black, scaly skin seemed to have moved further up his face.

"Hack..." May said.

He caught her as she fell back in a half-faint. The experience had drained him, but in her weakened state, May had clearly been pushed to the very edge by her contact with the Entity. Hack eased her down to the floor and was about to yell for some help, when he sensed movement just a metre away. He looked up and saw something happening to the hypersphere.

The black, mirror surface of the rock shimmered, as if it had become liquid. Then a single droplet of dark matter, no larger than a tennis ball, fell from the bottom of the sphere and hit the floor. As he watched, this new fragment from the larger sphere began to change. It elongated from the bottom to the top, became more angular in shape and actually seemed to grow in size. The molecular changes that Hack had sensed while connected to the Entity were now playing out for all to see. Placing his hands under May's arms, he began to pull her away from the hypersphere (which had once again become solid) and the tiny offshoot.

One of the technicians removed his camera from his tripod and advanced on the smaller object, trying to get a clearer shot.

Having retreated to the very edge of the square, Marlon Good said, "This is where it should start to get interesting."

The rock doubled in size. It pulsed and throbbed rhythmically and took on the appearance of the body of a squid – long and tapering to a point. Thin, tentacle-like protrusions began to extend from the base, probing the floor around it blindly. It was as if the rock had become a living organism and was feeling out its new, alien surroundings. Strange, delicate veins of light, like fibre-optic cable running through the rock, appeared all over the surface. Hack pulled May further away from the substance, which was beginning to look more and more like some creature from the depths of the ocean...

The technician with the camera was so focused upon the scene in his viewfinder that he didn't notice his shoe brush one of the searching tentacles...

The squid recoiled momentarily, as if shocked to make contact with a living organism, but then moved with terrifying speed. A tentacle whipped around the technician's midriff, lifted him clean off the ground and flung him to one side with amazing force. The technician flew across the square and was lost in the darkness. There was a sickening *splat* as the man hit something solid.

Technicians abandoned their posts and started running into the dark. One of the mercs stepped forward, machine gun raised. The squid reacted instantly. Another tentacle cracked through the air like a whip. The merc staggered back, clutching his throat and was dragged away by his partner. Hack looked round at Marlon Good, who was watching the scene with a kind of wide-eyed fascination from the sidelines, as if at once thrilled and terrified by the chaos he had set in motion.

"Do something!" Hack yelled at him. "It's going to kill us all!"

But it was Major Bright who stepped forward to take control. The squid threw itself at him as he approached, its eight tentacles entwining around his arms and legs. Bright fought it, muscles bulging through his uniform as if they were about to explode. With a cry of effort, he wrapped his hands around the newborn creature. Electricity danced from his fingers. The squid struggled for a moment, before the tentacles retracted. It slid to the floor and retreated under the hypersphere, like some kind of cub returning to the safety of a parent. Bright looked down at it with a triumphant smile.

"What is that?" Hack asked breathlessly.

Marlon Good stepped forward and joined Major Bright. "You just saw the future of weaponry, construction, engineering... Just about everything you can name. We have the power to harness this technology – turning alien matter harvested from the hypersphere into organic machinery of unlimited power. We'll build cities like this world has never seen. Armies to protect them..." He rubbed his hands together and looked at one of the cameras that was still standing. "And for people who stand against us, prisons."

# 18

Sarah trailed Commander Craig across the compound towards the two massive hangars. She followed his progress, sticking to the same shadows and cover that he used. Then, rounding the side of a tank covered with a tarp, she was surprised to find that the commander was no longer ahead of her. She spun round... His hand grabbed her arm and pulled her back beside the vehicle.

"What do you think you're doing?" Craig demanded. "You were supposed to stay with the others."

"You're going after Bright," she said. "I want to see him taken down just as much as you do. If not more."

Craig gave her a hard look, but then shook his head, as if deciding he didn't have time to argue. "Okay. Stick close to me. If I say run, you get the hell out. Understand?"

Sarah nodded and looked round at the hangar, which was less than thirty metres from their hiding place. The main doors were open only a couple of metres, revealing a darkened interior. A single sentry paced back and forth across the entrance. She tried to project her mind inside the building, but found the same block as before.

She thought, *This is all wrong...*

"I have to tell you something," she began, but Craig was already on the move. He crossed the ground between them and the hangar in a few seconds, grabbed the sentry from behind and jabbed him in the neck with a cylindrical object clutched in his fist. The guard went limp and the commander dragged him into the shadows at the side of the hangar. Craig reappeared a second later and beckoned to Sarah. She ran over.

"Is he dead?" she asked, looking to where the commander had dragged the guard.

Craig held out the object in his hand so she could see. It was a syringe gun, of a type she'd never seen before. "A throat-jabber," he explained. "Delivers a dose of tranquillizer direct to the carotid artery. Knocks an enemy out cold in less than three seconds. More accurate than a dart-gun in these situations."

"Cool," said Sarah, thinking she was glad the commander had decided to let her tag along rather than knock her out as well.

"It looks pretty dark in there," Craig said, meaning the interior of the hangar. "That should provide plenty of cover. Stay behind me and stay low."

Sarah nodded and followed him towards the entrance. Sure enough, as they slipped through the doors they found themselves in total darkness except for a brilliantly lit area in the centre. She strained her eyes and made out Major Bright. A few soldiers were positioned around the edge of this area, but their attention was focused inwards. There were lights and cameras, and a slim guy in a suit who looked out of place next to Bright. She also spotted two kids: a boy she assumed to be Hack, and a girl who was lying motionless on the floor.

"Stay here," Commander Craig whispered in her ear. She looked round and made out the shape of the night-vision goggles on his head. "There are snipers on the walkways above. I'm going to neutralize them and then take out Bright."

With that, he was gone.

Sarah crouched by the door and tried to hear what was being said in the centre of the hangar. The smaller man in the suit was speaking. The poor acoustics of the space meant that she was just too far away to hear. Slowly and carefully, she began to edge forwards in the darkness, until she had covered half the distance and could properly eavesdrop on what was being said.

"Well, I think we can count that as a success," the American in the white suit said.

"It will be a success when the *Ulysses* is sent to the bottom of the ocean," Bright replied. "My men have picked up the carrier headed for our location. Just as I predicted. The tracker they placed in the boy is leading them right to us."

"Why do you want to take on HIDRA?" the American asked. "We have our demonstration of the power of these machines. By the time the *Ulysses* has come within striking distance, we can be a thousand kilometres from here."

Bright snapped, "Because I owe them! They locked me in a cell in the bowels of that vessel and I will see it torn apart!"

"Fine!" the smaller man said hurriedly, in response to the major's barely controlled anger. "Another live trial of the technology can't hurt."

"Don't question me again, Good."

In the darkness, Sarah's heart missed a beat. The *Ulysses* was going to be targeted. They were sailing into some kind of trap. She had to warn Rachel...

Bright walked around a metallic sphere under which a squid-like creature cowered – its shape constantly changing, making it impossible to tell if it was an animal or a machine. The major said something Sarah couldn't hear and the American signalled for the remaining technicians to clear out. One by one, they left their posts and walked through the darkness towards the exit, flanked by the soldiers on the ground. Sarah watched two of the soldiers advance towards the unconscious girl and pick her up roughly by the arms.

"She needs medical help!" Hack exclaimed. "She's barely breathing!"

Bright snapped his fingers at two of his men. "Take her to Dr. Cameron."

The girl was lifted up and carried away towards an exit at the back. The boy made to follow, but Bright laid a hand on his shoulder.

"Not you. Return him to his cell."

Ignoring the kid's protests, two soldiers took his arms and led him in the other direction.

Now there was only Bright and the American left in

the lighted area. They launched into an animated discussion about how to handle the two prisoners. Sarah made out some kind of disfigurement on Bright's skin that she had not seen before. There was a reptilian quality to the black, scaly mark spreading up his face and she wondered what the cause was. Had Bright been experimenting with more serum, like the one he had created to give himself superpowers in the past? And if so, what new powers did he have?

She decided to send her brother a message. *Robert, they're taking Hack to the cells.*

There was no reply. Sarah had no sense of the others' presence and she was certain the message had not been received. Was something blocking her? Bright? He had shown no awareness of her presence in the hangar. She moved even closer so she could better hear what they were saying…

Commander Craig crouched at the top of the stairs and surveyed the catwalks criss-crossing the ceiling of the hangar. In the green-tinged viewfinder of the night-vision goggles everything had a flattened quality, but he was well used to working with the equipment. When it came time, he would have no problems moving in the seemingly

2D environment. Checking the machine gun was securely fastened at his side (he didn't want it knocking against one of the railings), he reached to his belt and extracted the throat-jabber once more. If he wanted to knock the snipers out, he'd have to get up close. Using a dart-gun would cause too much noise if they fell without him being there to catch them.

There were four snipers positioned on the catwalks. Since the girl and boy had been taken out of the hangar, they had visibly relaxed – switching from alert stances, eyes locked down the scopes of their rifles, to more comfortable positions, weapons cradled in their arms. Major Bright's voice echoed up from below and it was possible to make out every word. The usual madness that made Craig's stomach turn: *world domination, destruction, superpowers, blah blah, blah blah blah.* One piece of information that caught his attention was the talk about destroying the *Ulysses* with some piece of technology they had down there.

Craig smiled grimly in the darkness. *That isn't going to happen,* he thought. *Time to end this...*

The commander moved swiftly and silently as the nearest sniper turned his back. Craig's left hand clamped over the merc's mouth and twisted his head to expose the carotid artery. His right hand came up and the jabber hit the sniper's neck. For a second the man struggled violently, but Craig held firm, not allowing him to thrash around and alert the others. In three seconds it was all over. He lowered the unconscious merc to the floor of the catwalk, checked the jabber was ready to deliver another dose of tranquillizer and moved on to the next.

The second sniper went in much the same manner and just as silently. With the deed done, Craig looked round at the other two snipers, who showed no realization that their teammates had been taken out. The voices of Bright and the American continued to echo up from below. Craig moved on in the darkness.

The third sniper would be more of a challenge. He was leaning against the railing, facing Craig. The commander considered his position. He could go all the way down to the ground, up the stairs on the other side of the hangar, then approach him from the rear. *No, too time consuming.* Or he could just wait for the man to turn round. *By which time Bright might have left the hangar.*

It was now or never.

He went in, bent almost double. In the darkness, the sniper didn't even sense him until he was right in his face. The merc's eyes widened and he began to bring the rifle round. Commander Craig hit him in the throat with the jabber and clamped a hand over his mouth to stop his scream, but the angle was all wrong. The base of the sniper's spine hit the railing and he toppled back. Craig made a grab for him, but found only the barrel of the rifle. The man pitched over the side of the catwalk with the jabber needle still in his neck, but his rifle in Craig's hands. A second later, the merc's body hit one of the lamps below with a clatter and then a dull thud. The fallen lamp landed on the floor, casting its beam on the catwalk above – illuminating the commander's position.

Craig moved purely on instinct, pressing the stock of the sniper's rifle into his shoulder, one finger on the trigger. He spun and sighted through the scope in the direction he knew the last sniper was standing. The light from below was overloading the peripheral vision of the goggles, half-blinding him, but he saw the dark shape of the fourth man on the catwalk taking aim at him…

The commander pulled the trigger first. The sniper's body jerked round and disappeared into the darkness.

The floor of the catwalk exploded as a volley of bullets ripped through the metal. Someone was firing at him from below. Craig threw himself forward, running headlong for the darkened area. He didn't need to look over the side of the catwalk to know that it was Bright letting loose with a machine gun. He made the darkness as another round of bullets licked the walkway. He rolled into a crouch and waited. The shooting stopped as the major reloaded…

Craig ripped the goggles off his head, leaned over the railing and aimed the sniper rifle where he predicted the major was standing. His instinct was right and he sighted on Bright in the process of slotting a new clip into a Kalashnikov rifle. *One chance.* Craig sighted the middle of Bright's forehead and pulled the trigger. A red dot appeared in the centre of the major's skull and his head snapped back. Craig put two more rounds in his chest as he went down.

"Gotcha," the commander said as he lowered the rifle.

Bright was laid out on the floor below. The American guy had ducked into the darkness, presumably the moment the shooting started. Craig dropped the rifle at his feet and started moving back along the catwalk. It was time to clear out before the alarm was raised. He just hoped that Sarah had already made a break for it…

"COMMANDER!"

Craig stopped in his tracks at the sound of Major Bright's voice echoing up from below. *Not possible, I put a bullet in his head.* He moved to the side of the catwalk, unslinging the machine gun from his shoulder as he did so. But it was already too late...

The catwalk floor concertinaed as if some massive force had pushed it at both ends. The metal screeched as it was distorted and torn. Craig flew forwards. He grabbed the rail and managed to hang on for a second. He caught a glimpse of Major Bright on his feet again. *Impossible!* Bright was stretching his arm up towards the catwalk. He closed his fist and the entire walkway collapsed. Then Craig was falling through the air, the machine gun lost, completely unable to save himself. All he could do was roll into a landing position to minimize the damage.

He hit the concrete floor of the hangar hard. Pain exploded along his right leg. It felt as if someone had taken a sledgehammer to his spine. Craig rolled onto his stomach and looked down the side of his body to see a white flash of broken bone – it had ripped through the skin of his upper leg and the material of his combat fatigues. Nausea cut through the pain, but he fought to stay conscious as he sensed someone approaching. *Bright.* With the last of his strength, the commander grabbed the pistol from his belt and rolled onto his back...

He emptied the clip into the major, who barely flinched as the bullets hit his chest and shoulders. It was as if the rounds simply glanced off him. With a groan, Craig lowered the empty weapon and let it fall from his grasp. Through his swimming vision he saw Bright standing over him.

"Nice to see you again, commander."

The major's massive hands closed around his throat, lifting him to his feet. Craig screamed with pain from his broken leg. Then he passed out...

## 19

The mercs marched Hack back across the compound towards his cell. He'd protested about wanting to be with May, but the bigger of the two silenced him with a slap across his face. Now Hack walked meekly between the two men, head down as if he was beaten. Looking around, he saw the cells up ahead and thought about the stimulant injector in his pocket. He could wait until they were inside the building before striking, but he didn't want to give either of the mercs the chance to lock him inside. The spotlight swept the ground ahead of them and then moved on. There didn't seem to be any other soldiers in the immediate vicinity.

It was now or never.

Hack reached into his pocket and removed the injector. Without hesitation, he jammed the tube into the hip of the nearest solider and pressed the release trigger twice. There was a double hiss and the merc staggered forwards, making a gagging sound as the drug entered his bloodstream. *That's for May,* Hack thought. He spun round and jabbed the injector at the other soldier, giving him a dose of stimulant as well. The merc's eyes bulged out of their sockets and he stumbled, disorientated.

It was all Hack needed. He made a break for it, running fast for the nearest cover – a stack of metal crates. The boots of the first merc thundered after him, however, and he sensed the man right at his back. Hack turned and raised the injector to give him another shot, but the merc hit him full force, throwing him back against the crates. Winded, Hack slid down to the ground. The injector fell from his hand and was lost in the dark. The merc swayed before him, but shook his head, fighting to focus as the stimulant coursed through his body. He pulled his pistol and aimed it at the boy's head.

"Please," Hack said.

The merc looked at him through bleary eyes. His

finger tightened on the trigger…

Then he smashed into the crates beside Hack, as if he'd been pushed by some massive, invisible force. The merc fell back, laid out by the impact. A second later, the other merc smashed into the crates and fell beside his comrade. Still coming to terms with the fact he hadn't been shot, Hack pulled himself to his feet. A blonde-haired girl walked out of the shadows. He tensed, but she smiled to show everything was okay.

"Thought you could use some help," she said.

Hack looked down at the unconscious mercs. "Uh, thanks. How did you…?"

Robert materialized beside him, holding the hand of a Chinese boy.

"How do you think?" the girl said.

Hack grinned at Robert. "Am I glad to see you!"

"Told you I'd come and get you," said Robert. He quickly introduced his companions as Louise and Wei and turned his attention to the unconscious soldiers. "Let's hide these two before they're noticed."

Hack and Robert grabbed the nearest one by the arms and dragged him between the crates with some effort. Louise picked up the other like he weighed no more than a feather and tossed him down next to the first. It took Hack a second to understand that she hadn't really lifted him physically, but used telekinetic power to move the man's bulk. It was an impressive display.

"Right," Robert said as the searchlight swept the surrounding area, "we need to meet up with Sarah and get out of here."

Hack touched the collar locked around his neck. "It's not that simple."

He quickly outlined the situation with Marlon Good and the explosive devices placed around his and May's necks. Robert examined the collar.

"I wonder if I can teleport you right out of it," he suggested. "Transport you, but the leave the collar behind?"

Hack shook his head. "May has an identical collar. The moment this one is removed from my body, the detonation sequence is triggered in hers. The same if we get more than a kilometre apart. We have to rescue her too."

The sound of gunfire from the other side of the camp made them all turn. Hack moved to the edge of the crates and saw soldiers running in the direction of the hangar.

"Something's going on," he said.

"Sarah and Commander Craig getting in trouble," Louise said and Robert nodded.

"Let's get over there."

* * *

"Who is he?" Marlon Good asked, walking from his hiding place in the darkness. Bright had dumped their unconscious attacker in the metal chair May had occupied just a short while before. Good caught sight of the broken femur jutting from the man's right leg and had to look away. He'd always hated the sight of real blood.

"A HIDRA operative," Bright said. He reached inside his shirt and pulled out a misshapen lump of metal, which he tossed away. Good watched it skitter across the floor. It was one of the bullets that had been fired at him.

"Are you wearing a Kevlar vest?"

Bright looked round. There was a little red mark in the middle of his forehead where the sniper round had entered, but that was the only sign he'd been fired upon.

"Nobody can take that kind of punishment and survive, Major," Good said. "Tell me what's really going on here. Just how close are you to the Entity? Something to do with that black mark, is it?"

Bright took a couple of steps towards Good, who tried to hold his ground, but quickly shrunk back.

"You know exactly as much as you need to know,"

Bright said dangerously. For a moment Good thought the man was going to hit him, but then his eyes went blank – like they had many times before in conversation. Almost as if he was going into some kind of trance state. Or communicating with someone or something unseen.

Bright's eyes snapped back into focus. "Go and find Kotler," he said, jerking a thumb at the mercs standing in the entrance to the hangar, alerted by the earlier gunplay. "Tell him to put the base on heightened alert. There might be more assassins."

Good hesitated. "What about him?"

Bright looked at the commander. "Oh, we're old friends. Going to have a little catch up. You can stay and watch if you like."

Good took another glance at the protruding bone and decided there were some things he didn't need to see. He hurried towards the hangar doors.

Alone in the lighted square, Bright went to the medical cabinet beside the chair and removed a bottle of smelling salts. Unscrewing the top, he waved the bottle under Commander Craig's nose. With a splutter and a gasp of pain, Craig stirred. His eyes flickered open and he tried to focus on his surroundings, but he was clearly disorientated. Bright gave him another waft of the smelling salts.

"Wakey wakey."

The commander looked at him through bloodshot eyes. "Bright... Why aren't you dead?"

"I'd have thought you'd have realized by now that I'm invincible."

"But you don't have any serum... How...?"

Bright tapped the side of his nose. "That's my little secret. Tell me: is Colonel Andersen sending her men on suicide missions now?"

Craig looked down at his broken leg and winced. "It was my idea. I volunteered."

"And how many more volunteered?"

"I'm alone."

Bright laughed. "Please don't insult my intelligence." He reached down and tapped the jutting bone with the end of his finger. Craig screamed in pain and thrashed in the chair. "How many more are there?"

"I'm...alone..."

Bright tapped the bone again, more firmly this time. Craig screamed again.

"You're going to die, Commander. The only thing you can decide is how quickly or slowly. Tell me who's with you and how many there are."

Craig gritted his teeth, clutched the side of the chair and lashed out with his good leg. Bright caught his ankle with ease and twisted. Helpless, the commander cried out again as Bright increased the pressure.

"Would you like me to break this one too?"

"That's enough!"

Bright's head jerked round as the familiar voice rang across the hangar. He released the commander's leg and turned as the girl walked out of the darkness on the other side of the square.

"Sarah Williams," he said.

*There, I told you she would come back to us,* the Entity said in his head.

"You knew she was here," Bright replied. "Why didn't you tell me?"

*I didn't want to spoil the surprise. Now, I can be complete.*

"And I can have you out of my head."

Sarah Williams frowned, but then understanding spread across her face. "You're in communication with the Entity. How is that possible?"

Bright placed a hand against his chest. "When you left me for dead in Russia—"

"You *were* dead."

"Not quite, obviously. I woke up in the cold with a shard of the Tunguska meteorite lodged in my chest. The object that Makarov had used to communicate with the alien force is now literally a part of me."

"It saved you. Why?"

Bright grinned. "Why do you think? It needs me to carry on Makarov's good work here on earth. In return I get my life and lots of nice new superpowers without the need for serum injections. It's worked out fairly well up to now, but as you can see, there have been some side effects." He indicated the black mark spreading over his skin. "And that's where you come in."

Commander Craig shifted position in the chair. "Run, Sarah," he said, voice distorted with pain. "Just get out of here."

Major Bright ignored him and advanced on the girl.

"The Entity needs you, Sarah," he said. "It needs to bond with a true telekinoid. I get it out of my head and in return it gives me all the power I want. It won't be so bad. The alien seems to really like you."

She backed away. "You're crazy. All it wants to do is enslave the world, can't you see that?"

"Who cares? As long as I'm not one of the ones getting enslaved."

Bright reached out and grabbed her wrist. Sarah tried to pull away but he was far too strong. The major's eyes bored into hers, but then their usual fury was suddenly replaced with a blankness…

*Sarah, it's been so long.*

Sarah recoiled at the sound of the Entity's voice in her head, but Bright's hand kept its hold around her wrist. *How didn't I sense its presence the moment I set foot on this island?* she thought. *Stupid.*

*Don't be so hard on yourself. I shielded myself from you because I was afraid you wouldn't try to take Bright on if you knew I was here. In return I shielded your presence from him so you wouldn't come to harm. You see? I want to help you, Sarah.*

*Let me go,* she replied with her mind. *I'm not joining you. I'll never join you.*

*Don't fight your destiny. There's so much more for you than HIDRA or your friends can provide. And I can achieve so much more with you than a crude instrument like Bright. I realized that when we communicated under the ice in Russia. Your psychic potential is a thousand times greater than his.*

*You're shielding this conversation from his mind,* Sarah realized. *Does he even know what you've got planned?*

*The major thinks in terms of armies and territories. Battles won and lost. He has no real understanding of the true power that flows through us. He just wants to smash things and bend them to his will.*

From the corner of her eye Sarah saw movement. Commander Craig had shifted in his chair, reaching forward to remove something from one of the pockets of his combat trousers: a pair of grey, metal cylinders with pins set into the top. Grenades. He took one in each hand and met Sarah's eyes. She saw the deadly resolve there despite his terrible injuries.

*Why do you resist me, Sarah?*

She turned her attention back to the Entity, determined to keep it distracted. Bright would never have taken his eyes off Craig for so long, but the alien was in control and it was solely focused on persuading her to join forces with it. The legs of the chair scraped the concrete as the commander prepared himself to move.

*I don't know,* she said. *Perhaps I'm afraid.*

*I will make you ruler of all you survey.*

Sarah looked at the squid-thing sheltering under the hypersphere. *What are you planning? Your meteorites have been destroyed.*

*Now I have found a way to spread my virus without the need for such crude methods. The hypersphere is a method of transporting armies across the vastness of space. All it needs are suitable telekinoids to unlock it...*

Something clicked in Sarah's mind. *That kid, Hack. And the girl. You're going to use them. For what?*

*To create armies like your world has never seen before. And to spread my consciousness via the fall virus.*

*Then you plan to release the virus. Infect more people. Where?*

The Entity laughed. *Please, Sarah, why do you think I am a fool when I have so much respect for you? Surrender to me and you will be privy to all my plans.*

*If you're so powerful, why not just take over my mind right now? Control me like you controlled Bright and Makarov?*

*Because you are so much more than either of them. A being with your potential must surrender themselves to me willingly. Give their consciousness of their own free will...*

*That will never happen,* Sarah said.

*Oh, but it will. You're going to beg to become a part of me. Then you're going to help me kill all your friends.*

*No...*

*I told you before you would betray them...*

A terrible cry – part battle yell, part agonized scream – split the air as Commander Craig launched himself from the chair at Major Bright's back. In each hand he held a grenade. He had removed the pins a split second before he moved. Somehow, by sheer force of will, he managed to throw his arms around the major's shoulders and clung there.

"Sarah, run!" he cried as he dropped the grenades. They hit the concrete between Bright's boots. Face contorted with pain, Craig wrapped his fingers around the major's neck and clung on for dear life.

*No!* the Entity exclaimed. It pushed Sarah away and released the grip on her wrist. As she staggered back, she saw Bright's eyes snap into focus once again. He looked around, momentarily bewildered, then grabbed Craig's arm and swung him over his shoulder. The commander smacked down on the floor. Sarah turned and bolted for the darkness. As she reached the edge of the illuminated square she reached out and snatched a camera from its tripod. She clutched it to her chest as she flew headlong into the black...

The grenades exploded simultaneously, engulfing Commander Craig, Major Bright and the surrounding area. The computers, lamps and cameras were all destroyed in a brilliant flash. Sarah staggered towards the hangar exit, half propelled by the force of the blast at her back. The hangar was thrown into complete darkness with the destruction of the lamps, but she was guided by the outside lights showing through the gap in the hangar doors.

It was only as she made the exit that she stopped and turned. At the centre of the hangar an electrical fire burned, perhaps the remnants of one of the computers. In the flickering flames she saw wreckage from the blast, but sensed no life. For a moment she hesitated, wanting to know for sure that Commander Craig had completed his mission. Then the Entity's voice sounded in her head...

*Sarah.*

Something moved in the firelight.

She turned and ran.

## 20

"Sarah!" Robert cried, running towards her across the middle of the camp as she emerged from the hangar. As they met, the blazing searchlight beam whipped over them. They shielded their eyes against the light, which was shining down from a guard tower. A deafening siren wailed across the camp.

"Where's Commander Craig?" Robert shouted above the klaxon.

Sarah shook her head. "He didn't make it..."

Seeing the tears in her eyes, Robert placed a hand on

her arm as her voice trailed away. Hack, Louise and Wei approached out of the darkness.

"I hate to interrupt," Hack said, "but we've got company."

Sarah looked around and saw what he meant. Soldiers were running towards their position from all directions, drawn by the beam of the searchlight. A guard in a second tower angled his beam on them as well. She took a deep breath. With Craig gone, it was up to her to get them out of the base and back to the jet. She opened the back of the camera she'd grabbed from the hangar, removed the SD card and placed it in her pocket for later.

"We have to take out those searchlights!" she said, tossing the camera away.

"Allow me," Hack said. He took a step towards the nearest guard tower and threw out his hand. The giant bulb in the searchlight exploded, showering glass and electric sparks all around. The guard staggered back and fell over the side. Hack rounded on the second tower and blew up its light also. All around, the soldiers had stopped their advance and were taking aim with weapons. A burst of gunfire split the air and the ground before them tore up.

"They're using real bullets!" Wei exclaimed, moving closer to Louise.

"What did you expect?" Robert said, pulling the dart-gun from his backpack. "Water pistols?"

Sarah looked at the soldiers surrounding them, then spoke to her friends. "Okay. Stick close. Use your powers. And don't hold back."

"Finally!" Wei said, taking a step towards a group of mercs moving round the side of a truck. A line of fire burst from the fingers of his right hand, licking the side of the vehicle. The soldiers scattered as the fuel tank ignited, lifting the truck and depositing it several metres away.

"Nice!" Robert said, teleporting away as a volley of bullets flew in his direction. He rematerialized directly behind his attackers and calmly shot them both with the dart-gun. They were unconscious before they hit the ground.

Hack continued the job of knocking out the searchlights around the perimeter, while Louise created an invisible shield around them. Bullets flying in their direction turned in mid-air and flew back towards their attackers with silent, deadly speed. As the mercs were strafed by their own bullets, they began to fall back. Sarah concentrated on one of the final groups holding their ground, subverting the minds of several of them. Soon the soldiers were fighting among themselves in a melee of flying arms and legs. Robert materialized beside her and grinned.

"These guys are no match for us," he said. "What do you want to do next?"

Sarah thought of what she'd seen in the hangar, how Commander Craig had been tortured and killed, and said, "I want to destroy this camp." She turned her attention to Wei. "Burn it all."

Wei nodded, dark eyes flashing in the flames of the vehicles he'd already ignited.

"Wait!" Hack cried, running over as the last of the mercs retreated. "We have to find May first. She's in one of the buildings."

Hack stopped dead as a new sound filled the air: the *thrumm* of helicopter blades. A squat, black machine appeared over the roof of the second hangar and approached, nose angled down. Gun mounts on either side erupted, chewing up the ground before Louise. She managed to deflect a hail of bullets, but was driven back as the chopper swooped overhead and came round for a second pass.

"It's too powerful!" she said.

"Run for the wall!" Sarah shouted and they broke as the helicopter fired again. Robert staggered as the line of bullets almost ripped across his legs, but Hack grabbed his arm and pulled him on.

"That was too close!" Robert said as they made the edge of the compound.

The helicopter had stopped firing. It hovered above the middle of the camp, adjusting its position, taking aim at them. Sarah looked at the dark windscreen, unable to see the pilots beyond. Then she noticed the rocket launcher on the side…

"Oh, no. Louise!"

There was a *whooosh* and a missile flew. Louise stepped forward just in time, both hands out… The missile exploded in the air, halfway between them and the chopper.

Sarah nodded at Wei, who started burning a hole in the fence. "We have to do something about that helicopter!" she said, turning to the others.

"I'm on it," Hack said, moving in front of Louise. Dead ahead, the helicopter angled for another shot. He reached out with his mind, sensing the sophisticated computer-controlled steering mechanisms inside the machine… The missile targeting systems…

"Make it fast, Hack!" Robert said.

A second missile flew, but it veered wildly off course, over the top of the fence and into the jungle. Seconds later there was a distant explosion. Hack focused his concentration and the helicopter engine began to make a groaning sound. The blades started to tilt and the cockpit rotated clockwise and down in a dangerous fashion. The spinning blades tore into the ground and for a moment, through the open side windows, it was possible to catch a glimpse of the pilots desperately struggling against the joysticks, which weren't doing what they were supposed to.

"Move!" Sarah yelled as the helicopter hit the ground and kept on coming. Blades detached and flew across the compound, followed by lumps of jagged metal and broken glass. Sarah and the others piled through the opening Wei had made in the fence and into the darkness of the jungle. Only Hack held back, remembering the explosive collar around his throat.

"Come on!" Robert exclaimed, pulling him away.

"Wait—"

"No time!"

Behind them the helicopter exploded as it finally came to rest against the shattered fence. Robert, Hack and the others tore into the trees on the other side and instantly became lost in the blackness of the island night.

\*　\*　\*

Marlon Good found Major Bright standing amid the smouldering wreckage of what had once been the studio in the hangar. All that remained from the explosion was the hypersphere, the squid and the major himself.

"Are you okay?" Good asked uncertainly, looking over the tattered, burned remains of Bright's uniform. Strangely, his skin seemed completely unharmed.

Bright looked at him with distant eyes, then cocked his head to one side, listening to gunfire and explosions in the distance. His gaze snapped into focus.

"What's going on?" he said.

"Superhumans," Good replied. "The base has been attacked. Don't worry, I set the Black Hawk on them and they're on the run. Our men are going to chase them down in the jungle."

"You had the men use live rounds?"

Good looked at him incredulously. "Isn't that what all the guns are for?"

"Idiot." Bright turned his attention to Kotler, who was standing off to the side. "Call the men back. And start the evacuation."

Kotler saluted and moved out at the double, leaving a perplexed Good to follow the major as he crossed the hangar towards the containment field holding the squid.

"Those kids just tore up half the camp!" he exclaimed. "They blew up a chopper worth 5.9 million bucks!"

"So buy another," Bright said, eyes locked on the ever-changing shape of the squid as it moved beneath the hypersphere. "The boy is essential to our plans. As is Sarah Williams. And you would have gunned them down."

"Ah…"

Bright reached under the hypersphere, fingertips crackling with electricity, and placed his hands on the squid. Its tentacles, at once solid and yet liquid, metallic and yet organic, wrapped around his arms as he pulled it out. Good watched transfixed. As the squid struggled to envelop Bright, the major's eyes gleamed with a strange energy.

"Bring me the boy, Hack," he commanded the squid, which had stopped struggling against him. "And the girl, Sarah Williams."

With that, he dropped the alien machine-beast on the ground, where it simply lay for a few seconds. Then it began to change shape yet again. The writhing tentacles became thinner, more elongated. They gained definition, taking on a shiny hardness as they formed into segments, eight of them in all. These new legs lifted the black, central body from the ground. On the forward part of the body glowed red orbs, too many to count, set in the surface of the metal. Eyes.

"My god," Marlon Good murmured as he took in the transformation. "It's like a—"

"Spider?" Major Bright finished for him, taking a step towards the machine. He held a hand out to the creature, which was now the size of a large dog. "Hunt them down. The other children are expendable. Kill them."

With that, the robospider darted towards the open doors of the hangar, needle-sharp legs scuttling on the concrete...

## 21

After running through the humid darkness of the jungle for five minutes, Sarah looked back and, seeing no sign of pursuit from the camp, ordered everyone to stop. Breathing heavily and drenched with sweat due to the heat, they collapsed against the trees and on the giant roots spreading across the ground.

"Is everyone okay?" Sarah asked when she had her breath back. "Is anyone injured?"

Nobody spoke up. Either they were fine, or too exhausted from the flight to complain.

"Why aren't they following us?" Robert asked. In the distance they could see the flames of fires still burning and hear the sound of men's voices, but nothing closer. No torch beams flicking through the trees.

"We caused a lot of damage to the camp," Hack said. "Maybe they're too busy putting out fires."

"You should have let Wei burn it all," Louise said and her friend nodded vigorously at her side. "We should sneak back and finish them off. Right?"

Heads turned towards Sarah, but she said, "No, we need to get off this island. Bright is planning an attack on the *Ulysses*. We have to warn HIDRA."

Louise began to protest, "But if we get Bright first—"

"He's too powerful," Sarah interrupted. "He's not just using the serum any more for his strength. He's joined with the Entity and he's stronger than ever before."

"The Entity?" Robert said. "How's that possible? I thought we destroyed it when we flattened Makarov's Spire." He looked at Hack and said for his benefit, "Makarov was a Russian billionaire in league with the Entity. He wanted to take over the world from this giant skyscraper in the middle of nowhere. We blew it up."

"Okay," Hack said.

"But the Entity didn't die in the Spire," Wei corrected and Sarah nodded.

"We only destroyed the meteorite fragment the Entity was using as a transmitter here on earth."

Hack was becoming more and more confused by the conversation. "So, what is this Entity you keep talking about?"

"It's an alien force," Robert explained. "Like a kind of giant brain somewhere out there in the universe. We don't know where."

"The main thing is it's evil," Sarah added. "And incredibly powerful. It uses the fall virus to control beings on different worlds."

"Which explains us," Robert continued. "We get a little bit of the Entity's powers as a side effect of being immune to the virus. And it doesn't like it one bit."

Sarah nodded. "It plans to enslave the world and either kill or imprison anyone immune to its power." She smiled at Hack. "I guess all this must sound pretty far-fetched."

"Not really," Hack replied. "I think I've met this Entity of yours."

The others exchanged surprised looks.

"Back in the hangar," Hack explained. "Major Bright grabbed my and May's hands. That's when I sensed something else… Like a kind of presence coming from a massive distance away. It was the scariest thing ever."

"That sounds like the Entity all right," Wei said.

"What did it want with you?" Sarah asked, remembering the scene in the hangar, the cameras and the squid-like thing.

Hack frowned as he tried to explain. "Major Bright... I mean the Entity...used our powers on the hypersphere. The Entity manipulated May to change it into a different form and my ability to control machines to load it with data. Like programming a computer."

"What kind of programs?" Robert asked.

Hack looked at him. "Programs for creating killing machines. All sorts of killing machines."

For a moment everyone was silent. Once more, Sarah sensed something out there in the jungle dark...

"We should keep moving to the plane," she said.

They all stood, except Hack. He touched a hand to the collar around his neck and shook his head. "I don't think—"

Sarah threw out a hand to silence him and spun round, staring into the darkness behind her. Robert went to her side.

"What is it?"

"Something's out there," she replied, taking a step forward...

"FREEZE!" a man's voice yelled. Two mercs carrying

machine guns appeared. The taller of the two grabbed Sarah's arm before she could react and pressed the gun to the side of her head. "Try anything stupid, and she gets it. I don't think any of you can stop a bullet at this close range. Get 'em up."

The group raised their hands. The tall merc regarded them with a sneer. "Freaks," he hissed. "The sooner you're all wiped out, the better. Maybe we should start right now."

"Hey," the other merc warned, standing off to the side, gun trained on the rest. "We've got orders not to touch them."

His partner snorted. "I don't remember getting that order. Our comm must have been out of range." His cruel eyes met Sarah's. "A friend of mine was in that chopper you brought down."

Sarah sensed the tall merc's finger tighten on the trigger and she knew with absolute certainty that he planned to kill them all. Gun them down right there in the jungle and leave their bodies for someone else to find. She remembered her conversation with Commander Craig in the sparring room: *there are no rules for men like these.* She had to take control, but her fear for herself and the others was like a force paralysing her will to fight…

The other merc said nervously, "Perhaps we should just—"

"Shut it," the tall merc snapped.

*"GAKKKK."*

The tall merc looked round at the strange sound his partner had just made. The other man was still standing, but there was something jutting from the centre of his chest – a jointed, metal pole ending at a point. Blood glistened on the gleaming surface. It appeared to be straight through his heart. The merc's body went limp and his weapon dropped to the ground.

The tall merc released Sarah, pushing her away, and rounded on whatever was attacking them. His partner was flicked to one side and his body flew off the pole, far into the jungle. In the darkness, a dozen red orbs appeared, floating a metre off the ground.

"What is this?" the tall merc roared, letting rip with the machine gun. Bullets ricocheted off something in the shadows. The muzzle-flash of the gun illuminated a body and what appeared to be legs.

Sarah signalled everyone back as the remaining merc's gun clicked empty. He tore out the spent clip and grabbed another from his belt...

The thing in the darkness surged forward, swiftly and silently. One of its legs slashed the air in a smoothly efficient motion, the razor end merely a blur in the moonlight. The tall merc dropped to his knees, dark liquid spraying from his throat in a wide arc. Then he fell forward and hit the ground face first, blood still pumping from his half-severed neck.

Sarah and the others watched in horror as the robospider advanced out of the shadows. It positioned itself over the body of the merc and angled down at the front, red orb eyes scanning as if to make sure the man was dead. Then it rose again and turned its attention to them.

Unable to speak, Sarah used her mind to give the order...

*Run.*

The others didn't need telling twice. They dashed into the jungle, weaving between the trees and jumping treacherously low-hanging vines, their earlier exhaustion forgotten. Sarah sensed they were headed in the right direction for the plane, but it would be only too easy to get split up in their haste to escape.

*Keep together,* she warned them. *Look out for one another...*

There was a whoosh of air as something leaped overhead, jumping nimbly between the branches of the trees. Sarah looked up and caught sight of the spider hanging between two trunks, metallic legs splayed to hold it in place. Before she could react, the machine made a hissing sound and something dark flew from its lower body, hitting her full in the face. A sticky, black goo enveloped her nose and mouth and it was all she could do to stop herself swallowing the disgusting stuff. As she clawed it away, something wrapped around her ankles. She was pulled clean off her feet and high in the air. Struggling wildly, Sarah found herself dangling upside down two metres off the ground. She tried to cry out to the others, but the goo was making it impossible to breathe, let alone call for help.

The robospider descended towards her, hanging from a slender yet incredibly strong strand of black silk. The multitude of eyes turned on Sarah and she noticed pincer teeth for the first time. Her mind raced with images from the Discovery Channel: spiders biting their prey, paralysing them, wrapping them up for later. *I'm like a fly in the web,* she thought, beginning to panic as she struggled to get air into her blocked nose and mouth. *I can't breathe. I'm going to die...*

The spider reached towards her head with a claw sharper than a carving knife.

Sarah's eyes widened...

...and the spider sliced the smallest hole in the

substance hardening on her face. Suddenly she could breathe again. She gulped air into her burning lungs as the spider continued to regard her. *It wants me alive,* she realized. *The Entity isn't going to let me escape.* She looked up at the silk holding her by her ankles.

The jungle lit up as a line of fire whipped through the canopy, slicing through the silk strands. Both Sarah and the robospider crashed to the ground. She landed heavily on her shoulder and rolled to one side. Beside her the spider had landed on its back, legs thrashing wildly. As it managed to right itself, an uprooted tree hurtled out of the night, hitting the spider full force and sweeping it away.

"Sarah!" Robert exclaimed, appearing at her side. He grabbed her arm and they instantly teleported some fifty metres away. Wei approached and held up a hand to Sarah's face.

"Hold very still," he said seriously.

Sarah didn't move a muscle as heat emanated from his palm, melting away the hardened goo on her lower face. In less than ten seconds she was able to pull the rest away and take a relieved breath.

"Thanks," she said.

"What was that thing?" Louise asked.

"One of the machine plans the Entity had us load into

that rock," Hack replied. "It's a hunter. And a killer."

"Well, let's not hang around for it to return," Robert said urgently. But it was already too late. The robospider was scurrying back through the trees, forelegs a blur of motion, cutting through anything in its path. As it came within a few metres it jumped high into the air and arced down towards them. Louise held up her hands...

The spider stopped in mid-air above them, suspended, legs flailing. Louise looked at Wei, who already had the idea. Fire leaped around his hands and he pressed them together. The fire grew to become a blazing orb.

"Now, Louise!" he said.

She thrust her hands down and the spider slammed into the ground hard enough to create a mini-crater. At least one of the legs detached and went flying. The fireball ripped from Wei's hands and hit the spider dead centre. Its body exploded, showering the area with red-hot lumps of the alien metal.

"Nice work!" Robert exclaimed, lowering his arm from his face as the debris stopped flying.

Louise and Wei casually bumped fists. "Just something we've been practising," she said.

"That machine wasn't designed to be beaten easily," Hack said sceptically, casting his eyes around the trees.

"Then let's get out of here," Sarah said.

However, as they started in the direction of the plane once more, a high-pitched beep split the air. Everyone looked in the direction it was coming from: the collar around Hack's neck. He froze in his tracks as the beeping continued.

"What is it?" Robert asked as Hack took several steps back. The beeping stopped.

"The explosive in the collar," Hack replied with a groan. In all the excitement, he'd almost forgotten all about it. "I told you, it's triggered to go off if I get more than a kilometre apart from the one May's wearing."

"There must be a way to take it off," Sarah said, reaching for the collar.

Hack held up a warning hand. "Believe me, it's tamper-proof. I can't go any further."

Robert and Sarah exchanged a look. "Not without May, you can't," she said. "We're just going to have to go back."

Hardly believing what they were saying, Hack shook his head. "No. You have to keep going for the plane…"

Robert silenced him by placing a hand on his shoulder. "I told you I was going to rescue you and I meant—"

Something small and dark leaped from a nearby tree, landing on Robert's shoulder. *A spider.* He gave a cry of pain as its eight spindly legs dug into his flesh. It jabbed at his exposed neck and tiny teeth bit through his skin. Sarah moved fast, grabbing the spider and pulling it away. As she held it up, it was possible to see that the body was crudely made from a shattered chunk of the larger robospider – as if the broken pieces had sprouted legs and taken on a life of their own.

"In the air!" Sarah shouted to Wei. She threw the spider high. He hit it with a fireball and it disintegrated.

"What was that?" Louise said as they crowded round Robert, who was clutching at the part of his neck bitten by the spider.

"I told you that thing wasn't so easy to beat," Hack said. "Smash it up and the pieces keep coming. It's not like a normal machine. Each individual atom is part of the Entity's programming."

"And here come the rest," Wei said, pointing into the jungle.

They were like a dark wave washing over the ground and up the trunks of the trees – hundreds, perhaps thousands of palm-sized spiders – miniature replicas of the original made from its shattered remains. Each had a single eye, glowing redly. They swept forth, seemingly unstoppable. Wei blasted a wave back with a bolt of fire, but still they came, flooding in from all directions.

"There's too many of them!" Louise exclaimed,

looking all around. Sarah put herself between Robert and the approaching spiders.

And then they stopped.

It was as if someone had waved a magic wand over them. The spiders froze: tiny pincers in mid-snap, legs at all angles, blazing orb eyes locked on Sarah and the others. For a moment it was impossible to tell what had happened. Then Sarah looked at Hack, who was standing motionless, eyes closed in concentration.

"I've taken control of them," he said with great effort. "Don't know how much longer I can hold them off…"

Sarah turned her attention to Robert. There were two wicked-looking puncture marks in his neck and his T-shirt was wet with blood.

"Help me," she said, and Louise took Robert's other arm. They pulled him to his feet. Sarah turned her attention to Wei. "Clear a path for us. We don't have time to hang around."

The Chinese kid nodded and started blasting away vines and branches blocking their way back to the plane.

"What about you?" Sarah asked Hack.

"I'm…staying…here," he said, voice slow as if every word was a massive strain to get out. Sweat was pouring off his forehead and down his face, and his body trembled slightly. "They won't hurt me… The Entity needs me… Can't…desert…May…"

Between Sarah and Louise, the semi-conscious Robert mumbled something incoherent. Sarah's mind raced. She hated the idea of leaving Hack and the other girl behind at the mercy of Major Bright. But how else would they get off the island? Rachel Andersen had to be warned about the attack on the *Ulysses*. And Robert needed medical attention fast…

"Get…out…of…here!" Hack exclaimed as his grip on the spiders momentarily slipped. They surged forward half a metre before stopping again.

"We'll find you," Sarah said, making the decision to leave. "We'll find you both."

Wasting no more time, she and Louise pulled the weakly-protesting Robert in the direction Wei had cleared through the jungle.

Alone, Hack opened his eyes a fraction and looked at the motionless spiders all around. Every one of them regarded him with a piercing eye, as if willing him to fail. Taking a deep breath, he strengthened his resolve and just hoped he could hold them off long enough for the others to get away…

## 22

*Defensive systems disengage,* Sarah ordered the stealth jet as they staggered across the runway. Machine guns turned off and the entrance ramp slid down. They took Robert inside and through to a compartment in the back, fitted with an examination table and first-aid equipment. Sarah and Louise eased him up onto the table and he laid back, body wracked with shivers as if he were suffering from a fever.

*Run medical scan,* Sarah told the computer and a green laser swept Robert's body. Screens around the walls lit up with data about her brother.

"What's wrong with him?" Louise asked, looking at the bite mark on his neck. The puncture wounds had stopped bleeding, but they'd turned a nasty shade of black that seemed to be spreading.

"I don't know," Sarah said, feeling totally helpless.

"Sarah!" Wei called from the still-open entrance to the jet. "The spiders are coming!"

"Stay with him," she ordered Louise and tore towards the cockpit.

*Jets, power up!*

As she jumped into the pilot's seat the engines were already roaring. Wei strapped himself in beside her and pointed out the side window. Hundreds of the tiny spiders swarmed from the jungle and across the runway. They'd finally broken free of Hack's hold, Sarah realized and her heart sank. She had only met the boy briefly, but he had shown real bravery in holding off the spiders so they could escape. Her only hope was that the Entity still needed him and would not allow him to come to harm.

*Hang on, everyone,* Sarah told her companions. *Jets, full power. Emergency take-off!*

The engines screamed and the jet boiled down the runway. Sarah pulled back on the stick and the nose immediately began to rise. One of the spiders leaped at the windows and managed to cling on. As the jet lifted into the air, at least a dozen more found purchase on the plane.

"Look out!" Wei exclaimed as the spider on the window began using a diamond-sharp leg to draw a circle in the glass.

Sarah pulled hard left on the joystick, sending the jet into a violent turn over the jungle. Spiders went flying into the sky, but not the one on the window. Sarah banked right. This time the force of the turn and the wind resistance dislodged the remaining machine. With relief, she levelled the jet off. Below, the island jungle had given way to the unforgiving darkness of the ocean.

*Everyone okay back there?* she asked.

*Just about,* Louise replied.

Sarah looked at Wei. "Get the *Ulysses* on the comm."

He tried for a minute to get the carrier's signal, with no luck. "The computer says our communications are being blocked," he told Sarah. "Something on the island must be jamming us."

Sarah turned the jet towards the last known position of the *Ulysses*. "Then we'll just have to get out of its range."

\* \* \*

Hack walked back towards the camp, shattered by the mental effort of holding the robospiders back while his friends escaped. Now the machines surrounded him, urging him back towards his former captors. He stumbled on a tree root and went down on one knee. A spider flew at him, jaws snapping spitefully.

"All right, all right," Hack muttered, getting to his feet and continuing on. He heard the sound of a jet engine in the distance and hoped that it was Robert and the others. A few minutes later the party of spiders that had run off in pursuit emerged from the jungle and rejoined the ones herding him. He grinned. "Looks like they got away, huh?"

Soon enough the gap in the perimeter fence appeared through the trees and Hack walked back into the camp. Fires were still burning here and there and the wreckage of the helicopter and other vehicles littered the area. The soldiers were making no effort to clean anything up, however. They were busy moving crates and the remaining vehicles in the direction of the hangars. It wasn't too hard to work out the place was being evacuated.

The spiders led Hack towards the second hangar, where one of the massive transport planes sat. The ramp at the back was open and a constant stream of soldiers went in and out, loading equipment on board. As he walked under the wing of the plane, heads turned and a few of the mercs actually stopped what they were doing to look at the remarkable sight of the machines surrounding him for metres all around.

"Stop gawping and keep loading!" Major Bright snapped, appearing from the back of the plane, Marlon Good at his side. The men hustled back to their jobs.

"Well, well, well," Marlon Good sneered. "The prodigal son returns. And just as I was hoping to see a demonstration of the security collar."

Major Bright advanced on Hack, who held his ground. The robospiders parted to allow the big man to approach.

"You should have known there was no escape," he said.

Hack looked him in the eyes. "The others got away though."

Major Bright's right hand clenched into a fist. Hack tensed, but the man merely jerked his head towards a soldier who had appeared beside Good. "Put him in the plane with the girl," he ordered. "And make sure he doesn't try anything else stupid."

Hack was actually relieved when the merc grabbed his arm and dragged him away towards the ramp of the plane. Looking over his shoulder, he was amazed to see the robospiders merging together before Bright. Their individual bodies pressed into a mass on the ground and began to reform into the shape of the larger spider once more. *Incredible*. Then the merc pushed him onto the ramp and he saw no more.

"Hack!" May exclaimed as he entered the huge area of the plane. She was sitting on one of the benches that lined the side. "I thought you'd gone!"

He shook his head and took a seat beside her. "No, but the others got away."

"Others?"

He briefly explained to her about Robert and the other kids from HIDRA.

"You should have gone with them," May said. Then she touched the collar at her neck. "I guess this stopped you, huh?"

Hack shook his head seriously. "I wouldn't have left you even without the collar, May."

She smiled at him. Some of the colour had returned to her face and she looked a lot better than the last time he'd seen her. Hack turned his attention to the rest of the plane, which was now loaded with crates, weaponry and, at the far end, one of the helicopters – its blades folded back along the tail. In the centre of the plane was a large, open frame in which the hypersphere hung suspended.

"Wherever we're going," May said, "they're taking that thing with us."

Hack nodded. "It's big enough to create an army of those spider machines for Bright and Good."

The engines of the massive aircraft fired up, sending a vibration through the entire fuselage. Mercs ran on board and took their places along the walls or wherever there was space between the equipment piled inside. Finally, Marlon Good and Major Bright ascended the ramp. At the top, Bright stopped and looked round at the robospider (now fully reformed into its large incarnation) waiting at the bottom, as if for orders.

"Destroy the camp," Bright commanded above the noise of the engines. "Leave nothing."

The spider scuttled around and then disappeared as the ramp rose.

"What are they doing?" May said in Hack's ear as the two men strode past.

"Covering their tracks," Hack replied.

The plane juddered as it moved out of the hangar and taxied towards the runway. A few minutes later the engine noise rose to a howl. Hack and May held on to one another as the G-force of take-off thrust them back along the bench.

"Where do you think we're going?" May asked as the plane levelled off.

"Good said somewhere in Europe," Hack said. "But it could be anywhere." *Europe.* Suddenly his grandfather's little house in Tai-O seemed further away than it ever had before. He wished he'd never developed his power. Never followed Jonesey to the Goodware building. Never met Robert Williams even...

"Look, something's happening," May said, pulling him from his thoughts.

Two technicians were standing by the hypersphere at the back of the cargo bay. One held an object that looked like a cross between a chainsaw and a rifle. It had a rotating cutting blade at the end of a long muzzle that gleamed like hundreds of diamonds. This technician placed the cutting edge against the hypersphere and began to slice away a half-metre long shard. The rock squealed as the blade slid through it. The second technician stepped up with a suction clamp and caught the shard as it came away from the main body.

"This doesn't look good," Hack said.

The technician holding the rock moved to a smaller frame and dropped it into the magnetic field, where it hung suspended. Then he wheeled the cube over to Hack and May. The two kids exchanged a look.

Major Bright appeared from the front of the plane and beckoned for them to get on their feet.

"Time to do your chores," he said coldly.

Fifteen minutes out from the island of Oshino, the communication systems on board the stealth jet abruptly came back online, as if they'd reached the limits of the disruption system, or it had been disconnected.

Sarah nodded to Wei, who immediately began trying to contact the HS *Ulysses* again. As he worked away at the comm, an alert sounded on the control panel. Sarah punched up the holomap, which indicated the course of two planes heading west from the island.

"What are they?" Wei asked.

"Bright's transport planes," Sarah answered. "They're leaving."

"Then we should follow."

Sarah nodded, but then a red, flashing object broke away from one of the planes.

*Alert, alien object detected,* the jet's computer rang in her head.

"Something fell out of the plane!" Wei exclaimed.

"Or was dropped," Sarah said. *Computer, analyse object.*

The holomap zoomed in on the object and data

screens scrolled as it was scanned. Seconds later a new image appeared: it looked like the body of a squid – thin, tube body with multiple tentacles writhing at the back. The computer began its analysis:

*Object of unknown origin. Current length: 10.26 metres and growing exponentially. Current position: 20 metres below sea surface. Heading south-south-east at 400 kilometres per hour.*

"It's on a course for the *Ulysses*," Sarah said quietly.

"What is it?" Wei asked as the image seemed to grow by the second.

"Another one of those machines. A big one. We have to warn HIDRA."

"But they won't stand a chance against it!" Wei said.

Sarah nodded. The dilemma was clear: should they follow Bright's planes or turn to help the *Ulysses*?

*Computer,* she asked, *how long until the object reaches the Ulysses?*

*Estimated intercept time: 97 minutes.*

"If we follow it, we'll lose Bright!" Wei said. "And Hack!"

"I know," Sarah replied. "We'll just have to find them again with the GPS tracer when we've dealt with this problem. Get Rachel on the comm and warn them what's coming."

## 23

David Wisher let out a low groan and opened his eyes very slowly to look around the sickbay of the HS *Ulysses*. He was on a hospital bunk with a saline drip in his arm. His suit had been removed and replaced with a thin hospital gown. His head felt as if someone had hit it repeatedly with a brick.

"What happened?" he asked, voice thick and mouth dry.

A nurse approached with a glass of water, which he took and gulped at eagerly. "You had a nasty turn, sir," the nurse said. "You need to rest—"

Suddenly it all came back to Wisher. The kids stealing the stealth jet. Commander Craig shooting him with a dart-gun. He remembered that he was angry.

Very angry.

"*Nasty turn,* my ass," he said, ripping the drip needle from his arm and swinging his legs off the bed. His knees threatened to give out as he put his feet on the floor. The nurse stepped in to help him back to the bed.

"Don't touch me!" Wisher snapped, pointing a finger in her face. "I'll have you busted down to...whatever the hell is lower than your current position on this boat."

The nurse's eyes narrowed. She stepped aside and waved at the open door to the sickbay. "Be my guest. *Sir.*"

"Thank you."

Spying his clothes lying on a table by the door, Wisher grabbed his jacket and put it on hastily to preserve his dignity (the knee-length smock was completely open at the back). Then he walked into the corridor and paced through the ship in search of Colonel Rachel Andersen.

After getting a lot of odd looks from the personnel of the *Ulysses*, no doubt because of his strange attire, he found her in the war room. Commander Craig was nowhere in sight. He could wait for later.

"Mr. Wisher," Rachel said, showing little surprise at his sudden reappearance or the way he was dressed. "Good to see you back on your feet."

"I'm taking control of this vessel," he said, trying to keep his voice calm. "You're not fit to command."

If Rachel Andersen was flustered, she didn't show it. "That's a serious accusation, Mr. Wisher. On what grounds do you wish to relieve me of my post?"

"You allowed those children to steal a piece of classified military technology worth billions. I also believe you instructed your second-in-command to attack me with a dart-gun."

HIDRA personnel exchanged glances around the room. Lt. Kaminski appeared at Rachel's side.

"Would you like me to escort Mr. Wisher back to the sickbay, sir?" Kaminski asked.

Rachel held Wisher's eyes for a moment, before finally saying, "No. I want you to confine me to quarters. He's assuming command of this ship."

Kaminski and others around the room looked horrified. "On what grounds, sir?" Kaminski asked.

"Executive order number 345," Wisher said triumphantly. "Colonel Andersen knows I have every right to relieve her of her post if I believe she is no longer working in the best interests of HIDRA."

"Bull—" Kaminski began, but Rachel held up a hand to silence him.

"It's okay, Lieutenant," she said. "It was only a matter of time. Personally, I'd like to see how Mr. Wisher gets on commanding this operation. I'm predicting he won't last more than a day." She turned back to Wisher. "You finally got what you wanted, David. I hope you can handle it."

Wisher was about to say something smart like *Take her to the brig* or *Get her out of my sight*, but his moment of glory was interrupted. A kid's voice sounded from the communication speakers.

"This is stealth jet to *Ulysses*. Stealth jet to *Ulysses*. Come in!"

Kaminski moved to the central table and pressed an icon on the glass. "This is *Ulysses*. Identify yourself."

"Uh…this is Wei. I have to let you know there's a huge squid thing headed right for you."

Kaminski looked at Rachel, who went to his side. "Say again, Wei?"

Sarah came on the comm. "Rachel, Bright's using matter from an alien artefact to create war machines. That's why he wanted that kid, Hack. These machines are practically unstoppable and he's sent one to destroy the *Ulysses*."

Before Rachel could respond, Wisher slammed his hands down on the table and said to her, "First things first. I want to speak to Commander Craig. He's got some explaining to do—"

"Commander Craig is dead," Sarah interrupted.

Wisher fell silent. There were gasps around the room. Rachel looked away.

"He died saving me from Major Bright," Sarah said, her voice choking up. "He was…a hero."

"Right," Wisher said finally, sensing the hard looks aimed in his direction from around the room. "Right… Still, that doesn't change the fact you all have some explaining to do about the theft of that jet."

"Haven't you been listening?" Sarah said. "There's a piece of alien technology headed straight for your boat—"

"It's a ship," Wei's voice corrected.

"—and it's getting bigger. You have about ninety minutes before it starts eating you for breakfast."

"Okay, Sarah," Rachel said, "we're going to need a detailed briefing on this threat. Stay on the comm." She turned to the room and announced, "Code red. Full battle stations, all personnel."

The war room became a bustle of activity. In the distance a siren sounded through the ship.

"Wait a minute!" Wisher said, rounding on her. "I give the orders here now!"

Rachel looked at him calmly. "Not really. During a code red situation, a person of military rank cannot be relieved of command by a civilian. HIDRA executive order 214, as I recall."

Wisher's mouth fell open. Kaminski grabbed his arm and said, "Want me to throw him in the brig, Colonel Andersen?"

Rachel considered for a moment. "No. He can stay, as long as he behaves himself." She looked down at Wisher's bony knees below the smock and shook her head. "But for god's sake, find him some trousers."

The squid powered through the waters of the Pacific: sleek, silent, and familiar, yet totally alien. As it moved, it grew. An hour from its target it measured fifty metres from the tip of its black, shell-like head to the end of its longest tentacle. By the time it reached the *Ulysses*, it would be quadruple that size.

A single, reflective eye shone in the middle of its body, but to all intents and purposes this was mere decoration – a hangover from the amalgam of creatures this killing beast had been based upon. Its "sight" came from a sophisticated form of sonar that stretched far enough that it could pinpoint an object in an ocean on the other side of the world.

Every atom, every molecule of its body seethed with one single purpose: to destroy the target assigned by its master, the Entity.

And it would surely destroy that target.

Or destroy itself in the process.


"Hang in there, Robert," Sarah said, running a hand through her brother's blond hair. He was laid out on the diagnostic table in the sickbay at the rear of the stealth jet. A sheet was draped over his body, which was wracked with shivers from time to time, as if he were freezing up. The black mark surrounding the spider bite continued to spread, covering his left shoulder now and continuing out in vein-like patterns under the skin.

Robert mumbled something in his semi-sleep as a screen on the wall flashed a message in the periphery of Sarah's vision. She walked over and looked at the confusing array of data from the medical scans. A compartment slid open in the wall and a clear vial emerged on an arm, along with an injector gun.

"What is it?" Louise asked, hovering beside the table.

"I have no idea," Sarah replied. She slotted the vial into the chamber of the gun. "But it can't do any harm. The medical computer was thoroughly checked out by the HIDRA scientists. They assured me it's more competent than the most experienced doctor."

A diagram flashed on the screen, indicating that the drug should be administered near the bite. Sarah placed the gun against Robert's neck and pulled the trigger. He gasped in pain and his eyes flicked open, staring wildly. Sarah placed a hand on his shoulder, trying to ease him back down as he sat bolt upright.

"Sorry!"

Robert nodded it was okay and lay back. "What happened? Did we get off the island?"

"Yes, we're on the jet. Headed back to the *Ulysses*. Don't you remember?"

He shook his head. "What about Hack?"

Sarah and Louise exchanged a look. "We had to leave him behind," Sarah said. "There was no other way."

"We have to go after him," Robert said.

"We will. But first there's the *Ulysses* to protect. After that, we'll track down Bright."

Robert nodded and tried to get up once more. "You'll need my help."

"Uh-uh," Sarah said, holding him back down. "You need to rest."

Her brother attempted to argue, but his eyelids flickered and he was asleep before his head hit the pillow again. *Restraints,* Sarah ordered the computer and a series of straps appeared from the side of the table and wrapped across the top of the blanket, holding Robert secure.

"Keep an eye on him," she told Louise.

"He's going to be okay, Sarah," Louise said as Sarah headed back to the cockpit. At the door, she looked back at the younger girl and gave a smile, as if she believed it.

Wei was monitoring the progress of the squid on the scanners at the front of the jet. Sarah took her place in the pilot's seat and asked for an update.

"We're less than five minutes from the *Ulysses*," he said. "But so is the squid."

Sarah leaned in towards the holoscanner. It showed an image of the alien machine moving through the water somewhere ahead of them, its body elongated as it swam. Data indicated that it had almost tripled in size in the last thirty minutes.

"You mean we haven't overtaken it yet?" she said.

Wei shook his head. "It's moving too fast. Nothing

should be able to outswim this jet, right?"

"Nothing from this world," Sarah corrected.

She placed her hand on the control stick and disengaged the autopilot. "Warn the *Ulysses* the squid is four minutes from them," she said. "And let them know we're going to be late."

As Wei spoke to Lt. Kaminski, Sarah gave the jet computer another order. The standard HUD flashed off and was replaced by a red-hued holo-display, featuring a targeting system across the windows and air-touch commands such as *Air-to-Air Missile*, *Emergency Evasive* and *Depth Charge*.

*Tactical Systems Online,* the computer rang in her head.

Sarah took a depth breath and re-familiarized herself with the weapon systems loaded on the jet.

It was time to take it to war.

## 24

"Twenty seconds to impact," Lt. Kaminski called out across the war room, eyes fixed on a sonar screen showing the massive bulk of the squid heading directly for the *Ulysses*.

"It's going to tear right through us!" Wisher said on the other side of the command table, voice barely under control.

Rachel shot him a look – they didn't need panic in the command centre, but he was right. They'd already fired every missile they had at the thing and it didn't even slow. The hovercopters were in the air and the *Ulysses* was engaged in an evasive manoeuvre to get out of the way of the approaching monster...machine...whatever it was. But an aircraft carrier doesn't turn fast. There would be no avoiding the collision. In her mind's eye she imagined the thing smashing into the hull and carrying on out the other side as the *Ulysses* went down.

"Ten seconds!" Kaminski said.

Rachel grabbed a mic and spoke to the ship. "All personnel brace for impact. Look to your emergency stations—"

"Five seconds!"

The shape on the sonar screen was practically touching the centre...the point of impact...

"Two seconds!"

Rachel took a breath and grabbed the side of the table.

Kaminski yelled, "Brace! Brace! Brace!"

Every person in the war room clung on to something for dear life. Rachel closed her eyes...

And then opened them again. Nothing had happened. No explosions. No sound of the hull being opened like a tin can. No rushing water. Kaminski stared across the table at her and then down at the sonar screen.

The object had disappeared.

"Where did it go?" Wisher said, wiping away the sweat dripping from his face with the back of his hand.

Kaminski shook his head. "This doesn't make sense." He looked back at Rachel. "Nothing can pull up that fast. Can it?"

"We're not dealing with anything we've seen before, Lieutenant," she replied. "Assume it's moved under the ship."

Wisher gave a spluttering laugh. "Under? The ship?"

There was a groaning sound from deep within the *Ulysses*, as if the metal of the hull was being gradually compressed. The floor rocked and anyone who had relinquished their handhold was thrown to one side. Computer screens flickered around the room – one of them exploded in the corner, sending up a shower of sparks.

"That is not good," Kaminski muttered.

"Bring up the external view," Rachel ordered and the lieutenant changed the table screen to shots of the *Ulysses*'s exterior. Two giant tentacles – black, metallic and segmented – were rising out of the sea on either side of the flight deck and starting to wrap around the body of the ship. As they smashed down on the deck, the entire ship vibrated again. Crew members up top went running as the tentacles drew tighter, crushing the frame of the *Ulysses* as if it were cardboard. Another metal tentacle rose into view, further down the ship, and started to wind around the bow.

"It's squeezing us!" Wisher exclaimed.

Kaminski raised an eyebrow. "It could have torn us apart in one go."

"It looks as if it wants to play with us before the kill," Rachel said, reminding herself that this was Bright's revenge on them all for defeating him twice: once in Australia when he was under the command of Colonel Moss, and a second time in Russia when he tried to betray them after they defeated Makarov. And he would want his revenge to take time. She just hoped against hope that the delay gave Sarah the time she needed to get there.

Two minutes out from the *Ulysses*, Sarah and Wei spotted it in the middle of the ocean: hovercopters circled like gnats around the carrier, seemingly on the attack, but it wasn't the *Ulysses* they were attacking. It was the eight alien tentacles rising from the sea all around, as if the squid had positioned its body directly beneath.

*Enhance,* Sarah ordered and a magnified section of the heads-up display opened, showing a clearer view of the action. One of the tentacles swiped through the air at a hovercopter, swatting it the length of the deck. The flying machine skidded across the landing strip and flew off into the ocean. More hovercopters circled, firing at the writhing tentacles with tracer bullets that merely glanced off the surface of the alien metal.

"They're not even scratching it!" said Louise, who had appeared in the cockpit doorway.

"Let's see if we can do any better," Sarah said. With her mind, she adjusted the tactical HUD, focusing on a tentacle waving near the stern of the ship. A red targeting reticule flashed madly as it locked on.

*Fire,* she ordered.

Two missiles flew from the underbelly of the stealth jet, casting parallel white smoke trails in the sky as they zoomed towards the target. Seconds later, they hit the tentacle simultaneously, creating a massive fireball. The tentacle jerked back from the impact, but then rose again, unharmed.

"They didn't even make a dent," Wei said. "How do we stop it?"

"I don't know," Sarah said, sending the jet in a wide arc around the *Ulysses*. She didn't want to get close enough for one of the tentacles to knock them out of the sky. "But we have to find a way, or everyone on that ship is dead."

Up close, it was clear to see the *Ulysses* was listing dangerously to one side, as if the squid intended to pull it over and drag it to the bottom of the ocean. As they watched, a tentacle sliced across the flight control tower rising from the deck. The top of the tower flew away, casting bodies into the sea with it. Hovercopters rushed in to distract the squid from its attack, but were efficiently knocked out of the sky by the tentacles not engaged in pulling the ship over.

"What do we do?" Louise asked.

"Can't land on the ship," Sarah said, looking at the listing flight deck, which had four of the tentacles wrapped across it. "And our firepower isn't working."

"We need to get closer." They all looked round, surprised to see Robert appear beside Louise. His face was ashen and he seemed to be having problems just staying on his feet, but his eyes were determined. "I can get Louise and Wei down there."

Sarah gave him a stern look. "I thought we had you strapped down."

"You can't hold me that easily, sis," he said with a grin. "You know it's the only way."

"You're too weak," Sarah argued, but her brother shook his head.

"There's hundreds of people down there. We can't

just let them sink with that ship."

Wei rose from his seat and went to stand with the other two. Robert took Louise's and Wei's hands in his. It was decided.

"Okay, okay," Sarah said. "Just be…"

Robert and the other two dematerialized.

"…careful."


The floor of the war room now listed at a thirty-degree angle. Rachel Andersen held onto the side of the table just to stop from falling over. Objects that weren't held down had started to slide across the room.

"We've got multiple hull breaches," Kaminski said, examining a diagram of the ship. More and more areas flashed red by the second, indicating water rushing in from rips in the hull. "Too many to contain, sir. We're going down."

On another of the screens there was an explosion as another hovercopter got hit.

"Our pilots are getting killed up there," Rachel said. "Order them to pull back, Lieutenant."

Wisher gave her an outraged look. "But they're our last line of defence!"

"We have no defence," Rachel said, picking up the

ship-wide comm. "This is Colonel Andersen. I'm ordering a full evacuation. Repeat, all remaining stations, abandon ship immediately. Good luck, everyone." She killed the comm and looked around the war room at the operatives manning the defensive systems there. "Get to the boats. We've done all we can here. Move out!"

As the HIDRA personnel went for the door, Kaminski pointed at something on one of the screens. "Look!"

On the flight deck, three figures had appeared: Robert, Louise and Wei.

"What do those kids think they're doing?" Wisher said.

"What they always do," Rachel replied, "saving our backsides. Let's get out of here while we still have the chance."

As they hurried across the tilting floor, Wisher asked, "Isn't the captain meant to go down with the ship?"

"To hell with that," she replied, pushing him into the corridor.


"Maybe this wasn't such a good idea after all," Robert said, looking at Wei and Louise, who were standing beside him on the listing deck of the *Ulysses*.

Debris from crashed hovercopters lay all around,

and black, acrid smoke hung thick in the air. Here and there the bodies of crew members lay abandoned as the survivors desperately tried to make it to the escape boats. Sirens wailed.

Up close, the alien tentacles were massive and imposing – the impenetrable black surface so shiny it was reflective. The ones wound around the ship itself were as thick as a man was tall. The others, waving high in the air above the deck, towered as high as skyscrapers, ready to smash any resistance.

*How's it looking down there?* Sarah asked from the jet as it swooped low across the starboard side.

*Scary,* Wei replied.

One of the tentacles swiped at the plane, making the barest contact, but it was enough to send the jet flying off course. It swung round and out of danger as Sarah expertly managed to keep it in the air.

*It's scary up here!* Sarah said. *Just try to keep the squid busy while the crew gets off the ship. And don't take any chances.*

*Right,* Robert said as one of the tentacles began to swiftly descend towards them. *Watch out!*

They scattered. The tentacle slammed down before them, jarring the entire deck. As it rose again, Robert heard the sound of people crying out for help from the remains of the flight control tower. It had been cut in half earlier, but there were clearly people trapped inside still.

"You two keep it occupied," he said to Louise and Wei. "I'm going to get those people out."

He disappeared. Louise held up a hand as the tentacle descended again. It took all her mental strength, but she managed to hold the tentacle several metres above the deck. It writhed like a snake trying to escape from an invisible fist, but Louise wasn't about to let it go. The end of the tentacle was flattened and wide to allow greater damage when it struck – it hovered above Louise, ready to squash her like a bug.

"Wei!" she cried. "Heat it up!"

The Chinese kid unleashed a wave of flames along the length of the trapped tentacle, but this had no more effect than the bullets or missiles had. Then he focused all of his power, refining the flames to a single heat beam of incredible strength. He aimed his beam on a point of the tentacle halfway down. The metal began to glow red as it became superheated to an unbelievable temperature.

"That's it!" Louise said. With all her power, she wrenched the tentacle round with her mind. There was a terrific tearing sound and it ripped apart at the point Wei had been heating. With a cry, Louise cast the severed section of tentacle to one side, where it landed in the sea with a crash of water. Wei looked at her with wide eyes.

"We did it!"

Another tentacle smashed into the deck between them and burrowed into the ship. Seconds later it whipped backwards, tearing away a giant section of deck and almost taking the two kids with it.

"I think we just made it mad," Louise said as it came in for another strike.

As they fell back, the tentacle ripped open another great tear in the surface of the *Ulysses*. The stealth jet tore overhead on a pass through the waving tentacles, momentarily distracting the attack. As the arms of the squid tried to catch the jet, Louise focused her attention on two of them, bringing them together and twisting them round. Wei instinctively knew what to do: he fired a burst of heat along the tangled length of the tentacles, fusing the alien metal, reforming it. Cooling in the air, the melted-together tentacles gave a terrible groaning sound and then crashed down onto the deck, immovable.

*Good work!* Sarah's voice rang in their heads as the jet flew over again. *Weld it to the ship!*

Wei used his heat beam to melt the surface of the deck, while Louise reshaped the heated matter with her mind, forming great loops of metal around the tentacle. Now the squid was linked to the sinking *Ulysses*...

The five remaining arms of the squid now turned their attention towards Louise and Wei, but as they towered in the air, explosions erupted around them. The remaining hovercopters were firing upon them. The squid swatted at the tiny attackers, giving Louise time to grab another pair of tentacles and twist them together.

"The HIDRA crew are off the ship," Robert said, materializing beside Louise as Wei melted the tentacles together. "Time to leave."

"But we're winning!" Louise said.

Robert shook his head, having to lean against her for support. His face was ghost-white. "No, the ship is sinking. We can't prevent that."

Louise caught his arm and held him up. The black mark on his neck seemed to have spread even further. The entire ship rocked to one side as it went into the terminal stages of sinking into the ocean. A great plume of water, hundreds of metres high, exploded off the starboard bow and the bulbous body of the squid rose, its huge shining eye reflecting a distorted view of the ruined *Ulysses*.

"We have to get back to the jet," Wei said, helping Louise hold Robert up.

"Wake up!" Louise said, shaking Robert. "We have to get out of here!"

He nodded weakly and grabbed their arms as the deck tilted dangerously to one side...

...and they were inside the stealth jet again. Wei grabbed Robert and moved him to one of the leather sofas lining the main cabin. Louise ran through to the cockpit.

"Is Robert okay?" Sarah asked, not looking round from the controls.

"Wei's looking after him," Louise said, transfixed by the awesome sight outside the cockpit window. The tentacles of the squid were wrapped around and melded to the body of the *Ulysses*, which was now beginning to resemble a twisted lump of metal, kept afloat only because it was held by the monster. The head of the squid lay alongside the ship, giant eye facing upwards. On the other side of the *Ulysses*, a flotilla of yellow escape boats powered away from the wreck as fast as possible.

A howl split the air, audible even through the walls of the jet. The squid ripped one of its damaged tentacles free, and smashed it down into the sea, sending tiny boats flying.

"It's not dead yet!" Louise exclaimed.

"It soon will be," Sarah said, swiping her hand across a section of the HUD. The computer began to analyse the now-exposed head of the squid. The red reticule flashed around its eye.

*Weakness detected.*

*Target all missiles,* Sarah ordered. *Fire everything.*

A stream of missiles flew from the underside of the jet, locked on the head of the squid. Seconds later they hit the eye, shattering the glassy lens. The beast howled once more and went into a death roll, snapping the hull of the *Ulysses* in half as it went down for the last time. A series of explosions wracked the inside of the ship as the failing engines finally gave out. In a matter of seconds, the deep claimed it, along with its alien attacker…

The force of the two giants sinking sent a massive ripple across the surface of the sea, threatening to engulf the speeding escape boats. Colonel Rachel Andersen stood at the back of her boat and looked at the wall of water rising. She turned back to Lt. Kaminski, who was at the wheel.

"Is this as fast as this thing can go?" she demanded.

Kaminski shouted something that was lost over the sound of the two giant engines at the back. The hull of the boat slammed against another wave and the thirty or so crew members on board clung to the side for dear life. David Wisher lay flat on the floor and was starting to turn green.

Behind them, the wave receded. They'd escaped the massive forces generated by the sinking ship. As the sea settled, Rachel felt a pang of sadness as she looked across the water at where the *Ulysses* had been – now lost for ever to the depths.

The stealth jet ripped overhead, disturbing her thoughts. Rachel unclipped the mobile comm from her belt and switched it to the jet's frequency.

"Sarah!"

"Are you okay down there?" the girl asked.

"Yes," Rachel replied, shouting above the noise, "the remaining crew got off. Thanks to you."

The jet circled overhead. "What can we do to help?" Sarah said.

"Kaminski has already put out a distress call. We're heading for the nearest land. We'll be fine."

"Okay," Sarah said. "We're going after Bright."

"Is there any point in telling you to be careful?"

"None. We'll follow the tracker on Hack – it's our only lead. Whatever Bright has planned, this is just the beginning."

"I know," Rachel said. "Good luck."

The jet made a final pass over the emergency boats and the remaining hovercopters, before turning and heading east. Across the water Rachel heard a sound from the other boats: cheering. The surviving crew of the *Ulysses* were on their feet, waving Sarah and the others safely on their way. Rachel tapped Wisher on the shoulder and he got to his knees.

"So, Mr. Wisher," Rachel said. "Do you still want to take my command?"

He held up a hand as the boat hit another wave. "No!"

"Because if you want to take charge right now—"

"Keep your command, Colonel!"

"And the report?"

"Positive. It will be positive."

Rachel smiled with satisfaction. "And my authority isn't going to be challenged again? I get to run things how I see fit?"

Wisher nodded. "Just sort this out, Colonel. You can have anything you want."

Rachel bent down so she was looking into his eyes. "Get me another ship."

*   *   *

Hack dabbed at May's sweat-covered forehead with a tissue from his pocket. Once again, connecting with the Entity to manipulate the meteorite rock had been a traumatic, draining experience for him – but it had almost knocked the girl out. The demand on her power to change the very structure of the rock seemed to be so much greater.

"We need water and food and blankets," Hack said as Major Bright appeared from the front of the plane.

The major looked at him with a hard expression, but then nodded his assent. "Fine. We must look after our prize possessions, mustn't we?"

Hack looked away.

"There's just one thing I need first," Bright added. He removed a knife from his belt and flicked out a gleaming blade. "You've got something that I think we should get rid of."

Hack took a step back. "What are you talking about?"

Bright pointed the knife tip at where Robert had injected the GPS tracker. Before Hack could resist, two mercs stepped in and grabbed him by the shoulders, holding him firm.

"Don't worry," Major Bright said, advancing with the blade, "this isn't going to hurt a bit."

PART TWO

## 25

Nestor sighted on the target...took a breath...and followed through with the pool cue. The white ball shot towards the black over the top corner pocket, but at the last second veered off course and rebounded against the cushion. It rolled back and came to a rest in the centre of the table, perfectly lined up for the black.

"Man, that's too bad," said his brother, Octavio, a tall kid with a head of dark, shoulder-length hair.

"I thought we agreed, no telekinesis," Nestor protested, giving his opponent a hard look. "You moved it off course."

Octavio shrugged and chalked the end of his cue. "All's fair in love and war." He lined up on the shot, but as he struck through, the black ball lifted into the air above the table. The white rolled beneath it into the pocket.

"Hey!" protested Octavio. "Cheat!"

Nestor held up his hands to show it was nothing to do with him. The black ball continued to hover in the air. Then, the outline of a third boy appeared. Like Nestor and Octavio, he was fifteen, but blond and lighter in complexion that the Colombian brothers. As Alex Fisher became visible, he tossed the black ball in the air and caught it again.

"Just thought I'd even things up," he said with a grin.

Octavio threw his cue down on the table. "This game isn't fun any more."

"Because you never play by the rules," Nestor said.

Octavio rolled his eyes and Alex suppressed a smile. Although they were twins, the brothers were about as different as two people could possibly be.

Dunking the black in the corner pocket, Alex said, "Come on. We're wanted in the briefing room."

"At this time of night?" Nestor said.

Alex shrugged. "You know as much as I do."

"Great," Octavio muttered as he and Nestor followed

Alex out of the rec room. "Another lecture on HIDRA safety procedures, no doubt."

"Those procedures are there to make sure we don't get hurt," Nestor replied.

"Do you have any idea how lame you sound? Really?"

As his two companions continued bickering (some days they never stopped), Alex led the way out of their quarters, which was a block on the perimeter of the HIDRA UK centre of operations in the east of England. The centre was a disused RAF base that had been taken over by HIDRA some ten years before. There was an airstrip, hangars, storage facilities and barracks for the hundred personnel stationed there. To the outside world, the operation looked innocuous enough, but the real action happened underground.

Alex led the way from their barracks to an inconspicuous building that looked a lot like a rusty shed. The September night air was cool and the moon full. It would have been a lot easier for all of them to have lived in the main, subterranean part of the base, but the boys (like most of the other women and men from HIDRA stationed there) had requested quarters above ground.

It was nice to see the sky.

As they reached the building, the door swung open to

meet them and a HIDRA guard with a machine gun appeared. Alex held up his hand and they were nodded through. The inside of the shed was pretty much as you'd expect (rusting corrugated iron walls, dirt on the floor) with one exception: in the centre of the room stood a cubicle of gleaming metal with twin, automated machine gun turrets on either side. Alex removed a card from his pocket and swiped it through a reader on the side. As always, when the reader beeped and the light on the side went green, he took a relieved breath – he hated to think what the turrets would do to anyone trying to break in. Doors slid open to reveal the inside of a lift and the boys stepped in.

"Level 6," Alex said as the doors closed. The lift descended at high speed.

The HIDRA UK base had twenty underground levels, partly refurbished from a decommissioned bunker from the cold war days of the 1960s and 70s. However, the technicians had been to work on the site since then, massively expanding and refurbishing the network of rooms and tunnels hidden beneath the earth. The lift hummed to a halt on Sub-Level 6, the main command area of the base, and the doors opened onto a light, ultra-modern foyer. Halogen bulbs in the ceiling simulated daylight and there were even LED "windows" with incredibly realistic views of the East Anglian countryside.

The boys crossed the empty floor towards a reception desk, behind which a bespectacled woman sat, her hair tied back in a prim ponytail. As they approached, she gave them a careful look over before pressing a button on the desk. Glass doors to the right of the reception slid open. Alex had never spoken more than a few words to the receptionist (who never seemed to leave the desk), but one of the soldiers on site had told him that she was one of HIDRA's best sharpshooters and had a semi-automatic pistol strapped to the underside of the desk, right under a picture of her kids. The glass doors that slid shut silently behind them were made of a polymer so strong that a tank would bounce off them.

It was safe to say that HIDRA UK didn't want any uninvited guests.

The briefing room was the third door on the right: a circular chamber with giant screens along one curved wall and a ten-metre-long table in the middle – a black marble slab that reflected the images of anyone sitting around it. Several of the key personnel from the base were already seated, including Dr. Fincher, HIDRA's stick-thin head of science. As usual, he was dressed in a white coat and looked harried, as if he'd been interrupted in the middle of some experiment or other.

"Nice of you gentlemen to finally join us," a female voice said from one of the screens. They looked round at the image of Colonel Rachel Andersen as they took their seats. A caption in the corner of the screen read *Live Link via Satellite*. They were used to regular video briefings with Rachel, but today she looked tired and there were smudges of dirt on her face, as if she'd been in a scuffle. Yet her expression was as determined as ever.

"Sorry, Colonel," Octavio said hurriedly as he took his chair.

Nestor sniggered into his hand. *Sorry, Colonel,* he echoed.

*Yeah, Octavio's really sorry, Rachel,* Alex joined in. *He loves a woman in uniform.*

*I'll be a good boy. Promise.*

*Kiss kiss.*

Octavio looked daggers at them both. *Idiots!*

"Right," Rachel said, casting her eyes over the audience and pressing a button before her. Screens lit up around the wall. "There's been an attack on the HIDRA Pacific Base."

That got everyone's attention. "Who was it?" someone asked on the other side of the table.

"Who do you think?" Octavio said. "Major Bright."

Rachel nodded and brought up shaky footage of the *Ulysses* on the screen. It appeared to have been taken by a camera on a boat speeding away from the ship. Everyone watched in stunned silence as what appeared to be a giant sea monster crushed the ship in its tentacles and then, with a series of explosions, dragged it beneath the waves. The footage paused on an image of a dart-like object flying across the screen away from the wreck.

"The stealth jet," Nestor said, pointing at the screen.

"Sarah," Alex added quietly.

"That's why you're included in this meeting," Rachel explained. "Sarah and the other superhumans on the *Ulysses* were involved in holding off that monster long enough for most of the crew to escape." Her voice softened a little. "I also know you had friends on the ship among the HIDRA personnel. We all did."

"How many were lost?" Dr. Fincher asked.

"We're estimating over forty casualties at the moment," Rachel said. "The majority of the crew made it to the escape boats, however. A Korean military vessel in the area picked us up and that's where I'm speaking to you from. As soon as I can I'll be en route to the UK base."

"What about Sarah and the others?" Nestor asked. "Are they safe?"

"Yes. They were following Bright in the jet, but the GPS tracker went offline. We have intelligence that Bright and his men intend to strike somewhere in Europe. Judging by the monster they sent against the *Ulysses*, they have the capacity to inflict some serious damage. We need to find out where and what they intend to do."

"They're clearly using some kind of highly advanced technology," Dr. Fincher said thoughtfully. "Probably alien in origin."

"The Entity," Alex said and the doctor nodded.

Rachel addressed the HIDRA personnel in the room. "HIDRA Pacific is offline until further notice, so you're the first line of defence. Until we find out what's going on here, everybody is on continuous duty. For those of you who haven't familiarized yourself with the report on the Makarov incident, I suggest you do so at the earliest opportunity. Bright has killed our people. This time he isn't getting away with it. Dismissed."

As people rose around the table, she turned her gaze on the boys. "The stealth jet is rerouting to your base until we find out Bright's location. Sarah and the others should be with you at dawn. Get some rest."

With that, she started talking to Dr. Fincher as the footage of the *Ulysses* attack replayed. Octavio exchanged a look with Nestor and then both brothers turned to Alex.

*What?* he demanded.

*Looks like your girlfriend's coming back,* Octavio said with a wink.

Nestor sighed. *Get ready for World War III.*

*If you two need some time alone, just let us know, okay?*

Alex gave them both a withering look and rose swiftly from his chair. *Grow up. Both of you.*

The twins cracked up as he stormed out of the room.


Sarah sat beside Robert, who was laid out on the table in the medical bay of the stealth jet once more. She'd given him another injection and he'd fallen into a deep sleep, exhausted after the battle against the squid. Reaching out, she placed her palm on his forehead and immediately sensed his fervid, nightmare-wracked unconsciousness: dreams of spiders and all manner of killing machines.

*Easy,* she soothed, forcing the dreams away and replacing them with calming, neutral images. Robert began to breathe more slowly and she removed her hand.

"Sarah." One of the screens flickered on and Dr. Fincher appeared.

"Hi," she said, happy to see a familiar face.

"I've analysed the blood data you sent," Dr. Fincher said. "I'm afraid your brother has a very serious infection. It's some kind of mutant strain of the fall virus, but it seems to attack the host at the genetic level. Altering DNA strands. Hence the changes you can see on his skin."

"How do we stop it?" Sarah demanded.

Fincher shook his head. "We still don't have an effective cure for the fall virus, let alone this mutation. All we can do at the moment is slow the spread of the infection until we can run a proper analysis at the base. I'm sending data through to your medical computer for a series of injections that should slow it down."

"But what if we can't find a cure?" Sarah asked, looking down at Robert.

"Don't worry, Sarah. Robert has a natural resistance to the virus, as you all do. Don't forget that. We're going to do everything in our power to turn this around. I promise."

And HIDRA had promised a cure for the fall virus as well, Sarah thought, but after more than a year it had not come. What chance did Robert stand against this... What had Fincher called it? *Mutant strain?* The black mark on his neck was moving down his arm, making the skin reptilian, scaly. She thought the most horrible thing about it was the way it reminded her of the black mark spreading across Major Bright's face. How many hours did Robert have left?

Keeping these thoughts to herself, she looked round at the doctor as an alert flashed on another screen. "I have to go. See you in a few hours, doctor."

Taking a final concerned look at her brother, she walked through the cabin towards the cockpit where Wei and Louise were waiting. Ahead, a giant refuelling plane swung into view, flying above their position. Sarah took the pilot's seat and turned off the automatic pilot.

"Just in time," Louise said, pointing to a flashing fuel warning light. Any longer and the jet would have fallen out of the sky.

As Sarah made the fine adjustments necessary to the position of the jet, a refuelling nozzle emerged from the back of the larger plane. The nozzle stretched down towards them on the end of a hose over fifty metres long.

"That's it," the pilot of the fuel plane said in Sarah's headset. His accent was a heavy Texan drawl and she imagined someone in a cowboy hat. "Lookin' good."

Sarah tapped the joystick and the stealth jet moved perfectly into line with the nozzle. The coupling on the front of the stealth jet hit the nozzle and they locked closed with a *clunk*. Sarah reactivated the autopilot to hold them in position.

"Contact!" the other pilot said. "Beginning the refuel. Shouldn't take more than five minutes."

"Thanks."

"Just doing our job," the pilot said conversationally. "You sound kinda young to be flying that thing. Where you taking it?"

Sarah thought for a moment before saying, "We're going home."

## 26

The C-17s touched down at an airstrip eighty kilometres south of London just after dawn. The airstrip had been bought by Goodware Inc. two months before, ostensibly with the purpose of shipping PC games into Europe. However, the real intent behind its purchase was to act as the staging point for Major Bright's entry into the UK.

Mercs hurriedly offloaded the two UH-60M Black Hawk helicopters and started prepping them for departure. Less than twenty minutes after landing, Hack and May were escorted down the ramp to one of them. As the rotor blades whirred into life, May looked around their new surroundings: the mist hanging in the air and the early morning sun shining through.

"I always wanted to go to England," she said. "But not like this."

Hack nodded. After the heat of their jungle prison, the cool atmosphere was a shock to the system. Kotler, the merc leader, pulled open the back of the Black Hawk and ordered them to get in. As they took seats, a merc sat down opposite, gun cradled in his lap. Hack spied a pair of padded jackets on a rack in the ceiling and, without bothering to ask permission, grabbed one for May.

"Thanks," she said as he draped it over her shoulders.

"Keep your eyes open," Hack whispered, bending close to pull it around her. "We need to find a way to escape."

May nodded as the merc pushed Hack's shoulder. "Sit the hell down."

As the helicopter engine noise rose, Major Bright and Marlon Good jumped inside. Bright banged his fist on the back wall of the cockpit and the machine rose into the air. Hack looked out of the still-open back door at the flat English countryside below and then at the machine guns and rockets strapped to the side of the Black Hawk.

"Don't worry," Marlon Good said, reading his mind. "We've got flight clearance all the way into central London." He tapped a finger against the side of his nose and said in a fake English accent, "Friends in the Ministry of Defence, don't you know."

As they circled over the airstrip, Hack saw mercs loading equipment onto trucks, ready to ship out by road. He looked round at Good. "So, we're headed to London then? Where?"

Good opened his mouth to reply, but Bright cut him dead. "The less you know for now, the better."

Hack shrugged and looked at May, who shook her head – indicating that he should stay quiet. Bright's voice had a dangerous edge to it. The long flight had clearly done nothing for his temper.

After that, Hack contented himself with staring at the unfamiliar English landscape passing by outside. The fields and motorways soon gave way to an endless suburban sprawl. Despite their situation, he was fascinated by the landscape – row after row of two-storey buildings joined together, punctuated only occasionally by the tower blocks he was used to from Hong Kong. The streets were thin lines jammed with traffic.

"It's so different to where I'm from," Hack said, to no one in particular. "But similar too. So many people."

"Living like ants," Bright replied with no effort to disguise his contempt. "Eating and sleeping and working in an endless cycle. Pointless existence repeated day after day with no thought. No change."

Good laughed. "Well, not for much longer."

"Yes," Bright replied with a nod. "By the end of today we'll sweep it all away. Then the drones will serve us."

"How can you think about them like that?" May asked. "They're human beings."

Bright turned his piercing gaze on her. "Are they?"

May looked away. *They're both mad,* she sent to Hack. *We have to do more than just escape. We have to find some way to stop them.*

*Yes,* Hack replied. *But that's not going to be easy with these collars. One wrong move and Good will trigger these bombs around our necks. I know it.*

She glanced at him. *Maybe there's more at stake than just our escape. They're talking about enslaving an entire city. Then the rest of the world. We have to stop them even if it costs us our lives.*

Hack studied her face and saw the determination there. *I know,* he said. *How are you feeling?*

*Okay. Have you noticed? They haven't given me a shot since we left the island.*

Hack realized she was right. In the chaos of the evacuation of the island base, the mercs responsible for administering the drugs that held May's power in check seemed to have forgotten their job. Or perhaps they assumed the explosive collars would be enough to hold them in check. *Can you—*

*Not yet,* May replied, face betraying no emotion. *But I can feel the drugs wearing off. I just need a little longer until I'll be able to use my power freely again.*

*Good. Just don't take any unnecessary risks until you're at full strength. We aren't going to be able to do anything if we get recaptured as soon as we escape.*

May eyed the gun in the merc's lap. *Or killed.*

Hack nodded and rubbed the bandage on his arm. The crude stitches one of the mercs had sewn into his skin after Bright dug out the GPS tracker were really starting to hurt – and itch. He hoped that didn't mean they were infected. Seeing him fussing, May reached out and placed her hand over the bandage. There was a brief feeling of warmth, followed by a complete cessation of pain. Hack looked at her in surprise.

*What did you just do?*

*Healed your arm,* she replied. *But leave the bandage*

*on – we don't need them to know about that.*

Hack smiled. *Thanks.* The more he saw of May's power, the more amazed he was by it. He wondered what she would achieve with it in the future – if they survived the day, that was.

The helicopter powered on towards the very centre of the city, towards the taller buildings of the business district. Hack couldn't help craning his neck round the side of the helicopter to make out the famous landmarks below: Big Ben, the London Eye, Buckingham Palace.

"We're almost here," Marlon Good announced, clearly excited and showing off in front of Bright. "You're going to love the new base."

The major sniffed. "By evening we'll own London. All this place has to be is secure and low profile."

The helicopter passed over the Thames and turned to the west. Hack looked down at the great, dirty river cutting through the centre of the capital and then ahead as the helicopter began to descend. Marlon Good pointed to a structure on the south bank.

"There it is!"

The building was several storeys tall, rectangular and rather nondescript. However, it was the four white cylindrical towers stretching up from each corner that caught the eye. They gave the building the appearance of a giant, upside-down plug, dwarfing everything around it. From some piece of half-forgotten trivia, Hack recognized it as Battersea Power Station. He craned his head round to see better as the helicopter did a circle.

"Low profile," Major Bright said. "Right."

Marlon Good shrugged. "I got a good deal! They were going to turn it into flats!"

Bright shouted through to the pilot. "Take us down."

As the Black Hawk flew between the chimneys it was possible to see that the roof of the main building was open, revealing a single, giant room within. The space was large enough for them to fly inside. As the chopper descended into the belly of the building, the walls and towers rose high above.

Good grinned and then looked at Bright, who sat impassive. "Come on, Major! Don't tell me you're not impressed!"

Major Bright said nothing and, as the helicopter touched down on concrete, jumped from the vehicle and strode away towards a group of waiting mercs.

Good wrinkled his nose. "No pleasing some people."

Hack and May exited the chopper after Good, closely followed by their guard. May had the same dumbfounded expression on her face as Hack as she looked over the interior of the disued power station. The area where the chopper had touched down functioned as a landing pad and there was enough space for several more such vehicles. At each end of the building stood closed double doors – at least twenty metres high. Beams of light from windows set high into the walls fell across the centre, giving the place the look of a cathedral or the palace of some king. To the left and right were raised platforms linked by metal stairways. Technicians worked at computers and equipment here, while more armed soldiers patrolled.

*Great, more mercenaries,* May thought as she went to stand beside Hack. *So much for making an easy getaway.*

Hack nodded. *This place is a fortress.*

He pointed high up to the edge of the open roof, where it was possible to see sniper positions and even mounted machine guns.

"How did you manage to set up all this stuff in the middle of the city?" Hack asked Good.

The American grinned. "Money. And very influential friends. Come on. Let me show you around."

Hack looked at May as they followed him to a raised platform. *He wants to show off his toys. Let's see what we can learn.*

"Battersea Power Station," Good said, waving a hand

through the air as he strode ahead. "Initial construction completed in 1933. Almost burned down in 1964. At its peak it consumed a million tonnes of coal a year for electricity generation. Closed in 1975. Since then there have been suggestions for redevelopment as a theme park, shopping mall, apartments and museum, but without success. Now it belongs to me."

They stopped on a platform a few levels up and Good placed his hands on the railing, surveying the scene of mercs and technicians working all around. Hack looked towards the roof at the sound of another helicopter. The vehicle swung into view a second later, on a descent path into the building. Strung from the bottom of this Black Hawk was a net. It contained the hypersphere.

The helicopter hovered in place so the sphere was just a couple of metres above the ground. Technicians moved in with a cage on wheels. The sphere slotted into a cage like an egg into an eggcup, then the net was released. On the ground, Major Bright and a group of his soldiers watched the technicians wheel the cage to an elevated area packed with machinery in the very centre of the building.

"Do you really think Bright is going to let you live after you help him take over the city?" Hack asked, turning back to Good.

The American laughed. "The major needs me and my technology, as you might have seen."

May and Hack exchanged a glance. "For now," she said, going with Hack's lead. Anything they could do to drive a wedge between the two men would be to their advantage. "But what about after he owns London? He won't need you any more. It will be just him and the alien he's carrying around inside."

Good frowned at her, but then forced his expression into a smile. He waggled a finger at them both, as if he was telling off two naughty children. "Nice try, but Major Bright and the Entity need me far into the future. After London, there's Europe to be subjugated. Then the rest of the world. If I were both of you, I'd be more worried about my own necks…if you'll pardon the pun."

*He really believes he's too important for Bright to betray him,* Hack sent to May, who nodded slightly.

*He's too much of an egomaniac to see how he's being used.*

Before they could say anything else, Good turned and started up the next set of steps to a platform above. The merc gestured for both of them to follow.

"Welcome to the command centre," Good said as they stepped onto the upper level, a wide platform lined with workstations and banks of monitors along one side.

At each workstation a technician sat – twenty of them in all, each scanning CCTV footage of different parts of the city.

"We've hacked into the city's security network," Good said. "From here we can observe anything that happens within a fifty-kilometre radius."

Hack scanned the images on the screens: roads, shopping malls, underground stations, even the insides of some buildings. For the moment the technicians seemed to be merely snooping in on the security feeds for the city, but the controls before them suggested that when the time came they would be able to take over the entire system.

*Why is Good telling us all this?* May asked at Hack's side.

*Because he needs someone to show off to,* he replied. *And because he thinks there's nothing we can do to stop him.*

*I'd like to prove him wrong about that. Big time.*

Hack stepped closer to the nearest technician and looked over his shoulder at multiple views of rush-hour traffic crawling into the city.

"How's the convoy progressing?" Good asked the operator.

"We just picked them up heading past Croydon,"

the man replied, not taking his eyes from the screens. "They'll be here within half an hour."

"Excellent," Good said. "Let's speed them along, shall we? Give them green lights all the way. And turn every other intersection in the city red."

The operator grinned and started tapping away on the touch screen in front of him. Schematics of the traffic control system opened up and he began manipulating them at lightning speed. "All operators, prepare to go live in 5...4...3...2...1..."

He pressed the screen and it turned from red to green, indicating full control over the systems he'd previously been merely observing. Along the line, technicians began working away at their controls. The operator called up a screen labelled *Global Traffic Control Override*. He pressed a square flashing *Emergency Lockout*. On the screens, the traffic slammed to a complete halt as lights went red and stayed like that all over the city.

"How are you doing this?" May asked, shaking her head at the scene of chaos unfolding on the screens. Within a few seconds the city had been brought to a complete standstill.

Good replied, "A few years ago, the British government installed an override system that could take control of all security, traffic and communications within the capital in case of a terrorist attack. We've just taken control of that override. Right now, there's security guys spread all over the city wondering why their CCTV screens have gone dead. If they only knew." He placed a hand on the operator's shoulder and leaned over to look at the screen. "How are we doing?"

The operator grinned. "We own the city, Mr. Good. Traffic, police CCTV, even the Tube's automated systems."

"Listen," said May, nudging Hack's arm. He turned his head and strained to hear what she did. In the distance there came the faint sound of horns blaring as the giant traffic jam locked the city down.

*It's starting,* he thought.

With the touch of a few buttons, the takeover of London had begun.

## 27

Sarah watched with concern as the medics from the HIDRA UK base laid her unconscious brother on a stretcher trolley and wheeled him off the stealth jet to the waiting ambulance. She followed them down the ramp. Dr. Fincher placed a hand on her shoulder as the vehicle tore away across the landing strip towards the buildings in the distance.

"Robert will get the best care," Fincher reassured. "Now you're here, we can do a proper analysis of whatever's attacking him."

She nodded, but didn't feel much better. Although the last injection had slowed the spread, the black mark from the spider bite had infected Robert's skin all the way down his left arm by the time they landed the stealth jet, just after 9 a.m. UK time.

"Come on," Fincher said, leading her round the back of the jet to a jeep. "Let's get you all some food and clean clothes."

At the vehicle, Wei and Louise were already in conversation with two familiar faces: Nestor and Octavio. True to form, Louise and Octavio were already sniping over who had the greater telekinetic ability.

"Well, I did levitate a tank last month," Octavio was saying. "For ten minutes—"

Louise rolled her eyes at Wei. "Lame. Back at that island I used a tank like a fly swatter."

Nestor gave Sarah a quick hug and said, "Just like old times, huh?"

"Yeah," she said, looking around for the other member of their group.

"Uh, Alex had something to do," Nestor said.

"Right. So he's still mad at me then?"

"Are you still mad at him?"

Sarah shrugged. The last time they'd spoken there had been the usual argument about whether they should actively go looking for Major Bright themselves, or just leave it to HIDRA. Alex had been of the firm opinion that there was no point in waiting for the major to find them – Sarah had disagreed, at that time. After everything that had happened in the last twenty-four hours, it seemed that Alex had been right – not that she found it easy to admit.

Then there was the added complication of how close they'd become following their adventure in Russia – having faced death together. The time they'd spent on the *Ulysses* had formed an even stronger bond between them, to the point that it became clear that Alex wanted to be more than just friends... At which point she'd had to disappoint him. It wasn't that she didn't like him...it was just she didn't have time for a *boyfriend*. She had Robert to look after...a cure had to be found for her father...and her work with HIDRA tracking down other superhuman kids took up all of her energy...

Sarah realized this was an excuse, of course – she didn't need Lesley the psychologist's help to work that out. It was hard enough having to worry about Robert and her father and her friends in general, without letting her feelings for Alex get any stronger. She just couldn't stand the thought of losing another person she cared deeply about, so she'd pushed him away.

*Well, there's no sense in worrying about that now,* Sarah told herself. After she'd informed Alex there was no way they were going to be girlfriend and boyfriend, or whatever it was he'd got into his head, the arguments about the direction of the team began to get really bad. There was no going back to the closeness they'd shared before, even if she wanted to. Still, if circumstances had been different – if their lives had been normal, if they'd just met at school or a party rather than fighting for their lives – maybe things could have been different…

Seeing Nestor was waiting for an answer, she deflected the question by asking, "Is it always this cold here?"

Nestor grinned. "Most of the time. Come on. We'd better get you some food and somewhere to rest."

As they went to the jeep, one of the ground crew swarming over the jet gave a yell from the back of the plane. He'd pulled out an object that had been embedded in the fuselage: a half-metre long piece of jagged, black metal.

"It's part of the squid!" Wei exclaimed.

"It must have come off when it swiped the jet," Sarah said.

Dr. Fincher clapped his hands together. "Excellent! Get that to my lab immediately!" As the sample of alien metal was carried away, he turned to Sarah and the others. "Now we can analyse what these machines are made of. Find out how they work."

"And how we can fight them," Sarah added.

She found Alex in the recreation room, ferociously batting a ball against a piece of wood set up in the middle of the table-tennis table.

"Louise and Wei were asking after you," Sarah said from the doorway, by way of announcing her presence.

He jumped in surprise. The table-tennis ball went flying across the room.

"Yeah," he said with an embarrassed cough. "I was busy."

"I can see that."

Alex put the bat down on the table. "I heard about Robert. I'm sorry."

"He's not dead, you know," Sarah said.

Alex reddened. "I didn't mean—"

"It's okay. He's in the intensive care ward on Level 3. He'd like to see you."

"Sure. I saw the footage of that thing that sank the *Ulysses*. Looks like you had quite a fight."

"We did," Sarah admitted. "Bright and his accomplices

have plenty more of those machines. Enough to take on any army. We need to find out what Bright's up to and get to him before—"

Alex cut her dead. "I thought you didn't want to get involved any more. *Leave the fighting to the soldiers,* wasn't that what you said?"

Sarah sighed and looked away. "Are you going to make me say I was wrong?"

"It would be a start."

She took a breath, controlling her natural urge to start shouting. She wondered why it was that the people you care most about have the ability to wind you up so easily. "Okay," she said finally. "I was wrong. I thought that we could be part of HIDRA and not be involved in this war. I wanted to keep us safe, but you can't hide from your enemies. They always come looking for you. I've learned that now."

"Is that your apology?"

Sarah raised an eyebrow at him. "That's as much apology as you're going to get."

He cracked a grin and she actually found herself smiling too. The tension between them had broken.

"Fine," Alex said. "The last time we met…uh, sorry for calling you a…"

Sarah raised a hand. "Forget it."

"But—"

"Don't make me mad at you all over again. Come on, we need to meet with Fincher."

They walked side by side out of the rec room and towards the entrance to the lower levels of the base.

"So, now we're a team again," Alex said, "what do you want to do?"

Sarah gave him a quick, determined look. "I want to find a cure for my brother. And I want to stop the Entity and Bright. For good this time." She paused as they walked past the guards and into the lift for the lower levels. "But there's something else I need to do first."

Alex paused before he pressed the button for the level with the briefing room. "What?"

"I want to see Daniel," she said. "My father. They moved him here."

Without a word, Alex pressed the button for the level marked *Sleeper Containment*.

The lift whizzed down and opened onto a corridor that stretched ahead with many doors. Alex crossed to a panel on the wall and inputted Daniel's name. A map came up, directing them to a room three doors on the left, patient number 345.

"This way," he said, leading her down the corridor.

"You know your way around," Sarah said as they

reached the door and he swiped his ID card for access. "You've been down here before."

Alex didn't look round. "My parents are here. They were transported from Australia for observation."

They walked into another corridor that opened out into a larger chamber stacked with sleeper caskets – the sarcophagus-like containers used to keep the victims of the fall virus coma in a perfectly stable condition. The caskets were stacked high along all sides of the room. As Sarah stepped onto a raised platform, like a viewing deck, she cast her eyes over the rows and shook her head.

"I forgot there were so many," she said. "There must be five hundred caskets in this room."

Alex nodded. "And there are over twenty rooms like this." He said Daniel's patient number into a control panel on the deck and a pair of robotic arms emerged from the ceiling, deftly removed a casket from the stack and lowered it so that it was directly before them. Sarah walked to the edge of the platform and looked through the casket's window at the face of the sleeper inside – Daniel, her father. His beard had grown out and he looked strange without his glasses, but otherwise he was just as she remembered. He had only been back in her and Robert's lives for a short time when the fall virus took him from them, but a strong bond had formed. He'd saved their lives.

"We decided to have him moved here a few months ago," Sarah explained to Alex. "I was worried about having him on the *Ulysses* in case something happened to the ship."

"That was a good instinct," Alex said. "You can lift the lid if you want. These new caskets allow that for a short time."

"Okay."

He bent down and pressed a couple of buttons on the side of the casket. The lid gave a hissing noise and then swung up. Sarah reached in and touched Daniel's hand, which was warm.

*I don't know if you can hear me, Daniel,* she thought, *but we're in the fight again. Robert's in trouble too, but this being called the Entity has the secret to the fall virus. I'm going to get it and bring you both back. Do you understand? I haven't given up on you.*

She waited a while, kneeling beside the casket, imagining that at any second she would hear his voice responding in her head. But there was nothing. The expression on his face, which was strangely peaceful, didn't flicker. A warning beeped on the side of the casket.

"We have to close the lid," Alex said softly.

Sarah gave her father's hand a final squeeze and then let it go. As the lid descended, she rose and turned to Alex.

"Okay. Let's go meet the others."

28

The raised area in the centre of the power station was a hive of activity. Mercs with machine guns stood guard at the base, while technicians scurried around the hypersphere, attaching cables and sensors to its surface. They almost looked like doctors prepping a patient for surgery. Hack and May watched this work through the bars of a holding cage near the wall. They'd been placed inside it when Marlon Good finally got bored of boasting about his achievements. The technicians began setting up two tables, one on either side of the hypersphere.

Wires extended from these tables to the sphere itself and off to a set of control panels.

"What do you think they're for?" May asked.

"I don't know," Hack replied, keeping his real thoughts to himself: the tables were roughly the size of a person, had ankle and wrist restraints, and appeared to be linked to the hypersphere. And there were two of them...

One for him.

And one for May.

Hack recalled the mental and physical drain their earlier connection with the Entity and the hypersphere had exerted upon them. How much power did the Entity need to release the army of machines contained within the sphere? Would they be strapped into the tables until every last drop of their life energy was sucked out?

"We have to get out of here," May said, the rising fear in her voice making it clear that she was thinking the same thing. "Now."

"What did you have in mind?" Hack replied, eyeing the mercs patrolling the cage. The men were alert, but their heads were turned towards the activity on the podium.

"I think I have enough energy to do something," May said.

"But even if we get through the bars of this cage, we still have to escape from the power station."

"I'm not planning on going through the bars. Keep an eye on those mercs."

Hack moved so that he was standing in front of May, blocking the guards' view of her. He glanced over his shoulder and watched as she kneeled and touched the index fingers of her right and left hands to the concrete floor just a few centimetres apart. She closed her eyes and concentrated...

A black circle appeared on the floor, midway between her fingertips. The circle grew steadily, until it was about the size of a dinner plate. As Hack watched, it became clear what was happening: the solid matter of the floor was literally dropping away into the hole, as if it had suddenly become liquid. At the edge of the circle as it grew, it was possible to see concrete streaming down like a waterfall. May pulled her fingers further apart and the circle grew until it was a metre across.

"Wow," Hack said as she stood up and opened her eyes slowly.

"That's our way out."

"What's down there?" Hack said. The tunnel stretched down, but was perfectly dark. The bottom was not visible and for all he knew it stretched down for ever.

"I'm not sure," said May, voice uncertain.

"Great."

As much as Hack wanted out of the base, he didn't like the idea of jumping into a black void that led into… who knew where. Any protest was cut short, however, as one of the mercs gave a surprised shout.

"You two! What are you doing?"

Bootsteps approached the cage. *This is our only chance,* Hack thought. *If we don't go now, they'll sedate May again.* He grabbed her hand and pulled her towards the black circle. They jumped into the darkness…

And fell…

Hack had the sensation of the tunnel walls, melted concrete, whizzing past faster and faster as they descended, and realized that landing was going to be a problem. Then, amazingly, they began to slow. Rather than falling through air, it was like falling through treacle – an unseen substance slowing their rate of descent.

"What's happening?" Hack said. His words sounded muffled, as if he was speaking from behind a sheet of glass.

"I've changed the air density to slow our fall," replied May, her voice equally indistinct.

Hack looked up and saw light from the top of the tunnel. Guards appeared and one of them actually jumped in after them. He fell, but at the same unnaturally slow rate.

Then Hack felt solid ground beneath his feet. Above them the tunnel began to fold in on itself, closing up like the aperture of a camera as May stopped exerting her power upon it.

"Wait, May!" said Hack, but it was too late. There was a cry from above and then nothing as the tunnel snapped shut on the falling guard.

"Oh, no," she said quietly, putting her hands over her mouth. "I didn't see him. Hack, I didn't see him..."

"It's okay." He looked left and right and realized they were far from safe. Wherever they had landed was so absolutely dark that he couldn't even see May's eyes right next to him. The ground rumbled and then began to vibrate violently. To their left, a single beam of brilliant light cut through the perfect dark, illuminating curved tunnel walls...rails...

The hum of an electric engine rose... Warm, stale air rushed towards them... *We're in part of the London Underground system,* Hack realized...

"Come on!" he yelled, pulling May to the tunnel wall. They pressed themselves as flat as possible. Seconds later an underground train flew past at high speed, the carriages just centimetres from their bodies. In the lit windows of the train, Hack saw people passing in a blur, blissfully unaware of them down on the tracks.

The train howled down the tunnel and was gone as quickly as it had appeared.

"Are you okay?" Hack asked and had time to see May nod in the receding light from the train. Then the darkness was complete once more.

"What are we going to do?" she asked.

Hack scanned the area with his mind, sensing a series of emergency lights set into the ceiling of the tunnel. He placed his hand against the wall, just over where he knew a connecting wire ran, and concentrated. Lights flickered into life all along the tunnel, dimly at first and then stronger. Now it was easy to see the soot-stained walls and the three metal rails running along the centre of the tunnel.

"Don't touch the centre rail," Hack warned as he stepped away from the wall. "It's electrified."

May's hand slipped into his and he met her eyes. He could tell she was just about as terrified as he was following their narrow escape. He smiled reassuringly. "Well done getting us away from the bad guys. Now let's find a way out of here."

"But which way should we go?" May asked, looking left and right along the tunnel.

"You choose."

"Let's follow the train."

They started off in that direction, single file, careful to give the electrified rail a wide berth. As they walked, the lights ahead of them illuminated while the ones behind dimmed and went out.

"We need to get to a phone and call HIDRA," Hack said as he led the way. "Tell them the location of Bright's base."

"Right," May said, but then stopped moving.

"What is it?"

"Nothing. I thought I heard something."

Something brushed against Hack's leg. There was a squeak and the scurrying of clawed feet. A rat the size of a small dog scurried along the outer rail, jumped the middle one and disappeared into the darkness. May placed her hand over her mouth to stop from crying out. In the distance there was more movement.

"Let's pick up the pace," Hack said, trying to disguise the fear in his voice.

They began to jog along the tracks. After five minutes the tunnel seemed to be stretching on for ever, then a pinprick of light appeared in the distance. The light grew as they ran, becoming the arch of a tunnel exit – a station.

"Listen!" May exclaimed.

In the distance came the sound of rumbling. The rails began to vibrate again. Another wave of warm air pushed against their backs. Rats squealed and scampered for cover. A second train was coming.

"Run!" Hack cried.

They tore down the tunnel, sacrificing caution about the electrified rail for speed. The walls were closer here. If the train reached them before they got to the station, there would be no escape.

"We're almost there!" Hack called back to May, pointing ahead.

"So is it!" she replied, meaning the light of the train coming up behind them. Now the hum of the engine could be heard, rising in tone. The train lights appeared around a bend in the tunnel, brilliant and bearing down on them...

Ahead, the light of the end of the tunnel loomed closer...the tiled surface of a station platform stretching away on the right...

And the train bore down relentlessly...

Hack grabbed the edge of the platform and hauled himself up. Rolling round, he caught May's arm and pulled her beside him as the train tore past, slowing to a stop along the sixty-metre length of the platform. For a moment they lay there, breathing heavily. They looked at one another and laughed with relief as they staggered to their feet, ignoring the shocked stares they were receiving from people along the station.

"Okay," Hack said, checking out the name of the station: *Vauxhall*. "We need to find a phone."

"Over there," May said, pointing to an exit halfway down the platform with a sign indicating an emergency telephone. They walked along the platform, weaving between the commuters piling on and off the train. However, as they reached the exit, May grabbed Hack's arm and pushed him past it.

*Hey!* he protested, but she shook her head.

*Just keep walking. They've found us.*

Hack looked over his shoulder and saw two men step onto the platform behind them. They were wearing bulky leather jackets, but their merc uniforms were visible underneath. May thought fast.

*Let's get this train.*

They jumped through the nearest doors as they slid closed. Seconds later, the carriage pulled smoothly away. Trying not to draw attention to themselves, they moved to the opposite door and held onto the rail.

*How did they find us so fast?* May asked.

*The collars must have tracking devices inside,* Hack said.

*Do you think they got on as well?*

*I don't know,* Hack replied. *But if we don't get these things off our necks, we'll never get away from them.*

They both looked down the train. At the end of the carriage there was a window through to the next. The two mercs were weaving through the crowds of people in the next carriage, making their way towards the adjoining door. Without any discussion, Hack and May moved towards the other end of the carriage. There was a door there also. Hack grabbed the handle and mercifully it turned, opening to the rushing sound of the tunnel flying by. He opened the door of the next carriage and stepped through, closely followed by May. Hack looked round and met the hard, determined eyes of one of their pursuers.

*They've seen us. Run!*

They sprinted through the next carriage, getting plenty of nasty looks and cries of protest as they pushed past people, and made the next door. As May turned the handle, the train was already beginning to slow.

*Wait,* Hack said. *We're coming into a station. Time to get off.*

They moved to the automatic doors and prepared themselves. As the platform whipped past and they felt the pull of the brakes, Hack looked back again. Both of the mercs were in the same carriage as them now, positioned at the doors at the far end. One of them opened his jacket and removed an object: unmistakably a gun.

*Did you see that?*

May nodded. *Uh-huh.*

The train doors slid open…

They ran, using the crowd for cover and not looking back to see if the mercs were following. They made the nearest exit tunnel and jumped onto an incredibly steep escalator leading up to ground level.

*Keep moving!* Hack said and they continued to run. The escalator had to be fifty metres long at least…

At the top, two more mercs appeared, dart-guns in their hands. Thrusting people out of the way, they actually got onto the escalator and started running down. Hack looked round and saw the two mercs from the train running onto the bottom. And they were trapped in the middle.

*Get ready to move,* May said urgently, nodding at the escalator going in the opposite direction. There was about a metre of polished metal between the two moving stairways. *These stairs are going to get slippery,* she added.

Hack felt the metal steps under his feet tremble and lose definition, as if they'd been turned to jelly.

*Jump!* May cried.

They leaped across the divide and pulled themselves onto the down escalator. On the other side, the mercs and a few unlucky commuters tumbled towards the bottom as the metal of the stairs changed from a solid to a gooey, mercury-like liquid.

*Neat trick,* Hack said with a laugh as he watched the mercs slide down and land in a heap at the bottom. He touched a finger to the side of the escalator and changed its direction to aid their way to the top. Seconds later they ran off the escalator onto the upper concourse. Hack led the way towards a set of barriers as three mercs ran from the side, aiming to cut them off.

*Keep going!* May cried, stooping down to run her finger across the tiled floor as she ran. The tiles turned into a sheet of ice. The mercs' feet went out from under them and they skidded along in a heap. Hack held out his hand and all the ticket barriers sprung open before him. They raced through and up the nearest set of steps.

*We need to get to a phone,* May said.

*Not a problem.*

Passing a guy coming down, Hack reached out and snatched a mobile from his hand.

"Hey!" the guy cried out, turning to give chase. May

touched the steps as she flew past. The man fell back as they crumbled under his feet.

"Sorry!" she called down and they ran out into the sunlight at the top of the stairs...

...onto a bustling city street. Predictably, the road was jammed with cars, snarled up by the locked-out traffic lights. Horns blared. People leaned from the windows of their cars and yelled at one another. May looked round in confusion as someone bumped into her roughly.

"Idiot," the girl who'd knocked her snapped without even stopping.

"Let's find somewhere quiet to make this call," Hack said above the noise of the traffic and people all around.

"Good idea," May agreed and they started along the street, keeping to the side as much as possible.

"In there," Hack said, indicating the recessed doorway of a disused shop up ahead. He was already connected with the mobile, searching for a HIDRA UK contact number...

The sound of a helicopter rose, drowning out even the sound of the cars.

*Hack!* May warned.

He looked round and saw one of the Black Hawks appear over the roofs of the shops on the other side of the street. It looked out of place – a war machine hanging over a normal city street. The chopper angled round, twin machine guns aiming down at them…

May pushed him towards the doorway as the guns opened up. Shop windows exploded as bullets ripped through glass and wood. People screamed and ran. Others cowered behind vehicles. Hack and May collapsed into the doorway as the helicopter made a pass, spraying the top of the building with bullets. Lumps of brick and broken tiles rained down on the pavement. Then the shooting stopped.

"They're insane," May said. "They're going to bring the whole country down on themselves!"

Hack held the mobile to his ear. "They don't care any more. If they get us, they can unleash the machines from the hypersphere. And then no one will be able to stop them." Inside the phone he searched the internet for the protected area of the HIDRA portal and patched himself through the firewall.

"Watch out!" cried May, pulling him from the doorway as the helicopter opened fire again. They took cover behind a four-wheel drive as the place where they'd been standing was ripped apart.

The Black Hawk circled over the street and then descended, low enough so that Kotler and three of his men could jump down onto the tops of cars. In their hands they cradled automatic machine guns. With a word from their commander, the mercs opened fire, blasting out car windows and tearing through tyres. Helpless civilians cowered in fear and crawled for safety.

"What are they doing?" May yelled above the noise.

"Making a point," Hack said as the phone line finally connected to the HIDRA base.

"This is a secure line," a woman answered, "how did you get this number?"

"Shut up and listen!" Hack yelled above the gunfire. "I have a message for Sarah and Robert Williams—"

"Who?"

"They're superhumans! Just listen. Major Bright's target is London. His base is Battersea Power Station."

"I don't—"

"Just tell them to get here fast!"

The windows of the four-wheel drive shattered. Hack left the phone connected and threw it under the wheels of a nearby car. May gave him a questioning look.

"They'll be able to triangulate the location from the nearest cell phone towers," he explained.

She grinned. "Smart."

"Give yourselves up!" Kotler shouted from down the street. "Give yourselves up right now and nobody else has to get hurt."

Hack looked round the side of the four-wheel drive. The mercs had fanned out through the stationary cars, eyes scanning for them in every direction. Kotler jumped on the bonnet of a taxi and removed a grenade from his jacket. Ripping out the pin, he held it tight in his gloved fist, cooking it so it would explode shortly after being released. "We've got orders not to kill you," he shouted in the direction of their hiding place. "But if you don't give yourselves up right now, we'll kill everyone else on this street."

He threw the grenade through the back window of a parked car. The explosion lit up the petrol tank, lifting the burning wreck through the window of a nearby chemist. People scattered in all directions. The mercs fired into the air and they hit the ground again.

"I'm waiting!" Kotler screamed.

Hack met May's eyes. "No choice, huh?"

"No choice," she agreed.

Hack rose to his feet, hands in the air. May did the same.

Mercs moved in fast, grabbing their arms and pinning them behind their backs. Cable ties were drawn painfully tight around their wrists.

"We're not going to give you any trouble," Hack said as they were manhandled towards the waiting chopper, but it made no difference. They were thrown down on the floor of the vehicle and told to lie still or get shot. Seconds later, Kotler jumped on board and the Black Hawk lifted. The merc leader stood over them, pure malice in his eyes.

"You don't have to hurt us," May said as the chopper raced over the rooftops, back towards the power station. "We're going to do what you want."

Kotler crouched down beside her and bent his head close. "I don't like you freaks. You've caused me and my men a lot of trouble. And after the major's finished with you, you're going to pay for it."

He looked round at Hack and grinned viciously.

"Both of you are going to pay."

## 29

Every seat at the long table in the HIDRA UK briefing room was taken. There were HIDRA officers, Dr. Fincher and his science team, and Sarah and her friends. Rachel Andersen was on the satellite link-up again, this time from a HIDRA plane en route to the base. Everyone listened intently as the doctor spoke about the sample from the squid he had analysed – its holographic representation projected in the centre of the room.

"The material is a kind of polymer," Fincher said. "Alien origin, of course. But close examination revealed some interesting things happening at the molecular level." He tapped the table and the holo-image zoomed in. Magnified, it looked less like a metal, and more like the blood of an organism: circular microbes swarmed and multiplied within the substance. "We ran an electrical current through the object and things started jumping."

"It's like it's alive," Sarah said.

"Quite so," Fincher agreed. "We're looking at incredibly advanced nanotechnology. Microscopic robots can change the structure at the molecular level, turning it into basically any shape that the programmer dictates."

"You're saying this thing is active?" Rachel said.

"Well, not any more. As soon as we reactivated it, the nanites formed into a very nasty little killing machine. A kind of self-destruct mechanism. Tore apart the lab before we shut it down."

"Then you can control it," one of the military personnel suggested.

Fincher shook his head. "No. We have no way to interface with these machines. The technology is far beyond our present capabilities. It would be like trying to control a modern computer using an abacus, to use an analogy."

"That's why Good needs Hack and May," Sarah said. "To shape and control the material in the hypersphere."

"So it would seem," Fincher agreed. "With the proper means, this material can be formed into any configuration…any machine that the user desires."

"Like robospiders," Louise said.

"Or a giant squid," Wei added.

"And that's just the beginning," Fincher continued. "As we've seen on the video Sarah took from the island, the dimensions of the hypersphere suggest enough material to replicate a vast number of machines. The Entity must have fired the object at the earth with the express intention of releasing these robots."

"A fail-safe," Rachel mused. "In case the meteorite strikes failed."

"Which they did," Alex said.

"Tell us more about the machines, doctor," Rachel demanded. "We need a way to fight them."

"Ah," Fincher said, pulling up a video hologram showing recorded CCTV footage of the lab. "This is what that single fragment managed to do."

Everyone around the table watched the grainy footage of scientists in protective suits working on the fragment. As electrodes were attached, the materials immediately began to reform, sprouting spider-like legs. The scientists backed away as the machine split into two spiders and began tearing the table apart. HIDRA soldiers rushed in, firing upon the machines. The bullets glanced off their hard shells. There was a scream as one of the spiders jumped at a soldier's neck. The other scurried towards the corner of the room. A second later there was a brilliant flash of white and the recording ended.

"What happened?" Rachel demanded.

Fincher replied, "One of them turned itself into a bomb. Blew out the entire wall so the other machine could escape. We cornered it at the perimeter and managed to knock it out…by firing two Javelin missiles at it."

There were murmurs around the table.

"Those machines were the size of my hand," Octavio said.

"And they wrecked a substantial part of the camp," Fincher replied. "They're incredibly resistant to all forms of conventional weaponry. And, as you saw, they can split into multiple parts to avoid capture."

"Then how can we fight them?" Nestor asked.

"With our current weaponry?" Fincher said, looking around the table, his face deadly serious. "We can't."

"Well, we have to find a way, doctor," Rachel said, turning her attention to Sarah and the others. "Think you can help out with that, Sarah?"

Sarah looked around the others and then nodded as a harried-looking HIDRA officer burst into the room.

"Colonel Andersen," the officer said, looking at the screen in which Rachel appeared, "we've received a call from London. Someone claiming to know the location of Major Bright's base."

The Black Hawk helicopter had barely touched down on the floor of the power station when Kotler shoved Hack and May out with the butt of his rifle. Bent low, they stumbled towards the hypersphere with the mercs at their backs. Marlon Good waited at the edge of the platform. As Hack stopped before him, Good said, "You've caused us a lot of trouble." He drew back his hand and slapped Hack hard across the face. "Do you know why I did that?"

Hack looked at him with pure hate in his eyes but said nothing.

"Because," Good continued, "in a very short time there won't be enough of your mind left to understand if I broke every finger on your hand. Enjoy the pain, kid – it's one of the last things you're ever going to feel."

"You're insane," Hack said slowly. "And I'm going to make you pay for what you're doing."

Marlon Good looked at him, his face an emotionless mask for a few seconds. Then he laughed his high-pitched, giggling laugh. "Sure you are."

The mercs grabbed the kids' arms and led them onto the platform. May began to struggle as she was dragged towards the table on the left. Hack looked across at her as he was forced onto the other table and the restraints were strapped around his ankles and wrists.

"Just stay strong, May!" he called. "Hold on!"

She looked at him and nodded. Then a technician passed in front of her, obscuring his view. Hack turned to a technician at the side of his table.

"Why are you doing this?" he said. "Can't you see you're hurting us?"

The technician, a guy with thick glasses and long, straggly hair, couldn't meet Hack's eyes as he attached electrodes to his skull.

"I'm talking to you!" Hack persisted.

"I'm sorry," the technician said quietly as he finished his work. "We've got orders. We've got no choice."

One of the mercs pushed the tech away and Hack closed his eyes. The technicians were clearly too scared to disobey orders.

At the side of the platform, Marlon Good joined Major Bright at the control desks. Here, technicians oversaw monitors showing brain scan activity from the children on the tables. This data was linked into another scan of the hypersphere itself.

Marlon Good waved a hand over the computers. "From here we can control the hypersphere by channelling the combined powers of the two children. The tables are basically modified ECG machines, designed to manipulate brainwaves rather than just monitor them. Highly experimental stuff, of course."

"Very impressive," Bright said thinly. "Will it work?"

"Oh, it'll work."

"Then begin. Their little trip into the city will have alerted the authorities to our presence. It's only a matter of time before HIDRA finds us."

"By that time," Good said, "London will be ours." He signalled the nearest technician. "Link them up."

The tech nodded and pressed a series of keys on the panel. The thermal image of the sphere began to change, turning from blue to yellow to red, almost as if it was heating up. The surface of the hypersphere itself had become completely reflective, like looking into a perfectly calm lake. Then a single ripple passed across the sphere, from top to bottom. As the ripple disappeared towards the southern pole, a drop of mercury-like liquid fell from the hypersphere and hit the platform with a hiss. This drop instantly reformed into one of the metal spiders – eight sharp legs, pincers, and searching red eyes. Another ripple passed down the sphere and a second spider formed next to the first. The brainwave scans of Hack and May began to show increased activity. On the tables, the two children began to cry out, as if in pain.

"It's like it's feeding off them," one of the technicians said, meaning Hack and May.

Good nodded. "Using up their energy to create an army."

Major Bright smiled approvingly. "Your machine actually appears to be working, Good. I am impressed."

Good walked from the control panels and stood before the hypersphere. "It's beautiful," he said softly.

The ripples were coming at the rate of one a second now and speeding up. There were over fifty spiders on the floor of the platform. They moved forward in a kind of formation, like ranks of soldiers.

"By the end of this hour there will be millions of them," Major Bright said, appearing at Good's side. "All loaded with the modified fall virus and ready to infect the world. Ten times faster-acting than the original fall virus: it places the victim in a coma in seconds and allows full integration with the Entity's psychic control within less than an hour. You have done well."

Good beamed at the major, enjoying the compliments. Around the power station, mercs moved into position near the technicians working the computers, as if to make sure they stayed at their posts.

"When the Entity brought me into contact with you," Bright went on, beginning to pace around Good, "and told me using your money and technical knowledge was the only way to win this war, I was sceptical. But you've proved yourself a most useful ally."

Good cast a look at the hypersphere, which was now pouring spiders from its lowest point in a steady stream. On the tables one of the children screamed, but somehow it was impossible to tell whether it was the boy or the girl, the sound was so distorted by pain.

"Thank you," Good said, looking back at the major, who had stopped his circling and now stood right in front of him. A shadow passed over the American's face, as if he was experiencing an uncharacteristic moment of doubt. "I should really check on the readings..."

As Good retreated, Bright gave a sideways glance at Kotler, his second-in-command and said quietly, "Of course, all alliances come to an end at the appropriate time. Usually when a partner has outlived his usefulness. Make sure you keep an eye on Good and his people."

Kotler grinned and stalked away. On the floor of the

power station, the spider army began to surge towards the giant doors at the far end of the building. As the first of the spiders reached them, the doors slid open automatically to allow them out into the city beyond...

The mapped area of the Thames upon which Battersea Power Station stood was projected large in the centre of the briefing room table. Sarah and the others listened in silence as the telephone message played over the speakers.

"That's Hack's voice," Wei confirmed.

Rachel Andersen said, "The phone this message was sent from has been located just two kilometres from where he says the base is located. There are reports coming in of a helicopter attacking civilians in the same vicinity. We should assume this information is accurate and act upon it."

Sarah nodded. Thankfully there was no messing around with suits like Wisher this time. The time for uncertainty was over – it was something they could just no longer afford.

Rachel continued, "Bright and Good need these two children. Why? To control the hypersphere?"

"That's right," Sarah replied. "If we take them, we

take control of the sphere. Hopefully shut it down before they can release any of the machines."

"It's too late!" Dr. Fincher said, pulling up a new holo-window in the centre of the table. "Look what just came through!"

A live aerial view of the Thames appeared. Something was streaming along both sides of the river, sweeping between buildings and engulfing everything in its wake: a black mass, metres across and apparently unstoppable. "This is being streamed live from an observation drone over the city."

"What is that?" one of the HIDRA officers asked, leaning across the image. "Some kind of liquid?"

"No," Sarah said. "It's from the hypersphere. We saw this back on the island."

"Spiders," Louise said. "Thousands of them."

"Millions," Wei corrected.

The image zoomed in to a section of the river near the Tate Modern. People were running frantically as the mass of robospiders, none larger than the size of a man's hand, swept along the promenade towards them. The machines were so densely packed, the wave was almost a metre tall. As it engulfed people, they went down, lost in the swarming sea of machine legs. Here and there it was possible to see men, women and children being bitten by the robospiders before they disappeared.

"Just like they did to Robert!" Louise said and Sarah nodded.

There were gasps of shock around the table as people tried to take in what was happening in London. Thousands of people falling victim to the spiders within seconds.

"How can we stop it?" Nestor said quietly. "There's just so many…"

"We'll stop them," Alex said. "There has to be a way."

Sarah met his eyes and nodded, although she wished she felt more certain. The spiders on the screen constituted an army. And it would take an army to fight them, wouldn't it?

"Those spiders are spreading the fall virus with every bite, by the looks of it," Fincher said as he focused on another stretch of the river. Here the robospiders had passed on, leaving the bodies of unconscious people littered across the pavements. Sarah was reminded of a time when she had seen the survivors of a plane crash laid out in the desert, all victims of the fall virus. She had to look away.

"What's going to happen to them?" Wei asked quietly.

"They're infected with the fall virus now," Alex said. "When they wake up, they'll be the slaves of the Entity.

First the virus puts you into a coma, then it takes control. Just like Makarov was doing in Russia. Remember the servants in the Spire? That's what they're going to become – servants of the Entity."

Sarah nodded. She thought of Robert in the intensive care unit of the base. Would he too succumb to the power of the Entity? Was this new version of the virus powerful enough to turn even superhumans like themselves – who had been immune so far – into slaves?

Rachel said, "Someone tell me there's a military response being organized."

An officer nodded. "I'm getting reports this is spreading to multiple locations around the city. The emergency evacuation plan has been put into effect."

Sarah turned to Alex as the image cut to a different view of the city – spiders swarming down narrow streets, scuttling over everything in their path, leaving behind comatose bodies. "It's going to be chaos," she said.

Alex nodded. "And at this rate the entire capital will be infected within an hour."

"Current status?" Rachel demanded.

"The army is setting up road blocks on all major routes out of London," the officer replied. "The RAF has just scrambled a squadron of Typhoons." He listened to someone speaking in the headset. "They've got orders to fire on the spider swarm."

As they watched the screen, five arrow-like fighter jets zipped into view, flying low along the length of the Thames. They did a pass of the swarm moving along the river and then came round again. Lining up into attack formation, the fighters each fired two missiles at the mass of tiny robots. Yellow-orange explosions ripped through the seething black swarm, but did nothing to halt its progress.

"They're just going to kill anyone caught inside the path of those spiders!" Sarah said.

The fighters came round for a second pass. This time, however, part of the swarm rose into the air to meet them.

"What is that?" Alex asked, but it was impossible to tell on the grainy image what was happening. All they could see was a black cloud.

The first of the fighters hit the cloud and immediately went into a spin. As it rocketed down and smashed into the river, a second fighter was caught. The pilot ejected seconds before his jet exploded in mid-air. The third and fourth jets suffered the same fate. Only the fifth escaped, by conducting an extreme evasive manoeuvre and then retreating across the city to the west.

Then something dark flew towards the camera and the picture went to static.

"The observation drone just got knocked out," an officer at the far end of the table confirmed.

"I've seen enough anyway," Rachel said, looking around the shell-shocked faces of her officers. "We might not be able to fight these things, but we can make sure as many people get help as possible. Prepare your teams to move out immediately: we're going to assist in the evacuation operation." She said to Dr. Fincher, "I need you to keep working on a way to destroy these machines."

Fincher nodded and rose as the HIDRA officers hurried out of the room.

"What about us?" Sarah asked.

Rachel turned to her. "I don't know. What about you?"

Sarah looked around the faces of the other kids and saw they were waiting to follow her lead. "I want to take the stealth jet to Bright's base. If we can get Hack and May, we can shut down the hypersphere."

"The jet will be refuelled and ready in fifteen minutes," Rachel said without argument. "Do you want any HIDRA marines with you?"

Sarah thought of their attack on the island with

Commander Craig and shook her head. "No, this is our fight. We're the only ones who can stand up to Major Bright and the Entity." She turned back to the others, preparing to give them a speech about how they didn't need to come along if they didn't want to – but they were already all on their feet.


Robert Williams lay in the intensive care unit of the HIDRA base. A heart monitor beeped a steady rhythm at his side, while other machines were connected to his body via a tangle of wires and sensors. It was all Sarah could do to stop from crying aloud as she looked at him from the doorway of the room. She flashed back to memories of her mother and her slow, painful death from cancer almost two years before. And then Daniel, lying in the sleeper casket. She didn't know if she could take the loss of another member of her family, especially not Robert. The black mark had spread across the left side of his body – another cancer, of alien origin, attacking her brother's body from within. Killing him...or worse, turning him into something alien – a mindless slave of the Entity.

*That's not going to happen,* Sarah thought, wiping her eyes with the back of her hand.

"Is there anything I can get you?" a nurse asked, placing a hand on her shoulder.

"No," Sarah replied. "I just want a minute with my brother."

"Take as long as you like." The nurse padded back to her desk.

Sarah went to her brother's side and took his hand in hers. She searched his mind, but sensed only confused, dream-like thoughts. There would be no telepathic communication with him, so she spoke aloud...

"It's going to be okay, Robert," she said softly. "We're going after Bright and we're going to stop him. The Entity has the cure for the fall virus somewhere and I'm not coming back until I've got it for you. I promise."

Robert mumbled something in his sleep. Sarah squeezed his hand tighter. "Do you hear me? I'm going to save you, Robert, so hold on a little longer."

From the doorway, Alex gave an embarrassed cough to announce his presence. "Sorry, Sarah," he said. "It's time to go."

They strode across the tarmac towards the waiting stealth jet as the flight crew scurried around the undercarriage of the plane, detaching fuel hoses and closing access panels. Sarah and Alex walked side by side, leading the others. For once Octavio and Louise weren't arguing. Wei and Nestor were silent also – their faces serious as they reached the open access ramp to the jet.

"What's that?" Sarah asked as a technician deposited a suitcase-sized metal box in the back and hurried out again.

Alex gave her a sheepish look. "Uh…uniforms…"

"Uniforms!" Sarah exclaimed. "I thought I said no uniforms—"

"They've been developed by Dr. Fincher," Nestor jumped in, defending his friend. "They're made of a super-lightweight form of Kevlar. Highly resistant to bullet and knife entry."

"Water repellent," Alex added. "And designed to offer maximum insulation against extreme weather conditions."

"And they come in a choice of three colours," Octavio sniggered.

"Whatever," Sarah said, "I'm not wearing any stupid uniform. I told you before."

She looked around the runway as the flight crew backed off. It was just them and the jet again – no heroes' send-off, despite the fact they were about to take on the most dangerous force in the world…and not just theirs.

Unchecked, who knew how many other planets would fall to the Entity? How many other races would be enslaved? With the odds so high, it felt as if there should be more fanfare. But perhaps this was what it was always like for people going to war, Sarah wondered. The celebrations were only for those who came back alive...and victorious. She sensed the eyes of the others on her and turned to them.

"What?" she asked. "Do you expect a speech or something?"

Their silence clearly indicated that they did.

"Look," she said reluctantly, "the Entity has the cure for the fall virus. That means saving Robert and our families. So, we're going to get it and shut Major Bright down in the process. Right?"

Louise grinned and cracked her knuckles. "Right."

The others nodded too.

"Well," Sarah said, "what are we waiting for?"

A couple of minutes later the stealth jet blasted into the morning sky, did a turn over the HIDRA base and then headed south at full speed.

## 30

A pall of smoke hung over London, fuelled by five major fires burning around the capital. Here and there explosions lit up amid the sprawl, whether from spiders attacking or from army resistance, it was impossible to tell.

Sarah scanned the enhanced image on the cockpit HUD and dragged a finger round the collar of the uniform she'd finally been persuaded to put on. She'd originally envisioned something like you'd see on an ice-dancing show, but had to admit that the uniforms were okay.

Fincher had managed to work out their exact sizes for the creation of the dark-blue jumpsuit-like creations. As Alex had said, the material was lightweight, but clearly incredibly strong. The HIDRA logo was inconspicuously placed on the shoulder, but best of all each uniform came with a pair of very sturdy, but equally light boots. *Good for running,* Sarah thought. And, judging by the steel-reinforced toes, fighting. She hated to admit it, but you didn't go to war in a pair of jeans and trainers.

"Uniforms not so bad, huh?" Alex said, slipping into the co-pilot's seat.

She gave him a hard look. He wasn't going to get away with organizing the uniforms behind her back, even if it had turned out to be the right thing to do.

"I look like an idiot!" Octavio yelled through from the cabin.

"You always look like an idiot!" Alex shouted back and Sarah had to laugh.

Alex turned his attention to the HUD and called up an overlay showing significant landmarks around the city. A beacon flashed in the distance, showing the location of Battersea Power Station – Bright's base. Sarah sent the jet on an approach course from the east, following the winding course of the Thames for reference. She had grown up in London, gone to school there, but all that seemed like a long time ago. So much had changed for her since they'd left. And now the city was changed too: smoke and destruction evident everywhere along the river. It pained her to see her old home being torn apart, a place that had lived in her memory being invaded and defiled by the Entity and Major Bright. She gritted her teeth, all the more determined to drive them out.

*Offensive systems online,* Sarah ordered the jet and immediately began to get a stream of data. The jet had been reloaded with heat-seeking missiles and enough machine gun ammo to tear the city in half.

"How's it looking down there?" she asked, seeing Alex scanning satellite data of the city being fed through to the cockpit.

"It looks as if there are five major swarms in operation," he replied. "The spiders have formed a perimeter around inner London, trapping everything inside."

"What about the military response?"

"The land-based forces are concentrating on the evacuation efforts. All local emergency services have been knocked out or aren't responding. Reports out of HIDRA are that a battalion of marines sent in to retake the northern bank of the Thames has lost radio contact."

"Taken by the spiders."

Alex nodded. "And two more fighter squadrons just dropped out of the sky during a flyover. The whole city has been designated a no-fly zone until they know what's happening, even for the RAF."

Sarah glanced at the time on one of the control displays. Shortly before midday. How long had it been since the first attacks in the capital? Less than an hour for the Entity's machines to take control of an entire city. How long would it take for them to subjugate the world? Months? Weeks? And could they really be fought?

As if to answer her question, Dr. Fincher's face appeared on a section of the HUD. Sarah tapped the display to accept audio.

"Sarah, what's your status?" he asked, sounding urgent and to the point as always.

"We're on the approach to the power station."

"Very good," the doctor said. "I'm making progress with a way to shut down these machines. We managed to reactivate a small portion of one of the spiders that escaped the lab and are planning to upload a clonebot to the nanite stream."

"A clonebot?" Alex said.

"It's like a computer virus," Fincher explained, "but one adapted to attack the microscopic machines from the hypersphere. The clonebot orders a nanite to replicate its program, which is to shut itself down, but not before it's passed on the same instruction to its neighbours. This sets off a chain reaction of nanites going terminally inactive. Think of it as mass suicide for microscopic robots."

"Does it work?" Sarah asked.

"In theory. The spiders should literally crumble to pieces without the nanites holding them together. They won't be able to maintain their structure. There's just one problem..."

Sarah sighed. "Which is?"

"The delivery method. Uploading the virus to a single spider could prove very difficult – let alone to millions of them."

Sarah thought of Hack – what she'd seen herself and what Robert had recounted of the kid's abilities. "Don't worry about that, doctor. Just send us the...uh..."

"Clonebot," Alex helped out.

"Send that as soon as you've perfected it. We'll have the delivery method."

As she killed the video feed, a warning light flashed on the control panel. *Unidentified airborne objects,* the jet rang in her head. *Multiple targets inbound.*

"Look!" Alex exclaimed, pointing to one of the spider swarms on the bank of the river. It seemed to split, as it had when they'd watched the Typhoons attack, and rise into the air to meet them. The HUD automatically magnified a section, revealing that the spiders had transformed – sprouting silver, mosquito-like wings. They flew into the path of the stealth jet with alarming speed.

*Everyone hold on back there!* Sarah warned as she sent the jet into an evasive turn. The swarm was too fast and agile, however. Suddenly, it was like being in a car driving through a mass of locusts. Metal bodies smashed against the cockpit windows. Sarah pressed the fire button on the joystick and the forward machine guns blasted through the objects flying into them.

"What are they doing?" Alex said as Sarah sent the jet in another violent turn over the city. "They can't get in. Can they?"

There was a tearing sound from the outside of the jet. Alert signals began to flash all over the HUD.

"Sarah!" Louise yelled from the back. "They're ripping open the walls!"

The jet rocked violently and Sarah struggled to control the stick. "We're losing pressurization!" she said as a holo-image of the jet appeared showing multiple fracture points in the fuselage. One of the machines found purchase on the windows. Sarah and Alex watched helplessly as the mosquito began to drill into the thickened glass with a thin attachment from its jaws. On the other side of the cockpit, two more were doing the same.

"They're going to break through!" Sarah said.

"Now we know what happened to the fighter jets," Alex said as there was a crash from the back of the plane, followed by an explosive blast. *What was that?*

*Wei just took care of some machines that got inside,* Louise replied.

*And now we're on fire,* Nestor added. This was accompanied by the sound of a $CO_2$ extinguisher being triggered.

Sarah and Alex looked at one another. "Great," she said. *Everyone brace for landing. I'm going to ditch before we fall out of the sky.*

"Ditch?" Alex asked. "Where?"

"Where do you think?" she said, sending the jet into a dive towards the Thames.

"Great," Alex muttered as he fastened his safety harness around his body. "This mission is working out real great."

"I thought you craved excitement," Sarah said through gritted teeth as she pulled back on the stick, evening out the dive at the last moment. The machine on the window finished its drilling and drew back a slender leg, driving it forwards. The window shattered. Wind billowed into the cockpit, filling the air with tiny shards of glass and taking the breath from their mouths—

*Whoooosh...*

The jet hit the Thames, skidded off the surface once, and then ploughed into the water nose-first. Following the jarring impact, freezing water poured in through the broken cockpit window.

Sarah wasted no time in unlocking her safety harness and grabbing Alex's arm. "Come on!" she yelled above the noise of the rushing water as she dragged him to the cockpit door. "There's an escape hatch in the cabin."

The others were already on their feet in the back. Water was blasting in through multiple tears in the walls of the jet.

"At least the fire's out," Octavio said, holding onto the side of the jet as the floor listed to one side.

Ignoring him, Sarah moved to the exit door and ripped open a concealed panel on the wall. Beneath the panel was a handle with a warning above it: *Danger – Explosive Bolts, Emergency Exit Only*.

"Wait!" Nestor said as she gripped the handle. "Those machines are out there."

"Would you rather sink with the jet?" Sarah snapped

back, pulling free. She looked around the others, who were standing knee-deep in water now. "When I blow the hatch, hold on and wait for the water to stop flooding in. Then swim for it. Understand? Everyone get back from the door, it's going to fly!"

Octavio winked at Alex. "Getting bossed around. Just like old times."

"Tell me about it," Alex said, gripping the side of a chair as Sarah pulled down hard on the handle.

The explosive bolts triggered, blasting the exit door outwards. For a moment nobody moved as the dank, dirty river poured into the jet. Within seconds it had half-filled the cabin.

*Everyone go!* Sarah's voice rang in their heads as the water raced to the ceiling.

They swam for the opening, straining to see through the cloudy water. The jet itself began to tilt around, but Louise and Wei managed to swim through the door, closely followed by Nestor and Octavio. As Alex swam through, Sarah pushed herself off the wall and followed. Although her lungs were bursting for air, she looked back at the stealth jet – the plane that had saved their lives on more than one occasion. In the water it looked like a shark descending to the bottom to die.

*Goodbye,* she thought, before breaking the surface.

"Sarah!" Alex called, swimming over.

"I'm okay," she said and looked at the others bobbing in the water. Mercifully, the mosquito machines that had brought the jet down seemed to have followed it to the bottom of the river. She looked to the nearest bank and saw they had crashed just short of the Houses of Parliament. The London Eye and the Millennium Pier were just a few metres' swim away.

"We've got company!" Nestor called, pointing to the other side of the river. A giant swarm of spiders surged over the top of Parliament, their sleek, metallic bodies obscuring the aged stonework of the building – almost as if they were burying it. They poured down the side and splashed into the Thames, making the water churn.

"Go!" Sarah cried and they swam for their lives.

# 31

Sarah hauled herself over the side of the Millennium Pier, the metal-clad mooring area for tourist boats stopping at the London Eye. Alex pulled himself out of the river behind her and she turned to help him up, looking over his shoulder at the Thames. The river looked like a carp pool at feeding time – the surface bubbling wildly as thousands of spiders clawed their way across towards them. Here and there it was possible to see the machines, their bodies morphing and transforming to allow them passage through the water. They scrambled over the top of one another, forming a kind of moving bridge.

"How do we stop them?" Alex said, looking round at the others.

"Slowing them down would be a start," Nestor said. He held his hands out and immediately a powerful blast of air emanated out across the Thames. Sarah stepped back as the air became ice-cold – colder than anything she had experienced before, even in the sub-zero temperatures of eastern Russia. The water began to freeze across the surface under the extreme chill of the wind. Within seconds the entire river for a hundred metres in either direction was frozen solid. Here and there the spiders could be seen – trapped in the ice, stuck in mid-transformation.

"Cool," Octavio said at his brother's shoulder. "I didn't know you could do that."

"I don't tell you everything," Nestor replied. "And it won't hold them for long."

Sarah nodded. "We need to get mobile. We're still over three kilometres from the power station, so we'll need vehicles."

They ran along the covered walkway linking the pier to the embankment. Even as they jumped the barrier at the end of the walkway, the sound of ice smashing and the clatter of metal feet against the edge of the pier could be heard. The spiders were coming.

"My god," Alex said, looking down the wide pathway along the river. It was strewn with the comatose bodies of people caught in the swarm. He kneeled beside a woman and touched two fingers to her neck. "She's alive," he confirmed to the others, before pointing out bite marks and a spreading discolouration on her shoulder. "Infected with the fall virus."

"All of them are," Louise said. "How can we help them?"

"By getting to Bright and shutting down the hypersphere," Sarah said firmly. Behind them the spiders were beginning to surge along the walkway. Sarah looked up at the London Eye towering over them and then at the pier. "Wei, light up the walkway. Octavio and Louise, see if you can bring that down."

Louise grinned as she looked at the giant supports at the base of the Eye. "Finally, some destruction. Think you can manage it, Octavio?"

"Just try to keep up, huh?" he said, concentrating on the metal supports as well.

Wei threw out a hand and the roof of the pier became a blazing inferno, engulfing the first wave of spiders coming at them. A shearing sound split the air and all four legs of the London Eye ripped free of the concrete in a massive show of psionic force by Louise and Octavio. The wheel swayed and one of the glass-walled pods detached, crashing into the Thames.

"Push it, Octavio!" Louise yelled and the Eye tilted in the direction of the river. A second later, gravity took hold and the structure collapsed across the pier, driving it down under the water. Amidst the flames and twisting metal, spiders were pushed down too. For good measure, Nestor gave the mess another blast of freezing air, locking the swarm temporarily in place again.

"This is great!" Alex said breathlessly as they fled down the nearest street, putting as much distance between themselves and the river as possible. "I've always wanted to see London... Destroy a few famous landmarks..."

"And I'm just getting started," Louise replied.

"Check the cars," Sarah said as they passed parked vehicles. "Look for anything with a set of keys left in the ignition."

Alex laughed. "You clearly haven't spent much time in London recently."

"Let's take one of these!" Nestor exclaimed, pointing as they approached an intersection. Here the traffic was stopped dead, some of the engines still running – drivers and passengers slumped in their seats, doors open, windows smashed. He led them to a jeep stalled across the junction. Its windows were intact, but the door was open – a middle-aged man sprawled half-in, half-out of the vehicle.

"Sorry," Nestor said, pulling the driver out. As he dragged him to the pavement and laid him down, the man's eyes snapped open. Nestor gave a cry of shock as the man grabbed his arm.

"I SEE YOU!" the man hissed, eyes bulging out of their sockets. Nestor desperately tried to pull free as the man repeated, "I SEE YOU!"

"I see you too!" Octavio said, placing a foot on the man's shoulder and pushing him back down to the ground.

"What was that?" Nestor said, staggering back towards the jeep with his brother.

"Bad news," said Octavio, looking around the street. Around the pavements and in the road it was possible to sense a change in the atmosphere – almost like the coming of a storm. Over by the shattered front of a coffee shop an old woman sat bolt upright. She pointed a wizened finger directly at them.

"I SEE YOU!"

"It's the Entity," Sarah said as she ushered Louise and

Wei into the back of the jeep. "It's taking control of the infected. We have to get moving. Nestor, take the wheel."

"Where are you two going?" she yelled after Octavio and Alex as they went running towards the other side of the street.

"Creating a diversion!" Alex called back. He jumped over a previously comatose man who had risen into a sitting position. It was like the city was coming back to life – but now the victims of the fall virus had blank, zombie expressions.

Shaking her head, Sarah slammed the passenger door as Nestor gunned the accelerator. "Where's the power station?"

Sarah tapped the satnav on the dash and quickly inputted Battersea Power Station as their intended destination.

"Nestor!" Wei called from the rear. The side of the jeep rocked as a man appeared and slammed his palm against the back window. His mouth moved…

"I SEE YOU."

"*Turn around when it is safe to do so,*" the robotic woman's voice on the satnav ordered. A woman appeared in front of the jeep and placed her hands on the bonnet…

Nestor released the handbrake and floored the accelerator. The woman flew across the bonnet, but managed to grab onto one of the windscreen wipers for purchase. She drew her fist back and slammed it into the glass. The windscreen reverberated but didn't break. As Nestor spun the wheel, she raised her fist again…

Louise leaned through the front and pointed. The woman flew off the bonnet and into a pile of wheelie bins on the side of the road. As soon as she hit the ground, she began to get up again, unharmed by the fall.

"Floor it, Nestor!" Sarah ordered.

The jeep accelerated, weaving between the people rising to their feet and walking into the road.

"What are they doing?" Wei asked.

"The Entity is controlling them now," Sarah answered. "They're its eyes and ears."

Nestor wrenched the wheel to the left as a man threw himself in their path. The jeep scraped the side of a parked car. "It's using them as human shields!"

"The Entity is trying to slow us down," Sarah insisted. "It knows we won't hurt the virus victims."

"Very clever," Nestor said as he swerved again. Someone threw a brick at the jeep – it rebounded off the driver's side window, almost shattering it.

"*Turn left,*" the satnav ordered and the jeep screeched round the corner.

Ahead, people had risen and were crowding across the road, forming a barrier. "Hold on," Nestor said as he drove up on the pavement to avoid them. The jeep smashed through a telephone box and then ran back onto the road behind the wall of people, finding a narrow lane through the stopped cars.

"Nice driving," Sarah said, patting him on the shoulder.

To the side of the jeep, a motorbike engine roared and they both looked round. Octavio was riding alongside them on a brand-new, bright red Kawasaki. Alex was riding pillion, a weapon that looked like a plastic machine gun clutched in his hands.

"Show-offs," Nestor muttered. *Where did you get that from?*

Octavio winked at them through the window. *It's amazing what you find lying around during a disaster.*

Alex added, *We'll go ahead and clear the way for you. Dr. Fincher gave me something that could be useful. You might want to cover your ears...*

Octavio revved the bike and sped ahead of the jeep. They raced towards another wave of people rising to their feet. Alex aimed the strange-looking gun at them and pulled the trigger. Even from inside the jeep, Sarah and the others could hear a sound like a sonic boom.

The people blocking the road immediately flew back – hit by an invisible force.

"What was that?" Sarah asked as the jeep raced through the gap.

"Dr. Fincher's sonic impact gun," Nestor said. "It manipulates sound waves to—"

"Just concentrate on the driving," Sarah said as they picked up speed along Lambeth Palace Road. "The main thing is, it's working."

Up ahead, another wave of zombie-like people rose and moved to block their paths. Alex fired at them again… There was another boom and they went flying…

"*At the roundabout, go straight ahead,*" the satnav ordered. Alex and Octavio rode straight over the grass as Nestor sent the jeep round, expertly avoiding the stopped cars in the road. They were driving along the embankment now and Sarah noted their destination was less than two kilometres away. *We're going to make it,* she thought.

The engine of a heavy vehicle howled…

"Nestor!" Louise cried in warning from the back as a rubbish van sped across the road towards them. Nestor swerved to avoid it and the van carried on, smashing through the embankment wall and into the Thames. Another car drove at them down the wrong side of the street. Again Nestor managed to dodge it with a fancy manoeuvre, but only just. The Entity had clearly changed tactics – using cars driven by the infected as battering rams.

Nestor shook his head. "Ever get the feeling you're not liked?"

Octavio and Alex had turned their bike and were riding back to help. As another truck set itself on a collision course with them, Alex aimed the gun and hit it with a sonic blast. The truck careened off course and smashed into a parked car. Nestor gunned the accelerator over another junction and took a right onto Nine Elms Lane.

"We're almost there," Sarah encouraged. Less than a kilometre, according to the satnav display. Up ahead it was possible to see the familiar, white chimneys of the power station along the river.

"Look out!" Wei yelled from the back – but it was already too late. Something slammed into the back of the jeep, sending it flying off course. Windows shattered and they were all jarred in their seats. The jeep mounted the pavement, but Nestor managed to pull it back onto the road. The engine whined in protest. Sarah looked through the side mirror and saw a massive truck on their back. A bearded trucker stared vacantly through the windscreen, both hands locked on the wheel. The truck engine howled as it accelerated to ram them again.

"Get us out of here!" Sarah snapped.

"I'm trying!" Nestor replied – his foot was on the floor, but the jeep had taken a battering and was only just carrying on.

An object approached from the other direction – Octavio and Alex on the bike. A shiny, silver sports car raced across the road, intercepting them like a missile. Octavio saw it too late... The angular bonnet of the car clipped the back wheel of their Kawasaki and the bike spun round. Caught under the machine, the two boys were dragged along the road until it came to a rest against a tree. The sports car slammed into a line of parked vehicles.

*Octavio!* Nestor cried out in his mind.

The truck hit the ailing jeep a second time... In the back, Wei and Louise screamed as the jeep tumbled onto its side and ground along for several metres before coming to a rest in the centre of the road. The front airbags triggered, slamming into Nestor and Sarah as they jerked forward in their seats.

Then the truck hit them again... Sarah's world spun into blackness...

## 32

"*Wrong way,*" a woman's voice said. "*Please turn around. Wrong way…*"

"Huh?" Sarah groaned, opening her eyes.

"*Wrong way… Wrong way…*"

It took her a second to realize that it was in fact the voice of the satnav. She must have blacked out – maybe only for a few seconds. Looking round the shattered interior of the jeep, she saw the deflated airbags hanging like burst balloons over the twisted dash. Everything was at a ninety-degree angle because the vehicle was now lying on its side and her seat belt was the only thing holding her up. Below, Nestor stirred with a moan of pain.

Steadying herself, Sarah unclicked the seat belt and pushed open the passenger door, which now swung up like a lid. She pulled herself through... As she did so, a meaty hand grabbed her arm and yanked her over the side of the jeep. With a cry of surprise, Sarah rolled across the road and landed on her back. Beside the jeep stood the driver of the truck that had hit them – a greasy, unkempt beard hung down his neck and his gut poked out between his jeans and T-shirt. In one hand he held a crowbar, which he raised as he advanced on her.

"I SEE YOU," he said, completely without emotion.

"Sarah!" Alex yelled, appearing round the wreck of the jeep. He aimed the sonic gun at the man and pulled the trigger...

It made a whining sound and sparks cracked around the plastic. Alex dropped the gun as it started to melt. With his free hand, the trucker grabbed Alex by the scruff of the neck and threw him across the road. He landed heavily beside Sarah.

"That didn't go as planned," Alex said apologetically, looking at the melted remains of the sonic gun. "Prototypes, huh?"

The driver of the truck held the crowbar high and continued his slow, lumbering approach. Sarah closed her eyes… The trucker stopped. The crowbar slid from his hand. He fell like a stone.

"What just happened?" Alex asked, getting to his feet and helping Sarah up as well.

"I severed the psychic link with the Entity," she replied. "It must be using the hypersphere as a transmitter to take control of the newly infected. I should have thought of it sooner."

"Then you can shut them down."

"One at a time, Alex," she said. "There are going to be millions of infected all over the capital."

"Oh. Right."

Nestor emerged from the jeep and pulled Wei and Louise out after him. Sarah was relieved to see that aside from a few cuts and bruises they appeared unhurt. Octavio pushed the battered Kawasaki towards them as they regrouped. Sarah looked at him and Alex, remembering their slide along the road under the bike. Their uniforms weren't even torn. Alex grinned at her.

"Tough material," he said. "Told you uniforms were a good idea. How far are we from the power station?"

"Not far," Sarah replied, pointing at the white chimneys rising through the trees along the river.

"We can make it on foot."

Louise cast a nervous eye over people lying on the opposite pavement. "What about them?"

Sarah shook her head. She no longer sensed the Entity exerting its influence on them. Something had changed...

"The spiders," Wei said, pointing back down the embankment. Far down the road the black shape of the swarm was massing. The spiders had caught up with them.

"Great," Octavio said. "If it's not zombies in trucks, it's mechanical spiders trying to kill us." He threw his leg over the battered Kawasaki and managed to kick-start the engine into life. "Everyone get moving. I'll take care of this."

Sarah placed a hand on the handlebars of the bike. "What do you think you're doing?"

Octavio shrugged. "Just being a total hero. As usual."

"Not alone, you're not," Nestor said, jumping on the back. Down the embankment, the spider swarm was getting closer. He turned to Sarah and the others. "We'll hold them off for as long as possible. Just get to the power station."

Knowing they had little choice, Sarah stepped aside.

As Octavio throttled up the engine, Louise ran forward and threw her arms quickly around both boys. "Be careful."

Octavio winked at her as she pulled away. "We won't."

The Kawasaki roared down the street towards the wall of robospiders. Sarah watched them go and then turned to the others.

"Let's make this count," she said, breaking into a run. The others kept pace with her – sprinting the final few hundred metres to their confrontation with Major Bright and the Entity…

The Kawasaki powered along the embankment, picking up speed as it approached the wall of robospiders.

"Are you sure this is such a good idea?" Nestor yelled over the roar of the engine.

"No," Octavio said, applying the brakes and turning the handlebars. The back wheel spun out and the bike screeched to a halt a hundred metres from the swarm. He turned to his brother on the back of the bike. "Want to go back?"

Nestor sighed and climbed off. "I guess not."

Octavio swung his leg over the bike, kicked out the

stand and went to his brother's side. Ahead, the swarm surged forward and it was possible to see the reds of the spiders' eyes.

"So," he asked, "what's the plan?"

Nestor looked at him in disbelief. "What's the plan? *What's the plan?* I thought you had the plan!"

Octavio shrugged. "It didn't get much further than where we are now."

"*Of course.* I'll freeze them. You...do whatever it is you do."

The swarm was now fifty metres away and seemed to be picking up speed, as if sensing fresh prey...

Nestor held out his hand and an arctic blast of air howled down the embankment, freezing the foremost spiders in place. Octavio closed his eyes and the road before them cracked open, as if hit by a mini-earthquake. As the ground split, the frozen machines began to fall into the hole. Seeing this, Nestor froze the swarm into the pit.

"It's working!" Octavio said, opening his eyes. "I think we can actually—"

A deep rumble went through the ground under their feet...

The iced-over top of the pit exploded in all directions as the machines escaped – transformed into locust-like creatures once more. They filled the air, so black it was almost impossible to see.

Nestor saw his brother desperately trying to hold off the swarm, but there were simply too many of the machines to combat.

"Octavio!" he screamed as the other boy disappeared into the swarm.

Then the machines were all around him... Crawling over his body... He tried to blast them back, but it was no use...

One of the machines sunk its teeth into his neck. Nestor's legs crumpled, as if they had lost all strength.

Another machine bit him, injecting its poison into his bloodstream.

Then there wasn't anything at all...

## 33

It took five minutes for Sarah and the remainder of the team to reach the edge of the disused land surrounding their destination, by which time they could hear the approach of the swarm once more. As they came to a chain-link fence sporting signs for a construction company and announcing a *New development soon!* the metallic buzz of thousands of spider feet approached. Wei blasted a hole in the fence and they ran through onto muddy ground. Ahead, the industrial hulk of Battersea Power Station towered over the landscape.

"Over here," Sarah said and they ran for the cover of a stack of building materials. The spider swarm reached the chain-link fence but, rather than surging over it as it could have easily done, the mass of spiders paused there, so densely packed it was difficult to distinguish one from another. Thousands of blazing red eyes stared at them.

"Why have they stopped?" Wei asked, crouching down by a stack of bricks.

"There must be some kind of barrier around the base," Alex said. "To prevent the swarms from getting inside."

Sarah nodded. "Luckily for us."

"But what about Nestor and Octavio?" Louise asked. "They've been bitten by those spiders, right? Just like Robert was."

Sarah placed a hand on her shoulder. "We'll go back for them. We're going to find a cure for the virus and save everyone."

"What about the Entity?" Alex asked. "It must know we're here."

"No," Sarah said. "I'm shielding our presence from it."

Alex glanced at the thousands of spider eyes fixed upon them and gave her a sceptical look, but said nothing. He peeked around the edge of the bricks at the power station. On the roof area between the giant chimneys it was possible to make out the shape of sentries walking back and forth.

"It's well defended," he said.

"Can you get us inside?" Sarah asked.

"Not a problem." Alex put his hand in Sarah's. She in turn clasped Louise's hand, who held onto Wei. Alex began to fade out... In less than five seconds both he and the others were completely invisible.

*You're getting faster at that,* Sarah said.

Alex gave no reply, but pulled on her hand to indicate they should move. He led them from behind the bricks and out across the open ground towards the front of the power station. As they drew closer, they made out two giant doors at the front, open the width of a house.

*This is weird,* Louise said, meaning the sensation of walking while being unable to see your feet or legs.

*Yeah,* Wei agreed. *What happens if you eat something while you're invisible? Do you see it go into your stomach?*

*Don't be stupid,* Alex replied tersely as they approached a ramp leading up to the entrance. The ramp was wide enough to drive two trucks up side by side and bore a multitude of tiny scratch marks – no doubt made when the spiders trooped out of the building to take over the city.

A merc walked out of the station and down the ramp. Alex and the others paused as he passed, then carried on through the entrance and through the doors...

*Wow,* Louise said as she and the others looked over the inside of Bright's base. Technicians sat on raised control decks along one side of the interior, while heavily armed mercs patrolled all around. Two helicopters sat ready for action at the far end of the building. Sunlight streamed down through the open roof...

And in the very centre was the hypersphere, its liquid surface reflecting and distorting the world around. Next to the sphere were two tables, upon which lay Hack and May.

*Let's get closer,* Sarah said.

Alex led them into the station, keeping near the wall to avoid any technicians wandering around or mercs on patrol. They stopped level with the hypersphere. It was possible to see the straps holding Hack and May in place. Electrodes attached to their bodies stretched to monitoring equipment, which was in turn linked to the hypersphere itself. The surface of the sphere rippled and the shape of a newly formed robospider dropped from the bottom. It scuttled along the ground to join a group of a hundred or more on the floor, waiting to be mobilized like a battalion of tiny soldiers.

*We have to get them free,* Sarah said, looking over Hack and May. *Remove them and the hypersphere will shut down.*

*Easier said than done,* Alex replied. The raised area upon which the hypersphere sat was exposed to the entire base and packed with personnel – both scientific and military.

*I'll create a diversion while you get them free,* Sarah said urgently. Her plan was hastily thought out, but they just didn't have time to waste. *Louise and Wei – be ready to give Alex backup if he needs it.*

*And who's going to give you backup?* Alex asked, concern in his voice.

*Don't worry about me.* Sarah began to pull her hand free, but froze as a figure approached the hypersphere… Major Bright.

"Why has the spider production slowed?" Bright demanded as Marlon Good turned from one of the machines controlling the hypersphere. "I need armies."

"The system is still bedding in," Good replied. "You can't expect one hundred per cent efficiency from the get-go."

One of the technicians swivelled in his chair and indicated monitors showing brainwave activity in the two children strapped to the hypersphere.

"We're pushing these kids too hard, sir," the technician said. "Carry on like this and they'll be vegetables within a few hours." As if to prove the point, Hack gave a feeble cry from the table. On hers, May's whole body jerked in pain.

Major Bright nodded, as if mulling over that point, before bending in to speak softly to the technician. "Poor little children. We mustn't push them too hard, must we? Perhaps we should order in some pizza? See if they want to watch a *Harry Potter* movie?"

Marlon Good took a step back. The technician looked nonplussed. "I... Uh..."

Bright grabbed the technician's head and slammed it onto the workbench. The man's skull bounced off the table and he fell to the floor in a crumpled heap. Around the base, Good's people looked on in shocked disbelief. Marlon Good himself had gone a greenish colour at the sight of blood pouring from the technician's broken nose.

Bright addressed the entire base, yelling as he did so. "Anyone else want to tell me how to run my plot to take over the world?" He paused for silence. "No? Then get back to work!"

Around the base, technicians suddenly found something important to do. Bright stepped up to Good, who swallowed heavily, no doubt expecting the worst.

"Do what you have to do," Bright said quietly, keeping himself under control, "but get me more of those machines. When the world finds out what's happening here, they're going to throw everything they've got at us. We'll be lucky if we just get nuked by China. We are going to need all the firepower we can manage. Understand?"

Good nodded. Bright stalked away to the other side of the base, where Kotler and more of his men were waiting. Laughter broke out among the mercs as their leader made a comment.

"Turn up the power on the ECG drain," Good said to the nearest technician. "No arguments." He looked at the unconscious tech on the floor. "And someone take care of him."

At the side of the hypersphere, Alex led the others over to some cover by the wall. Sarah placed Louise's hand in his and then pulled away. She immediately became visible again. *We have to do this before they kill those kids,* she said urgently. *Wait here for my signal.*

*What signal?* Alex asked.

*Trust me, you'll know it when you see it.*

## 34

Sarah ran along the wall in a crouch, keeping to the shadows as she approached the helicopter landing area at the back of the base. In the distance she made out Major Bright. Although he was in contact with the Entity, the man showed no sign of sensing her. She'd told Alex that she was shielding their presence from the Entity, but this had been a lie – this close, there would be no hiding from it. Clearly the alien did not want Bright knowing she was there – but why? Once again she had the feeling of being drawn in... *This is what the Entity wants,* she reminded herself. *It needs me more than Bright. It's letting me get close, just like it did on the island...*

Putting such thoughts aside to concentrate on the job in hand, she stopped near the two helicopters. It was relatively quiet at this end of the base and a single pilot stood guard over the Black Hawks, sitting on the open back of the nearest, smoking a cigarette. Sarah reached out with her mind and connected with his. The pilot's head raised and the cigarette dropped from his lips. He stood and walked slowly over to her hiding place. Checking they were unseen, Sarah placed her hand against his right cheek, fingers splayed...

And scanned his mind for the information she needed – his expertise in piloting the chopper. It took less than ten seconds for her to learn everything the man knew about flying one of the Black Hawks.

"Return to your aircraft and get it in the air," she ordered, lowering her hand.

The pilot nodded dumbly, completely under her control, and turned back to the landing area. Sarah watched from her hiding place as he climbed into the cockpit of the nearest machine and powered up the engine. The blades began to spin, picking up speed until they were whining away, ready for take-off. Sarah gave a concerned glance towards the other end of the base, but both the technicians and the mercs were too occupied with the hypersphere to pay much attention. No doubt they assumed it was just another patrol taking off.

The Black Hawk rose several metres, and then turned so it was facing down the power station. Rather than continue towards the open roof, however, the pilot sent the helicopter on a slow approach towards the other end of the base, where the majority of the mercs were stationed.

*Fire your weapons, pilot,* Sarah ordered.

The machine guns on both side of the Black Hawk opened up. The far wall of the power station exploded as hundreds of rounds ripped into the brickwork. Mercs scattered as debris rained down around them.

*Rockets,* Sarah ordered, smiling with satisfaction at the chaos she was causing.

The pilot fired two rockets down the length of the power station. They flew with a scream and hit one of the raised platforms. Technicians and mercs jumped free just in time as computer equipment exploded...

"That's the signal, I guess," Alex said as he, Louise and Wei watched with wide eyes the destruction being wreaked by the helicopter. "Stay here and cover me.

I'm going after Hack and May."

He released the hands of the other two children. They became visible, but during the present chaos, no one in the base was going to notice them crouched in the shadows. Alex remained faded-out as he ran onto the raised platform holding the hypersphere and the monitoring equipment. Marlon Good's people, unused to barrages of machine-gun fire over their heads, had abandoned their posts and were sheltering under their desks. Good himself had retreated to the other side of the base and had tucked himself into a ball on the ground – all that was visible was two terrified eyes between his fingers. Mercs were firing their machine guns at the Black Hawk, but the pilot inside seemed oblivious to the danger as he strafed another area of the base with the twin machine guns.

Wasting no time, Alex moved to the table upon which Hack was strapped. The boy's face was deathly pale, as if the machines had been sucking the very life out of him. Tearing away the fastenings on his legs and ankles, Alex then proceeded to rip off the electrodes attached around the boy's forehead. Hack's eyes flickered open as the connection with the hypersphere was severed and he looked around in confusion. Alex placed a hand over his mouth as he began to rise.

*It's okay,* Alex said. *Just stay still for a moment. I'm going to free the girl.*

Hack nodded his understanding and lay back to gather his strength. Alex moved past the hypersphere to May's table and began to repeat the operation of freeing her. If anything, she looked even more deathly than Hack. As Alex freed her from the machine, she barely managed to open her eyes as he wrapped his arms around her and lifted her from the table.

"Hey!" Marlon Good yelled, no doubt surprised to see the girl levitating off the table. The American took a step towards them, and then flew back violently, as if pushed. He rolled into a heap on the floor. Louise appeared at the opposite side of the platform.

*Hurry up, Alex!* she said.

Becoming visible once more (there was little point in expending the energy now), Alex moved back to Hack, who had swung his legs off the table and stood, looking shaky on his feet.

"Can you walk?" Alex asked and the boy nodded.

The Black Hawk roared overhead, guns still firing wildly around the base. Mercs fired from every direction. Major Bright strode across the floor of the station, seemingly oblivious to the danger. He raised an open hand at the helicopter and its engine made a terrible groaning sound…

"Come on," Alex said. "I don't think the diversion is going to last much longer."

They ran to the edge of the platform as Major Bright closed his fist... The fuselage of the helicopter crumpled inwards and the blades spun into the body of the vehicle. Bright twisted his fist and the vehicle compressed further, as if it had been put through an invisible crusher. The major opened his hand and the remains of the Black Hawk crashed to the ground. Around the station, the mercs stopped firing.

"The hypersphere!" Marlon Good shouted from his prone position on the floor as Alex and the others made the wall. Bright shouted an order and the guns opened up again. Alex ducked behind cover with May, closely followed by the others, as bullets ricocheted around them. A merc came running, but Wei threw up a wall of fire between them.

*Over here!* Sarah's voice rang in their heads. *The other helicopter!*

Alex looked round and saw her waving from the landing pad. He didn't need to tell the others – they started running for the back of the station. Alex carried May, while Hack leaned on Wei for support. As they went, Louise turned her attention to the hypersphere, which was now a dead lump of metal in the centre of the power station. As mercs approached on the other side she gave it a mental shove – the sphere detached from its frame and went rolling, crushing equipment and newly-formed robospiders as it went.

"Do you know how to fly this thing?" Alex asked Sarah as he put May in the back of the Black Hawk. Behind them, Louise was holding off the advancing mercs by deflecting their bullets and throwing anything that wasn't bolted down at them.

"I'm not going to fly it," Sarah said. "You are."

Without warning, Sarah leaned in and placed her lips against his in a kiss. As they made contact, Alex had the strangest sensation of learning a vast amount of information in a matter of seconds as Sarah pushed the know-how she'd previously extracted from the pilot's head into his.

"Now get the others out of here," she said, pulling away.

He looked at her without responding, a stunned expression on his face. She punched him hard on the shoulder.

"Wake up, Alex!"

Alex came to his senses and grabbed her arm as she started across the landing pad. "Where do you think you're going?"

She met his eyes. "Bright and the Entity will never let you out of this building unless I give them what they want."

"And what do they want?"

"Me," she replied. "The Entity wants to join with me like it has with Major Bright."

Alex shook his head. "That's crazy. You can't surrender—"

"It's the only way. You have to get Hack and May as far away from the hypersphere as possible – and you'll need them to destroy the robospider swarms."

"But what about you?"

"The Entity thinks it can control me," Sarah said defiantly, "but I think differently. Somewhere in its consciousness is a cure for the fall virus. A cure for Robert and all the others who've been infected. This is the only way we're going to get it."

"And what if you aren't strong enough?" Alex asked. "What if you become part of the Entity for ever?"

"Then you'll just have to find a way to kill me."

Alex looked away. "You planned this all along, didn't you? You knew you weren't coming back with us the moment we boarded the stealth jet."

Sarah placed her hand on his and gently pulled her arm free. "It's the only way, Alex."

"I'm not letting you go—"

"Please, Alex. The others need you now."

*Sarah! He's coming!*

It was Louise's voice calling urgently from where she and Wei were fighting off the mercs. Both Sarah and Alex looked round and saw Major Bright stride through a wall of flame. Louise threw a computer tower the size of the man at him, but the major brushed it aside like it was made of cardboard.

*PLAYTIME'S OVER, CHILDREN,* he said with a smile.

Sarah looked at Alex and said, "You know what to do."

With that, she ran towards Louise and Wei and ordered them back to the helicopter...before turning to face Major Bright.

## 35

"Sarah," Major Bright said. "You finally made it." He held up a hand and the mercs ceased fire.

"Let my friends go," Sarah said, glancing back at the landing pad. "Then I'll give you whatever you want."

Bright laughed. "You're in no position to bargain."

"And I'm not talking to you, Major."

A look of confusion passed over Bright's face... His eyes went blank...

*Sarah,* the Entity said. *I told you this was inevitable. I see that now. Let my friends leave.*

*Why? The end of their world is at hand. You only prolong their agony by saving them.*

*Do it for me… And I'll cooperate. I know it's me you need, not Major Bright and not anyone else in this building.*

*You overestimate your importance to my plans.*

*Do I?*

*Very well,* the Entity said finally. *I will not stop them leaving the base. Once they are outside, however, they are on their own.*

Sarah nodded. Eyes still blank, Major Bright raised his right hand and held it out to her, palm up. Sarah hesitated.

*Well? Do we have a deal or not?*

Taking a deep breath, she placed her hand in his… His fingers closed around hers…

And the world began to melt away…

Inside the helicopter, Alex and the others watched Sarah standing before the major.

"What's she doing?" Louise demanded. "We have to help her!"

"No," Alex said, flipping a series of switches on the ceiling of the cockpit. The giant blades began to turn. "She told us to get out of here."

"But we can't—"

"This is the only way," Alex said, looking Louise hard in the eyes. "Do you understand? Sarah is doing this so we can escape."

Louise opened her mouth to argue, but Alex cut her dead.

"Do you think I can stand the thought of leaving her behind?" he said, turning his attention back to the Black Hawk controls – an array of buttons and switches that were oddly familiar (thanks to the information Sarah had placed in his head) and yet at the same time completely alien.

Seeing the tears forming in his eyes as he worked the helicopter controls, Louise finally accepted what he was saying. She reached out and touched his shoulder. "We'll come back for her."

"Yes, we will."

In the back, Hack brushed the hair out of May's eyes. She was lying on the floor of the helicopter, barely conscious.

"Is she going to be all right?" Wei asked at his shoulder.

"She's going to be fine," Hack snapped back, but he wished he could be so certain. Being plugged into the hypersphere was like a slow death, every drop of energy being drained in the service of creating the Entity's machines. It had been bad enough for him, but in her weakened state, May had been pushed to the very edge.

Outside the helicopter, the mercs were keeping their distance while Sarah and Major Bright stood hand in hand, unmoving. Whatever was happening between them was unseen – passing between their minds. As Hack watched, he caught sight of a single figure moving along the wall of the station, bent low and keeping to the shadows so as not to attract attention.

Marlon Good.

"Look after May," Hack told Wei, jumping out of the helicopter.

"Where are you going?" Wei protested.

Hack ripped an emergency crowbar from a bracket on the side of the chopper. "I've got someone to take care of."

He moved swiftly to intercept the fleeing American, who was too preoccupied with his escape to notice. Hack swung the crowbar across the back of his knees and Good went down with a yelp of pain. As he rolled over onto his back, Hack smashed the iron bar across his protectively raised right arm.

"No!" Good cried.

Hack hit him again, and again…then jumped on him,

pressing his knees into his ribcage and forcing the crowbar down across his throat. Good struggled, but it was a weak effort.

"You're hurting me!"

"Good!" Hack exclaimed, pressing down harder with the crowbar. Marlon Good choked and flailed at his attacker with his hands, but Hack grabbed a fistful of his hair and slammed his head against the concrete. Although he was no fighter, he'd learned to defend himself well enough on the backstreets of his grandfather's village.

He slammed Marlon Good's head against the floor again.

"Enough, enough!" Good spluttered, tears and snot pouring down his face. "Just let me go. All this killing is a mistake! I just wanted to have fun! It was supposed to be a game!"

*It was supposed to be a game.* Remembering everything that had been inflicted upon him and May, the words only made Hack angrier.

"What?" he spat, hitting Good again. "Your game not so much fun any more, huh?"

"I… This is wrong… I just want to get out of here…"

Repulsed at Good's snivelling, Hack reached into the man's shirt and ripped free the trigger on the chain

– a silver rectangle with several buttons and a keypad. "Show me how to unlock the collars."

"Uh-uh. You'll kill me."

Hack held the trigger in front of Good's face and put his thumb over a red button on the side. "What happens if I press this?"

"Then your neck explodes."

Hack held up the trigger as if he was about to press the button...

"Wait!" Good cried. "What do you think you're doing?"

Hack bent over his prisoner so their noses were almost touching. "At this close range, the explosion would rip you apart as well. How about it?"

"Nice bluff. I don't buy it."

"I'll do it," Hack said. "If it's the only way to stop you, I'll do it."

Good's eyes widened. "What about the girl? She's wearing a collar too. You'll both die."

"We're willing to sacrifice ourselves to stop your plans. To keep our families safe." Hack waved the trigger in front of Good's face. "We'd die heroes. Probably make a film about us and everything. Cool, huh?"

"You're crazy," Good said, sounding as if he actually believed it.

"Last chance." Hack began to depress the red button...

"435892!" Good yelled. "That's the release code! 435892!"

Hack took a deep breath. What choice did he have? He thumbed the six-digit code into the keypad. His collar began to beep shrilly...

Hack closed his eyes, waiting for the explosion...

With a click, the collar snapped open at the back and fell into his hands. He laughed with relief.

"Now get out of my sight," Good said, squirming on the ground.

Hack weighed the open collar in his hands. "You know what? I think it's about time you tried out some of your own technology...Marlon."

He placed the collar around Good's neck, clicking it shut at the back.

"Wait!" the American cried, twisting round into a kneeling position, as Hack ran in the direction of the waiting helicopter. "Don't leave me like this! Where are you going? We can work together! We'll be bigger than Microsoft!"

Hack raced across the landing pad, where the rotors of the helicopter were running at full speed now. Jumping into the back, he found May sitting up – her explosive collar in her lap, open. She looked at Hack and, seeing that the collar was gone from his throat also, managed a weak smile.

"Where's yours?" she asked.

"Marlon Good is trying it out for size," he replied.

May nodded…and clicked her collar closed. It emitted a beep as it twinned with the other…

"Time to get out of here!" Alex yelled from the cockpit. He pulled back on the stick…

Hack looked round. "Sarah?"

Alex shook his head. Outside, Major Bright's hand opened and Sarah's fingers slipped from his. The major blinked like someone awaking from a sleep and looked round in surprise. Before him Sarah stood with her eyes closed still, as if in a trance. Bright looked over her shoulder and saw the Black Hawk powering up for take-off…

"Open fire!" Bright screamed at his men as the vehicle began to lift into the air. "All weapons!"

The mercs, who had been holding off, awaiting orders, now let loose with everything they had. The air became alive with flying metal. The chopper tilted to one side as Alex struggled with the stick. On the floor in the back, everyone held on for dear life as one of the walls loomed dangerously close to the blades. Bullets ricocheted off the fuselage and a few tore through the floor as mercs ran from cover and fired upon them.

*They're going to tear us apart!* Wei cried as a round flew through the floor between his legs…

On the ground, Sarah Williams's eyes opened. She looked over the mercs firing upon the helicopter and said one word:

"*No.*"

Every mercenary in the power station was instantly thrown back several metres. Major Bright rounded on Sarah and pulled a pistol from his belt.

"That would be a very stupid thing to do," she said as he levelled the gun at her head.

"What are you?" Bright demanded. Sarah Williams's outward appearance had not changed in the slightest, but her eyes… They were infinitely old and full of malice. Major Bright lowered the gun.

"You understand what I am?"

Bright waved the gun at the chopper. "Why are you letting them escape?"

"Because I made the girl a promise. Don't worry, Major. You can kill them later."

Bright shook his head and watched the Black Hawk pull out of the spin. Now it rose swiftly, through the open roof of the power station and into the sky.

\*   \*   \*

Beside Alex in the cockpit, Louise exclaimed, *You did it!*
The chopper cleared the edge of the power station
and arced over the Thames, putting as much distance
between them and the power station as possible.

*We're not home yet,* he replied. *One of those bullets
has ruptured the fuel line. We're not going to make it more
than a few kilometres.*

As if to prove his point, the engine juddered and the
rotor blades gave a dangerous screeching sound as they
slowed.

*Just put us down somewhere safe,* Hack said. *I'll see
what I can do to fix it.*

"Right, somewhere safe," Alex yelled back. "The
whole city is swarming with robospiders. There's a small
army of mercs on our back. Should be easy."

As the others began to argue about where to put down
before the Black Hawk fell out of the sky, Hack moved
closer to May, who was sitting against the back wall, the
collar in her lap.

"We need to get rid of that," he said. "It's still live."

"I know," May replied softly. The detonation warning
sounded on the side of the collar as it approached the
limits of safe distance from its twin. "I'd say we're almost
a kilometre away by now, wouldn't you?"

Her eyes met his and sparkled with some of their old life.

"I'd say so," Hack replied. "We could just let it go off."

May shook her head. "No. We're better than him."

As the beep rose to a whine, May threw the collar out of the side of the helicopter. Caught on the wind, it arced through the air like a frisbee and came to rest on the top of a building...

Inside the power station, the mercs regrouped, grabbed fresh ammo and surveyed the damage. A group of them set to work with the technicians to roll the hypersphere back onto the platform and into position. Major Bright strode past the wreckage of the second helicopter towards Kotler.

"I want them tracked down!" he ordered. "I want them dead!"

"Yessir," Kotler replied. "I'll lead the—"

A high-pitched yelp interrupted him. They both looked round as Marlon Good staggered into the centre of the building. His jacket was soaked with sweat. The explosive collar was clamped firmly around his neck.

The collar beeped loudly.

"Somebody do something!" he screamed. "Get this thing off me!"

"Where's the key?" Bright asked with minimal interest in Good's fate.

Good looked at him, wild-eyed, perspiration pouring down his face. "They've got the key! And they've got the other collar. Don't you understand, you idiot? They've got the only key!"

A rare smile passed across Bright's lips. "You only made one key? And you're calling me an idiot?"

The beeping rose in intensity until it was almost a constant tone.

"It's gonna go off!" Good cried, starting to run around the mercs and technicians, who stood watching in terrible anticipation. "Help me!"

People stepped back, not wanting to be close to the walking bomb. He fell against a merc, who pushed him away roughly.

"Please!" Good begged. "Somebody do something! Somebody…" He fell to his knees, closed his eyes and clasped his hands before him, almost as if praying.

The beeping stopped. Good gave a spluttering cry of relief. He opened his eyes and looked around wildly.

"I have to find the other collar," he said manically. "I have to find it…"

Without another word, he turned and bolted towards the other end of the power station. Kotler moved forward, raising his rifle to take him down, but Bright shook his head.

"Let him go," the major ordered.

"Why?" Kotler demanded, clearly itching to take the American down.

Bright looked at his second-in-command as if the question was stupid. "Because it's amusing. Haven't you ever heard of poetic justice?"

"I don't like poetry."

Bright sighed and said, "Prep a team to track down those kids. They can't have gotten far in that chopper."

Kotler nodded. "I'll prepare the elite force."

Without another word, Bright strode towards the edge of the landing pad, where Sarah Williams sat cross-legged on the floor, eyes closed, apparently oblivious to everything happening around. As he approached, she spoke…

"You have done well, Major Bright. You will be rewarded."

The girl rose to her feet and looked around the interior of the power station. She flexed her fingers, as if testing them out. "Yes, this mind will be a much more suitable channel for my powers. Now I will be truly unstoppable on this planet."

"Where's Sarah Williams?" Bright asked. "What happened to her?"

The girl's head turned and those evil eyes regarded him in a way that made even Major Bright shiver.

"I have sent her someplace far away," the Entity said. "And trust me, she is never coming back."

*Sarah Williams is falling through layers of darkness... A seemingly bottomless void with only the sensation of air rushing against her skin giving the impression of descent...*

*She has long since given up calling out for help. There is no one here to hear her. No one to help. The memories of the battle against the Entity are fading. Her friends. Even her name. Everything is becoming cloudy, obscured...*

*Finally, just as she has given up hope that there is anything but herself and black space left in the universe, a light pierces the dark. A light so brilliant it's almost impossible to look at. The light grows, becoming a single beam stretching for ever. White tendrils stretch out from the beam, reaching across the universe for her.*

*Unable to resist, Sarah allows the tendrils to wrap around her body, drawing her closer to the beam, which is shining more intensely than the sun...*

"Sarah," a voice says as she is drawn closer. A voice she recognizes, but can no longer remember where from. "At last. You have returned to me."

She has the strangest feeling that she should draw away, but it is far too late for that...

The tendrils pull her into the beam and she clamps her eyelids shut to avoid being blinded. She opens her mouth to scream as the white light burns away her clothes, her hair, her skin, and everything she ever was...

## 36

The helicopter made it less than ten kilometres along the river before Alex was forced to put down, picking the one safe spot he could see: an open space in the midst of a sprawling scrapyard. It was a bumpy landing and the terminal-sounding screech as one of the slowing blades collided with the shell of a van suggested that the Black Hawk wouldn't be going anywhere in a hurry.

Leaping out of the cockpit, Alex looked around the mountain of junk with a despairing expression. The wrecks of cars piled on top of one another in stacks ten high towered over them. Piles of vehicle parts, smashed computer components and broken white goods were littered all around.

"Very appropriate," he said. "We've ended up with the scrap."

Hack appeared at his side. "There must be a working vehicle somewhere in this dump. It's only a matter of time before the robospiders find us. Or worse: Sarah."

"What about Sarah?" Louise snapped, jumping off the helicopter and stepping into the middle of the boys. "We're not leaving her!"

Alex placed his hands on her shoulders. "Sarah did what she did so we could get away. The Entity is just too strong now. We can't risk letting Hack and May fall into its hands again. It's what Sarah wanted. The professionals can take care of this now."

"Leave the fight to the army?" she said incredulously. "You know they're no match for the Entity. We're the only ones who can stop it!" She looked around the others as if they just weren't getting it. "Come on!"

Wei looked down at his feet. "Maybe they've got a point, Louise," he said.

Her eyes flashed anger. "Fine. Run away. But I'm staying here. I'm not giving up on Sarah."

Wei took a step towards her, but she turned away.

At the helicopter, Hack helped May to her feet.

"What about you two?" Louise demanded.

"We've fought enough for one day," Hack said.

Louise's head jerked round at him. "We came to save you. But I guess you're free now you've got your collars off."

Hack sighed. "Now that the Entity has bonded with Sarah, it doesn't even need us to control the hypersphere any more. It's over."

"What do you mean?" Alex asked.

"I sensed it when I was linked to the hypersphere," Hack explained. "With enough psychic energy it can become a portal. A link to the Entity's home-world. Combined with Sarah's power, the Entity can use it to bring a limitless number of machines through into this world. An infinite number of robot armies. And no one will be able to stop them. Not even you." He looked around the yard. "I'm going to find somewhere for May to rest and try to find a way out of here."

With that, he helped May walk in the direction of a mobile office. Wei hesitated a moment before following them. Alex moved closer to Louise and put his arm around her shoulder.

"It's okay," he said to her softly. "We won't give up. There has to be some way to stop this."

She nodded. But when she looked up at him there were tears in her eyes. "I'm not leaving Sarah," she said resolutely.

*The train is passing over a bridge. Sarah stands on the observation platform on the last carriage watching the rails receding into the distance. Grey painted girders fly past and she can see the odd flash of ocean beyond, but other than that, the landscape is expressionless. How long has she been standing there? She tries to remember...*

*Moving to the edge of the train, she cranes her head round the side. The old-fashioned wooden carriages stretch ahead, too many to count. There is no end to the bridge in sight. It seems to go on for ever.*

*"Nice day," a voice says behind her. There's something about the clipped accent that she recognizes. She looks round at the man leaning against the opposite rail. His face – short hair, firm jaw, determined eyes – is strangely familiar, but she just can't place him...*

*"Do I know you?" she asks.*

*The man smiles. "We've met before. You don't remember me?"*

*She shakes her head.*

"It's okay," he continues. "You just have to concentrate more, Sarah. Hold onto this for me, will you?"

He reaches out and deposits an object into Sarah's hand: a white stone the size of a penny. The stone is perfectly smooth, almost warm to the touch.

"What is..." she says, looking up, but the man is gone. She moves to the other side of the viewing platform and looks round, half expecting to see him hanging off the side of the train. He isn't there. Just the endless view of the carriages stretching ahead into the distance.

Turning the stone over in her hand, Sarah opens the door into the carriage. There's plush carpet on the floor and people sitting on leather couches in old-fashioned dress. Like something from the early twentieth century. Her jeans and T-shirt stand out in the crowd, but no one seems to notice as she walks past people drinking at the bar, towards a table at the back.

An old man is sitting, facing away from her. She can tell he's old because of the thin, grey hair stretched over his scalp and the hunch of his shoulders. Moving past his shoulder, she notices the object on the table before him: a wooden board with a grid of squares and various white and black stones laid out. The stones are identical in shape and size to the one she has in her hand.

"Were you talking to someone back there, my dear?"

the old man asks, not looking away from the view of the bridge passing the window.

Something tells Sarah to keep the stone a secret, so she slips it inside her pocket before taking the seat opposite.

"Just some guy," she says.

"You shouldn't talk to strangers," the old man says, turning to face her. His skin is pale and lined, the texture of old paper, but his eyes are intelligent and alive. Sarah tries to remember who the man is as he begins to remove the black stones from the board, putting them into a velvet bag on his side of the table. She starts collecting the whites. There's a bag for them as well.

"What is this?" she asks, meaning the board. "A game?"

"Yes. A very old game. It's called Go. I first came across it in eighth century Japan." With the board clear, the man removes a black stone from his bag and lays it on the board at a point where lines intersect. "It looks very simple. But it fact, it's incredibly complex."

Sarah leans forward and examines the board. It's old – an antique. "What's the game about?"

The man's thin lips stretch into a smile. "War. Would you like to play?"

"Does it take long?"

*"Don't worry," the old man says softly. "We have all the time in the universe."*

*She frowns again, trying to remember something. Something she had to do. With a shake of her head, she removes a white stone from the bag and places it on the board.*

*It can't have been that important anyway.*


"Put your foot on the gas!" Alex called to Wei. He had his head stuck under the bonnet of a rusting SUV they'd found near the junkyard office. Compared to the wrecked vehicles all around, it looked in usable condition. Just.

In the distance there was a flash of lightning followed by a rumble of thunder. The temperature had dropped several degrees in the last few minutes and there was humidity to the air which suggested the coming of a storm. Another flash in the distance. More thunder. Alex turned his attention to Hack and May, who sat in the doorway to the yard office. Hack had found a blanket from inside and had draped it over the girl's shoulders in an attempt to stop her trembling.

"Is she going to be okay?" he asked.

"She'll be fine just as soon as we get out of here."

"Well, make yourself useful then," Alex said, waving a hand at the engine.

Hack rose and walked over. He placed his hand against the battery and electricity sparked around his fingers. "Try it now," he said.

Wei turned the key and pumped the gas again. The SUV protested, but the engine fired and kept turning over this time. Hack grabbed the edge of the bonnet and slammed it down.

"It won't get us far," he said. "Maybe just to the edge of the city."

"That's far enough," Alex said, moving to the driver's door. "We need to get back to HIDRA. Regroup and work out some way to stop all this. Let's get out of here."

Hack returned to May and helped her to her feet. They climbed into the back of the SUV as the first giant drops of rain began to spatter against the van roof. Wei slid across into the passenger seat as Alex took the wheel.

"What about Louise?" he asked.

"I don't think she's coming with us, Wei."

"Then neither am I." Wei half-opened the passenger door, but Alex placed a restraining hand on his shoulder.

"We won't help Sarah by getting ourselves caught or killed today," he said. "Sometimes the best thing to do is retreat. She understood that."

As Wei thought this over the downpour started – a waterfall of rain fell over the yard, turning the ground into mud in seconds. Finally, the younger kid hauled the SUV door shut against the storm. Alex breathed a sigh of relief. He had no intention of leaving Louise behind, but he was certain that she would come with them the moment she saw them driving out of the yard. It was his instinct to go after Sarah as well, but rationally he knew this was not an option. They'd lost Nestor and Octavio already. Now Sarah. Who would he lose next? For the first time he was beginning to realize what Sarah had gone through all those months. The responsibility of being in charge. The fear of losing members of the team. Of putting them in danger.

Alex threw the vehicle into gear. The ageing tyres spun in the mud before finally finding traction. The SUV's broken suspension threw them around inside as it bumped over the uneven ground. Alex turned round a stack of semi-crushed cars and headed towards the open gates leading out to a road…

The SUV skidded to a halt, throwing everyone inside forward violently. Wei braced himself against the dash to stop from being thrown through the windscreen.

"Go easy on the brakes!"

"It's not me," Alex said. He put his foot down on the

accelerator. The engine howled. Wheels spun in the mud, throwing up dirt against the windows.

"Look!" Wei exclaimed, pointing ahead.

Louise stepped in front of the vehicle. She was already drenched with water, long blonde hair hanging in straggles around her head and shoulders, but she seemed oblivious to this. Alex eased off on the gas and gave a sigh. "Looks like we aren't going anywhere."

"What do you want, Louise?" he said, jumping out of the SUV. The rain soaked his clothes in an instant.

"I can stop you from leaving," she said.

"I know," Alex said softly. "But you won't. You know this is the right thing to do. We need to get back to HIDRA and tell them what we know about the hypersphere. They need to be warned it's going to become a portal for the Entity's armies. We'll come back for Sarah."

"And by that time she might be lost for ever! The longer we leave her under the Entity's control, the stronger it gets! How can you leave her, Alex?"

His face reddened. "She made me promise to get you all to safety. If it was up to me I'd go back right now. But Sarah's the leader—"

The sound of the back door of the SUV sliding open made them both look round. To their surprise, May was standing in the rain now. "Louise is right," she said. "We can't leave."

Alex shook his head. "Staying is completely the wrong decision. I made Sarah a promise to look after you all—"

Wei climbed out of the passenger door. Hack emerged a second later and said, "It *is* the wrong decision. And it's the one we've got to make."

In that moment Alex knew that they weren't going anywhere. Louise slipped her hand into his. "It's going to be okay. Sarah's rescued us enough times – don't you think it's about time we did the same for her?"

He smiled at her through the rain. "Let's go after her then," he said, looking round at Hack and May. "I take it you two can make yourselves useful in an impossible fight?"

The two looked at one another and grinned. "Actually," Hack said, "I think we've got just the thing."


*"Two armies go to war," the old man says as he lays another black stone on the board, adjacent to one of his others. "Black and white. Justice and injustice. Good and evil."*

*Sarah reaches into her velvet bag and removes a white*

stone. She places it to the left of the last stone laid. They are sitting beside a fountain amidst a city of towering skyscrapers. All around, people in business suits half-run from one location to another, never stopping.

Time passes. More stones are laid on the board.

"The aim is to keep your forces unified," the man says, laying a black stone on the other side of Sarah's. "To become surrounded, cut off from the mass is... to die."

She lays another white stone and looks him in the eyes. "Who are you?"

Another black stone goes down. "Don't you remember?"

"No." She places another stone, forming a complete barrier of whites, trapping two black stones within. With a triumphant grin, she picks up the three captured, or "dead", stones. "But it's coming back to me."

"You won a small victory, but lost the war," he says, placing another black stone – cutting off a group of twelve white stones. He picks the whites off the board and lays them down on the edge of the fountain. His pile of captured stones is three times the size of Sarah's.

"Who are you?" she asks, studying his ancient face.

"Who do you think I am?"

*"I think… I think…"*

*Sarah rises swiftly as a memory of another time, another places rushes across her mind and then disappears. Her knee catches the edge of the board and it goes flying. Stones skitter across the concrete.*

*"I think I don't want to play with you any more."*

*The old man's eyes twinkle, at once playful and full of spite. "But you have nowhere else to go, Sarah."*

*She looks around the towering skyscrapers… The bland, uniform faces of the people walking by…*

*"None of this is real."*

*The old man gives a cackling laugh. "It's as real as you want to make it."*

*"I want to go home."*

*"This is your home now."*

*"No. It isn't."*

*Before he can respond, she turns and runs across the square, into the mass of people. Shoulders jostle her as she runs against the tide of men and women. Every way she turns, they seem to be going in the opposite direction.*

*"Get out of my way!" she cries, pushing a woman aside.*

*Someone grabs her arm and spins her around. The man from the train. "You're beginning to remember, aren't you?" he says, pulling her out of the middle of the pavement.*

*She nods. "I remember..."*

*"Go on, Sarah. Think."*

*"My friends," she says. "We were in a battle. Against a man called Major Bright." She looks back in the direction from which she came. "And that old man."*

*"The Entity," the man says, squeezing her arm. "Do you remember why you're here?"*

*She shakes her head.*

*"You're here to kill him. Don't be deceived by the sheep's clothing he wears. He's more powerful than anything you can imagine."*

*"Then how can I—"*

*"You're powerful too. This place is yours to manipulate. Learn how to control it and you can do anything you want." The man looks round as someone shouts from the other side of the pavement. Two uniformed police are pushing their way through the crowd.*

*"Remember what you have in your pocket, Sarah," he says urgently. "I don't have much longer."*

*"But—"*

*"Find out where he hides," the man says as his arms are grabbed by the police. "He's weak there. You will know what to do..."*

*As the cops drag him away, Sarah suddenly remembers who the man is.*

*Her father.*

*"Daniel!" she calls after him.*

*But he's gone. She starts to run after him, but stops at a mighty thunderclap and a cracking sound. Across the street, the lower levels of one of the skyscrapers explode outwards, casting a cloud of debris into the air. People run in all directions, desperate to escape the destruction as the building begins to fall.*

*Sarah backs away along the wall, watching in horrified fascination. The skyscraper hits another as it comes down, setting off a domino effect of falling buildings. One collides with another in a chain reaction of destruction. She knows she should run, but cannot tear her eyes away as a building lists over the street, blotting out the sun…*

Major Bright stood before a giant world map spread out on the floor of the power station. Since the Entity had surrendered his body, the black mark across his skin had begun to recede to the point that it was no more than a bruise-like discolouration around his neck. The Entity had been as good as its word. He still sensed the alien power coursing through his veins, but the mutation was receding. *You can have your cake and eat it,* he thought with satisfaction. He was indestructible and he had a whole city to play with... Soon, the world.

Pacing around the map, he tapped North America with the end of his boot.

"How about the good old US of A?" he said. "Could make a nice residence."

Standing on the other side of the map, Kotler said, "Great idea, sir. Good climate. Plenty of natural resources."

"Good skiing too," Bright added. "We'd get Hawaii thrown in. When the Americans see there's no way to fight us, I'll have them make me president."

Gunfire burst out at the far end of the station as a merc opened up on a pair of technicians deserting their posts. Kotler watched with contempt as they went down. "It seems Good's people would rather die than join the winning team."

"Let them go. The spiders will get them if the mob doesn't. We have everything we need."

"Sir," Kotler said, calling the major's attention to the figure of Sarah Williams walking towards them. Although her feet touched the ground, she almost seemed to glide across the floor. Ghostlike.

"What is it?" Bright asked.

"I have sensed the girl, Louise, using her powers ten kilometres to the west of here," the Entity spoke through her. "I will send the spider army to deal with them."

"No," Bright said. Kotler grabbed a machine gun from the edge of the map. "I want my elites to deal with them. They've been waiting six months for a live fire exercise."

The Entity regarded him with expressionless eyes. A slow smile spread across Sarah Williams's face – it was an unnatural motion. Human…and yet totally alien. "As you wish," it said.

Bright nodded for Kotler to assemble the men. His second-in-command moved off and started shouting orders. Bright looked back at the girl. "And don't smile. It's creepy."

*A subway platform. Men, women and children huddle along its length, clinging together for safety as the walls rumble. Dust falls from the ceiling and the lights flicker as there is another crash. High above, the city is destroying itself.*

*Sarah sits against the wall, face and clothes dust-covered after her escape from the falling skyscraper. She must have fled into the subway at the last minute, but she can't remember how. The old man picks his way* through the crowd of people taking shelter, and crouches down beside her, bones cracking with the effort.

"You shouldn't have run away from me, Sarah," he says. "See what happens? The city is falling apart."

"You did this," she says accusingly.

He holds up his hands. "Nothing happens here without you wanting it. But you'll find life is a lot easier if you work with me." He leans closer and she can smell his breath – a rank odour of stale tobacco and meat. "There's so much I can teach you, Sarah."

She backs away, suddenly wishing she could get far, far away...

Wheels screech against rails as a train brakes along the length of the platform. Leaping to her feet, Sarah jumps over people on the platform and through the automatic doors.

"Come back!" the Entity calls after her, its voice a scream.

The doors snap closed and the train tears out of the station at high speed. For a split second black tunnel walls fill the windows. They zoom away, revealing brilliant blue sky and flat countryside in all directions. Here and there, people work in the fields, little specks in the distance. On the horizon, snow-capped mountains rise through the haze.

*Taking a breath, Sarah walks down the length of the empty carriage – the ultra-modern interior of a bullet train. Outside, the landscape passes by at 200 kilometres per hour.*

*Doors open at the far end of the carriage and a man appears. Daniel. With a cry, Sarah throws her arms around him. For a moment he hugs her back, before pulling away.*

*"Well done, Sarah," he says. "I see you're beginning to learn how to control this place."*

*"How can you be here?" she says.*

*"I'll explain everything," he replies, leading her to a seat by the window. "You need to rest now. You'll need your strength for tomorrow."*

*She looks at him questioningly. "What happens tomorrow?"*

*"We're going to kill the Entity."*

## 37

Standing in the junkyard now the rain had stopped, Hack explained, "When we were linked to the hypersphere, the Entity channelled a huge amount of information through us. Plans for machines – their electronic—"

"And molecular," May added.

"—structures," Hack finished. "And it's all still in here." He tapped the side of his head.

Seeing the confused looks on the faces of the others, Hack and May smiled at one another.

"Let us show you," she said, taking Hack's hand and

leaning in to him to say quietly, "This had better work."

"Of course it will work," he whispered back. "Probably."

They walked over to a stack of crushed cars. May closed her eyes and placed her hand against the crumpled metal of the one on the bottom. Hack took a deep breath and concentrated as they began to combine their powers once more – but this time it was to their own design...

*He calls up the thousands upon thousands of machine designs the Entity loaded into his brain. Spiders... squids...killing machines so strange in appearance they defy easy description. Finally, he settles on one: a skeletal frame that looks almost human, having arms, legs and a head. It's a battlesuit, designed to hold a humanoid within and to provide an incredibly strong exoskeleton. Its hydraulic limbs are incredibly powerful and within the suit is an array of tactical systems designed for war. Perfect. Channelling May's power, he begins to re-form the raw material of the assorted junk into the shell and inner components of the suit...*

The others looked on in amazement as the pile of cars began to morph together, almost as if the metal was melting in the sun bursting through the clouds. There was a crunching sound from within as matter was rearranged, re-formed into new configurations. New shapes became apparent from the mass – a torso...crude, oversized legs...thick arms and hands with clawlike digits...a rounded helmet with two red slit eyes, sitting atop the broad shoulders. A shiny outer layer of metal began to form over the skeleton. This protective skin now hid the innards of the machine.

"Very nice," Alex said. "What is it?"

"Can't you see?" Louise said. "It's a gorilla."

The comparison was an apt one. Its thick arms, which hung down to its knees, and rounded torso indeed made it look like some kind of giant primate.

"It's a battlesuit," Hack said, stepping forward. The front of the machine opened in multiple places to allow access to the cavity within. As the others watched, he grabbed one of the arms and swung himself inside. Then the front closed over him, the helmet slipping down over his head. Hack was gone – only the machine remained. For a moment nothing happened. The moment stretched on...

"Hack!" May shouted finally, the concern obvious in her voice.

The machine stirred, raising its arms and straightening its legs. It stumbled to one side, knocking down a stack of cars. Then its head swivelled towards the group of kids and it took a step in their direction. Everyone stepped back.

"He does know how to control this machine," Alex said to May. "Right?"

"Er..."

The machine took another step, this time putting its foot down so heavily the ground shook. The battlesuit swayed...and then crashed forward. The group scattered as it smacked down on the ground, sending dust flying. The gorilla-like robot gave an ear-splitting groan and pushed itself up into a kneeling position. The helmet swung open again, revealing Hack from the neck up.

"It's going to take a little time to get it completely right," he said apologetically.

"Well, you'd better make it fast!" Wei called over – he'd climbed the side of another stack and was looking across the junkyard in the direction of the entrance. "There's two vans coming into the yard! One stopped at the main entrance. One moving round to the south!"

"The mercs have found us," Alex said, and turned to Hack. "You and May work out how to use that suit." He looked at Louise and Wei, who had jumped back down to ground level. "It's up to us to buy them some time. Wei, you're with me covering the main entrance.

Louise – think you can deal with that second vanload?"

Louise grinned at him. "Let me at 'em."

*As the sun is setting, the train arrives at a village by the ocean. Daniel leads Sarah through the tiny collection of wooden houses to one on the outskirts of the hamlet. Here a family (an ageing man with a younger wife and two small children) greets them and lets them into their home. As Sarah and her father take cushions on the floor of a spare room in the back, the sound of a meal being fixed can be heard from the other side of a sliding screen door.*

*"Who are they?" Sarah asks. She has so many questions she hardly knows where to begin.*

*"Just villagers who have suffered under the rule of the Entity for too long. They want to help any way they can."*

*The door slides open and the woman carries in a tray with tea and soup. Sarah nods her thanks as the tray is placed between them and the woman hurries out, closing the door against the inquisitive eyes of her children.*

*Daniel regards her with his intense gaze as she sips the soup. "What do you remember of your life before you came here, Sarah?"*

*"I remember…Robert was sick. I have to find a cure for*

the virus he's been infected with. Alex and the others... they're fighting against the Entity on my world. But I can't remember their names."

"It's okay," Daniel says softly. "Your memory will start to return the more you fight against the control of the Entity."

"But I have to get back," she says. "I've been gone days and days. The Entity will have taken over the world by now..."

Her father shakes his head. "That's not how it works in this place, Sarah. Hours here are only minutes in the real world. Days are hours. Trust me, you haven't been gone long."

"Then there's still time," she says, almost to herself. "Is this an illusion?"

"This place is called the construct. It's a platform through which the Entity controls the minds of individuals with which it is linked. Think of it like an interface – a way for your brain to interact with the Entity. While it keeps you busy here, it can control you completely on your own planet – access your powers."

"Then none of this is real."

Daniel shakes his head slowly. "That's a dangerous way to think, Sarah. The construct exists in the link between your mind and the Entity's. What happens here *is of as real significance to you as anything that has ever happened in your life. If you want to escape, you must fight."*

*"And what if I don't?"*

*"Then you become completely subsumed by the Entity over time. A shadow. No free will. You become part of the illusion, not a participant in it."*

*She shivers as a cold breeze blows through the window. Daniel sets the bowls to one side, rises and slides the screen shut over the window.*

*"What about you?" she asks.*

*He thinks a moment before answering. "Beings on other worlds have found ways to fight the Entity: to infiltrate the construct and subvert parts of the Entity's own consciousness. When I first came here they helped me. Showed me how to manipulate the system."*

*"Like taking over a computer."*

*Daniel nods. "The Entity has grown strong by gorging on the consciousness of other beings, but this has also led to a weakness. Its mind is so vast, it can hardly monitor itself. There are many back doors into the construct. Many ways that its own agents can be turned."*

*Sarah nods, processing everything she's learned since stepping off the train.*

*"We've been trying to find a cure for you, Daniel," she*

says finally. "We didn't give up on you. But it's been so hard..."

Daniel reaches out and strokes a hand down the side of her face. "I know. I sensed it. You and Robert have been very brave. And you have to be brave for a little longer if you're going to free us all."

Sarah looks at him. "But why me?"

"You should sleep," he says, blowing out the candles around the room. "There'll be time for more questions tomorrow. We attack the ocean fortress at dawn."

"The ocean fortress?"

"A guarded structure out to sea where we will find the Entity," he explains. "I'll get you in. Then you can kill it."

"How can you be so sure the Entity will be at this... fortress place anyway?"

"If you seek it out, it will be there. Everything around you is merely a sensorial representation of your experience with the Entity. We are in this village now because you are shielding your thoughts from it. Tomorrow at dawn we will make contact again – but at a time and place of our choosing. Now, get some rest."

She nods and lays back on the thin mattress, pulling the sheet over her body. "Daniel," she says as he walks to the door and slides it open halfway. "What happens if I kill the Entity?"

He pauses and looks round, a silhouette against the light from the other room. "Then the construct will fall apart. All links will be destroyed."

"And what about you?"

He frowns. "I'm not sure."

"You could die. All the sleepers could die."

"It will be a worthwhile death to defeat the Entity." With that, he slides the door closed, leaving her alone in the darkness.

# 38

The passenger door of the lead van swung open and Kotler stepped out onto the muddy ground of the junkyard. Around him, men from his elite team of mercenaries piled out of the vehicle, checked their weapons and assumed defensive stances, as if expecting to be attacked at any moment.

"I want every one of the fugitive children brought to me," Kotler said. "Dead or alive, I don't care – except for the two we brought from the island. They're mine, understand?" Around him, the men nodded. "A bonus for every kill! This is your chance to prove yourselves."

"These freaks are already dead, sir," one of the mercs said, flicking the safety off his weapon. Kotler signalled the men to move out.

The elites formed two teams, one heading straight into the yard, while another followed the first at a distance, ready to back them up. Kotler watched the movement with satisfaction. After all the messing around with the hypersphere and that idiot Marlon Good, this was just like old times: sending men off into battle to live or die, win or lose.

He felt alive.


The elite team from the second van rounded a stack of crushed cars and saw the nine-year-old blonde girl standing out in the open, as if she had no fear. The leader went down on one knee and sighted down his rifle, while his three teammates did the same on either side. This was a routine they'd practised many times since joining Major Bright's elite army: drills designed to overcome the unique powers of the children they'd been trained to defeat. Each of the mercs knew the girl's name was Louise and had been told again and again that she was just about the most dangerous of the superhuman group, despite her youth – a high-level psionic who wasn't afraid to use her powers.

The leader fired a burst of rounds at her head. The bullets glanced off course as she used her psionic powers to deflect them. A rumble went through the broken cars stacked around the area where the soldiers had taken position. The leader looked around and realized that he and his men were surrounded by the precariously stacked wrecks... *Just where the kid wanted us to stop,* he thought grimly...

"Move!" he yelled to his men as the girl raised her hands...

The stacks crashed down around them as they broke in all directions. One of the men disappeared behind a falling van, but the others managed to dodge the toppling cars. They regrouped in the centre of the clearing. Before them, the girl turned her attention to another stack and it began to list towards them.

"Flash-bangs," the leader said. Both he and the others reached for flash-bang grenades from their belts, throwing them at the girl. Distracted by trying to bring the stacks of vehicles down on them, she looked momentarily confused as the grenades landed in the mud before her. *They're powerful, but they don't have military training,* the group leader thought with satisfaction as he averted his eyes.

The girl backed away...

The flash-bangs exploded loudly with a blinding burst of light. Louise cried out and threw her hands to her eyes.

"Take her down!" the leader snapped. He and his men took aim and fired freely at the girl, who was staggering, blinded, towards the cover of the nearest stack of scrap metal. As bullets ricocheted off the broken cars, she fell to her knees, throwing one arm out to desperately block the volleys.

"Hit her again," the leader ordered. "Live grenades."

His men threw two grenades towards her. The girl was crawling on her hands and knees now in a hopeless attempt to escape...

The grenades exploded, throwing up mud high into the air and bringing cars crashing down all around. The mercs rose to their feet and started firing freely into the devastation. After a few seconds, the leader held up a fist and they stopped. He pointed forward and they advanced on the heap of twisted metal, rifles at the ready. The words of Major Bright rang in their ears from so many training sessions: *they are not to be underestimated.*

The leader reached the edge of the blast area and saw the girl lying face down in the mud, either unconscious or dead, it was impossible to tell. The merc leader pulled a pistol from his belt...and shot Louise in the back. The kid jerked. For good measure, the merc leader took aim at her head. Better safe than sorry...

The giant fist of the battlesuit hit him with the force of a wrecking ball, lifting him off the ground and throwing him ten metres across the yard. His body landed in a crumpled mass.

The gorilla-like robot howled as another merc reached for his weapon. It sideswiped him and he flew into a pile of twisted scrap metal, disappearing amid the razor-sharp fragments, never to rise again. It swept its arms around and caught the remaining soldier, who was in the process of fleeing. The blow lifted the man from his feet and threw him into the distance.

The battlesuit shuffled around the prone body of Louise, as if afraid it was about to step on her, and looked down with its giant, strangely sad eyes. It kneeled down beside her and the helmet section opened up, revealing Hack inside.

"Louise!" he exclaimed. Her face was covered in mud and blood, but her eyes flickered open. May ran from beside one of the junk stacks.

"Louise?" she asked, then saw the body of the girl. "Oh, no. We shouldn't have let her take them on alone."

She met Hack's eyes and he could tell from her expression that it wasn't good. May placed her hands on Louise's shoulder. She moaned in pain weakly and spluttered blood from her mouth.

"You have to do something, May," Hack said. "Heal her."

"I don't know if I can," May said, looking down at the bullet wound in Louise's back. There was blood everywhere. "This is more than a cut…"

"You can do it," Hack said. "I believe in you."

May nodded and closed her eyes. As Hack watched, the bullet hole began to change shape, becoming smaller and less defined. May passed her hand over the wound and held up a twisted piece of metal that she threw to one side.

Louise's eyes flickered open. "Ouch."

"You're okay," May reassured. "Take it easy."

"They shot me."

"I know."

"Let's get them."


On the other side of the junkyard, Alex and Wei had managed to get themselves cornered in a broken-down static caravan that was used as an office. Wei tried to blast the soldiers back, but they were too mobile. Whenever they hit one team, another would flank them from a different location. These mercs were smart.

Now they crouched on the floor of the office as bullets ripped through the cardboard-thin walls and the shattered windows. Wei took advantage of a lull as one group reloaded to stick his head up and direct a blast of fire-wind through the nearest of these windows. A merc flew backwards, but the gunfire resumed from all directions immediately, driving him back down again.

*What happened?* Wei said. *We're supposed to be the ones with superpowers, not them!*

*They're too well trained,* Alex replied. *They out-manoeuvred us.*

*How do we get out of here?* Wei added as a line of bullets tore up the floor beside him.

Alex looked around for something they could use, some magic weapon lying there in the junkyard office. There was an ancient computer. A filing cabinet spilling papers from the drawers. Two dead pot plants.

*Hey!* Wei exclaimed, shoving him in the shoulder. *What's the plan?*

Alex looked at him angrily. *Why do I always have to come up with...* Then he stopped, looking round at the flimsy walls of the caravan. The main thing was that they were keeping the majority of the mercs busy and away from the others. That's all that mattered. Wasn't it?

*Think you could blow up this caravan?* Alex said.

Wei gave him a look. *What?*

*We have to get out of here somehow,* Alex continued. *How long do you think we can hold out like this?*

Wei looked like he was about to argue, when abruptly the firing stopped. They looked at one another.

"That is not good," Alex whispered now they could hear one another talk again.

One of the merc leaders shouted an order and there was a sound of metal pins being pulled. Seconds later a grenade flew through one of the open windows. And another. And another...

"That is really not good," said Alex, eyes wide. "Tear this place up!"

Wei closed his eyes... Alex moved closer to him as the temperature inside the office increased. Wei held out his arms, one pointed towards the front of the office and one towards the back. A fireball was forming on each hand that he allowed to grow until it was the size of a table and letting off intense heat. Then he let each of them fly in opposite directions...

The front and back of the caravan exploded, wooden walls splintering into a million tiny shards. Office furniture, papers and electronics became pieces of shrapnel flying out from the epicentre, where the two boys huddled. The grenades went flying as well – exploding in mid-air. The noise was deafening. Alex stole a look up and saw mercs running for cover from the wave of fire and debris. One grenade exploded near a group, sending them hurtling across the yard.

"Move!" Alex yelled, grabbing Wei and pulling him to his feet. All that remained of the office now was a raised floor with no walls. They were completely exposed, but the mercs were still in disarray...

They jumped off the remains of the office and hit the ground running. The cover of a scrap pile was only a few metres away...

"HALT!" Bullets tore up the mud before them. Alex and Wei skidded to a stop and turned as another volley cut off their retreat...

Kotler advanced across the open area, Kalashnikov locked into his shoulder. Around him, his remaining elites turned their guns on the boys. They were surrounded.

Kotler smiled and gave an order to his men.

"Shoot them."

The Black Hawk helicopter sailed across the yard and smashed down in the mud before the boys. They ducked as bullets glanced off the wrecked machine between them and their attackers. On the other side, Kotler looked round in time to see what had just thrown the helicopter...

A four-metre tall robot made of re-formed junk and looking strangely like a gorilla was bowling towards the mercs. As the men turned their weapons on it, the battlesuit picked up a car and used it as a shield. Then, when it was within a few metres of the first group of mercs, it twisted the car in its huge hands and used it like a club, swiping all three soldiers off their feet and into the air.

"Fall back!" Kotler screamed and the men began to retreat. The robot slammed its fist into the earth, knocking a soldier down. Then it raised its foot and trod him into the ground.

"Back to the vehicle!" Kotler yelled at the six remaining elites. "Use the heavy artillery!"

In the centre of the yard, Alex and Wei stood up and looked from the fleeing mercs to the towering robot in disbelief. As they watched, a section of the battlesuit's chest folded open, revealing the compartment inside where Hack sat. He was surrounded by wires and components and was grinning back at them.

"Finally managed to get this thing working properly," he said.

"Wow," Wei said.

A second giant stomped across the yard, followed by another. The breastplate of one of them opened in the same way Hack's had – revealing Louise sitting inside.

"What are we standing around for?" she said to the open-mouthed Wei. "The mercs are getting away."

"She's right," Alex said. "If we don't fight them now, we'll have to fight them all over again later."

"Then let's do it," Hack said. He scanned the two vans up ahead using the battlesuit HUD. A thermal image showed up five remaining mercs, Kotler among them. *Kotler.* The man who had abused them worst of all of Bright's men. And the one who had promised to kill him and May when the time came. Hack opened the battlesuit's left hand and punched the right fist into it.

*That isn't going to happen.*

"You guys might want to sit this out," Louise said to Alex and Wei on the ground. "Wouldn't want to step on you." The chest of her suit folded closed around her, but as she moved off Hack placed a giant hand on her chest.

"Stay here and protect the others," he said, voice piped through the mouth of the machine. "These are mine."

Before Louise could protest, he headed off in pursuit

of the mercs. Wei looked at Alex. "I *really* want one of those."

Inside his battlesuit, Hack sat in a space that was claustrophobic at first, but which he was fast getting used to. The leg movements of the robot were controlled by thought impulse – a kind of telepathic link-up. He imagined moving his legs, and the legs of the battlesuit moved. Vision was provided, not by the eyes in the helmet, but by an incredibly sophisticated computer rendering of the outside world being beamed directly onto his retinas. Within the suit, he had the strange sensation of wearing no helmet at all, the illusion was so real. He turned his head to the right and the display floating before his eyes turned across the yard. The vision highlighted fleeing mercs in red as they raced to their vehicle and started to unload more guns...and rocket launchers. Warning markers generated by the suit flashed in the air around the threats.

*They're getting serious.*

He sent his battlesuit stomping across the yard, knocking down car stacks as he went. A group of mercs peppered the suit shell with bullets. Hack opened the arms of the machine wide and brought them together in a sweeping motion, crushing the soldiers together. They fell to the ground in a groaning, mangled heap – alive, but out of the action.

A rocket flew from beside the van and hit him full in the chest. It felt like someone had driven a bus at the outside of the machine. Hack cried out in pain as warning messages flashed across the display. He realized that he was actually sensing mild pain around his body. *I'm telepathically linked with this machine,* he thought. *If it gets hurt, I feel it too.* Shaking his head to clear his thoughts, he focused on the van: the merc was slotting another rocket into the launcher.

With a battle cry that echoed across the yard, he raced forward and kicked out. The foot of the battlesuit connected with the van. Three of the mercs disappeared, caught in the path of the tumbling vehicle. A fourth dodged to one side, raising a launcher in his hand...

The rocket hit the battlesuit full in the face. Stars exploded in Hack's eyes and he was aware of the machine's knees buckling as he lost all control. Warnings blazed all around...

Kotler stepped forward with his own rocket launcher, calmly took aim and fired...

The explosion ripped the right arm from the battlesuit. Inside the shell, Hack screamed in agony. It felt as if someone had ripped his own arm out of the socket. A message rang in his head: *Emergency – full system shut-down imminent – escape procedure activated...*

The chest plate slid open automatically and Hack spilled out of the machine and onto the muddy ground. Minus an operator, the battlesuit staggered away and came to rest on its back. Still in pain, Hack looked at the face of the robot and gave it a final order before the telepathic link was severed. The red eyes went dim...

Hack pushed himself up, running for the nearest available cover. He almost made it before Kotler grabbed him by the shoulder and drove him down to the ground.

"That's far enough!" the merc leader hissed, pressing the barrel of a pistol into the back of his skull. Metres away, the only other remaining merc jumped on the broken carcass of the battlesuit, rocket launcher still in his hand. The merc gave a whoop of triumph and started poking around at the exposed operator cavity of the machine.

"Get the others to shut down their suits," Kotler ordered, his cold eyes glittering with satisfaction. "Tell them to show themselves or I'll shoot you right now."

*Everyone stand down,* Hack said, looking back to where Louise and May stood in the distance, still suited up, while Alex and Wei ran to catch up. *I can take care of this.*

*Yeah, looks like it,* Louise said.

Hack looked up at Kotler. "Two of you? Against the rest of them? You'd better run…if you want to live."

Kotler sneered. "I make the threats around here."

Hack shrugged. "Don't say I didn't warn you."

At that second the battlesuit sent him its final message: *Self-destruct ready… Activating…*

Atop the battlesuit, the merc looked up as a high-pitched alert sounded. Kotler turned fractionally as the merc shouted, "Sir, I think it's going to—"

The machine exploded, throwing its remains in all directions. Hack hit the ground and threw his hands over his face to protect his eyes.

He lay on his back for a moment, catching his breath as he looked at the sky. The storm clouds had passed and now there was blue up there. Rising to a sitting position, then to his feet, he looked around and saw Kotler's pistol lying in the mud. He picked it up and turned towards the merc, but saw that he would not need it. Kotler was lying face down in the mud, his body burned from where it had taken the full force of the explosion. With a deep breath he tossed the pistol far into the junk pile.

"Are you okay?" May asked, as she ran over, having climbed out of her battlesuit. She looked over at Kotler. "You got him."

"Yeah, I got him," Hack said quietly.

"He would have killed you," she said, taking his hand in hers. "He would have killed us both."

"I know. That doesn't make it any better though, does it?"

"Come on." She led him over to where the others were waiting and they all fussed about for a while before he convinced them he was okay.

"I can't believe it," Wei said, looking around the group. "We beat them."

Louise grinned from the open front of her battlesuit. "Yeah."

"It's not over yet," May reminded them. "We still have to get back to the power station if we're going to rescue Sarah. And now the mercs are out of the picture, the Entity will throw everything it has at us. The only way we can stop it is to destroy the hypersphere."

"Then we're going to need more battlesuits," Wei said, unable to keep the excitement from his voice. "Right?"

## 39

*Sarah awakes to early morning sunlight streaming through the gap between the window and the screen. Rising, she opens the screen to crisp dawn air and notices that at sometime in the night a new set of clothes has been placed next to the mattress. She picks them up to examine them: a black uniform fitted with multiple pockets that look designed to hold an array of tools or weapons. She finds the weapons wrapped up in a cloth case on the floor: throwing stars, knives, utility items such as a mini-torch, and a set of nunchaku. The uniform fits perfectly, designed to facilitate easy movement, while the soft material makes no noise as she moves experimentally around the room.*

*"What do you think of the outfit?" Daniel asks as she slips open the door.*

*Sarah smiles, remembering Alex's uniforms. "It's an improvement on the last one I was given, I guess." She delicately removes one of the shuriken throwing stars from the case. The edges are razor-sharp.*

*"Everything a budding ninja could want," Daniel says.*

*"It looks as if you've been planning all this for a long time."*

*Her father's face darkens. "You have no idea. Being in his place is like...an eternity."*

*Sarah looks at him and feels suddenly sad. "Has it been very bad for you here?"*

*"No," he replies. "Because I knew you would come."*

*She looks down. "Perhaps you've got too much faith in me. I'm not sure if I can use any of these weapons."*

*"Don't worry," he reassures her. "If you need to, you'll use them. And I haven't got too much faith in you. You're the only person to take on the Entity. I believe that more than anything else." He steps into the room and places his hands on her shoulders. "I know I wasn't there for you and Robert when you were younger, but neither of you*

*gave up on me. I promise when all this is over, I'll be a proper father to both of you."*

*Sarah smiles at him, seeing there are actually tears forming in his eyes. "I know, Dad."*

*Daniel steps away and coughs noisily. "Well, anyway… We move out in ten."*

*With that, he leaves her to finish getting dressed. Spreading out the weapons case on the floor, Sarah removes several of the stars and slips them into her pockets. She takes a couple of throwing knives and the torch, but leaves the rest.*

*In the next room she finds the family eating breakfast with Daniel. As she joins them, they look at her, nod and smile, but say nothing. When they finish the meal and the woman removes the bowls, Sarah leans over so she can whisper to her father.*

*"Do they know?"*

*He raises an eyebrow. "They know you're not part of this place. They've seen the different ones before."*

*"Are they…"*

*"Sleepers," he replies. "Just like me. Maybe not human, of course."*

*Sarah looks at him in confusion.*

*"The construct links all of the victims of the Entity's virus," Daniel explains. "From millions of different planets.*

There are billions upon billions of beings here. Only a few thousand from Earth, so far. We have to keep it that way."

"You're saying they're aliens?"

"Shh. They'll hear."

"But they don't…you know…look…"

"No tentacles and six heads?" Daniel asks wryly.

"Yeah."

"The construct is partly created from the memories of the individual," Daniel explains. "How it appears to you, might be different to me. And they appear to you as human, because that's what you expect."

"So I might look like I've got six heads to them?"

"I would say almost certainly."

"Then none of this is real?" Sarah asks again.

Daniel picks up one of the remaining breakfast bowls and places it in Sarah's hands. "Does that feel real? Did the rice taste real?"

She nods.

"Everything here is as real as it needs to be. The Entity makes it so."

"So if we get hurt here…"

"The damage will seem completely real to you. You can feel pain. You can die."

Sarah frowns. "Die?"

"Trust me," he says, "you don't want to die in the

construct. You'll fall into a kind of limbo. The link between you and the Entity will be severed, but you won't be returning to your body on Earth. Your physical form will grow old and die, while your mind will be trapped here for ever."

Sarah takes a moment to let that sink in. Somehow the unreality of the place – the Japanese setting, almost a copy of the images she'd seen in her karate books, and the presence of Daniel when he was really back in the sleeper casket at the HIDRA base – had convinced her that this was all some kind of a game. Ninja uniforms. Throwing stars. Back in the real world, her friends are fighting and probably dying without her.

"Are you okay?" Daniel asks, seeing the seriousness on her face.

"Yes," she replies. "I just feel like I haven't been thinking straight... I..."

"It's okay, Sarah. Just remember that the construct is designed to do that – lull you so the Entity can keep control over your mind. You must be mindful that this is not your reality at all times."

"How?"

"By fighting."

* * *

The streets of London were filled with the comatose bodies of men, women and children. Through the thunderstorm that had lashed the city they had lain, oblivious to the rain and cold, but now they began to rise…

All across the capital people flicked their eyes open and, staring blankly, they stood. To an observer they might have appeared like a set of dominoes that had been knocked over, simultaneously rising up again…

And they waited, as if for some command. Unnaturally unmoving…

Then…

They began to hum.

First just a few, but like a virus the noise spread from one person to another. Young and old, all made the same noise… The same tone…

They were one…

"What *is* that?" May said as a buzzing noise rose around the junkyard. It almost sounded like an engine of some sort, but the sound was unnaturally even. Louise levitated to the top of one of the stacks and looked around.

*It's the infected people,* she said. *They've all risen up and they're…humming.*

May looked at Hack questioningly, who was in the

process of checking over another of the battlesuits. They had five now – one for each of them. They'd need the advantage the suits provided if they were going up against the base defences.

"The Entity is booting up its slaves," Hack explained as he worked. "Like computers in a wireless network."

May said, "Then that means…"

"…they're probably about to attack."

Just then, Alex and Wei came running. "We've got trouble!" Alex yelled.

Behind them a line of people appeared, advancing slowly in a uniform progression. Each one of the people – be it a man, woman or child – had the same fixed expression. Each one was emitting the same low hum.

"What do they want?" May asked as they regrouped in the centre of the yard. A second line of people had entered from the other side of the yard and it was possible to hear the sound of others clambering over the corrugated iron fencing that surrounded the area. One of the men at the head of the first group picked up a rusty pipe as he approached. Others snatched up bricks, broken bottles, lumps of metal…

"I'll give you three guesses," Alex said. He and the others had formed into a circle facing out at the threat appearing from all around.

"I can take care of them," Wei said and a fireball appeared in his hands.

Alex turned to him and shook his head. "No. They're just being used by the Entity. We can't hurt them."

"The suits are ready," Hack said as the nearest group came within just a few metres. They clambered into the machines and Hack sent them hurried instructions as to how to use them, explaining the telepathic link between their minds and the suit controls.

The man with the pipe raised it above his head and ran at the nearest battlesuit, which was Wei's. As the man started smashing the pipe ineffectually against the leg of the machine, Wei stumbled back clumsily and almost went over.

"Be careful!" Hack snapped. "You'll crush one of them!"

The five children, made gigantic in the cumbersome robot suits, stumbled away from the approaching mob. The machines were designed for fighting and to protect the user, not to pacify crowds. Hack realized they were in serious danger of accidentally doing damage to the innocent people the Entity was using as its puppets as they swarmed ahead.

"Everyone, go high!" he commanded, leaping over a line of civilians in a single bound. As he touched down, he sprang again, hooked his metal claws into the side of one of the junk stacks and clambered to the very top. The others quickly got the idea, running and jumping onto high ground, away from the people crowding into the yard.

"What now?" May asked, crouching precariously atop one of the stacks and swivelling her head around.

Inside his suit, Hack brought up a scan of the city on the internal HUD – a holo-image highlighted Battersea Power Station in the distance.

"We keep moving," he said, leaping to another stack and then another. Bricks, metal and wood were thrown at him, but bounced off the hard exoskeleton of the battlesuit. The main thing was no one got hurt as he reached the outer wall of the yard, leaped onto the road beyond and then hauled himself up the side of a building. On the roof, he turned and waved to the others, who were watching him from their vantage points in the junkyard.

*Come on! Race you to the bad guys!*

40

*They say their thanks to the family and leave quietly by the back door to the house on the outskirts of the village. It's early, but already the main street is coming to life with men and women in work overalls going about their daily business. Suddenly Sarah feels conspicuous in the black uniform. Both she and Daniel look like fighters amidst the farmers. Out of place...*

*"Over there," Daniel says, nodding towards an open-top jeep standing at the other end of the street. They move towards the vehicle as quickly as possible. Sarah*

*notices that no one in the village meets their eyes.*

*They're afraid of us, she realizes. We're not like them. We're fighters.*

*Without warning, a woman only a few years older than herself steps around one of the buildings directly into Sarah's path. Taken aback, Sarah looks into the eyes of the woman – and sees only blankness there. The woman stares back at her with no comprehension, but equally does not move.*

"Come on," *Daniel says, taking Sarah's arm and leading her away.*

"Who was that?" *Sarah asks, looking back at the woman, who hasn't moved. She feels a strange fascination towards her.*

"She was another visitor here," *he says quietly as they reach the jeep.* "Like you."

"What do you mean, like me?" *Sarah asks. Daniel starts the jeep and they pull away from the village onto a bumpy dirt track leading down to the sea.*

"She came of her own free will so she could fight the Entity on its own turf," *Daniel explains.*

"So what happened to her? She's like the walking dead."

*They reach the end of the track and pull onto the sand.* "Like you, she had the power to take on the Entity at its *own game – a being with the psychic strength to actually defeat it. But she was not successful."*

*They have entered a bay surrounded on all sides by hills, providing some seclusion from the ocean beyond. The water of the bay is brilliant blue. The jeep heads towards an inflatable boat pulled up on the sand.*

*"What do you mean?" Sarah presses. "Not successful?"*

*"She fought the Entity. She lost."*

*"And so now she's stuck here for ever?"*

*"Or until someone shuts down the construct."*

*"Someone like me."*

*"That's right."*

*The jeep stops by the boat, an inflatable with two powerful outboard motors attached to the back. Sarah helps Daniel push it into the sea and they jump aboard. He angles the outboard on their boat down into the water and rips the starter cord. The engine roars into life and the boat powers across the bay. In less than a minute they pass a narrow inlet and are suddenly in the open sea.*

*"Where did you get all this stuff from?" Sarah asks her father. Sitting at the back of the boat, he looks like some guy out of an action movie.*

*"Friends," he says. "There's a large resistance movement. They've been training me ever since they*

found out I was your father. You're quite a celebrity, you know."

"Among the aliens?"

"Once in a while someone comes along with the ability to challenge the Entity. That's you. They sensed it after the Entity's meeting with you under the ice in Russia. The cost of bonding with so many beings – the Entity can't keep many secrets."

Sarah frowns, thinking it over. "So you've been living off my fame then?"

Daniel grins. "Free meals. All the military equipment and training I could use. It has been kinda cool."

"You're a big kid!"

Sarah grips the side of the inflatable boat as it bounces over the water. Daniel sends it on a course around the headland. As they round a jutting outcrop of rock, he points ahead.

"Look," he shouts over the engine and Sarah sees what he's pointing to...

Three giant structures rise from the sea just a few kilometres from the land. They look like oil rigs – made up of platforms sitting atop iron legs rising a hundred metres from the water. These platforms, however, are a maze of walkways, observation decks and buildings. Here and there it is possible to make out mounted machine guns...

satellite communication arrays...landing pads... But there is also an odd mix of Japanese-style wooden structures, twisted trees and vines hanging down from the structures... Massive, black birds circle both above and below the rigs...

"What are they?" Sarah asks.

"Unknown," Daniel replies. "They appeared in the construct the day you arrived, which makes me think we'll find the Entity in one of those things. Which one?"

Sarah gives him a confused look. "How should I know?" Then she remembers his earlier words: If you seek it out, it will be there. "The middle one."

Daniel nods approvingly and steers towards the central rig.

A whistling sound fills the air...

An explosion of water rises above the sea, just a few metres to the right of the boat. She looks towards the rigs again as they speed past. There is a flash from one of the mounted guns. A second explosion rocks the ocean, dead ahead this time, but Daniel expertly sends their boat around it.

More shells hit the ocean, creating a wall of flying water ahead of them.

"What do we do?" Sarah cries as the boat is almost capsized.

*"Swim!" Daniel yells.*

*He pushes her off the side of the boat. Hitting the water is like falling against concrete, then Sarah is sinking as the boat is destroyed with the* whumpf *of another shell. She gasps for breath. Daniel grabs her arm and pulls her towards the surface where they gulp air into their lungs for a few seconds, before he pushes them down again, away from the explosions hitting the surface all around.*

*Diving, he produces a silver tube that he places in her hand. Sarah watches as he takes another and puts it in his mouth – a mini breathing tank. Copying him, she sucks air from the mouthpiece and breathes out through the side of her mouth. Daniel looks at her and she gives the thumbs up to show it's okay.*

*Her hand in his, Sarah swims towards the rig…*

Hack and the others ran across London, jumping from one rooftop to another, powered by the hydraulic strength of the battlesuits. They made it into a race to see who would make it back to the enemy base – mainly to distract themselves from the thousands of slave humans lining the streets, looking up as they leaped across the gutters.

"I SEE YOU!" was the cry that greeted them wherever

they ran, along with the strangely inhuman humming of the masses – the signal that seemed to link them together under the control of the Entity. At the edge of a building on Clapham Road, Alex paused as the others leaped on, crashing across the tiled roofs of the shops opposite. He cast his gaze over the motionless crowd below – a throng of people looking up at him with one vision – their only purpose to relay information back to the Entity. *This is what we're fighting against,* he thought to himself. *This is what it would turn us into...*

*Keep up, Alex!* Louise called as the crowd began to throw missiles up at him. He jumped on.

A few minutes later Alex caught up with the others as they ran along the railway track towards the gasworks opposite the power station. Leaping onto the side, he used the hooked metal of the suit's feet and hands to claw his way up to the top of the highest structure. Here he stood, alongside the others, on the circular frame and looked out over the site of the power station.

The place was eerily still. No mercs moved around outside. The crowds of slave people had moved away from this area as well.

Hack opened the helmet of his battlesuit and took a breath of fresh air, as did the others. "It's quiet down there," he said. "Do you think they know we're—"

He stopped dead at a terrifying sight from the river beyond the power station. The five spider swarms were crossing the Thames, churning the water as they converged on the base.

"Yes, I think it's safe to assume they know we're here," Alex said as the swarms breached the side of the Thames. On dry land each swarm seemed to shrink suddenly, as if the millions of spiders were folding in on themselves. "What's happening?"

"I've seen this before," Hack said, remembering back on the island when the swarm had formed into a single spider. "The Entity is reconfiguring the spiders to protect the base."

Within seconds they had reformed into five gigantic spiders, each towering several storeys tall. Three of these spiders climbed the side of the power station, taking up positions around the open roof, while the other two scuttled round to the open ground at the front of the base.

Wei said what everyone was thinking: "Suddenly these battlesuits don't look so big."

## 41

By the time they reach the underside of the rig, Sarah's arms and legs are burning with fatigue, but she knows they cannot stop. The explosions have long since ceased on the surface of the water above. Either the gunners from the rig believe they have been killed or have realized their weapons are ineffective against an enemy approaching underwater.

Breaking the surface, Sarah and Daniel swim towards a platform at water level and clamber up the metal steps on the side. They crouch and Sarah looks up. The underside of the main rig platform is at least fifty metres above – accessible by ladders stretching up along the side of the four support legs.

Daniel removes the breather from his mouth and says, "Come on, we have to keep moving."

Sarah nods, although all she really wants to do is sit down and rest – preferably for a week. Instead, she runs to the nearest ladder and starts climbing, closely followed by Daniel.

"When we reach the top, let me take care of the guards," Daniel says behind her. "Your job is to find the Entity. It's somewhere up there."

They are halfway up the ladder when a shot rings out. A bullet ricochets off the metal rungs. A uniformed guard has appeared at the top of one of the ladders and is taking aim with a rifle again...

Daniel removes one of the shuriken and throws it with a single, swift motion. The star-shaped blade blurs through the air, hitting the guard dead in the chest. Sarah watches, wide-eyed, as the man falls all the way to the lower platform and bounces off into the sea.

"Keep moving!" Daniel hisses.

Sarah doubles her pace, her earlier fatigue forgotten, as more gunfire erupts from above. Daniel responds with volleys of throwing knives and stars, fired off with deadly *accuracy. More guards fall. Reaching the top, Sarah finds herself on an empty level with stairs leading up at one end – obviously to the upper areas of the rig. She instinctively knows that's where she has to head...*

*The Entity is waiting.*

*Movement to one side alerts her to the presence of a guard. She rolls, removing one of the throwing knives as she does so. The metal floor where she was just crouching lights up as bullets glance off. The guard aims again... She throws the knife, but it whistles past his head...*

*The guard's eyes bulge from the sockets as the end of a sword blade bursts from his chest, straight through his heart. The sword withdraws smoothly and the guard falls, revealing Daniel standing behind him, a full-length samurai sword in his hands.*

*"Sarah," he says urgently, going to her side as an alarm starts to howl. "Just go for the Entity. I've got your back."*

*With a nod, she runs for the stairs leading up, even as the guards come running from all directions...*

Up close, the newly formed spiders were massive. As Alex and the others ran across the hundred metres of open ground in front of the base, the two sentries on the ground raced towards them – their black front legs raised in the air as the others worked furiously, propelling them forward.

*I don't know if this is a good time to say this,* Wei said, *but I'm afraid of spiders.*

*We all are,* Louise replied. *Now.*

Alex was up front, so he reached their attackers first. One of the spiders swiped its leg at him, knocking his suit to the floor. Pinning him, it raised another leg high, clearly aiming to drive the ultra-sharp point right through the body of the battlesuit.

*No!* Louise leaped onto the spider's back and, wrapping the thick arms of the battlesuit around its thorax, yanked its head back. The spider howled with rage, red eyes blazing. Wei ran in and grabbed another leg, yanking it away as Alex rolled to safety. The spider hit the ground as its partner circled menacingly to one side. Wei drew back one giant foot of the battlesuit and brought it down on the head of the spider he and Louise had trapped. The blow didn't even make a dent.

*It's going to take more than this to defeat them,* Alex said. *Our suits are made out of iron. They're made out of alien metal, remember?*

The Chinese kid nodded his helmet and turned back to the spider Louise had pinned. Its eight legs flailed wildly, but she held firm.

*Get out of the way when I say,* Wei instructed, putting his hands together. *Now!*

Louise's battlesuit jumped back, releasing the spider as a beam of fire with the intensity of a laser burst from Wei's hands. The beam hit the spider in the head and burned through the incredibly hard matter. The machine thrashed on the ground, trembled mightily and then to everyone's surprise split into two, right down the middle. Louise and the others backed away as the two separate halves of the spider sprouted extra legs and scuttled back to regroup with the other sentry.

*Great,* Louise said. *How do we fight them?*

Everyone looked at Hack, who shook his head. *I don't know if we can.*

Over the side of the power station the other three spiders appeared and began to crawl down towards ground level. They moved slowly, deliberately – taking their time, as if knowing their prey wasn't going anywhere.

*Wait,* Alex said, remembering the clonebot. *Hack, do you think you could deliver a virus to these things?*

*Sure,* he replied. *If I had one.*

Alex continued, *Dr. Fincher said he was getting close to perfecting something that would shut down the nanites in these machines.*

*Whatever we do, we'd better make it fast,* Louise said,

looking around as the two smaller spiders circled to the back, cutting off their retreat. *I think they're gearing up for the kill.*

Alex nodded. *Hack, contact the HIDRA base and get a copy of the clonebot. The rest of you hold off the spiders for as long as possible.* He put his battlesuit down on one knee and placed the splayed fingers of both hands on the ground, like a runner preparing for a sprint start.

*What are you going to do?* Hack asked.

*I'm going after Sarah,* Alex replied as he powered forward, running directly at the spider blocking their path to the entrance of the power station. The spider rose up as he approached, but Wei blasted it back. Running past, Alex made the ramp of the station and carried on through the doors...

...into a volley of bullets fired from the platforms surrounding the interior of the base. Rolling to one side, he took cover behind a post as a rocket flew from a launcher in the hands of one of the mercs. The shell exploded against the wall. Alex looked round as the battlesuit HUD picked out seven remaining mercs taking cover at strategic locations inside the base. Major Bright crouched at the far end of the building, a weapon in his hands. And in the very centre of the base, next to the glowing hypersphere, stood Sarah.

Momentarily taken aback by the sight of Sarah standing out in the open, undefended, Alex emerged from his cover and looked at her. The mercs stopped firing as she raised her hand and walked towards him. He approached also, until they were standing just a couple of metres apart. In the suit, he towered over her.

*Sarah,* he said. *Are you all right?*

She looked up at him and nodded, expression impossible to read. Then she reached out and placed a hand on the arm of the battlesuit.

*Sarah, we have to—*

In a show of supernatural strength, she dug her fingers into the metal of the battlesuit and yanked the machine round. Alex gave a cry of shock as his suit was thrown across the floor of the base and came to a rest on its side before the hypersphere, which was now shining brilliant silver. Placing one hand against the ground, Alex pushed his battlesuit into a kneeling position and looked back at Sarah. She raised a hand and pointed directly at him. All around, the mercs took aim on his exposed position.

Alex shook his head at her. "Sarah, no."

"Kill him!" she yelled.

## 42

*The upper levels of the rig are made up of one chamber after another. They're like the rooms of a museum, crowded with glass display cases containing all manner of strange and wonderful sights: stuffed animals, some familiar, some completely alien; elaborate suits of armour, some designed for human body shapes, others sporting multiple arms, legs, or even heads; weaponry ranging from simple swords to guns to cruelly-shaped implements that look like a cross between the two.*

*The cases explode as Sarah runs through another*

*chamber. On the balconies above, guards are firing automatic weapons – strafing the room below indiscriminately. She dives for cover as another pane of glass shatters, showering her with shards. Inside the broken case a suit of samurai armour disintegrates as it is flayed with bullets. Behind her, Daniel dispatches another pair of guards with his sword, then starts fighting the enemy on ground level.*

*"Keep moving!" he yells, pointing to the far wall as he rips the sword through another guard's stomach. Sarah looks where he is indicating and sees a set of silver doors set into the wall. A lift.*

*Having seen it's an effective weapon, she grabs one of the samurai swords from the shattered case and runs for the lift at the other end of the floor. A few metres away, the doors begin to close, but she puts her head down and leaps through as they slide shut. Breathing heavily, she leans against the mirrored wall of the lift car as it begins to rise, shocked by her own reflection: drenched with sweat, hair matted from the sea, wild eyes, the sword clutched in both hands as if she would use it at a moment's notice. She hardly recognizes herself.*

Who am I? *she wonders.* To win this battle, what have I become?

*The lift slows...*

*...and the doors slide open...*

*...onto a blandly pristine hospital corridor. Stepping out of the lift, Sarah blinks at the surprising surroundings. The acrid smell of bleach in the air reminds her of other such places she's been in the past. The ICU where her mother died of cancer. Robert's sickbed at the HIDRA base. Even the white rows of caskets housing her father and the other sleepers.*

The Entity is trying to manipulate me, *she realizes.* Using my memories to throw me off balance.

*A dark-haired woman in a spotless uniform bearing the name* Nurse Bowen *appears at her side. Seemingly unworried by Sarah's general appearance and the fact she is holding a samurai sword in one hand, the nurse says,* "You're cutting it fine for visiting hours, you know."

*Sarah barely looks at her as she scans the closed doors along the corridor.* "Huh?"

"You're here to see your grandfather, I take it?"

"My grandfather?"

"He's in one of our private rooms," *the nurse says, gently taking Sarah's arm.* "I'll show you."

*Sarah allows herself to be led down the corridor to a numberless door.*

"Now, you must promise not to get him worked up," *the nurse says, opening the door.* "He needs his rest."

"Don't worry," Sarah replies. "I'll make sure he gets plenty of rest after this."

"That's nice, dear." The nurse backs away as Sarah slips into the room…

Inside, the room of her "grandfather" is as bland as they come: walls painted magnolia, brown curtains drawn over the window, a vase of wilting daffodils on the bedside table. In one corner a television on a bracket is showing a daytime soap with the sound turned down. Surrounding the bed, monitoring equipment flashes and bleeps, all linked up to the ancient man lying under the covers. As Sarah approaches he wakes from a half-sleep and looks at her in confusion for a moment, before recognizing her face.

"Ah, Sarah," he says. "You've finally come to visit me."

She tightens her grip on the handle of the sword, which feels suddenly massive and unwieldy – an alien weapon to her. In the confines of the cramped private room, it feels ridiculous to be standing there with it in her hand.

"Well, are you just going to stand there all day?" the old man asks, patting the side of the bed.

Self-consciously, Sarah approaches and sits on the mattress. After a second's consideration, she leans the sword against the bedside table, point down.

"You weren't seriously thinking of using that, were you?" the old man asks. "Look at me. I'm no threat to you."

She meets his eyes and says, "I'm not fooled by this. I know what you are."

The Entity smiles, yellowed teeth flashing. "I'm dying, Sarah. If you really want to kill me, all you have to do is pull out a few leads." He waves a hand around the machines monitoring his heart and lungs.

"You're not dying," she says. "This is an illusion. A trick."

"I wish it were. But I'm ancient, my dear. I was spreading out of my first galaxy when your world was still just a ball of dust forming in the void."

Sarah leans towards him, genuinely interested. "What are you?"

He shrugs his bony shoulders. "I remember…being like you once. Part of a species – a race of humanoids, not unlike your own. And like you and your friends, we evolved. Developed new powers. Augmented our bodies with machines. Eventually we developed beyond the stage of needing humanoid form altogether."

"What happened to the others of your race?"

The Entity waves a hand dismissively. "Without physical form they soon lost interest in the matters of this universe. They disappeared, one by one – migrated to parallel dimensions. Until I was the only one left."

"Why did you stay?"

"Because I saw all the suffering in the universe. Pain and despair spread across millions...billions of planets. For a time I merely watched, then I realized that it was within my power to put an end to that suffering."

Sarah shakes her head. "By turning people into slaves? By taking over their worlds?"

"By freeing them from the struggle of having to exist in an uncaring universe," the old man insists. "I look after them. Make sure they come to no harm. In my world no one dies in wars, or of disease, or of a broken heart."

"And what about those who don't want your protection?" Sara asks. "What happens to them?"

He gives her a hurt look. "They come to understand that it is for the best...in time."

"Or they die."

The old man sighs and lays a bony hand on hers. "I won't tell you I haven't made mistakes, Sarah. Which is why I need you. I am dying. I feel my consciousness stretched thin over worlds and galaxies...and so much time. Things are breaking down. Falling apart."

"And you expect me to help you keep control of your slaves?"

"What do you think will happen to the universe if I die? Your planet is young – just at the beginning of its association with me. Older civilizations came under my protection millions of years ago. It is all they know. If I cease to be, they will fall into chaos. It will be an apocalypse on a universal scale – a dark age that will last an eternity. Billions upon billions of life forms will die in agony and suffering. They cannot exist without me any more." He tightens his clawlike grip around Sarah's hand. "I need your potential, Sarah. Your youth. I've searched for millennia to find a being like you. Someone with the ability to replace me."

Repulsed, Sarah tries to pull her hand free, but he holds tight. "I'm nothing like you…"

"But you are," he insists. "Wouldn't you like to experience everything I have? To know all the worlds I know? I've sensed you trying to fight your destiny. Concerning yourself with the petty worries of your friends. Always putting them first." He rises in the bed and his voice becomes a hiss. "You're so much more than that. With my help you'll rule everything…"

Sarah eyes the sword leaning against the table. Sensing what she is thinking, the Entity changes tactic…

"Wait!" it hisses. "If you kill me you'll never find the cure to the virus afflicting your father and brother."

*Rather than snatching up the weapon, she looks back at him and the old man grins at his little triumph.*

*"What do I have to do?" Sarah asks finally.*

*Pushing himself up in the bed so he is in a sitting position, the old man points a withered finger at the bedside table. "In there."*

*Sarah opens the door and sees the Go board they played in the train lying there. She removes it and lays it down on the bed between them.*

*"Let's play a final game," the Entity says. "If you win, I'll give you the cure and let you take it back to your planet."*

*Sarah opens the bag of black and white stones, but the old man holds up a warning finger.*

*"But if I win... Well, you're going to be here for a very long time. Sure you want to take the risk?"*

*She turns the bag upside down on the bed, emptying the stones out.*

*"Let's play."*

Hack smashed the metal fist of his battlesuit hard into the head of the spider that had rushed him just seconds before. To the left and right, his companions were holding off the machines any way they could: Wei with fire,

Louise by using her telekinetic power to smash the metal arachnids into the ground, and May by making the ground crumble under their feet...

But the spiders just kept on coming.

Cut them in two with a laser and both halves formed into individual units and attacked again. Smash them so hard their legs flew off, bury them under the earth, hammer them down with the wrecks of vehicles... They always rose again... Renewed.

And Hack and his friends were getting weaker.

The battlesuits were getting gradually battered and slower in their reactions, like a computer being pushed to the edge of performance over a long period of time. Rather than being made of the super-strength matter of the hypersphere, they were formed from earthly metals. Vulnerable. It was only a matter of time before they shut down, and then they would truly be at the mercy of the Entity's machines.

The spider reared up on its hind legs and spat a glob of venomous liquid directly at the eye slits of Hack's helmet. Immediately the HUD flashed warnings, showing that the liquid was in fact acidic and slowly burning through the metal of the battlesuit. Retreating, Hack tried to wipe the liquid away with one hand, with limited success. The acid was sticky and immediately began to burn into the battlesuit's right hand. More warnings flashed on the HUD.

"Hello?" a human voice echoed in Hack's ears – the spider raced at him again. "Please identify yourself."

As the spider swiped the battlesuit's legs, Hack realized that it was the voice of the man Alex had instructed him to contact at HIDRA: Dr. Fincher. The thin-faced scientist appeared in a window on the HUD, looking with some confusion at the webcam of his computer. The battlesuit slammed onto its back and before Hack could move, the spider pounced upon him, pinning the arms and legs down.

"Dr. Fincher!" Hack told the image. "I'm with the superhuman team you sent into London…"

The spider drove a foreleg down with amazing force. It punctured the stomach of the suit and carried on right through, ripping out the back and into the hard earth. Now Hack's suit was impaled on the leg of the spider. Warnings blared inside and pain shot along Hack's side in sympathy with the suit.

"Are you okay?" Dr. Fincher said with concern. Whether the HIDRA scientist had visual or only audio from the link Hack had established with his personal computer (by bouncing a signal from the suit around three satellites, passing ten layers of encryption and then triggering an alert in the HIDRA UK labs to get the doctor to his workstation) he had no idea. The main thing was to get the clonebot.

"I need you to upload a copy of the weapon you've been developing," Hack said urgently. Above him, the spider repositioned itself and raised another leg...

"The clonebot? We're still testing—"

"No time!" Hack yelled as the second leg ripped through the suit, near the right arm. This time the sharpened foot tore not only the metal, but sliced through Hack's shoulder. He screamed in agony and felt warm blood stream into the operator cavity...

"Okay, okay!" Fincher exclaimed, hustling in the window to open up files on his computer.

"I don't have long," Hack gasped. The visual sensors of the battlesuit helmet finally failed as the acid burned them out. Now the acid began to eat through the inner shell of the helmet and he could see daylight through the cracks...

*WARNING... SHUTDOWN IMMINENT... HULL BREACH... MULTIPLE SECTOR FAIL...*

The breastplate of the battlesuit opened automatically as it went into the terminal stages of shutdown. Hack's helmet fell back as it disintegrated. The spider towered above him, even more threatening now that he lay exposed. He could have run, but he had to wait for the clonebot to upload...

"I'm almost there," Dr. Fincher said in the comm system. "Just give me a couple of minutes..."

*I don't have a couple of minutes,* Hack thought, gritting his teeth as the spider violently withdrew the leg that had sliced his shoulder and raised it high. Ready for another strike...

The air inside the base was alive with the crossfire of bullets. All seven remaining mercs were simultaneously emptying their machine guns at Alex. The battlesuit was holding up, but the sheer force of the bombardment was making it difficult to stand.

He threw himself forward, through the hot metal flying from all around, until he was under a platform upon which one group of mercs was positioned. Grabbing the nearest support in the battlesuit's massive hands he pulled... The iron post wrenched free of the concrete floor and the wall, and the platforms crashed down, spilling soldiers into the air. They landed hard on the floor of the power station.

Having taken out half of his attackers, Alex picked up one of the fallen platforms and swung it round his head, before hurling it across the top of the hypersphere. It sailed towards one of the control areas, where a group of four mercs were firing upon him. The men scattered too late to avoid being hit full on by the object. The platform upon which they were standing collapsed, taking out the lower levels with it.

Silence fell. Those mercs still able crawled for cover as Alex walked into the centre of the base once more. Sarah stood there, waiting for him.

"Impressive," she said, her voice oddly flat. "Most impressive."

Alex opened the helmet of the battlesuit. "Sarah," he said, keeping a distance between them. He didn't want her to grab him again. "I know you're in there somewhere. It's me, Alex."

The girl tilted her head to one side. "Alex?"

"That's right," he encouraged, listening for any show of emotion in her voice. Any sign of humanity beyond the Entity. "You remember me?"

She nodded. "I remember you, Alex. I remember everything Sarah Williams has experienced."

Alex shook his head. "No, Sarah—"

She pointed at the floor. "Kneel before me, Alex, and I will spare your life."

He backed away and flipped his helmet back on,

suddenly at a loss as to how to fight her. The Entity was in control of Sarah now, but what use was the battlesuit in this situation? He couldn't clobber her like he had the mercs. *But how could he get through to her?*

WHAM... WHAM... WHAM... WHAM...

Something with the force of a sledgehammer hit the outside of the suit repeatedly. Alex could actually feel the exterior metal being dented out of shape.

WHAM... WHAM... WHAM... WHAM...

He turned and saw Major Bright advancing, the biggest machine gun Alex had ever seen in his hands – a cannon ripped from the side of a wrecked Black Hawk. No normal man would be able to hold the giant weapon, but the major was hardly normal any more...

WHAM... WHAM... WHAM... WHAM...

Disorientated and unable to control the suit during the onslaught, Alex went to his knees. Bright smiled with satisfaction and let loose with the gun, ripping into the left arm of the suit. Alex pulled his arm back, just in time to avoid having it torn away.

WHAM... WHAM... WHAM... WHAM...

As the battlesuit began to disintegrate around him, Alex held up the remaining robot arm for mercy. It didn't come.

As Sarah looked on dispassionately, Major Bright pounded the battlesuit into a misshapen lump of metal. Inside, Alex screamed...

43

"Your friends are dying," the Entity informs her as it lays another black stone on the Go board. "They came to rescue you. A suicide mission."

As Sarah lays a white stone, she wants to call the old man a liar. To say that she instructed Alex to get the others away... But she knows they wouldn't do that. However much Alex tried to follow her order, she knows he wouldn't have deserted her.

"Ah, you see it's true," the Entity chuckles, laying another black. This move isolates four of her stones, which the old man plucks swiftly from the board and lays on the mattress. The pile of white stones is almost double the size of the blacks. She's losing.

"They put up a good fight, I'll give them that," the Entity continues, trying to distract her as she contemplates her next move. "But they're no match for my forces. The hypersphere portal is almost complete, by the way. No army on your planet will survive the infinite number of forces I will have at my disposal after that."

Sarah takes a white stone from her bag and is about to lay it...

"Of course, I could save them."

She pauses and looks at the old man questioningly.

"Just join with me and we'll put an end to all the fighting. Swiftly and cleanly."

Sarah lays the white stone, capturing two of her opponent's. A look of uncontrolled anger passes across the Entity's face.

"The longer you resist," it snaps, placing another stone, "the worse it will be on them. In fact, I'll make sure the one who came to save you...what's his name? Alex? I'll make sure he dies by your hand."

She wants to pick up the board and smash it across his face. But she remembers the sessions with Commander Craig in the sparring room of the Ulysses. Losing control is the first step towards losing completely, *he always told her.*

*Taking a deep breath, Sarah calms herself...*

*And lays another stone...*

*The game goes on...*

The spider had impaled Hack's suit once more, this time narrowly missing his neck. The machine's control systems had shut down completely, but with his power Hack was managing to keep in contact with Fincher via the uplink. It was the only hope he had.

"How much longer?" he asked into the comm. He'd lost visuals with the doctor since the helmet had fallen apart, but he could hear.

"Almost there," Fincher replied. "Just preparing the data packet."

The spider withdrew its foot and raised it again – this time for the true killing blow.

"Doctor!" Hack cried.

"It's there!" Fincher exclaimed.

Hack immediately sensed the data upload to what remained of the suit's internal drives. As the spider leg descended, he forced the arm of the battlesuit to raise one last time...and caught it by the foot. The spider howled, but the battlesuit fingers held it firmly.

Transferring the clonebot into his head in a nanosecond, Hack connected with the machine that was attacking him and passed on the program. He had the briefest sensation of the virus spreading from one microscopic organism in the machine to another, before the spider ripped its leg back, pulling the arm off the battlesuit in the process.

Pushing himself out of the shattered suit, Hack stumbled away as the spider smashed its leg down again, breaking the suit in two. The spider rose up and turned to face him now he was exposed and out in the open. In the background he saw Louise, Wei and May fighting their own desperate battles – their suits impaled and shattered as his had been. Turning his attention back to the spider, he held his ground as it approached, pincer teeth snapping for an easy kill…

But it didn't come.

There was a crack, like the sound of a brittle twig breaking, and the spider listed to one side. Two of its legs had simply snapped in the middle. The spider half-turned, as if surprised by the event, and in doing so snapped off two legs on the other side. Unsupported, the machine's abdomen crashed to the ground and split in two. Then, in a sudden chain reaction, the entire body of the spider began to crumble into dust.

Hack grinned, sensing the clonebot virus spreading from one nanite to another within the machine's structure – the order to shut down spreading like an unstoppable plague. In less than ten seconds, the spider was no more than a pile of black dust that began to blow away in the wind.

The rest of the spiders stopped attacking the others in that moment and, seeing the fate of their companion, turned to face Hack. They scuttled forward to make a joint attack.

Flexing his fingers – feeling the power in them – he ran to meet the remaining spiders...


The outer shell of Alex's battlesuit had become little more than a battered sheet of metal, but somehow it managed to deflect the rounds from the oversized machine gun in Major Bright's arms until the chamber clicked empty. Tossing the spent weapon to one side, Bright looked round at Sarah, who had been observing the scene without emotion.

"Let me show you how I deal with my enemies," Bright said and strode across to where Alex was kneeling. He placed his hands on either side of the battlesuit helmet and, with a violent twist, wrenched it free, throwing it across the base.

"Hi there," he said and took Alex's head in both hands. "I don't normally kill children... But for you and your friends, I'm going to make an exception."

He began to exert pressure on Alex's skull – a pressure that increased slowly until it felt like a vice closing around his head.

"Stop!"

Bright groaned in frustration as Sarah advanced towards them.

"Release him. I want to kill him with Sarah Williams's hands."

The major's annoyance at the interruption gave way to a look of amusement. "Ouch. That's cold." He released the boy, who fell back heavily. "All yours."

The suit opened and Alex pushed himself out, bruised arms and legs barely working. Sarah moved in swiftly...

"Sarah, no—"

His words choked as she grabbed his throat, crushing his windpipe.

"I told you," she spat, "Sarah Williams is gone. You obey me now."

Alex grabbed at her arm, but the grip was unbreakable. Stars exploded before his eyes as the oxygen to his brain was cut off. "I know you're in there… Sarah…"

The doors at the end of the base smashed open as one of the spiders crashed through. The machine staggered left and right, as if disorientated… Then collapsed on the floor, where it immediately disintegrated…

Hack walked through the opening as the dust remains of the machines blew away on the wind. Louise, Wei and May appeared behind him protectively – still wearing the battered remnants of their suits.

Major Bright tapped Sarah, who had not taken her eyes from Alex, on the shoulder. "Hey. If you've finished strangling the kid, we've got problems."

Sarah looked round, as if surprised to see the other children. "They defeated my spiders."

"No, really?" Bright said.

Louise stepped in front of Hack, flipped back her helmet and pointed a finger at Sarah. "Let him go!"

Sarah released her grip on his neck and Alex fell to his knees, gasping for breath. May and Wei moved to Louise's side. The younger girl gave them each a nod and then looked back at Bright and Sarah.

"Get them."

As the kids in the remaining battlesuits ran at them, Sarah casually opened her hands. There was a rush of air and the suits disintegrated into a million tiny shards of metal that flew out in all directions around the base. Louise and the others, stripped of their protection, dropped to the ground. Sarah glanced at Major Bright.

"Let me show you how *I* deal with my enemies."

Blue electricity sprang from her fingers, hitting all the children simultaneously. They fell to their knees, faces twisted with pain, unable to fight back or even flee…

*"This game is almost over," the Entity says, laying its penultimate stone on the Go board. "You have lost. As have your friends."*

*Sarah looks into the old man's evil, black eyes. "It's not over until I say it is." She removes her last stone from the bag and lays it down, isolating a group of the Entity's stones. She plucks then from the board and lays them on the bed. The two piles of captured stones are even.*

*"This is a draw. So what now?"*

*The Entity shakes its head and, to her surprise, produces another black stone from its bag. "But I still have a piece to play." It lays it down, taking a final white and adding it to the pile. The Entity's leering smile widens.*

*"You've lost…"*

\* \* \*

Alex held up a hand against the electricity surging over him, but it was no use. The sickening smell of singeing hair was in the air all around. Then, abruptly, the agony ceased.

Sarah lowered her hands and looked around the beaten children. Louise, Wei, Hack and May lay where they had fallen, paralysed by the after-effects of the electrical blast. Sarah turned to the hypersphere and fired off a bolt of electricity. The silver sphere immediately began to turn and then fall in on itself, revealing a tunnel stretching down…for ever.

*She's opened the portal,* Hack said weakly in Alex's head.

Alex tried to move, but Sarah grabbed him by the shoulder and lifted him to his feet with supernatural strength.

"Sarah, don't do this," Alex begged as she dragged him towards the opening of the portal. Up close, he could see the silvery sides of the tunnel rotating and feel an uncanny pull – almost like a gravitational attraction to the thing. "Sarah, please."

The girl tightened her grip on his shoulders, digging her fingers in until he cried out. "I'm going to send you a long way away, Alex. Perhaps when your friends see what happens to you inside the portal, they'll realize that surrender is the best option."

With the last of his strength, Alex attempted to pull away, but it was no use. Sarah pulled him to the edge of the gap in reality that the hypersphere had become. But on the threshold she paused...

*"Wait!" Sarah exclaims as the Entity makes to pack up the board, suddenly remembering something important... "I have one last move."*

*The old man stops his hand and looks at her. "Not possible."*

*Sarah reaches inside her pocket and retrieves the white stone Daniel gave her back on the train...*

*She lays it on the board...capturing two of her opponent's stones...*

*"I win," she says. In the centre of the Go board, the polished white surface of the stone shines, becoming a brilliant point of light between them. The Entity grabs Sarah's arm, digging its nails into her flesh.*

*"Cheat!" it hisses, voice full of bile.*

*Sarah wrenches her arm free, drawing blood as the nails rake her skin. "Since when did you fight fair? You played with one extra stone and so did I! Now give me the cure."*

*The Go board is engulfed in white light now, so brilliant*

*it is impossible to look at directly. The Entity cringes back in the bed, away from the brightness. Sarah grabs the handle of the samurai sword and rises swiftly. The light is so intense now it is almost impossible to see the bed, but she can make out the Entity's black eyes staring at her in rage.*

*"I cannot be defeated!"*

*"Let's see about that." Sarah holds the sword handle in both hands and brings the blade down, severing the leads and tubes connecting the old man to the machines. There is a howl from the bed and warning lights flash. Sarah raises the sword again and strikes a second blow, this time cutting the heart monitors in half. They explode in showers of sparks.*

*"Noooooooooooooooo!"*

*It is the Entity – screaming for its life. The door to the room bursts open and the nurse flies in, a knife in her hand. Sarah barely looks round, sweeping the sword back with her right arm as if she has been using it all her life. The blade slices through Nurse Bowen's neck and she dissolves into nothingness... Sarah brings the sword back, raises it high... And advances on the bed for the killing blow...*

*"You cannot destroy me!" the Entity screams. "The universe needs me!"*

"The universe needs you?" Sarah says. "You're nothing but a cancer. And I'm going to cut you away. Give me the cure right now, or I will destroy you."

The Entity cackles through its pain. "You won't do it. You wouldn't dare..."

Sarah swipes the blade down, cutting through the light, the bedclothes...

The room explodes in all directions...

Suddenly the floor and walls and ceiling are gone, replaced by the blackness of the void. But there is also the Entity. It is no longer a thing of light, but an insect – its true form. Its bloated body is dark with infections, while its massive limbs hang uselessly, too weak to support the overgrown bulk. As she falls towards it, the creature's eyes look up at her.

She angles the blade down and pierces the monster's brain...

The body of the Entity splits along the middle from one end to another. Its abdomen spills dust across the emptiness of the void, choking and engulfing Sarah, blotting out everything. She fights against the tide, sensing what remains of the alien consciousness as it is torn apart.

"Give me the cure!" she screams. "Give it to me!"

The Entity makes contact with her one last time. It says one word...

534

*"Never."*

*"No!"* she cries trying to hold its shattered consciousness together, sifting the mass of memories, twisted thoughts and desires. As she does so she becomes aware of her own body – so very far away in another dimension. Going into freefall, she senses Alex and the others, in desperate need of help and diverts all her power towards one final act...

"What's the hold-up?" Major Bright demanded, pushing Sarah aside in order to throw the boy into the portal himself. The girl turned as he pulled Alex from her grasp.

"Leave him alone."

Something in her tone made him stop and look round. His eyes widened as he saw something in her expression. Something different.

*Something human.*

He snatched his pistol from his belt and brought it round. Sarah was too fast, however, catching his hand in hers. She squeezed...

...and every bone in his hand broke.

"Arrrrgh," Bright gasped, releasing Alex and grabbing at Sarah with his other hand. She caught his wrist, giving it a violent twist. The arm dislocated with a sickening pop. Major Bright's eyes rolled into his skull and he sank to his knees. Somehow he managed to stay conscious, however, fighting the incredible pain. His mouth moved…

"How?"

"This is for Commander Craig," Sarah said as she released him. She looked at Louise and gave a command.

*Put him in the portal.*

With that, she collapsed to the ground. Bright staggered to his feet, both arms hanging uselessly at his side. He looked around wildly, seeking an escape route.

"Bright!" Louise yelled at him, rising into a crouch and holding out her hand. "Where do you think you're going?"

The major groaned and turned to face the girl. Preparing for the inevitable, he pulled his shoulders back and straightened into a defiant military posture. His mouth twisted into a final, contemptuous sneer.

"Bloody kids."

Louise hit him with every drop of telekinetic power she had. The major was lifted from his feet and thrown backwards. For a split section it was possible to see him caught in the mouth of the portal, being stretched and torn apart by the massive forces within. His dying screams were loud enough to be heard above the maelstrom...

...then an explosion within the tunnel itself shook the power station a second time. The mouth of the portal became a vacuum, sucking in everything from all around. Bricks, fallen weapons, computer components, torn sections of metal – all flew into the gaping hole. Alex leaped across the mouth of the portal and threw himself on the unconscious Sarah, saving her from being caught up in the vacuum. A few metres away, Louise and the others clung onto anything that wouldn't move to stop themselves from being pulled in.

*Everyone, get out of here!* Alex cried out. *Louise, help them!*

Using the last of her strength to fight against the forces pulling them towards the portal, Louise managed to stand. She walked slowly to where Wei was clinging onto a post and took his hand. As she led him over to Hack and May, she looked round at Alex, holding on to Sarah below the mouth of the portal.

*What about you?* she cried out.

Alex looked up and shook his head. *Get the others away! You can't come any closer.*

Watching Louise lead the others towards the gap in the wall, Alex turned back to Sarah and shook her roughly.

*Sarah, wake up!*

She did not respond. Above them the portal's inexorable force continued to draw in everything in the surrounding area. A section of wall crumpled and flew towards the mouth, bricks detaching and whizzing past their heads like missiles. Alex shook her again.

*Sarah! I'm not leaving you!*

**44**

*She feels like she has been falling for centuries. All around her, the dying embers of the Entity are slowly losing their light and soon there will only be darkness. A voice splits the silence...*

Sarah, wake up!

*She wants it to stop... To leave her alone for ever in the dark and stillness of the void...*

Sarah! I'm not leaving you!

*A light appears in the distance and she suddenly knows that she must go towards it – to fight the numbing effect of the void. Clawing her way through the tide of choking ash, she finds the light, grabs it and pulls it open...*

*With a rushing sensation, she falls out of the darkness and onto the floor of the hospital room again. The walls are black with soot now, the tiled floor misshapen and cracked. Pushing herself up, she flies through the door and out into the corridor as the ceiling begins to cave in.*

*The construct is falling apart.*

*Ahead, the lift doors are open, but there is no car – only an empty shaft. She leaps through and falls as the level above collapses. Catching the thick metal support cable running down, she slides – ignoring the tearing on the flesh of her hands – and hits the roof of the lift...*

*Above, the lift shaft crumples and folds in on itself.*

*Kicking open the emergency hatch, Sarah slides through, hits the ground and starts running. The museum chamber is littered with the bodies of dead guards, weapons still in their hands. She leaps over them, runs down the steps and out onto the platform with the ladders leading down...*

*The rig shudders and tilts violently to one side.*

*Sarah runs past the nearest ladder, jumps onto the rail surrounding the edge of the platform and leaps off. As she falls, she manages to turn herself in the air, stretch out her body and execute a dive into the sea. The height is still enough to make the impact so hard it almost knocks her out. Stunned and gasping for breath, she fights to the surface in time to see the legs of the rig collapse and the upper platforms crash down towards the ocean.*

*In desperation, Sarah turns and swims as the platform hits the sea, triggering a mini-tsunami that rushes over her, obliterating everything...*

Outside the power station, Louise and the others turned back to see the portal dragging everything inside, like the mouth of a black hole. Directly beneath the swirling force, Alex huddled over the unconscious body of Sarah.

"We have to go back for them!" Louise cried, moving back towards the ramp.

Hack grabbed her arms and held her firm. "No! Nothing can survive in there!"

"We have to get further back," May said, looking up at the four giant chimney stacks. Tiles were beginning to fly off into the middle of the station and it was only a matter of time before they came down too.

*Sarah!* Louise cried out.

\* \* \*

*She opens her eyes, aware of water rushing around her face and sand against her cheek. Someone takes her arm and lifts her to her feet. Disorientated, she looks around and finds she's standing on a beach – no doubt where she was washed after the wave hit. Out to sea, only one of the rigs remains, and as she watches, it crashes down, exploding as it hits the water. Sarah looks at the person who lifted her from the sand.*

*Daniel.*

*"You made it," she says.*

*He smiles at her as other people approach across the sand – men, woman and children she's never seen before. There are hundreds of them, maybe thousands. Overhead the sky flickers, momentarily, like a glitch in the picture on an LCD screen.*

*"What's happening?" she asks.*

*"We're holding the construct together for as long as we can," her father replies. "It will be the last time many of us can communicate."*

*"Who are they all?" Sarah asks.*

*"Beings from many worlds, spread across the universe. All places that the Entity enslaved over time. Now they're free." His face darkens. "But they're also alone."*

*"They used the construct to communicate," Sarah says and he nods. "Before I killed it, the Entity said that*

billions would die without its protection. Have I done the right thing?"

Daniel lays a hand on her shoulder. "The life that the Entity gave its slaves was no existence at all. The road ahead will be hard for many of them. But they've chosen freedom."

"I didn't get the cure for the fall virus."

Daniel takes her hand and presses his other palm against her lower arm. For a moment there is a burning sensation. When he removes his hand, she seems symbols and numbers on her skin, like a tattoo.

"They gave me this formula," he explains. "It will stop the infection from the spider bites. With some modification it can also be used to combat the original fall virus. The HIDRA scientists should have the technology to modify it for humans."

Sarah runs her fingers over the markings on her arm. "But how did they get this?"

"Many of these beings have been trapped in the construct for a very long time – linked into the Entity's consciousness. They've known where to find the cure, but the Entity has always been too strong – guarded it too closely. That all changed when you started fighting it back there. And when you killed it, all the doors were opened." Daniel places a hand on her shoulder. "Use the formula,

*Sarah. Use it to save Robert. Use it to save us all."*

*Sarah looks up at him as the sky begins to dim. "I'll bring you back, Dad. I won't give up."*

*"I know," he says, stepping back as darkness spreads across the sand, hiding the faces of the others.*

*He fades into the darkness and Sarah has the briefest sensation, like you get when you've just fallen asleep, like a sudden sensation of falling...*

...back into her body, lying on the cold, hard concrete floor of the base. Alex was crouched over her as a storm raged all around. Above, the portal was about to swallow the entire base.

"Sarah!" he cried, all sound lost in the howling wind.

Grabbing his shoulder, she pulled herself up and was immediately caught in the force of the portal. The gaping hole in reality beckoned, ready to engulf them both. She raised her hand and summoned the residual power left behind by the Entity.

With a cracking sound, the portal began to shrink, closing up like the aperture of a camera until it was only a few centimetres wide. Then it simply disappeared.

Immediately, the howling ceased and silence fell over the base. She looked at Alex and smiled, who was looking back at her with a stunned expression.

"You called me back," she said.

He opened his mouth to say something, but stopped with a gasp. One of the massive chimneys, weakened by the portal, was finally falling – directly towards them...

Just metres above them and disintegrating as it fell, the chimney simply stopped. The broken bricks, tiles and general debris simply hung in the air – in suspended animation. With wide eyes, Alex looked around the interior of the base. Projectiles hovered in space, unmoving. It was as if someone had taken a photograph of the destruction at the point of total collapse – and that photograph had frozen reality.

"I don't believe it," he whispered, as if afraid speaking too loud would bring the power station crashing down around them like a pack of cards. Sarah slipped her hand into his and they rose slowly to their feet.

"Are you doing this?" he asked as she led him towards the open front wall of the station.

"A little something left over from the Entity," she replied, ducking under a wooden beam hanging across their path – suspended by nothing.

"Cool," he said, voice hoarse. "Can we run now?"

"Yeah."

They ran.

"Get back!" Alex ordered Louise and the others as they tore down the ramp. "The whole place is coming down!"

They dashed into the empty space in front of the power station and only when they were at a safe distance, turned to look. The four chimneys were in the process of coming down, smashing through the remaining walls of the structure. The picture was frozen just a few seconds before the final destruction. There was something frigidly beautiful about the scene.

"Weird," Wei said.

"Sarah, it's you?" Louise asked, looking at the older girl.

Sarah stroked a hand through Louise's hair. "Yes. Thanks for not giving up on me."

"Look!" Wei exclaimed, pointing across the Thames. In the distance, four objects had appeared in the sky: hovercopters bearing the HIDRA logo. As they approached, Sarah looked down at the markings on her lower arm. Alex noticed them too.

"What's that?"

"I'm not sure," she replied. "A way to save Robert and the others, I hope."

The hovercopters made a wide pass around the half-destroyed building and landed on an open stretch of ground. As the children ran to meet them, Rachel Andersen emerged from the lead vehicle. HIDRA marines fanned out to secure the area.

"Is everyone okay?" she asked.

"We need to get Nestor and Octavio," Louise said, jumping into the back of the hovercopter. "We left them along the river."

Rachel nodded and looked at Sarah. "Is it over?"

Sarah took a look back at the remains of the power station and closed her eyes, letting go of the last of the alien consciousness that had invaded her soul. With a mighty crashing of bricks and mortar falling, the four chimneys fell into the building, sending up a cloud of dust that would be seen for kilometres. All that remained of the base, the hypersphere, Major Bright and his men was buried for ever under the rubble.

"It is now," she replied.

## 45

Octavio groaned and shifted in his hospital bed. Licking his parched lips, he opened his eyes and squinted against the light.

"Sleeping beauty's awake," said Nestor, who was lying in the bed next to him.

"About time," Robert added from the other side.

Octavio looked at them in confusion, then at the drip in his arm and the monitoring equipment surrounding their beds on the medical level of the HIDRA base. "What happened?"

"You were being a hero, remember?" Nestor said wryly.

"Oh, yeah," Octavio said, touching his fingers to the point on his neck where the spiders had bitten. The flesh was now all but healed over. "That didn't work out so well."

"It worked well enough," Sarah said from the door of the room where she had appeared a second before. "You bought us the time we needed to get to the base."

Octavio raised his eyebrows at Nestor. "See, we did all the heavy lifting as usual." Then he had a thought. "What happened to my Kawasaki?"

Sarah walked in and stood by Robert's bedside. "Sorry, we didn't have time to pick it up when we went looking for you. There were about three million other infected people to take care of. You're lucky we found you so soon."

"Thanks."

Sarah examined her brother's neck, which now showed only the slightest discolouration. "The infection is receding nicely. How are you feeling?"

"I'm fine!" Robert said under his breath. "Stop fussing over me!"

"Okay," Sarah said, backing off a little.

"You can fuss over me, if you want," Octavio said and Nestor laughed.

Sarah gave him an unimpressed look. "I'll send in the male nurse on my way out." She kissed Robert on the forehead and moved back to the doorway. She paused there to look back at Nestor and Octavio. "Thank you. Both of you."

For once Octavio didn't have a smart reply. Nestor smiled and nodded at her.

"And you," she said, speaking to Robert, "no more sneaking out of your bed. The nurses tell me everything that goes on down here."

Robert rolled his eyes.

"Hey!" Octavio said as Sarah left, noticing the strange markings on her arm. "Since when did she get a tat?"

In the days following the defeat of the Entity, the meeting room had become a kind of open area for personnel passing by wanting to catch up on events in the capital. The wall screens were on constantly, broadcasting feeds from multiple news sources. The BBC was showing aerial footage of the devastated site of Battersea Power Station – now a cordoned-off high security zone surrounded by tanks. Sky News had a story about the humanitarian operation around the city. Amid a sea of temporary medical tents, a reporter was talking to doctors administering injections to infected civilians. Al Jazeera was broadcasting a press statement by the Prime Minister, talking about the clean-up operation.

Sarah entered and went over to Alex, who was seated at the conference table, newspapers spread out before him.

"What's new?" she asked.

"Nothing," Alex replied. "They've been showing the same footage for hours. There was this though." He pressed a remote and a recording of a news story began to play: Marlon Good, head of software giant Goodware Inc., had been found wandering in a confused state along the Thames. The reporter stated that he was currently being held for questioning in relation to the London attack. Footage showed him being led into a van between two police officers. His suit was grimy and tattered, his eyes wide and staring and he was clutching a single object in his hands: a metal collar which matched one around his neck. Good appeared to be saying something to himself over and over again as he was pushed into the van.

"I was wondering what happened to him," Sarah said.

"How are the patients?"

"Doing well. The antidote has been a success and

Fincher is working on a version to treat the previous fall virus victims."

"What are you going to do with that?" Alex asked, meaning the mysterious symbols that had appeared on her arm following the incident with the Entity. Upon their return to the base, Dr. Fincher had instantly recognized them as instructions for the creation of a chemical compound. Sarah had insisted the compound would be a cure for the strain of the fall virus in the spider bites and she'd been right.

She ran her fingers over the symbols on her arm and remembered her last moments in the construct, standing with Daniel and the strangers on the beach. She wondered what was happening to all those beings on all those other worlds now they were finally free of the Entity. "I don't know," she said. "I'm kinda getting used to them."

"You should see some of the tattoos the HIDRA grunts rock up with after a weekend on the town," Lt. Kaminski said, appearing in the doorway. "That's nothing."

Sarah smiled and looked at the screens, her attention caught as one by one they flicked to the same image: blurry footage that looked as if it had been taken with a handheld camera. The scrolling titles below the BBC screen read: *BREAKING NEWS – leaked video footage of "superhuman" team responsible for saving London.*

"Oh, damn," Kaminski said quietly as they watched the twenty-second movie play out. It had clearly been taken with some kind of distance lens and showed the hovercopters touching down on the runway at the HIDRA base. The image zoomed in to show Sarah and the others, less than an hour after their defeat of the Entity and looking grimy and worn-out, emerge from the machines and be escorted into waiting ambulances.

The screens kept on playing the video in a loop, either full screen or as an insert while people talked in the studios. Images of Major Bright (*"Rogue military commander implicated in city assault"*) appeared intermittently. One channel had isolated Sarah, Alex and Louise's faces from the video and had them superimposed in the background with the caption *"Friends or foes?"*

"Well, this is going to be a little bit more difficult to cover up than the last one," Alex said.

Sarah nodded. "They know who we are now."

"And they'll start demanding answers," Kaminski said. "God knows what we're going to tell them."

"How about the truth?" Alex suggested.

"I wish it was that simple," Kaminski replied, before disappearing down the corridor. Alex shrugged and looked at Sarah.

"Perhaps it's not a bad thing," he said. "People should know what happened. What almost became of the world."

Sarah didn't take her eyes from the screen. "Maybe there are some things they're better off not knowing."

"I don't believe that."

She looked round at him. "Well. I guess we'll soon find out, won't we?"

Alex nodded, then said, "There was just one thing I wanted to ask you…"

"Yes."

"Back in the power station, when you kissed me…"

"When I transferred the information about how to fly the helicopter to you," Sarah corrected. "We had to be in physical contact for me to be able to do that."

"Right," Alex said. "I was wondering why you didn't just grab my hand or something."

Sarah coughed. "Well, I thought…it seemed the easiest way to get your attention. I needed you focused. Did you mind?"

"No! It was great!"

"Great?"

"I mean, it was very effective… As a means of transferring information."

They sat in silence for a moment.

Alex finally said, "If you'd ever like to…um…"

"Transfer information?"

"Yes. If you'd ever like to transfer information again, I wouldn't mind. I mean, that would be fine by me."

Sarah gave him a quick glance. "I'm sure it would."

"If you wouldn't mind, that is."

She thought for a moment and then smiled. Their enemies were defeated. Her friends were safe. Maybe it was time, like Commander Craig had told her that last day on the *Ulysses*, to stop worrying so much.

"No," she said. "I don't think I'd mind at all."


Hack and May walked across the runway towards the private jet sitting ready on the tarmac. What few items of luggage she had were already loaded on board and the engines were humming, ready for the flight that would carry her back to Australia – and her parents. Unlike the other kids, May had been kidnapped and she had a family to return to. It was time to go home.

A little distance from the plane, they stopped. May rubbed her hands together and blew on them.

"I'm not going to miss this cold," she said.

Hack grinned. "Tell me about it. You'd think a country this freezing would actually have decent central heating. But, oh no..."

She laughed, but then became serious. "You can come with me, Hack. Mum and Dad said they want to meet you. We have a spare room where you can stay for as long as you want. And it's summer in Western Australia right now. Beaches, barbecues. I'll teach you how to surf."

Hack thought it over for about the hundredth time. Then he shook his head. "I don't know what it is, but I feel like I've still got stuff to do here."

"What about your grandfather? Isn't he going to miss you?"

Hack laughed. "He's flying out next week. First time he's been off his island in about fifty years. I think he's quite excited about it."

May laughed and said, "Try to look after yourself, huh? I won't be around to patch up any cuts and bruises in future."

"Yeah."

Behind them the sound of the jet engines rose. They embraced hastily and May ran towards the plane. Hack waved to her as she went up the steps, but she didn't look round – mainly, he sensed, because she didn't want him to see the tears in her eyes.

A few minutes later the jet blasted into the morning sky as Hack watched from the edge of the runway. He followed its path until it was just a speck in the distance, eventually becoming aware of someone standing beside him.

*Aren't you supposed to be in sickbay?* he asked, glancing at Robert.

*By the time they miss me, I'll be back. Are you okay?*

Hack nodded and they started back towards the main buildings of the base. "I never thanked you properly for saving us," he said as they walked. "May and I owe you our lives."

Robert shrugged as if it was nothing. Then he said, "Well, there is one way you can pay me back."

"Yeah?" Hack said.

"I've been stuck on the lower dungeon level of *Portal War* for the last two months—"

"Trying to find the proton shield?"

"Yeah! How did you guess?"

Hack shook his head. "All the newbs go looking for that one..."

"Yeah... Wait a minute. *Are you calling me a newb?*"

"Yeah, I'm calling you a newb. Everyone knows the proton shield isn't in the dungeon. Look, you have to double back to the control room on level 5 and... It's probably easiest if I just show you...*newb...*"

*   *   *

The doors to the sealed sleeper chamber opened with a hiss and a warning light flashed red on the wall as the monitored temperature within began to rise. Dr. Fincher and Sarah passed through quickly and they slid closed again. Lights illuminated automatically, showing the rows upon rows of caskets containing victims of the original fall virus outbreaks. They stepped up to the raised platform.

"Patient number 345," Fincher said into the control panel and the robotic arms went to work, retrieving the chosen casket and carrying it towards the platform.

Sarah stepped forward and checked the window, confirming that it was her father, Daniel. The read-outs on the side indicated a perfectly stable coma, as always. Dr. Fincher laid out an aluminium case on the panel and flipped the lid, revealing a syringe gun and vials of liquid. He slotted one of the vials into the gun.

"Are you sure you want to do this, Sarah?" he asked. "There are plenty of other patients whose families have given us research permission. We don't know how your antidote is going to affect victims of the original fall virus, or even if it will have any result at all."

To answer his question, Sarah pressed the release code on the side of the casket. Magnetic locks shot open and the lid rose slowly, revealing her father lying inside. He was draped in a sheet, covering the sensors attached to his body. She reached out and touched his hand.

"It's what Daniel would have wanted," she said. "He never ran away from a fight."

Fincher nodded and offered her the gun. "Would you like to do the honours?"

Sarah took the instrument and placed it against Daniel's upper arm where she knew the vein was.

"Come back to us, Dad," Sarah said as she pulled the trigger.

# Epilogue

It was one of those incredibly bright, crisp winter's days. The frost was still on the ground as the two limousines pulled through the automatic gates at the edge of the estate and started the two-kilometre drive through the woods down towards the Georgian mansion at the centre of the grounds. As they passed the lake, the cars stopped. Presently the back doors of the vehicles swung open and an assortment of teenagers piled out, taking in their new surroundings.

Sarah Williams walked to the edge of the road and

looked across the lawn at the three-storey building up ahead. It looked like something out of a period drama – all high windows and stone steps leading up. Her friends stood alongside her and it was a moment before anyone spoke.

"I thought we were going to the city," Alex said.

Octavio sniffed and added, "This place looks... educational."

Colonel Rachel Andersen emerged from the other limo and walked towards them, smiling at the confused looks on their faces.

"What is this?" Hack asked, leaning against the car.

"This is your new home," Rachel said. "I thought you could all use a little more space to run around in."

"It looks ancient," Louise said and beside her Wei nodded sceptically.

Rachel grinned. "Just on the outside. We've added some modern features for all of you." She reached inside her pocket and produced a set of keys. "Why don't you go and check it out?"

She tossed the keys and Nestor was the fastest, snatching them from the air. He looked round at Sarah, who shrugged.

"Race you," Nestor said and started running across the grass, closely followed by the others – even Octavio, who hesitated just a moment for show. By the car, Robert looked at his sister and shook his head.

"When will they learn?"

He disappeared and in the distance Sarah saw him reappear instantly on the steps in front of the building. She smiled and turned to Rachel.

"What is this?" she asked.

"The leaks to the media have made it increasingly difficult for us to keep you at HIDRA," Rachel continued, referring to the small army of reporters camped out around the perimeter of the base. "You're not prisoners, but that's how we're having to keep you at the moment."

"And that's bad for publicity, right?" Sarah said wryly, thinking of some of the nastier news headlines she'd seen online. The world seemed torn between portraying them all as saviours or as dangerous forces that should be locked up underground.

"Something like that," Rachel said. "Which is why we've decided to relocate all of you. With you and your parents' agreement, of course."

*Your parents.* It was something they were all having to get used to again – most of the kids in the team had lost their family to the fall virus, but now, with the antidote, they were all making slow but steady recoveries at the

HIDRA UK base. And being back on the scene, their parents naturally wanted a say in what their kids were up to – even if those kids had changed a lot since they'd seen them last. A door on the other side of the limo opened and Daniel eased himself out, leaning on a stick for support (over a year in the sleeper casket had weakened his muscles).

"What do you think?" Rachel asked him as he cast his eyes over the mansion rising before them.

"Well, it's not as nice as my flat in Melbourne," he said wryly. "But I guess it will have to do. I'm just glad you picked somewhere discreet."

Rachel laughed. "Trust me, this place is isolated enough not to attract attention. To the outside world it's a school – a charitable organization set up by HIDRA to educate those children affected by the fall virus."

"A school?" Sarah said.

"I'm putting Dr. Fincher in charge of the institution, but there'll be proper teachers and everything else you and your friends need. And there are more like you out there, as you know. Kids who need help and guidance with their powers to make sure they don't run off the rails."

Sarah raised an eyebrow. "Dr. Fincher running a school?"

"Okay, okay," Rachel said. "So there'd also be the

opportunity to engage in some…extra-curricular activities. If you want to."

"The Entity is dead," Sarah said. "So is Major Bright. What else is there for us to do?"

Rachel stopped walking. "The moment the fall virus came to earth, the genie was let out of the bottle, Sarah. We're identifying increasing numbers of kids with virus-related powers every month, all over the world. Not all of them are intent on using their powers for good."

She handed Sarah an iPhone showing a series of security pictures. They showed a military base of some kind with soldiers being blasted left and right by what appeared to be a pair of fourteen-year-old girls.

"That's a US military facility in Kandahar Province," Rachel explained as Sarah flipped through the pics. "A team of superhumans hit them last week – ripped through the defences and made off with over ten million dollars' worth of equipment – equipment that showed up on the black market three days ago. The security footage suggests they had a teleporter, a psychic and two pyros."

Sarah handed the phone back. "They've teamed up."

"And they're not the only ones," Rachel said. "There'll be more." She paused for a moment, then said, "We're only asking you to consult, not get involved in another fight or—"

"Rachel, it's okay," Sarah interrupted. "There'll always be another fight – Commander Craig taught me that. I'm not afraid. And neither are my friends."

"Then you'll stay?"

Sarah glanced at the house up ahead. "I'll want a say in how things are run."

"You've got it."

"And we don't get involved in anything we don't like. No taking on people over oil wells or a border on a map."

"Fine."

"And no more weekly meetings with counsellors."

Rachel smiled. "So you're in?"

Sarah looked at Daniel, who held up his hands. "It's your decision, Sarah. How could I presume to tell the *saviour of the known universe* what to do?"

She rolled her eyes and looked back at Rachel. "Let me take a look at the place first."

The interior of the house was exactly as you'd imagine based on the outside: wood-panelled walls, an elaborate staircase in the hall, plush carpets all round. Sarah expected to hear her friends running around, arguing and generally tearing the place up as she entered – but the building was silent.

Searching with her mind, she sensed they were together and close by – although almost thirty metres below her feet.

It didn't take long to find the concealed panel on the wall and the lift doors behind it. *HIDRA must have a deal with a bunch of underground builders,* she thought as she looked over the sub-level names:

*Private Suites*

*Swimming Pool and Gym*

*IMAX Cinema*

*Games and Recreation*

*Training Zone*

She smiled to herself and pressed the button for *Training Zone*. The lift descended smoothly and a few seconds later the doors opened onto a massive, circular chamber. It seemed that the others had been drawn there first as well, because they were scattered around the floor, engaged in various activities.

Wei was throwing fireballs at targets on a range…

Louise was levitating various different-sized blocks and interlocking pieces and arranging them into shapes in the air…

Hack was tinkering with the remains of their battlesuits, which were laid out in a lab area…

Octavio and Nestor were looking over a row of

motorbikes, arguing over who got to ride what first...

And Alex was just standing in the middle of the area with a big, stupid grin on his face. Sensing her enter, he looked round and his grin only widened.

"So what do you think of this?" he said.

"It's okay," she replied, playing it cool.

Seeing that she'd arrived, the others temporarily left whatever they were doing and walked over. They all looked at her expectantly. She sensed they had made up their minds, but were waiting for her cue. *You're their leader,* she reminded herself.

"Okay, it's better than all right," she admitted, then turned and started walking back to the lift.

"Hey!" Robert called after her. "Where are you going?"

She turned to face their concerned faces as she stepped into the lift.

"Well, if we're staying, I thought I'd better grab the biggest bedroom."

The others exchanged glances and then scrambled madly for the doors as they closed... Sarah laughed and then closed her eyes in relief as the lift rose...

*Looks like we're home,* she thought.

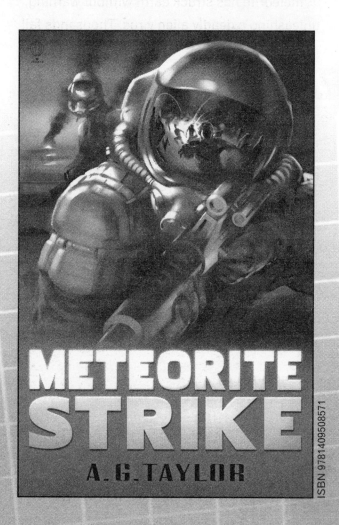

A meteorite has struck earth without warning, unleashing a deadly alien virus. Thousands fall victim…but not Sarah and Robert.

Instead they develop strange side effects – psychic abilities. And that makes them a target for HIDRA, a rogue international agency determined to turn them into lab rats, just like the other kids they've already captured – kids who can control fire, create storms and tear steel with their minds.

If they work together, these kids might just stand a chance against HIDRA…

**SHORTLISTED FOR THE
WATERSTONE'S CHILDREN'S BOOK PRIZE**

*"A heart-racing, breath-stopping thriller."*
***The Bookseller***

# ALIEN STORM

## A. G. TAYLOR

ISBN 9781409520184

**The thrilling action-packed sequel to METEORITE STRIKE**

A freak virus released by a meteorite storm has given Sarah, Robert and their friends amazing superpowers. But such powers are both a blessing and a curse...

Deadly meteorites are heading to earth, but mysterious Russian billionaire Nikolai Makarov seems gleeful. What is his secret and can the group of friends thwart his master plan?

**"Takes the reader on a nerve-wracking ride filled with...more moments of nail-biting tension than you will find in many a Hollywood action film..."**
*bookzone4boys.blogspot.com*

**"Brilliantly stunning sci-fi from beginning to end... A definite must-read."**
*Teen Titles*

# About the Author

A.G. TAYLOR was born in New Zealand and grew up in East Anglia. He studied English Literature at Sheffield University and teaching at Cambridge. For the last ten years he has worked as a teacher in England, South Korea, Poland and Australia. He currently lives in Melbourne with his partner, her whippet, his Italian greyhound and numerous computer games consoles.

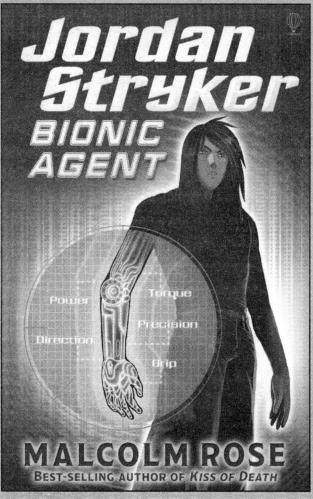
ISBN 9781409509752

A massive explosion destroys the south-east
of England. The near lifeless body of Ben Smith
is plucked from the carnage…

Deep within the secret headquarters of the
mysterious government agency, Unit Red, Smith is
rebuilt as…Jordan Stryker. New technology gives him
unbelievable new powers, and now he has a mission: to
hunt down the perpetrators of one of the biggest crimes
ever known.

Can Jordan outwit the evil masterminds and
violent gangs who will use any means to destroy
their enemies?

**"Buzzing with the thrills and spills
of a James Bond blockbuster…"**
*Lancashire Evening Post*

**AND THE GRIPPING
SEQUEL IS ALSO
OUT NOW…**

ISBN 9781409509776